THE SUMMERLANDS SERIES

EXPEDITION: SUMMERLANDS

NATHANIEL WEBB

Published by Level Up in the United Kingdom in 2019

Cover by Claire Wood

ISBN: 978-1-83919-299-9

www.levelup.pub

To Jack.
For teaching me how to walk.

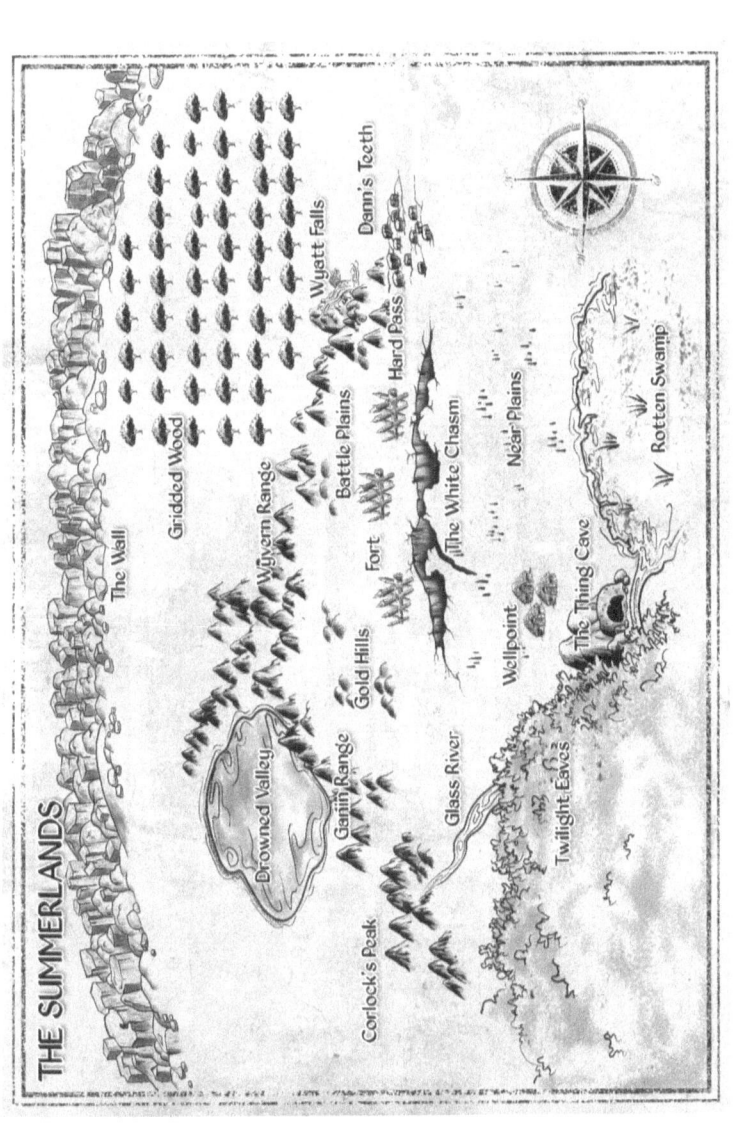

THE SUMMERLANDS

The Wall
Gridded Wood
Wyatt Falls
Dann's Teeth
Hard Pass
Battle Plains
Wyvern Range
Fort
The White Chasm
Near Plains
Gold Hills
Rotten Swamp
Ganin Range
Wellpoint
Drowned Valley
The Thing Cave
Corlock's Peak
Glass River
Twilight Eaves

THE MERCHANDISE MACHINE

At the exact moment I earned my Summerlands fee I was deep in the guts of a merchandise machine, ringing a bell. I'd worked out the day and hour months ago: at 4pm Hollywood Adjusted Time, my daily paycard incremented just enough that when I swiped it into my bank account that night, it would put me over ten thousand dollars.

The price of a ticket to the Summerlands.

I swept the bell through a complex pattern that supposedly, if I performed it in the Summerlands, would produce a small flame capable of lighting a candle or lantern. At the final flourish, I flicked my wrist a little too vigorously, and the bell slipped from my fingers and landed with a clatter on the floor of the narrow maintenance access tube where I sat.

I picked up the bell, wiped off a little machine oil, and stowed it in a plastic freezer bag with a few quarters and a folding pocket knife. I crammed the bag into a pocket of my uniform as I double-checked the solders I'd been sent in to make, which were solid and shiny. Satisfied, I scooted down my butt until I lay flat on my back.

I took a breath, reached up, and clicked a glowing orange switch above me into the on position. The machine roared to life around me. I could feel its gears getting up to speed as I wiggled my way down the maintenance tube, the tip of my nose almost scraping the oiled metal above me. By regulations, I had thirty seconds to get out of the tube before the merch machine started running again, but most managers had their techs shorten this startup time, and mine was no different. I'd done the work myself on this one.

1

I dropped out of the tube with five seconds to spare and found my manager Mr Fessy waiting for me. He stood with his arms crossed, a phone in one hand, in front of a small mob of impatient customers. He was a round man with a red face and a bushy white mustache that almost distracted from his thinning hair. At my full height—about five feet seven inches, tall for my parents' income—I looked him right in the eye. We wore identical black shirts stitched with the silver badge of Expedition Games, our mutual employer, but mine ballooned out around me while Mr Fessy's threatened to pop its buttons.

The cracked touchscreens on the merch machine flickered and came to life, and the shoppers surrounded me and Mr Fessy as they surged forward. I watched them for a moment as they swiped their paycards into the machine, then tapped through touchscreen menus to find the products they wanted. T-shirts, shot glasses, posters, video cards, plush monster toys, and boxes of hair dye dropped from the machine as quickly as their buyers could snatch them up.

Mr Fessy cleared his throat and smoothed his mustache with his free hand, a nervous tic that I had learned to associate with big news, usually layoffs.

"That was very good, Emma," he said, glancing at his phone. "Target completion time for that procedure is seventeen minutes. Took you only fourteen thirty-five." I'd actually had the job done in less than eight and spent the rest of the time working with my bell, but I wasn't about to mention that. The interior of the merch machine was the only spot in the Expedition store not watched by security cameras, which made it perfect for some secret magic practice.

"Anyway, end of shift," Mr Fessy continued. "Here's your pay." He handed over a paycard, which I pocketed, repeating the mental math I'd performed a hundred times in the last week: ninety-two fifty for a ten-hour shift, less twenty percent in federal taxes, five percent in zone taxes, five percent police insurance, two percent fire insurance. In all there should be sixty-two ninety on the card, just enough to get me to ten k after the bank took its insurance cut.

"One more thing," said Mr Fessy, pulling me from my mathematical reverie. "Mr Schneider died yesterday."

"Oh, I'm so sorry," I said. Mr Schneider had been an uncaring assistant manager, happy to arrive late and leave early. He was quick with a cruel word when he didn't like my performance, but I most often found him in an opiate haze in the employee bathroom, his acne-cratered face slack, far beyond words for me or anyone else.

Still, I wouldn't have wished him dead. We all had our methods of escaping the real world. I spent every day dreaming that I would make it to the Summerlands and I had the gift of three best friends who shared my plan. Jason, Cass, Noah and I could count on each other for encouragement when gray reality pressed in and the Summerlands were too far away. I suspected Mr Schneider had had nobody to fall back on.

"Anyway," said Mr Fessy, "I clocked you out. See you tomorrow."

I made my way towards the front of the store, weaving around eager Summerlands fans as they picked through the display merchandise. I'd long since learned to tune out the blare of advertising all around me. Rows of flatscreens played up-to-the-second livestreams from all the big-name adventurers: Valkyrie and Rad were sparring, their feeds showing alternate views of the same fight. Pixie was talking directly to her camera, a pink bra strap and soft white skin showing where her tunic had slipped artfully from her shoulder. St George was sleeping.

A knot of kids, too poor to afford to watch at home, stood staring at the feeds as flickering colors played across their rapt faces. I couldn't blame them. If they missed something especially thrilling or momentous on the feeds, they'd be completely left out at school tomorrow. One of them, a girl in oversized clothes, turned and gave me a little wave that said *thanks for not kicking us out.* I smiled and waved back.

I was almost to the front doors when a boy cut me off, stepping from behind a T-shirt display to put himself between me and the exit. I recognized him instantly: Jamie Bullard. He lived in my apartment block, and had been a couple years behind me in high school. His crisp haircut, round red cheeks, and little gut hiding under a brand-name Valkyrie T-shirt all illustrated the most important fact about Jamie: his father was the chief of police, which made him the richest kid on the block.

"Hey Burke," he said, "you pull anything out of the prize machine for me?"

"It's not a prize machine, it's a merch machine." I tried to stand up as tall as I could. "If you want something, you can buy it."

"Come on, I know techs get full access." He had a sort of whiny voice for such a big guy. "My allowance ran out. Just hook me up, I won't tell."

"You know I can't do that, Jamie."

"Ah, fine." He deflated a little, letting air out of his tough-guy posture. "How's training going? You're looking fit."

I blinked at the sudden change in tone. "Oh, thanks. Cass works us hard."

"You must be close to having enough, yeah? You guys really gonna do it?"

That's the ten-thousand-dollar question, I thought. We'd spent five years saving, and now the Summerlands were within reach. With my own fee banked, I could start putting money towards the others'. Cass was almost as close as I was. Jason made decent money working swing shift at a factory, but he was still in school, so he couldn't work full-time. Noah... Noah was lagging behind, but now I could help him.

"We're not there yet," I said.

"Yeah, I have a hard time seeing you killing rats." Jamie shrugged. "Be cool if you were famous, though."

"I guess." I looked at my sneakers, which really needed replacing.

Jamie crossed his arms. "You better give me free Hearthhammer merch."

★★★

4

It took me the better part of an hour to get home, walking my usual route along a broken and abandoned highway. The anticipation of telling my friends was a buzz of fear and elation in my stomach and I couldn't keep my right hand from diving into my pocket to touch my paycard every few seconds. It sat there like a stone and yet I was constantly certain it had disappeared.

I walked past a clutch of big white houses that sat in a wide bowl of dead grass just off the street. Their windows were mostly cracked or missing and a dozen black power lines made a drooping spiderweb between the houses and a half-fallen electrical pole. Jason and Cass's dad—Mr Keats, though I had always just called him Keats—had told me once that the houses were all owned as investments by rich folks waiting for the prices to rebound. They'd been waiting longer than I'd been alive.

A policeman stood on the weedy shoulder of the road between me and the abandoned homes, tapping his fingers on the butt of an Armalite slung across his chest, his head swiveling to follow me as I passed. I gave him a wave—I'd passed him at this same spot nearly every day for years—but his expression, hidden behind black shades, didn't change.

Between the brown grass, the black asphalt of the neglected highway, and the orange-gray clouded sky, it was a dismal landscape I walked through. Even I could see that and I'd never known anything else. But today, the money in my pocket made me feel daring enough to call unnecessary police attention to myself. Not because it made me rich, but because it made me a promise: a better world.

★★★

Between the strip mall and my apartment block, one crisp rectangle of bright color showed against all the washed-out gray. A billboard for the Summerlands stood about half a mile from my block and it looked quite literally like a window into another reality.

5

On the billboard, a skinny, handsome, light-skinned man with salt-and-pepper hair and a neat beard stood holding a sword in one hand and a bell in the other. Behind him were the perfect blue sky and rolling green hills of the Summerlands. He wore lush red wizard's robes and a necklace of sea-green jewels. His name was Dr Agony and if anybody was the face of the Summerlands, it was him.

Because the Summerlands wasn't just a place, it was a game, and he was the man who'd built it.

Back in 2055, Expedition Games was the leading developer of VR and sensurround games. Dr Agony—also known by his real name, Dr James Agostino—was their chief designer and coder. So it fell to Dr Agony to make the announcement that changed everything: Expedition Games had found a portal to another world.

The portal was in the European Union, on a craggy island in the North Sea, at the northernmost extremity of a country my History text called Scotland. In a patch of reclaimed wilderness that was part of Expedition's real estate holdings was a small crofter's homestead that had collapsed long ago. Beside the low stone rectangle that had once been a peat-roofed house, there was a well. At the bottom of the well was a ring of luminescent moss. And on the other side of the ring was a world they called the Summerlands.

At first, people were just confused. Most of us took it for a marketing tactic: Expedition had probably come up with some slick new VR technology and the whole "different world" thing was metaphorical. Then, once we all understood what they were claiming, nobody bought it. But soon the feeds started. A team of Expedition employees called the First Ranger Group, led by Dr Agony, sent back live HD video streams of a world with green grass, blue skies, clear rivers, and gleaming white ruins.

And then we had to believe, because nowhere like that existed on Earth anymore.

For months, the world was enthralled just watching the First Ranger Group explore this new Eden. Expedition Games claimed all the territory the rangers covered in the Summerlands. They certainly owned the well and the portal and their lawyers argued convincingly that the laws of Earth's nations ended where other worlds began. Then, just as the secondhand thrill of the rangers' exploration feeds was wearing off, tragedy struck.

A ranger group led by Dr Agony himself made camp at the outskirts of a huge forest. They shut their cameras off for the night. The next time their feed came online, some twenty hours later, every ranger was dead except for Agony himself. Expedition weathered a tsunami of demand from the public to explain what had happened, even stared down a congressional investigation, but they refused to disclose the fate of what became known as the Lost Expedition. Instead, they marked off a wide circle of land, built a huge wall along the border, and revealed Dr Agony's master plan: he was making a game.

First, they built a city. Called Wellpoint, it was a full-scale model of a fantasy medieval town, all plaster and stone and exposed beams. Some of the materials were brought over from Earth, but most were harvested from the seemingly endless resources of the Summerlands. In the center of Wellpoint, surrounded by a cobblestone town square, stood a green-glowing moss circle that matched the portal in our world.

Next, Expedition started hiring. Noah, Cass, Jason and I were too young to apply, but it probably wouldn't have mattered anyway: they received something like half a million applications for maybe two hundred jobs. They quickly filled out seven more ranger groups, whom they sent off to map the new world, with a particular eye for caves, ruins, and dungeons where treasure might hide. The rangers were the first to find the monsters that seemed to lurk anywhere there were riches to be found. They named them: gold dogs, trash snakes, giant hell rats.

The town of Wellpoint grew and Expedition took on applicants to act as the everyday people of the world. You could be a town guard, a ditch digger, a blacksmith, a shopkeep, anything Expedition needed to keep their new fantasy world running. If you had the skills, all they asked was a lifetime contract.

It was during this period that Dr Agony discovered magic. A cache of books in what appeared to be an ancient temple suggested a codified system of spells, but the texts resisted translation for weeks, until one day Dr Agony announced that he could speak and read the language of the people who had once occupied the Summerlands.

The Book of Elvish Magic was published a month later and rode the bestseller lists for a year. I read my copy over and over until it fell apart, learning that magic came in two types and relied on the help of ritual implements. Dr Agony was what he called a red magician, casting flashy spells with coins, swords, bells, and jewels. I also practiced red magic, not that I could afford jewels. Noah was our white magician; he amassed a small trove of wands, bracelets, cups and gloves as he practiced from his own copy of the *Book*.

Finally, after three years of frenzied anticipation and round-the-clock media coverage, Expedition opened their new game to beta testers. A spot on the beta list cost a quarter-million dollars; it filled up in four hours. One by one, the new players passed through the portal to the Summerlands. They were stripped of all their possessions and sent through with nothing but some pseudo-medieval clothing, a handful of copper coins, and a camera drone.

The drones were the only concession to modern technology in the game and Expedition Games was notoriously strict about enforcing the rules of their new wonderland. (A would-be player once tried to smuggle in a handgun and he'd been caught and banned for life. No refund on the ticket fee, which was a hundred-fifty thousand at that point.) Before you passed through, you were implanted with a subdermal RFID chip and on the other side you were given a drone keyed to your particular signal. Twenty-five hours a day—time worked a little differently in the Summerlands—your drone sent back a live feed of whatever you were up to.

With the beta open, Dr Agony quit his job with Expedition to become a full-time adventurer, handing over the reigns to his protégé, a woman named Blomhaugen. Some fans complained that he had an unfair advantage, but as the earliest players learned how to navigate their new world, Agony swiftly established himself as having the most interesting and exciting feed to watch.

The beta players quickly formed adventuring parties and the most talented ones started guilds to share their knowledge (for a fee, of course). The less talented chickened out and opened shops and restaurants rather than risk their lives. Others returned home via the portal and hit the talk-show circuit. But the adventurers who stuck with it soon found that there were really only two good ways to get rich in the Summerlands.

The most obvious was to go out adventuring and make it back to Wellpoint laden with treasure. The ranger groups did their job well and there seemed to be no shortage of abandoned buildings crammed full of coins, jewelry, and other treasure. The other way was to have a popular feed. Advertisers were happy to pour cash into the accounts of big-name streamers like Dr Agony and, in return, plaster their likenesses across any and all merchandise. The more viewers you had, the more you could make in sponsorships, but if you turned off your stream, your fans would change channel.

Still, some players lived mostly off the airwaves, streaming only in the midst of something exciting. Most killed their streams when they were doing something really mundane, like sleeping or using the bathroom. (Some didn't. There was a market for that.) Some people streamed their lives in confessional form, showing everything twenty-four/seven and talking nonstop about their emotions through every gold coin found and every friend lost to a monster. A few had even made the leap to porn, teasing, stripping, even sleeping with other players and beaming every detail back to a thirsty public. They always had the nicest clothes.

The Summerlands had been open for five years. Beta-tester spots were a quarter million each; tickets were down to two hundred thousand at the official launch. After the early adopters and rich kids had bought in, and especially once people started getting killed, the real price cuts began.

My friends and I had spent that entire time saving money. We'd played a lot of other games: Expedition's VR offerings,

9

old 2D games that Keats had collected, even some pen-and-paper roleplaying games. But the Summerlands captured our imagination instantly. It promised an exit from the gray landscape around us and, more than that, it was a place with a whole new set of rules.

In the Summerlands, it would be us against the world. The treasure that hid underground was ours for the taking. The monsters that stood between us and glory could be slain. Everyone started with nothing; everyone lived or died by their skill alone. That was more than could be said for real life.

HEARTHAMMER

All four members of my would-be adventuring party lived in the same apartment block, a cross made up of four twenty-story buildings with a small shared outdoor space in the center. As I turned from the street to the weedy cement path that led to my door, a few kids from the block ran past, laughing as they chased after a dust-caked ball.

"You there!"

I had my head down as I rounded the last corner between me and my door, so I saw the cop's gleaming black boots first. My heart choked and froze. As I looked up in resignation I took in the heavy slate-grey jodhpurs, black leather belt slung with gear, Kevlar vest, and rifle butt jutting out from behind it all, but when I finally saw the deep scowl creasing the cop's face, I burst out laughing.

"Christ, Keats, you scared me!"

"I got you, didn't I?" David Keats's face split in a grin. Raising Cassidy and Jason on his own had given Keats a knack for throwing on a serious face at a moment's notice, but if you knew him well enough, you could see the laughter in his pale blue eyes no matter how hard he tried to hide it.

"God, I really bought it, too. I should have known." I shook my head to try and hide my own smile. "And you shouldn't be lurking around scaring people."

"Lurking around scaring people is half my job," said Keats. "But actually I just wanted to invite you to dinner. You eaten yet?"

"You know I haven't. Stopping for fast food isn't on the Cassidy Keats fantasy adventure diet plan."

"Perfect." He slapped me on the shoulder. "Come on, you can wake Jason up for his shift."

"You know," I said as Keats held the rusting metal door of our building open for me, "you probably don't have to personally invite me to dine every single night."

"No?" he asked, following me in. The long hallway light flickered and buzzed above our heads as the door clicked shut and I thought for the hundredth time that I really ought to rewire it.

"I mean, I think Noah and I have just assumed a standing invitation for the last few years."

"Well," said Keats, adjusting the shoulder strap of his Armalite, "there's nothing wrong with a little etiquette. Even if the world is rude, we can still be polite."

"That's very deep, Keats," I said, and he laughed. "Speaking of polite, any chance tonight will be the night?"

We were side by side on the clanging metal fire stairs now—the elevators had been busted since before I was born—and I could see the shine of sweat at Keats's receding hairline. He was a strong man, a full six feet tall with thick arms, but over my lifetime I'd watched his belly grow steadily out over his belt. He took a wheezy breath before he replied, "Night for what?"

"The night you finally let me pay for dinner. Or at least some of it." Keats was already shaking his head, but I soldiered on. "C'mon, I just got paid. Let me cover my part, at least."

"No chance," he puffed. "Least I can do is feed my kids, Emma."

"You know I'm not actually your kid, right? And neither is Noah. At best we've got squatter's rights."

David Keats just shrugged and shifted his assault rifle on his shoulder.

★★★

12

Jason, the younger of Keats's two kids and the junior member of our adventuring party, was snoring terribly, tangled in the sheets of the upper bunkbed in the room he shared with his sister Cass. I reached up and shoved the metal lattice beneath his mattress, bouncing him awake as I sang, "You gotta get up in the morning, you gotta get up with the sun…"

Jason half-fell, half-slid down the ladder, his eyes still closed. He was naked except for a pair of ratty boxers; the Keats family's apartment captured a lot of the heat from the lower floors, a blessing in winter and a curse the other ten months of the year.

As Jason stumbled around his room, looking for pants and quietly cursing me, I couldn't help but appreciate how much he'd changed. His father's pale blue eyes still shone bright against his mother's brown skin, but he'd grown a few more inches in the last year. Between his factory job, our relentless combat practice, and a decent diet—we had Cass to thank for the last two—he'd put on a lot of muscle as well. He'd recently buzzed his thick brown hair, and the short cut drew attention to the sharp angles of his new cheekbones and jawline.

I wasn't about to say all that, though, so instead I told him he was a lazy bum who slept all day.

"All day? All day?" he grumbled from behind his open closet door. I watched the old boxers come flying over the door and saw a foot and a hint of calf as he stood one-legged to pull new ones on. "*All day* I'm in school. All night I work."

"Yeah, what are roll bars, anyway?" I teased, but he ignored me.

"Not being a dropout makes Dad happy, so school, that's Dad Time. I work four hours a night and save every penny for my ticket, so that's Summerlands Time. But afternoon—that's naptime. That's Jason Time." He came out from behind the closet door, wearing a blue factory jumpsuit with the name "Buck" stitched onto a tag on the chest. "Why am I awake, Emma? What happened to Jason Time?"

"It's not Jason Time," I replied. "It's dinner time. C'mon, Buck."

He sighed dramatically. "Only one more year to graduation. Then I can go full-time and really live my dream of being a factory worker."

"I won't stand for that kind of talk, adventurer!" barked Cass from the doorway. Jason stiffened to mock attention, then ducked sharply as Cass flung a sweaty towel at him. She was two inches shorter than her younger brother and slimmer and she looked like a color-inverted photo of him with her father's sun-reddened white skin and her mother's deep brown eyes. They shared the same cheekbones, though, and in a sweat-darkened gray tank top her muscles stood out just as sharply, toned from five years of drawing a heavy yew longbow. Her hair was clipped as short as Jason's on the sides, with an unruly brown tangle on top.

"How are the piggy banks?" I asked, just as Cass dove her sweat-gleaming face into a fresh towel. Cass was a personal trainer, trying to reverse years of neglectful parenting that had led the children of wealthy families to obesity. The job had always struck me as a ridiculous luxury. It was hard to blame the kids I'd grown up with for being so unhealthy, considering a sugared meat patty at Cluck-a-Duck's was the cheapest meal in town by far, but surely the few rich families, the ones with houses to themselves, could put real food on the table every night.

"I get paid to work out," replied Cass, coming up for air. That was how she always deflected the question, but she loved to run and jump and climb on obstacle courses she built for kids who were, like all of us, huge fans of Summerlands streams. I'd once watched her grab a wooden sword and chase a group of eight-year-olds in a circle for half an hour as they shrieked with laughter, yelling that she was an elf come back to steal their gold.

"Hey," said Jason suddenly. He was looking down at his phone, his dark eyebrows pressed together. "Do you guys remember Terra?"

"Your online girlfriend?" said Cass.

"She's not—" Jason started.

14

"She's just a girl who's your friend. Online." Cass laughed as Jason blushed. "Oh, and I've never met her because she's from the EU."

"What about her?" I asked.

"Well, we haven't talked in a while," Jason said. "I've been busy with school and work and everything. But she just messaged me out of the blue. It just says 'Summerlands Discovery, 2054.' And..." He held up his phone. "There's like ten megs of files attached."

"It's probably a virus," I said. "Her account got hacked or something. You shouldn't open it."

"I guess." Jason stuck his phone in a pocket of his jumpsuit. "Come on, I'm hungry."

★★★

With Jason and Cass more or less dressed and clean, we crossed the hall to the Keatses's little kitchenette-slash-dining room. Their apartment was cozy and simple. The front door opened into a hallway with four doors: Jason and Cass's room was on the left, followed by the bathroom, and on the right were the kitchen and Keats's room. As an only child I could only guess at the morning havoc in the bathroom, but otherwise it seemed like a nice place to grow up.

In the kitchen, Keats stood at the stove, flipping protein slabs on a frying pan like a chef in an ad for an upscale pancake house. On the second burner a pot of pasta was boiling.

"Looks perfect, Dad," said Cass as we came in.

"Looks boring, you mean," said Keats with a laugh. He uncomplainingly cooked Cass's training diet for us morning and night, but during the day I think he had no compunctions helping himself to whatever snacks the police department's corporate sponsors had left at the station.

"Where's Noah?" asked Jason. "He's never late for dinner." Noah García Benatar was the fourth member of our party and Jason was right; Noah never missed a meal at the Keatses's place.

"Good question." Keats banged on the wall above the stove with his spatula. "Noah! Food!" A moment later, Noah appeared at the door of the kitchenette, an open book in one hand and two more in the other. He had thick, wavy black hair and thick eyebrows, and a long nose below wide, brown eyes. He was shorter than even me, but much broader, another of Cass's training success stories.

"Noah, how long have you been in my room?" Keats asked. His bedroom was on the other side of the wall, just big enough for a twin bed and a tall bookshelf overflowing with science-fiction novels from the last century.

"You said I could look at the new books you got," said Noah matter-of-factly.

"That was…" Keats glanced at his police-issue phone on the counter. "Nine hours ago."

"Oh," said Noah. He had a funny sort of straightforwardness to him, like he didn't really understand everyday concepts such as boredom or fatigue or laziness. When he found a book he liked, he would read it until he finished it or somebody told him to stop. When Cass told him he needed to start doing an hour of cardio and two of weights daily, he was out in the dust fields the next day lifting and running in the hazy orange sunlight. It was as though the idea of not doing something simply never occurred to him.

Naturally, this made it hard for most people to understand him and Noah had been pretty badly bullied at school until he found us. On top of his dedication to our training, he was our walking encyclopedia, even more obsessed with the Summerlands than the rest of us. He usually didn't say much, but if you got him going on some piece of lore he could talk forever. Two years earlier, we'd taken the bus to San Diego for a Summerlands fan convention. I sat next to him and he spent the entire three hours telling me how every mountain in the Summerlands had gotten its name.

We adored him.

★★★

16

Protein chopped into pasta made a filling, if bland, meal, and after we'd all had enough we sat around the Keatses's chipped formica table, momentarily too full to move.

"So, I have an announcement," I said, breaking the contented silence. Cass sat up straight, her eyes keen. Jason raised an eyebrow. Even Noah looked up from his book. I cleared my throat a couple times, then, deciding to go for forthrightness over showmanship, dove in.

"Once I put today's paycard in the bank, I'll have a little over ten thousand—"

The room went off like a fireball spell. Cass leapt up with a whoop, knocking over her chair; Noah was smiling and clapping; Jason and his dad were shouting "Did you know? I didn't know!" back and forth at each other. I just sat there, feeling my cheeks grow red-hot.

"It's not that big a deal," I eventually interjected. "We still have to get you guys to ten k."

"Are you excited?" asked Noah. "You don't seem excited."

"No, I'm excited," I insisted. "Just... it's just a lot more real now, that's all."

"What?" Cass yelped. "Don't tell me you're getting cold feet now! It's finally happening for us!"

"No, no, of course not," I stammered. "I just..." I trailed off.

"I have a question," said Keats, changing the subject with merciful bluntness. "Before you actually get there—what are you all looking forward to most about the Summerlands? Cass?"

"Kicking ass, obviously," said Cass, still standing over me with her hands on her hips. She hadn't noticed her dad's act of conversational mercy, or maybe she just couldn't stand to miss a chance to boast. "We're going to be the best adventuring party the Summerlands has ever seen. Untouchable."

"Untouchable is good," her dad agreed. "Jason?"

"Well, honestly..." Jason wrinkled his nose. "It'll be kinda nice not to worry about money for once. When we start winning it, I mean. I think there's a lot of gold still sitting out there for us to grab."

"Oh yeah?" said Keats, smiling. "What's the first thing you're gonna buy when you're rich?"

"A house for you," said Jason, not meeting his dad's eyes. "A real one."

"I can't wait to meet everyone," said Noah. "Dr Agony will be there. St George. Rad is a Hecker, you know."

"We know!" laughed Jason. "Hecker" was the slang term from someone from the HECZ, the Hollywood Economic Cooperation Zone. People like us. "Why do you want to meet St George? That dude's a psycho."

"He seems interesting," said Noah. "And he has more confirmed kills than any other player."

"How 'bout you, Emma?" asked Keats. "What are you excited about?"

"Everybody took mine," I hedged, but Keats held me pinned by his stare, refusing to let me off that easily. "But I guess—okay, has it ever bothered you that there are no scientists in the Summerlands?"

"Huh?" Cass looked blank, as did her brother, but Noah seemed attentive.

"Well, think about it," I went on. "The Summerlands was gamified immediately after it was discovered. Aside from the rangers, nobody's ever really studied it, right? I mean, this whole other world and we made it into a theme park. There's all kinds of plants and animals and elven architecture—we don't even know for sure that the elves are all gone."

"Elves? Seriously?" Cass's eyebrows drew together. Expedition Games had concluded that the elves were long dead and that was enough for her.

"Or whatever," I said. "But don't you think someone should be, I don't know, taking notes?"

"First scientist of the Summerlands," said Keats. He smiled, but there was a sadness in his crinkled eyes, the look of a man watching his kids grow up. "I have a feeling we're all going to remember tonight. The first, biggest step on the road of the rest of your lives. So let me give you some fatherly advice, if that's

18

okay." We all nodded, his sudden serious turn cutting through our jangled nerves.

"Whatever happens on the other side—whether you guys get rich or get famous or decide to just stay in town and run a shop, which is fine by me, by the way, seems a lot safer than dungeon-diving—once you get to the Summerlands, you've already won. Just being there is a victory, a big one. That's a better life than anything I could give you here."

He waved a big hand vaguely at the window at the back of the room, which looked out on a battered metal fire escape and a dust-choked alley beyond it. "Look at the ground. Look at the sky. You're too young to remember how things used to be, but I'm not. I remember how it was before we all went too far as a society. So when you get there... don't go too far."

★★★

After dinner, we crammed into Cass and Jason's little room. Jason and I shared Cass's bunk as she paced back and forth, all nervous energy. Noah sat on the floor, his nose in one of Keats's books. There was always a calm period after dinners at the Keats apartment, perfect for just hanging out: too early for Jason to go to work, too late for me to get my paycard to the bank.

I resolved to get up a bit early and deposit the card before practice the next morning, but for now, Noah and I both had no urge to head home. I would have just spent the night on Cass and Jason's floor, but a gentle word from Keats had nudged me into thinking I ought to go home and give my own parents the good news... in a bit.

Jason had his phone out again, his brows a heavy line. I'd forgotten all about his mysterious message in the excitement of my announcement, but he obviously hadn't.

"Seriously, don't open that file," I said. He tapped at the phone screen a bit but didn't respond. I nudged him gently. "Jason, did you hear me?"

He looked up as though he'd just realized I was sitting next to him.

"My phone's blank," he said.

"It's what? Blank?" I asked. Noah looked up from his book, and Cass stopped pacing.

"Look at this, it's the startup screen." He held his phone up, and we all peered at it. He was right; the display showed a basic user data form.

"The only way to get that on an old phone is to do a full wipe," I said. "I haven't seen that screen since I bought my own after graduation. You opened the file, didn't you?"

"I did not!" said Jason defensively. He dropped the phone in his lap. "Okay, maybe I was thinking about it, but I can't. All my messages are gone."

"Noah, is your phone wiped, too?" I asked. "Maybe the school did something."

"No, mine is fine," said Noah. Like Jason, he was still in school, though a year ahead and about to graduate. They both had school-issued phones, which meant the school had final control over their contents.

"You're sure you didn't open the file?" said Cass.

"I said I was sure!" Jason snapped, and Cass put her hands up in a don't-bite-my-head-off gesture. Jason shook his head. "What if something happened to Terra?"

"Phones glitch all the time," Cass said. "Especially school phones. Don't sweat it."

Jason sighed and stood up. "I have to get to work."

★★★

To get from the Keatses' place to mine, I didn't even have to leave the building. The apartment where I'd grown up was three floors down and two halls over. I knew every stain and patch on the plastic carpet, had probably contributed more than anyone to the worn-in path down the center of the hall. I was less familiar with the walls and ceilings, since I tended to walk with my head down, but I could still identify any of the intervening hallways by the holes in the yellow plaster or persistently dripping leaks.

I was walking on autopilot. The business with Jason's phone had been strange, but I just couldn't focus on it. Instead, I was thinking about names. Despite the stark differences between the Summerlands and every game that had come before, one tradition had survived across realities: gamertags. The most famous were household names. Dr Agony, Rad, Wolfheart and Valkyrie, the members of the legendary party Golden Apple, could be seen on T-shirts, VR headsets, and, on one memorable occasion, a condom ad that ran only once during the Super Bowl.

Our party had a name, of course: Hearthammer. We'd picked it up in a Dungeons & Dragons game that Keats had run for me, Jason, and Cass when we were kids and it had naturally carried over to our Summerlands party.

We also had our own gamertags, just as we had agreed-upon roles in the party. Cass went by Jessamine (the name of her first D&D character and more feminine than I would have expected from her) and had gotten dangerously good with a longbow. Noah was called Sepharad, a great name for a wizard, which he would be in the Summerlands. He was learning white magic the same way I was learning red: by mastering the essential Elvish words and practicing the moves hour after hour and hoping we were doing it right.

Jason was our muscle, literally as well as figuratively after years of training with a heavy steel bar in place of a sword. He insisted on calling himself Yukon, even though Cass hated it; not fantasy enough, she said. I think he'd heard once that the Yukon Territory far to the north was a place of blue water, green grass, and mild sunlight, like the Summerlands itself, and it had stuck with him.

As for me, I'd gone through a few tags, but that night's conversation had helped me finally settle on one. I would be called Linnaea, after an eighteenth-century naturalist who'd invented taxonomy, the discipline of categorizing and organizing living things. It seemed like an appropriate handle for the girl who aimed to be the Summerlands' first proper scientist. I could imagine the cover of my first book, with LINNAEA across the top in big letters and EMMA BURKE underneath it.

The halls of our apartment block were normally crowded with a bustling mixture of neighbors and squatters. A lot of folks sat out in the halls to eat their dinners, some out of a sense of community, others to use the public plugs to power their hot plates and rice cookers. Having grown up on the block, I knew most of them, especially on this walk, but I was too caught up in being pleased with myself to notice that the halls were silent and empty. It was later than I had thought and the only people still out were squatters curled up under thin blankets in the corners. So I was alone when I heard a familiar whiny voice.

"Hey Burke, did you get paid today?"

Jamie Bullard came around the corner of an inset doorway, an oversized hunting knife held loosely at his side. He looked the same as he had at the Expedition store earlier and he certainly had a habit of popping out at you, but there was something new in his eyes that made the back of my neck prickle.

"I get paid every day," I replied.

"Perfect," said Jamie. His grip tightened on the hunting knife, though he kept his hands down. "Then you won't mind sharing with me."

"Come on, you're not a criminal. Why don't you get a job? Then you can share with yourself." My voice was steadier than my nerves. Jamie had bugged me plenty in my life, but never with a knife in his hand, and never with that look in his eyes.

"Don't say that. Everybody knows you're a bleeding heart." Jamie brought his hands up, spread wide in a mock *why the hell not* gesture that I guess he thought was an impressive display of casual insolence. In reality it just exposed a bit of his overhanging belly. "You give stuff to your Hearthhammer friends all the time. Christ, you even give stuff to the street kids. I've seen you. So give some to me."

"Jamie, let's talk about this." I took a step back and dared a glance over my shoulder. I wasn't too far from the door to the

22

nearest stairwell, but if I ran, I would expose my back to Jamie and his knife. Plus he knew the block as well as I did and no matter where I hid, would find me.

"Talk about it?" His gleaming eyes narrowed. "Nah. Wanna fight about it?"

There it was, the unspoken threat that he held over my head. However big he was, I had spent the last five years learning to fight. The way he was standing, I was pretty confident I could get inside his guard, grab the knife, and walk away. The problem was that I would have to hurt him to do it, maybe even break his wrist. I didn't want to in the first place, and, if I was successful, I'd feel the full weight of the police on my back within an hour. They wouldn't care that it was self-defense, not with the chief's kid crying and clutching his arm.

I couldn't even just hand over my money and trust the law would get it back for me. Despite the police insurance I'd dutifully paid since my first job as a kid, there was no point in filing a complaint that Chief Bullard would just toss in the trash.

"No thanks," I said, just like he knew I would.

"Come on," he whined. His eyes were hungry and his hand on the knife was white and shaking. "I've seen you out there running around with your little adventuring party. Don't you think it's time to fight a real man instead of imaginary gold dogs?"

"I said I'm good," I said tightly.

"Then give me your paycard," he said.

So I gave him my paycard.

POLICE STATEMENT

"It's not a big deal, Cass," I said for the hundredth time. Sitting in the dust field behind our block, I was rolling a quarter over my fingers and she was putting a new string on her bow. Behind us, Noah murmured the same word of Elvish over and over as he made little arcs with a stick. Cass stood and aimed at me, arrowless but with the string drawn back to her ear.

"It is a big deal," she insisted, glaring at me down the length of her arm. "You should have kicked his ass. We'll be out of here before long anyway."

"Not if I'm in jail." I passed the coin to my other hand in a satisfyingly smooth motion.

"Why aren't you bothered by this? I'm sick of having to be upset on your behalf all the time. It's exhausting." Cass loosed the string, piercing my heart with an imaginary arrow and a real thrumming snap.

I sighed. "You shouldn't do that. Without an arrow to absorb the force of the string—"

"It all goes into the bow," Cass finished for me. "I know, professor. Loosen up."

I unleashed a string of Elvish gibberish and flicked the quarter at her, nailing her square in the chest. "Bang. You're dead." If we'd been in the Summerlands, it would have exploded... maybe.

"You had the last word wrong," Noah said.

"No I didn't." I twisted around to look at him. "*Gíru.* That's what the book says, *gíru.*"

24

Noah shook his head. "It's not *gíru*, it's *girú*."

"Sure, if you go by Ringler, but on Agony's feed—why do you even know this? It's red magic!"

"Emma Burke, you're coming with me." It was Keats's voice, snapping like a whip. I looked up to see Jason standing at his father's side, his shoulders hunched and his eyes locked firmly on his shoes. Keats's neck was red and his mouth was working like he was trying to chew a particularly heinous piece of protein gristle.

"Bathroom break my ass," I said to Jason as I stood. "You sold me out, you rat!"

Jason just shrugged, but at least he had the decency to look a little embarrassed.

"Come on, Emma." Keats's voice was still tight. "We're going down to the station. Now." I knew he wasn't mad at me personally, but it was still unnerving to see him like this.

"Keats, it's really not a big deal," I tried.

"Like hell it's not." He was already walking away, expecting me to follow. I'd always guessed Cass got her stubborn streak from her dad; this was just confirmation.

"What's happening right now?" Noah asked.

"Jason told Keats about Jamie Bullard," I said, then pointed at the boy trying to avoid my eyes. "Do the crime, do the time," I told him. "You're coming too."

★★★

The police station was a classic example of lowest-bidder brutalist architecture. The front was all glass, stuck with translucent posters for the department's corporate sponsors; a picture of a gleaming, greasy Cluckin' Turducken Meal from Cluck-a-Duck's made my anxious stomach flip over. Behind the station, the attached jail was a pile of concrete boxes, cell blocks placed like building blocks.

The Turducken split in half and we were hit with a puff of canned protein scent as glass doors whooshed open to let us in.

The interior was sticky with the body heat of two dozen cops, citizens, and handcuffed criminals. No AC in here, which Keats had once told me was an intentional choice to discourage people from hanging around.

"Welcome to Hollywood Precinct Five!" chirped a disembodied female voice from somewhere above our heads. "The current wait time is seventy-eight minutes. Please feel free to return any time between eight a.m. and six p.m. if you do not wish to wait."

If it were possible for so busy and crowded a room to fall completely silent, it would have. Clearly, rumor of the mugging had arrived ahead of us. Between the cops, the perps, and a well-dressed woman who looked up as the touchpad where she was entering a complaint began to play a video ad, every face in the lobby turned toward us.

I hesitated, half in and half out of the doorway. Grabbing me by the wrist, Keats led me past the reception screens and through a frosted glass door deeper into the station. Jason trotted along sheepishly behind us.

The cops in the bullpen stared openly as we passed. Some watched with anger etched into their stony faces, others with fear. One absolutely huge officer stood bent over with his hands planted on the desk of a dark-haired female colleague. His biceps strained against his uniform shirt; his face was red beneath the open visor of his riot helmet, which had the name PORTER stenciled on it in worn white paint. He let his gaze linger on us for an intentional moment, then leaned in and whispered something that made the woman laugh, a staccato bark that still hung in the air after she covered her mouth. As he looked back at us, I got the weird but distinct feeling that he wasn't watching me or Keats: he was looking right at Jason.

Keats arrived at his desk and quickly opened a new report file on a tablet chained to the desktop. He entered the basics on a touchscreen menu: the date; my name; Jamie's name. From a series of dropdowns he selected "Misdemeanor," then "Theft," then "Petty."

Finally he looked at me for the first time since we'd entered the station. Far from the growl I was expecting, his voice was soft when he said, "You need to make a statement for the camera."

"Is that—" I hesitated, feeling my neck and cheeks get hot, keeping my eyes locked carefully on the tablet in Keats's hand. "Is that safe?"

"Yes," said Keats. "For you, at least. The report, the statement, the warrant, everything goes under my badge number. That way you won't be held responsible. And it can't be ignored."

"Okay," I said. "If you're sure."

"I'm sure."

I did my best to look the camera in the eye as I made my statement. I tried to stick to the basics, leaving out the times Jamie Bullard had bugged me and my friends in the past, but spilling out a nervous overflow of detail about the exact time, the floor and hall and nearby room numbers where he'd mugged me, and the sixty-two ninety he'd taken. I caught myself a moment before divulging exactly why that money was so important to me. Instead I coughed and finished, "And anyway, that's what happened. Uh, thanks. Good luck."

Hearing myself say "good luck" was the worst moment of the whole ordeal, or so I thought for about thirty seconds as Keats hit a few buttons to log the report. It submitted with a soft ping and I was just thinking about getting the hell out of there when a door in the back of the bullpen crashed open.

"Keats—office—now!"

The look in Keats's eye as he dragged me and Jason behind him to the chief's office told me that he had known this storm would come, but even so he seemed a bit surprised at how quickly it had whipped up.

"Who the hell is this?" asked Chief Bullard as soon as we entered. He was looking at me, not Jason; my attempt at passing unnoticed had obviously failed. Invisibility was a white magic spell in the Summerlands anyway. Bullard wasn't a big man, but his uniform was too small; the collar cut into his flushed neck and the Kevlar vest strained its straps. He was loud enough to fill the room anyway.

"This is Emma, the girl your son mugged," said Keats.

"One of yours?" Bullard was straining to keep his temper.

"Friend of the family, sir," said Keats.

"*Friend of the family*," repeated Bullard. His voice was quiet, the rage tucked away for now. "You think you're a good parent, Keats?"

"Yes, sir, I do," said Keats. It was the closest I'd ever heard him come to bragging.

"Think I'm a good parent?"

"I wouldn't know, sir." Keats stood at parade rest, hands behind his back, looking Bullard square on. Behind me, Jason kept his eyes down.

"I think I am," said Bullard. "I'm a decent man, Keats. A good member of the community." He snorted. "Against the advice of every sergeant on the force I haven't fired you. You know why? Because on the whole you make my life easier. You bring crime down. That's good enough for me. But then you go and do this"—he indicated his desk computer, which showed the report we'd just filed—"and it makes my life harder. A lot harder. You know why?"

"Why, sir?" said Keats.

"Because your family is all you got, Keats. And since Anna died, my boy Jamie is all the family I have. Now look, I know you love your kids. And these strays you pick up, God knows why. So if you had a chance to give your kid an advantage in life, any advantage, wouldn't you take it? You would. You'd do the same."

Keats was silent as Chief Bullard began to pace.

"So when my own kid breaks a little law, has a little teenage fun, well, I could bring the hammer down on him or I could let it slide. And if I let it slide, then when we batch up our records and sell 'em up for background checks, my kid won't get a red flag or a black mark."

Bullard was crossing and recrossing his office now, looking at the floor, one hand behind his back and the other jabbing at the air as he went. It was really a monologue rather than a conversation, getting louder and louder as it spun on.

"But then you had to go and do this"—he waved at the computer again—"and screw it all up! Can't erase a report entered by an officer, God knows why. Good luck ever finding a job with this on your record, Jamie. Poor kid." Bullard turned on us. "Got anything to say in your defense, Keats? Jason, care to stick up for your old man? How about you, girl? Feel good that you ruined a boy's life over, what was it, sixty bucks?"

I could barely put together a whole thought, but Keats was more composed. He put his chin up, but all I could see was a man about to get hit on the jaw.

"My job is to stop crimes if I can, and report them if I can't," he said. "I did my job."

"That's how you're gonna play it, huh?" Bullard was quiet again, but his voice was tight with menace. "Fine. Fair's fair. My boy won't be able to find work with this on his record. I'll be stuck supporting him for the rest of my life. So let's say no more work for you, Keats. Let's say your perfect little golden kids can support you until you die. Pack up your things and get the hell out of here, and don't come back. Fair?"

★★★

By the time we made it back to the apartment block, I was late enough for work that I couldn't walk. Luckily there was a bus that could get me to the Expedition store with four minutes to spare, but I had to rush for it, so I couldn't be there when Keats broke the news to Cass. I wasn't sure whether to feel guilty or relieved to miss the awkward scene, so I settled on both.

To distract myself on the bus, or maybe to pretend for five minutes that it was still yesterday, I pulled out my phone and called up one of my favorite Summerlands clips. It was from Dr Agony's stream, and captured a short fight between his party, Golden Apple, and a group of monsters called trash snakes. It

29

was a pretty exciting video, but I loved it because it captured him performing a particularly amazing piece of magic.

As the clip began, the four members of Golden Apple—Dr Agony, Rad, Wolfheart, and Valkyrie—were slogging through what appeared to be an arcane garbage dump. They sloshed through waist-high filth, shards of pottery and bones floating in brown muck. Rad was in the lead, a huge maul in his hands, and he looked back and winked at Dr Agony's cam. Rad was a mountain of a man with dark skin and a shaved head, and his trademark grin flashed bright in the drone's headlight. He was a Hecker like us and had actually starred in a few Hollywood action movies before the Summerlands went public. He'd signed up immediately.

Far out on Rad's left flank stalked Valkyrie. She was a pale, slender woman with hair dyed jet black and chopped short. Her face sported war paint in a matching deep black, and two long knives glittered in her hands. I'd always thought that if she hadn't made it to the Summerlands, Valkyrie would have been a serial killer. She enjoyed killing more than any other adventurer; her stream was always noisy with her excited panting while Golden Apple fought, and her eyes gleamed bright and wide in the aftermath. She took her name seriously, and often talked (in Icelandic) about delivering the souls of the slain to Valhalla. Her fans were more like worshippers; a few had even killed themselves in hopes that she would gather up their souls. No word on whether it worked.

Wolfheart was behind Dr Agony's drone, so he was out of view of the stream, but I could hear his voice faintly as he rattled off an endless string of patter to his own viewers. He was a small man with a sardonic smile perpetually plastered on his face. In fights he often hunched to one side, chatting casually with his viewers as he waited for a teammate to need healing magic. He was also notoriously impossible to interview, as he took reporters about as seriously as he took everything else.

Valkyrie was the first to spot the trash snakes, when a scaly tentacle topped with a snapping, toothy head shot up from the water a few feet ahead of her. Shouting something in Icelandic, she leapt forward, her knives glittering in the gloom as she neatly decapitated the tentacle and came to a splashing stop a foot beyond it.

A dozen tentacles thrashed up from the roiling water where she had just been standing. Their heads snapped as they began to move towards Valkyrie in an undulating roll, bobbing up and down above the waterline with neatly synchronized movements. That was the trick with trash snakes: they looked like individual beasts, but were actually the many tentacles of a single wide, flat creature pressed against the floor beneath your feet. If Valkyrie had stayed put or moved backwards when the first snake popped up, she would have been caught in a forest of grasping arms.

Rad waded in among the tentacles without fear, his massive arms flexing as he swung his maul. Snakeheads shattered with each swing and backhand, spraying long teeth everywhere. He was laughing and mugging for the camera when another full set of tentacles, twenty or more, shot up around him. Half a dozen wrapped around the arm that held the maul; the others began nipping at his torso, taking out palm-sized chunks.

Wolfheart appeared in the frame, his hands making arcane symbols as he spat out a staccato series of words with no cognates in any Earth language. Wolfheart cast from the so-called "white group" of spells, so there was nothing I could learn from him, but Noah had gone over this section of the video at least two dozen times.

Wolfheart was suddenly as entangled as Rad, as what must have been a third trash snake erupted around him and dragged him under. My favorite part was coming up and I felt my heart thudding in my chest despite knowing exactly what would happen.

The video's point of view pulled back as Dr Agony stepped away from the fight. His hands dipped to his waist and came up with a palm-sized bronze bell in each. His drone hung over his right shoulder as he stuck his arms straight out at his sides and began to swing both bells. They clanged through swooping arcs and sudden jerks as Dr Agony twitched his hands and wrists almost imperceptibly. His fine motor control was incredible, especially considering he was shouting a string of magical commands at the same time.

From the roiling chaos of the fight at the top of the screen, dozens of tentacles stood suddenly rigid, like soldiers at attention. The other members of Golden Apple appeared from under the surface, gasping and shaking water from their eyes and hair. The tentacles quivered as though struggling against the spell that bound them. Muttering, Valkyrie slashed them down two at a time, misting the air with white blood.

The clip ended just as the bus pulled up at the strip mall where my job waited. My head was clouded with awe as I hopped off. It was such an incredibly precise piece of magic, taking such control, even if you ignored the less-than-ideal circumstances. But to my immense joy, the camera had captured it all in perfect high definition.

Dr Agony's *Book of Elvish Magic* included a handful of spells and more had leaked since the game opened, making their way onto fansites and into third-party books that were usually equal parts reprints and BS. The spell in this clip wasn't one of them. Whether Agony had dug it up somewhere or it was his own invention I had no idea, but I'd been trying to master it since the clip had come out.

Mr Fessy greeted me at the doors of the Expedition store. He was already smoothing his mustache as I came in. My stomach lurched: more bad news?

"Ah, Emma, I'm glad you're not late," he said. "One thing before you clock in. You remember Mr Schneider died?"

"Sure," I said. It felt like a year ago that we'd had that conversation.

"Well, we need a new Assistant Manager. Mr Sorolla thought you might be a good fit." Mr Sorolla was our Regional Manager, a step above Mr Fessy. "No need to respond. This isn't an official offer. That would be from HR. Just letting you know that you're under consideration. The final decision is Mr Sorolla's, not mine."

"Sure."

"Would you accept some advice?" asked Mr Fessy.

I nodded, only half-listening. A promotion? Me?

"Good. I suggest that you try your best to get the position. The pay increase is notable." With his head cocked to one side, he looked like an attentive dog.

"Uh, thanks," I said.

"Can I share a personal thought?"

"Sure."

"I believe you're capable of the position. A number of managers started as techs. From a compensation perspective, if you're given an offer and accept it, the higher wage might enable you to afford an apartment of your own rather than living with your parents. Perhaps you might even support another person or two, such as a family, for example. If I may, the quality of life can be quite high in a management position."

"I see." I nodded. "Um, thank you."

"Okay, good," said Mr Fessy. "Oh, you understand that this conversation can't count towards your clocked time? Okay. Go get clocked in." He walked away, tapping at his phone.

★★★

"Emma, that's great!" Keats's genuine smile stabbed me deep in my gut. It felt wrong that I should have a chance at a promotion when I'd just cost him his job and it felt even worse that he should be so happy about it.

"Do it," said Jason, passing me the bowl of yesterday's leftovers, which was all we had for dinner. "Whatever the raise is, you can give me the extra since you're already flush with cash." I wasn't quite at ten thousand, but that day's pay had gotten me close. If only Keats hadn't gotten involved, the incident with Jamie Bullard could have been forgotten in another day or two.

"I need the money more," said Noah around a mouthful of pasta. "You should give it to me."

"How about we wait until she actually gets the job before we loot her corpse?" said Cass. "Buncha vultures. Jason, bowl please."

Three sharp knocks sounded on the front door of the apartment, freezing Jason in the act of passing over the food.

"Who's that?" asked Cass.

"Dunno," said Keats. "Everyone I like is already here."

"I'll get it," said Jason.

"Better let me," said Keats, standing. As he left the kitchen, shutting the door to the hallway behind him, the four members of Hearthammer shared a look.

"I smell trouble," said Cass. "We should go out there."

Noah stood and eased the door open a few inches. Through the gap I saw a slice of bicep, thick neck, red face in a battered black riot helmet, the butt of a gun: the huge cop who'd stared at us that morning. Out of uniform, but with the same riot gear strapped over a black T-shirt and jeans.

"—he's not here—" Keats was saying, but he was cut off as Noah shut the door and put his back to it, his eyes wide and white.

"Keats'll handle it," I said, looking at Jason and Cass. "I'm sure that guy just came to give his condolences." Nobody laughed. Jason was rubbing his thumb along the blade of a butter knife in his hand and Cass was glancing around as though a longbow might suddenly appear in the kitchen.

There was a crash, then silence.

Keats's voice came suddenly clear through the door, "Don't worry about it, Porter. It's only a vase."

Cass stood up. Jason stood, too, putting his hand on her shoulder.

"He'll handle it," I repeated.

There was another crash, then something hit the door. Noah stumbled forward as it swung half-open, revealing Keats with his back to us, his hands up, palms out. He looked over his shoulder for a second that lingered for an eternity as his wide eyes held each of us in turn.

"Run," he said.

Instinct took over. By the time I had my hands on Noah, pulling him across the room to the window, Jason was already shoving it open. Only Cass hadn't moved. Noah climbed out the window onto the fire escape balcony beyond, then clanged across it to let the ladder down.

"He needs our help," Cass said.

"He knows what he's doing, Cass," said Jason in a strained whisper.

"He needs our help!" his sister shouted.

"Not the time, guys!" I cast around the room for some inspiration. "Cass, listen! Listen. We'll take the fire escape down now. Then we can circle back to the front door and come up if we need to."

"Promise?"

"Promise."

Jason was next out the window and I was right behind him. At the far end of the balcony, Noah was banging the emergency ladder back and forth within its clamps, shaking the fire escape as he tried to get it loose. It broke free suddenly and roared down to hit the seventh-floor landing twenty feet below.

The noise of the ladder covered the sound Cass, still in the kitchen, made as she slammed the window shut and locked it from the inside. I only realized what had happened when Jason screamed her name. He darted back across the balcony as I grabbed Noah's shoulder to stop him halfway over the edge of the fire escape.

"Cass, open it!" Back bent, Jason was straining against the locked window.

"I got this!" Cass shouted back and disappeared into the kitchen.

The windowpane exploded into shards as Jason kicked it in. He reached through the hole and undid the lock, threw the window open and went in feet-first, heedless of the broken glass gleaming everywhere. Noah pushed past me and before I could grab him he dove after Jason, making it halfway through and kicking his legs to shimmy in and spill onto the kitchen floor.

There was the bang of a gun, a hundred times louder than in a movie.

At the window I brushed away the worst of the glass with my hand tucked into the sleeve of my shirt. Across the kitchen, Cass threw open the hall door. Jason had a hand out, trying to stop her, but the table was between them. I slipped through the window head-first and stumbled to my feet next to Noah.

Out in the hallway, Porter stood over Keats's body, rifle dangling from one hand. I could see red and purple all over Keats's face beneath his shielding hands, but couldn't tell if he was moving. Porter looked up, and even under the mirrored faceplate of his riot helmet, I could see his eyes lock on Jason. "There you are," he said.

Cass took a swing at him. He grabbed her wrist with his free hand and twisted savagely, forcing her to her knees as she screamed and spat in defiance. With his other hand he lifted his rifle, braced it against his shoulder and fired three shots.

If Jason screamed, I didn't hear it. The rifle was deafening in the little kitchen and my ears rang as I watched Jason slump to the floor, his head looking one direction and his legs twisted the other. A pool of blood crept out from underneath him. It crawled closer to my feet, but I couldn't get away. I was frozen amidst the noise and violence.

"Stay back!" Porter's shout cut through the ringing. "And don't follow me!" He covered me and Noah with his rifle as he dragged Cass back through the door into the hall. He gave Keats's body one last kick, threw Cass down the hallway as though she were weightless, and walked out the front door.

"Daddy!" Cass's voice was an animal yowl. In a scrambling crawl she got to her father.

"Jason," Keats said. His voice was clogged and nasal. "I'm okay. Jason."

"He shot him," said Noah. He was kneeling over Jason, his shirt red and sodden. "He shot him. He shot him. I don't think he's alive."

JASON

In the days that followed Jason's death, I was like an animal. Not a tiger, snarling and snapping at the world, or an eagle, cold and aloof; I was an insect, a creature without intelligence, relying on numb instinct to respond to the stimuli of the world around me in only the most basic way.

I went to work. I fixed the machines and any time I was out of the view of the security cameras, I cried. I didn't answer my phone; I deleted voicemails. I took the bus, staring out at mirror-faced policemen guarding empty houses. Their windows reminded me of Jason's dead eyes: portals that passed through a solid object to reveal nothing inside.

Keats was still in the hospital. Every night, I ate dinner at home with my parents then walked mechanically through the halls of our block to slip the day's paycard under the Keatses' apartment door. Sometimes after I did I would sit against the wall, hugging my knees up to my chest, staring at the door. It never opened.

I lay awake at night, my thoughts playing out the night of the killing like a movie. Porter had been watching Jason at the police station, I was sure of it. But why? Why Jason? My mind went around and around like a computer caught in a recursive loop.

First, I would wonder if it had anything to do with Jason's phone being wiped. Then I would shove that aside and think it was some sort of sick revenge for Keats getting Jamie Bullard in trouble: killing one man's son in vengeance for another's. Then

I'd circle back to the mystery of the phone, the cryptic message from Jason's friend Terra, the file he hadn't had a chance to open. Inevitably, around one or two a.m., I would pull up Terra's contact info from an old group message and call or email her. When she didn't answer, I would start thinking of Jamie Bullard again.

Locked in this endless cycle, I spent every night tossing and turning until morning.

Finally, after two agonizing weeks, there was a knock at my parents' door during dinner. I nearly bent the fork in my hand as my heart began to hammer. My mother went to answer it and I watched her unblinking. I wanted to run, but I was frozen as she opened the door.

"Hello, Mrs Burke," said Keats from a wheelchair. "Is Emma home?"

"Emma!" my mom shouted, but I was already there. Keats had lost weight. The worst of the bruising had faded everywhere but around his eyes, revealing pale greenish skin and dirty stubble. His nose was hidden by a gauzy white splint. The lines of his face were twice as deep as the last time I'd seen them.

"Keats," I started, "I'm so—" Keats held up a hand. Two of his fingers were splinted as well.

"It's okay, Emma." He grimaced and shifted his weight in the wheelchair. "I just came by to invite you to the funeral."

"Does Cass know you're here?"

"No." Keats looked away. "She hasn't left their room—her room—very much. I was hoping you could talk to her at the funeral."

"I'll try," I said, but I had no idea what I could possibly say.

★★★

Jason was buried in a plain wooden coffin at the back of a large municipal cemetery. It was a dismal place: a few scraggly, leafless trees still clung to life here and there, but for the most part it was a flat, unbroken plain of gray grave markers in thin dirt.

A bigger crowd than I had expected watched as the coffin was lowered. Jason had been respected at work and popular in school, where everyone dreamed of going to the Summerlands. But all those old friends of his were strangers I had no desire to meet, just a shapeless mass at my back.

Cass, Noah and I stood together under a rare blue sky. Cass was as pale and drawn as her father, who watched silently from his wheelchair at her side. Noah was sobbing openly. I thought I had done plenty of crying in the private corners of the last few weeks, so I bit my lip and kept my face still.

It only took a few minutes for the gravediggers to cover Jason's coffin, then fill the hole completely. One of the dirty-handed men looked over at us as if to say *are we done here?* I had to look away. Cass let go of my hand and stepped forward to stand beside the fresh grave.

"Jason..." She cleared her throat and wiped her eyes. "Jason never got to know our mom. He was only two when she died and he said he remembered her, but I think he was lying. Not really lying, but... I think he knew it made me feel better.

"Mom would have been so proud of him. The man he was becoming. She was an athlete, too, until she got sick. I used to think it was so unfair that she didn't get to watch him grow up. Now..." She closed her eyes. "I had no idea what *unfair* really means."

Cass opened her eyes and looked at the crowd, catching us one by one with her iron stare. Most people, the ones from Jason's school and work, put their heads down rather than hold her gaze. "We were attacked. My father was put in a wheelchair and Jason was murdered. We've been paying our police insurance my entire life, but can we go to them? No, we can't, because the man who murdered them is a cop. It's no big secret. I don't know why he did it, but I know that nobody's going to do anything about it.

"I'm sure they don't want me to say that and I don't care. I'm done with this world. With all of this, all of you. I'm leaving. I'm going somewhere where nobody can hold me

39

down." Her eyes met mine. "Anybody who wants to come with me is welcome. If not, I'll see you on the feeds."

★★★

As the funeral broke up, I stood aside, watching schoolmates who had teased Noah for years line up to give him their condolences. Cass was already waiting at the bus stop, so Keats and I were alone together when he rolled up beside me. We looked on in silence as Noah hugged a sobbing girl, patting her back awkwardly, and I remembered how she used to call him "Big-Nose Benatar" before he'd become friends with Jason.

"My parents wouldn't come," I said as the girl moved on, wiping at her tears. "They said they didn't really know Jason. They said I should have brought him over instead of spending all my time at his place."

"Every time you went home you looked like you were leaving for a business trip," Keats said. His voice sounded like it had in the hallway that night, stuffed up thanks to the padding in his broken nose. "*Emma's packing up to go to the hotel,* I'd always think."

"I guess that's how it felt," I said. I couldn't look at him, so I pulled on my fingers, making my knuckles pop gently one by one. "Uh... did you get the money?"

"It helped us pay for all this," Keats said, waving his splinted hand vaguely at the cemetery. "I guess cremation is cheaper. You take up less space afterward... but then I thought of when Jason was three and he burned his hand on the stove and I—I just couldn't."

"Thanks for that," I said.

"Thanks for helping."

"I always thought you and Jason would've made a nice couple," Keats said. "He idolized you, you know. I used to think—I used to think, if they get married, Emma will be part of the family officially."

"There's always hope for Cass and Noah," I said. He laughed, but it quickly turned into a cough, and then a hiss of pain.

"How is it?" I asked.

"It hurts," Keats said. "A lot. All the time. But the pain meds are expensive, so…" He shrugged.

"How long are you in the wheelchair?"

Keats shook his head, looked up at the blue sky. "Forever, probably."

"What?" I could feel tears starting from my eyes. "Forever? Does Cass know? There has to be something—"

"Emma, I can't even pay the emergency room bill. I can't afford an elective surgery." He snorted. "And what would I gain? Even if I could walk, I'll never work again, thanks to Bullard."

"Do you… do you have any money saved?" I knew how stupid the question was even as I heard it leave my mouth.

"A little," Keats said. "A month, maybe." He left the rest unsaid: after that month was up, he and Cass would be homeless. My parents certainly wouldn't take them in and the shelters were all perpetually overflowing; he and Cass would likely be split up anyway. And even if they had somewhere to live, there was the question of Keats's medical bills, which would continue to pile up even if he didn't have any more checkups or surgeries.

In the space of a few days, everything had collapsed. Even under the blue sky, the world was gray and barren. My hands were shaking as I knelt to put them on Keats's arm.

"Take my money. My savings." He tried to say something, but I rolled over him. "Please. I'm serious. Ten thousand can get you out of debt, right? More or less? And as far as the future, we'll figure something out. Cass and I are still working and Noah had that job interview last month…"

"Can you hurry up, please? The bus'll be here any minute." Cass stood over us with her arms crossed.

"Patience, kid," said Keats. "I just need to tell Emma no thanks and we'll be on our way."

"No thanks to what?" asked Cass.

"Cass, I know you don't want to talk to me—" I started.

"No thanks to what?" she repeated.

"I was just telling your dad he should take my money. All of it. For the bills, and… and stuff."

A dozen expressions flew over Cass's face like a fighter jet formation passing overhead. One or two of them looked like the friend I remembered. And then, to my amazement, she began to laugh. She laughed up at the blue sky and as she fell to her knees and laid her head on her father's arm, she was still laughing, but she was crying, too.

"I'm such an idiot," she said at last. "Of course you should. Of course you should. And mine. And Jason's, too."

"Mine, too," said Noah as he came upon our scene. He had a tentative smile on his face, as though he were just waiting for permission to be happy again. "Even though it's less than everyone else's."

"And so what if we don't get to go to the Summerlands?" I said. "We'll always have the feeds."

"Better," said Cass. "We'll always have each other."

★★★

We spent the afternoon getting our various accounts transferred over to Keats. We all shared a bank so the fees were minimal and, as I watched my savings tick over from ten thousand to zero, I felt as though I'd just dropped a hundred-pound sandbag off my shoulders. No price could be put on Jason's life, no amount could bring him back, but giving away my dreams at least felt like a penance of the appropriate kind.

We had dinner together for the first time since the attack. Keats paid and for once I didn't argue. We talked about everything except the Summerlands, but mostly we talked about Jason, telling stories and sharing memories. And if we all compulsively looked at the door every time there was a noise in the hall, nobody admitted it.

Keats's constant pain showed most clearly in the way he held his body when he laughed, tense and angled as though it would fall apart if he shook too hard. I don't think I expected him to be cured immediately upon receipt of our money in his bank account, but it was disheartening to see him clenching his jaw each time he shifted in his wheelchair. Aside from all the cuts and bruises, he'd had his nose and four fingers broken and a few teeth knocked out. But the worst damage was to his spine, where a bullet from Porter's rifle had lodged between two vertebrae. A long series of expensive surgeries promised to win back his mobility, but until and unless they happened, Keats would stay half-hunched in the chair.

After dinner, Cass asked me to stay over in her room. I climbed the ladder to the top bunk and nestled into Jason's sheets, which were still unmade from the last morning he'd gotten out of them. His scent hovered around the bed like a protective spell. As his warmth settled over me, I let myself hope that this might be the first night I didn't spend chasing my anxieties in a circle.

"Emma," said Cass from below me. Her voice was barely more than a whisper.

"Yeah?"

"We have to start again."

"Saving money?"

"Yeah," said Cass. "Jason would have been pissed if we just gave up. Hey, by the time we get the money together, maybe ticket prices will have dropped again."

"That would be nice," I agreed. "But, Cass..." The words I wanted to say caught in my throat. I took a deep breath and tried again. "Cass, I don't think it's a good idea."

"It's okay to be scared," she said. I rolled onto my side and propped myself up with an elbow. Cass's face was poking up from the lower bunk and our eyes locked.

"I'm not scared," I said.

"It's okay," she insisted. "Summerlands is a dangerous game. And it's hard to train as a spellcaster without ever seeing the results of your practice. Noah doesn't care, but I know you have doubts."

"That's not it," I said. "I mean, it is, but it isn't. I've watched so many feeds over the years... I've seen people get killed. We all have. But it's not the same up close. It's not the same when it's someone you... care about. I couldn't lose you or Noah too, not after this. I just can't do it. I don't want to be responsible for your lives."

"Responsible?" Cass shoved her sheets away and sat up. "You're not my mom. You're not my dad. You're not my teacher or my tutor or my boss, Emma, you're my *friend*. I'm not asking you to carry me. I just want you to watch my back."

"Cass—" I choked as tears welled up without warning. "Jason would still be alive if not for me. That big cop that killed him, he saw us at the police station the morning after Jamie mugged me. Your dad would be fine. He would still have his job. You have no idea how good it felt to give him all that money. All of this is my fault."

"Ha!" Cass reached up and shoved the bunk springs above her head, bouncing me. "You wanna play the blame game? Get in line, sister! Did you forget who was so hell-bent on helping Dad that she *locked the window*? Jason came after me when he should have been running." She snorted. "I haven't slept in weeks. *I locked the window*. This is why I need you with me, Emma. You're the only one with any common sense."

"I'll think about it," I said, and I meant it. I rolled onto my back and looked up at the ceiling only a few inches away.

"Practice starts again tomorrow," said Cass as she climbed back into bed.

"Go to sleep."

★★★

"So yeah," I concluded, "I guess we won't be going to the Summerlands after all."

Coming home had been a mistake, that much was obvious. My dad hadn't moved from the couch, where he now grunted something that might have been the word "sucks" as he fiddled with a plastic bottle of painkillers. At least he'd bothered to mute the TV on the wall, where Pixie was chattering into the camera as she strolled down one of the main streets of Wellpoint, ducking into all her favorite clothing stores.

Mom at least had stood up to talk to me. "Maybe it's for the best," she said. "The Lord works in mysterious ways. I never liked you playing those dangerous games anyway. Now you can focus on your promotion." In her hand, her phone showed St George kneeling down with his sword like an ancient Crusader. He was praying and the soft murmur of his words floated under our conversation.

"I haven't gotten the promotion yet, Mom," I said.

"You better," said Dad from the couch. "You're twenty now. Can't be mooching off us and the Keatses forever."

"This might be a good opportunity to live a more quiet life," Mom added. "It can't be good to be running around in the sun so much. Oh, you can get a good job, start a family…"

I felt a nasty reply boiling up and choked it back. We'd had this argument a hundred times before, many of them in the fragile last few weeks. It wasn't worth going another few rounds with them now. I'd lost everything else; I couldn't bear to lose this fight, too.

"Okay," I said. "I'm going to work. Just wanted to tell you the good news."

"Okay, sweetie," said Mom. She looked at her phone, where St George had stood up from his prayers and was now saying something to the camera. "Oh, Hector, didn't somebody call for Emma last night? Aren't you answering your phone, Emma?"

"Yeah," said Dad. "Your boss from the restaurant. Wanted to invite you to some party tonight."

★★★

45

"Some party" was right. Mr Fessy filled me in on the details at work and even let me leave a little early (after clocking out, of course) so I'd have time to shower and change.

I spent my last few dollars on bus fare and as I approached the wide white house of Regional Manager Roger Sorolla and family, I was glad I hadn't walked. The paint was clean and fresh, the windows unbroken. The front door was a cheerful red and stood open. In a small yard of healthy green grass to the left of the house, a handful of men stood around a grill.

From that grill came the most mouth-watering scent I'd ever smelled. As I came up a walkway of neat paving stones, I tried to categorize it. At its base, it reminded me more of reconstituted beef than the extruder chicken we usually bought for dinner, but it wasn't too much like either. Laid over that was something that made me think of the char-broil flavor in some of the grilled chicken meals at Cluck-a-Duck's, but it had a depth and complexity that made the char-broil chemicals of memory seem sickly and green.

I ignored the open front door and headed straight for the grill. The men all looked up as I approached and I felt my stomach go fluttery as I glanced from face to face. They were all at least as old as Keats, dressed in clean, sharp button-downs and khakis. Gold gleamed from the watches on their wrists and the rings on their fingers.

I blew out a relieved breath as I recognized Mr Fessy smiling at me. It had taken me a second: his bright white, well-fitted shirt was like a party hat on a dog. The thought was funny enough to propel me forward a few more steps, until the tallest of the men shifted a long, pronged skewer to his left hand and stuck out his right for a handshake.

"You must be Emma," he said. His smile gleamed white and made lines in his tanned face; his flat blue eyes bored into mine. His hand was big and dry as I shook it. "I'm Roger Sorolla, Regional Manager. Fessy says you're a little genius, isn't that right?"

"Oh, I don't know—" He was still holding my hand; I had the feeling he wouldn't let it go until I'd agreed with him. "I try to work hard."

"Of course you do," said Mr Sorolla. He gestured behind him. I saw an open sliding door, and beyond it, a group of women holding tall, slender glasses in a tidy living room with floors that looked like real wood. "Like the house?"

"It's beautiful," I said, and meant it.

"The entire ground floor is ours. We're supposed to share the yard with the upstairs, but you know how it is. Takes me two hours every other Saturday to mow it. Two hours! The wife complains, but I'll go to Hell before I let this lawn get out of hand. Want some cow?"

"Some what?" I said. He gestured to the grill with his skewer. Sizzling above a low gas fire was the source of the smell that had drawn me over: six gleaming meat patties, dripping fat, with black char lines where they met the grill. Mr Sorolla stuck the tongs into one and tore it partially open to reveal a wavy pink pattern that reminded me of pictures of the human brain I'd seen in school.

"Cow. Cow. Beef? Real beef? Not that extruder shit." The surrounding men all laughed at this. "You ever eat real beef, Emma?"

"No, sir," I said. My stomach sent a message that I roughly translated as *I sure hope we're about to.*

"He's so bad!" A woman was coming through the sliding doors, glass in hand. She was skinnier than I was and for a moment I thought she was taller, until I realized she was wearing high heels. Her skin was white and her hair was blonde and held back by a purple headband that complemented her close-fitting lavender dress. "I said, Roger, there's no need to splurge. Who are you trying to impress? But of course he went ahead and got the good stuff anyway. That's my Roger."

"Emma, this is Mrs Sorolla." Mr Sorolla pointed at each of us with his skewer. I couldn't help but notice that this brought the implement farther away from getting me a piece of cow. "Kate, Emma."

"Aren't you sweet," said Mrs. Sorolla. "Goodness, look at those muscles!"

"Emma is a big Summerlands fan," interjected Mr Fessy, his bald head popping up between the Sorollas.

"Who isn't?" asked Mr Sorolla, and the men all laughed again.

"Oh, the boys love it!" chirped Mrs Sorolla. "I couldn't tell you what we spend on T-shirts, action figures, exclusive feeds, even with Roger's discount. Oh, it's criminal. But we must have the best for the boys. They've got their own bedrooms, would you believe it?" She took in the house behind her with a gesture that slopped a bit of fizzy, tan drink from her glass. "But it's only what any parent would do."

"Well said, darling," agreed Mr Sorolla. He put an arm around her. "Parenting is hard. Kate was so upset by that business with the police chief. Little bleeding heart, this one."

My appetite disappeared as my hungry stomach filled with butterflies. *Maybe they're talking about something else. Please.*

"Well, just imagine!" Mrs Sorolla made another messy gesture with her glass as she pleaded her case to the men around the grill. "Poor Chief Bullard. Jamie will never get into college now, not with that on his record. And forget about a job!"

Shut up, shut up, shut up. My hands were in fists, clenching and unclenching reflexively. My body had put itself into a fighting stance without being asked: feet spread, back straight, knees slightly bent.

"The cop who brought in Jamie," said Mrs Sorolla in a hoarse mock whisper, "I heard his son was killed. Got mixed up with a bad crowd."

Relax. Relax. Start with one hand… let's let go of that fist. There you go. Now the other one…

"I mean, what kind of terrible father lets his son get killed?"

"*Shut up!*" I slapped the glass out of her hand, feeling it shatter under my palm. Bloody shards sprayed across the grass. And as I looked up at the cold, white faces of the men around me, I realized I'd made a terrible mistake.

GREEN AND GOLD

Everyone was shouting, their faces red with anger or white with shock. Their voices roiled around each other like orange clouds, words and phrases breaking through like scorching sunbeams.

"Public decency violation—"

"How dare she!"

"Assault—assault with a deadly weapon—"

"Ungrateful little—"

Mr Sorolla was the only one keeping quiet. The Regional Manager looked at me with naked disgust on his face, then took his wife in his arms as she sobbed noisily over her hand, which had a few scratches from which red was beginning to show.

"Fessy," he said. His voice tolled like a church bell and the men around him fell silent. Even Mrs Sorolla's crying became more subdued.

"Yes, sir?" said Mr Fessy.

"This was your recommendation to replace Schneider?"

"Sir, I had no idea—such breeding—I thought—" As he spluttered, Mr Fessy swept at his mustache again and again in a compulsive, robotic motion. Finally an entire thought surfaced. "Obviously not *now!*"

"This shows quite a lack of judgment, Fessy." Mr Sorolla's voice was cold.

"You're fired!" shouted Mr Fessy suddenly. "Emma—Miss Burke—your services are—don't come in tomorrow!"

"You may join her at the job kiosk, Fessy," said Mr Sorolla.

"Sir!" squeaked Fessy. "Sir, seventeen years, seventeen years I've worked for you—"

"And? So?" Mr Sorolla was stony-faced. "You think you can't be replaced, you little scut? You bring this wild animal to my home and you expect me to give a shit for your loyalty? Get out. You're lucky I don't include you in the charges. Get out. Get out!"

Mr Fessy slunk away across the lush grass and I turned to follow him. Mr Sorolla's big hand fell heavy on my shoulder. I froze.

"Not you. That's a public decency violation easy. Assault and battery. Stay here until the police arrive."

I looked around me. I was more or less surrounded by strong, healthy men who served Mr Sorolla. Half of them looked eager to please; the other half, terrified of making a mistake like Mr Fessy.

"She looks like an escape risk to me," said one of them, an older man with tight skin and slicked-back silver hair.

"Get a chair," said Sorolla. The silver-haired man hurried through the sliding door into the house.

"What are you doing?" I asked. My voice sounded tiny. Mr Sorolla's lackey reappeared with a wooden kitchen chair, which he dropped in front of me. Sorolla pointed to the chair.

"Now, you can either sit here and wait, or we can make you sit."

"You can't do that," I said.

"Miss Burke, my police contract entitles me to one citizen's arrest per quarter, with application of necessary force. You should feel honored that I'm wasting it on you. So I say again: sit or we'll seat you. Your choice."

I collapsed into the chair and doubled over. The fight had gone out of me quicker than it had come and I cursed myself for opening my big mouth. There was no doubt that Sorolla would honor Mr Fessy's final act of firing me.

I could practically see the Summerlands fading away before me. The cobbled streets and white plaster buildings of Wellpoint, nestled beside an azure river that wound between emerald hills; the shadowed eaves of forests that lay at the feet of red mountains stabbing the eternal summer sky; the bright gleam of yellow gold slipping between the dusty gloves of adventurers returned from daring journeys. Jason was there, holding a real sword. All of it turned to gray as the weight of my actions settled on my slumped shoulders. The gray turned to ash and crumbled. What little remained was caught by the wind and floated away on the sound of approaching sirens.

★★★

The police station was a blur. A young, gentle officer processed me and helped Mrs Sorolla make her statement as a rat-faced cop put a blanket over her shoulders and brought her a mug of coffee. The lines on her hand were already white and closed. Officer Porter, Jason's killer, was nowhere to be seen.

All of Sorolla's men made statements as well. They'd made a game of it, laughing and sharing pocket flasks with the cops as they competed to see who could exaggerate my assault most dramatically.

I gave my statement, my confession, to a touchscreen recorder. It played my voice back to me for confirmation and I heard a dead monotone speaking words I had already forgotten. I confirmed the statement. It hardly mattered. A court date popped up on the screen, just a week away, but there was barely even a need for me to show up. The verdict was obvious; only the sentence was left hanging open like a waiting noose.

The police finally released me around three in the morning, long after the Sorollas and their friends had gone home. There was no bus that late, so I steeled myself for the walk back to the apartment block, the final indignity of a day that seemed hell-bent on breaking me. The station doors whooshed open with a chicken-scented puff of air.

Cass and Noah waited just outside. Cass was pacing, hands in pockets; Noah sat against the concrete wall, making complicated hand motions over a paper cup on the ground. They both looked up as I came out and Cass immediately drew me into a bear hug. There were tears in her eyes as we broke apart.

"God, I thought they'd never let you out! Are you okay?"

"Hungry," I said. Noah stood, put his cup carefully in a pocket, and hugged me as well. "It's so good to see you guys. How'd you know I was here?"

"They never took Dad's police scanner back." Cass laughed. "Come on, we've got a long walk home."

As we walked, they peppered me with questions. I had to describe slapping the glass from Mrs Sorolla's hand a dozen times. Finally, I wound up in a detailed recollection of the sight and smell of the cow on Mr Sorolla's grill. I'd come closer than any of Hearthammer to eating real meat, aside from Keats himself, who'd had it as a kid. Dreams of sizzling patties carried us back to the block and if I was starving by the time we made it to Cass's apartment, at least I was feeling something other than numb misery.

★★★

I woke up just as hungry as I'd gone to bed, and as Cass stirred in the lower bunk and Noah unfolded himself from the floor, we quickly found we were all feeling the same way.

"Can't wait to get at that refined protein," said Cass as she reached down to touch her toes. "I don't have any clients today and Emma is on permanent vacation. You working, Noah?"

"No," he said, imitating Cass's stretches.

"Then it's a training day. Eat big and get ready to hurt."

"Cass." I slid down the ladder from Jason's bunk. "We need to talk about this."

"Talk about what?" She stood on her right foot, pulling her left leg up behind her back.

"The Summerlands. Guys, I was there when they booked me. They're putting me up on assault charges. That's serious. Do either of you really, truly think I'm gonna be found innocent?"

Cass looked at the floor, but Noah just kept his steady brown-eyed gaze on me, waiting for the other shoe to drop.

52

"I'm going to—" I choked, unable to finish the thought. After a deep breath, I tried again. "I'm going to jail. Not forever, but... long enough."

"We'll wait," said Noah.

"It'll take years to save up the money again," Cass agreed.

"So I get out, then what?" I spread my empty hands. "I'll have nothing saved. I won't be able to get a job. I'm dead weight, guys. You need to find someone else."

"I *need* to eat some goddamn breakfast," said Cass, clapping her hands. She pushed past me and opened the bedroom door. "Dad! Dad, you up?"

Silence answered her.

"That's weird," said Cass. "He usually has breakfast on by now. Maybe he's still asleep."

"Maybe he didn't feel up to cooking," I said. "I know he can still reach the stove and everything, but it obviously hurts more than he lets on."

"Let's make breakfast," said Noah.

"Sure," said Cass. "I can—hey, what's this?" She bent down to snatch up an unmarked white envelope from the hallway floor. "Emma, you leave this?"

"No, I was going to start putting my paycards into the bank again." I came up to peer over her shoulder as she opened the envelope. It was lined in green and contained a folded sheet of white printer paper. Cass pulled it out and unfolded it to reveal a single sentence written in blue pen.

"*I refuse to stand in the way of your dreams,*" Cass read. Her voice started strong and ended in a whisper.

She dropped the envelope on the floor as I started yelling for Keats. There was no response. The three of us ran into the hall. I tore the kitchen door open to find it empty. A glance down the hall to where Cass and Noah stood at her father's bedroom door earned me a quick shake of the head: *no.* They disappeared into the bedroom anyway and I followed.

Cass stood by the single window. Like the kitchen window, it looked onto the fire escape and, beyond that, a collapsed chain-link fence that separated the back alley from the expanse of brown grass and dust that we used as our training grounds.

A single tree still lived in the field, gray and leafless. Beneath its skeletal branches we could see a seated shape next to an empty wheelchair.

"Dad!" Cass screamed out the window, across the empty space of alley and field. Her father did not respond.

★★★

Panicked memories of the last time I was on the fire escape rushed up my throat like vomit, but I swallowed them down as I helped Cass shake the ladder loose. Cass hoisted herself over and slid down twenty feet to the seventh-floor landing, shedding rust flakes as she went. I followed only a few seconds behind, Noah's sneakers inches above my head. From the next balcony we took a series of switchback staircases that rattled and banged as we pounded down them two at a time.

At the third floor landing another ladder waited. Cass kicked it loose and clambered aboard as it was still falling. She rode it down to the alley and tumbled off as it clattered home. She was on her feet by the time Noah and I caught up. We leapt the fallen-down fence together and sprinted across the field.

Keats looked up from where he sat, his back against the bare tree, the wheelchair off to one side.

"I thought you'd be excited, but this is a bit excessive, don't you think?" he said, but his smile fell as he saw Cass's horrified face. "What? What is it? Are you okay?"

"Dad—Dad!" Cass fell to her knees and threw her arms around her father. "We saw your note and I thought—I thought you—"

"Thought I what?" Keats's face was a perfect mask of bemusement.

"Oh, nevermind." Cass slumped to the ground next to Keats. "So what *did* you mean?"

"I thought it was pretty obvious," said Keats, still puzzled. "You could say thank you, you know."

"For *what?*" Cass seemed ready to explode.

"For the love of all that's holy, Cassidy Keats, did you not look in the envelope?" Keats began to laugh. Cass looked back at me and Noah, and her face said she felt about as stupid as I did.

"Go," said Keats, and he was still laughing as we slunk away. The trip back up to Cass's room took much longer than our mad dash down the fire escape, but as our mutual embarrassment wore off we began to move faster, drawn by the mystery of Keats's words.

In the hallway, Keats's note still lay half-open by the baseboard. Cass beat me to it, snatched up the envelope, and tore it nearly in half in her eagerness to get it open. Three fat cards, lush green printed with glittering golden whorls, fell into her hands.

I grabbed one before she could stop me. "*Noah Garcia Benatar,*" I read from golden letters stamped deep into the green. "Are these—"

"*Cassidy Keats,*" read Cass. She was holding the other two cards, one in each hand, her eyes flickering back and forth between them. "*Emma Burke.*"

★★★

"How did you even get out here?" Cass asked. "I know they didn't fix the elevator."

We were together around the tree in the back field; Cass snuggled under her father's arm, I sat cross-legged on his other side, and Noah paced a little circle in the dust. I fingered the heavy card that was my ticket into the Summerlands.

"Mr Vogler carried me," said Keats. "He's pretty strong for an old guy."

"When I read your note and then you weren't in the apartment, I thought…"

"Got you," said Keats.

"Why do you think they print these cards?" I asked, holding mine up so the golden letters glittered in the thin morning sun. "You had to give them our SSNs and everything, right, Keats? And I'm sure when we get there we'll have to do some biometric ID validation. Why the physical tickets?"

"That seems like the sort of thing Noah would know," said Cass, but he just continued pacing, staring at his own ticket.

"They missed the accent mark on the 'i,'" he said.

"I'm sure they'll still let you in." I shook my head in wonder at his total nonchalance about the whole thing. Good old Noah.

"I can't believe we're really going," said Cass for maybe the hundredth time.

"How is Keats going to pay his medical bills?" Noah said.

Cass and I looked at each other. She opened her mouth, closed it, opened it again. I'm sure I looked about the same. He was right. The money Hearthammer had saved was enough for three tickets, but that left Keats at square one with no job and no savings. Cass wriggled out from under her father's arm.

"Dad, what did you do? That money was for you—we all agreed! I know it wouldn't pay for everything, but we could live—we could live—*there are no refunds*!"

"Nope," said Keats. He put his hands behind his head and leaned back against the tree.

"How are you going to pay your bills?" asked Noah.

"I'll think of something," said Keats. "I've got a month or so still saved up, so I've got time."

"You'll never be able to get a job," I said. I was starting to feel that terrible weight again.

"Ye of little faith," said Keats.

"We can make the money." Noah stopped and turned to look at us straight on.

"What?" said Cass.

"In the Summerlands," Noah said. "We can make the money. The rangers are turning up new ruins all the time. We

56

just have to be the first to reach one of them and bring back all the treasure."

Cass leapt up and took over the pacing. "We'll have to hit the ground running," she said. "We can support Dad while we're still here, but once we get to the Summerlands we'll only have a month. We're not even ready to get in the game yet, not really. We've got so much more practicing to do. And I think we can afford the plane tickets, but there are gonna be travel expenses… dammit!" She kicked at the dirt. "Dad!"

"If my worst sin as a father is that I believe in my kids too much, I think I'll be okay," said Keats.

"Okay, everybody settle down," said Cass as though her father hadn't spoken. "Six weeks? Six weeks. I'll take on as many hours as I can and we'll practice every night. You two"—she jabbed fingers at me and Noah—"practice twelve hours a day. Actually, Noah, get a job. Get a job *and* give me twelve hours a day. Any spells you've been putting off, learn them. Even the ones from the Golden Apple videos—*especially* those ones. Emma, we need firepower. Noah, without Jason, you're our tank, so get your buffs and heals straight. Emma, you'll be exposed now, so we're gonna step up your combat training. I want you to pick up something for a shield and carry it every-where—"

"Cass," I said.

"Don't complain, it's good for you!" she snapped. "I can see it now. One-handed magic, shield and bell, like a hybrid thing—"

"Cass!"

"Don't interrupt me! We don't have time!"

"We *don't* have time!" I shouted. Cass stopped pacing. "My court date is in a week! Maybe, *maybe* if we leave now I can slip away if they haven't put me on the no-fly list. But six weeks from now? I'm gonna be behind bars. It's now or never."

THE COMPLEX

My heart pounded nonstop for hours as Cass, Noah, and I threw what little we could bring with us into a single duffle bag, took the bus to LAX, and bought our plane tickets. I kept my eyes down in the security line, willing the cops not to notice me, and we made it through without a word about my arrest. It seemed the HECZ police hadn't thought to put me on the no-fly list after all.

We spent seven hours in the air, then another three on a layover in New York, during which they wouldn't let us off the plane. From there we crossed the Atlantic to Glasgow, a city in the western islands of the European Union. None of us had ever flown before and we spent the trip peering out the windows as thousands of miles of farmland, coast, and ocean unspooled below us. But by the time we were on our last connecting plane, from Glasgow to Expedition Games's private landing strip, the novelty of flight had worn off along with our adrenaline.

"I wish we'd had time to explore Glasgow," I said. We were alone on the flight, which served only Expedition employees and new players for the Summerlands, and I was sprawled across two seats with my feet up, eating a bag of soy nuts that they'd given me completely free.

"It has a long history," said Noah. He was sitting upright and proper in his seat, his seatbelt buckled neatly across his lap. "The proximity to the Summerlands portal really revitalized the city's economy."

"Oh, who cares?" said Cass. She lay across an entire row with a sweatshirt over her eyes. She'd said she wanted to sleep, but hadn't moved out of earshot of me and Noah. "Get me to the Summerlands as fast as possible. I've been waiting my whole life for this."

"You've been waiting five years for this," corrected Noah and Cass laughed.

"Right as always, nerd." She rolled onto her side. I threw a soy nut at her, but she didn't notice as it bounced off her sneaker.

"There's the Isle of Lewis!" I said. We'd left the mainland and spent the last few minutes over gray ocean. Now the rocky cliffs and yellow grass of a large island were just visible out my window.

"Technically it's Lewis and Harris," said Noah, crowding in behind me. I sat back to give him a proper view. "It's one island with two names."

"The whole thing is owned by Expedition, right?" asked Cass. She'd given up on her nap and had her face pressed up against the window in the row behind us.

"That's right," said Noah. "They bought the whole island right before the announcement about the Summerlands."

"Lucky them," said Cass.

The island quickly grew larger as the plane banked around for the approach to Expedition's landing strip. We came in over the hilly southern reach of the island and headed directly towards a wide plateau of yellow and brown grass dotted with shallow ponds. I was watching for the runway and it appeared suddenly, a long stretch of gray between two flat pools that reflected the belly of the plane.

For the third time in twenty-four hours my stomach lurched as we swept in towards the runway. The pilot brought us down neatly, but our little plane felt every bump of turbulence much more than the big airliner from the HECZ had. As we taxied to a stop, it took every ounce of my self-control to keep from throwing up the soy nuts I'd been enjoying not long before.

"You can open your eyes, adventurer," said Cass. I did, and saw her standing above me holding our duffel bag. "Come on, the limo is waiting."

"Limo?" I said as we made our way between the seats. Noah was at the end of the aisle, chatting with the pilot.

"I know!" said Cass. "Noah can cross two more off his 'modes of transportation' checklist."

We caught up with Noah just as the plane door hissed open. The pilot unfolded metal stairs down to the tarmac. Cass went first, fairly leaping down the steps. Noah followed close behind her. I took a breath and went after them.

As promised, a limo waited for us on the runway, sleek and black. The driver stood by an open rear door. He was dressed in black, but the boxy cut of his suit resembled a medieval herald's tabard. The logo of Expedition Games was stitched over his heart in silver thread. If not for his mirror shades, he might have fit in nicely at some king's court.

The driver gestured us into the limo. He reached out for the duffel bag in Cass's hands, but she pulled back from him sharply and he relented. As we got seated, the driver peered back at the plane.

"Missing somebody?" he asked. He had a rough local accent. My heart leapt in my chest, and I could see Cass stiffen beside me.

"What do you mean?" asked Noah. He was seated across from Cass, facing her, and he looked more intrigued than anxious.

"I was told there'd be four on the plane—ah, there we go." He swept his hand toward the limo as a young man dressed in black came down the stairs.

"Where the hell did he come from?" Cass whispered. "I thought we were alone on the plane."

"Me too," I said. "Was he hiding?"

He was small, shorter than me and with a slimmer build, though he looked about my age. High cheekbones and a sharp, smooth chin gave his face an elfin look beneath hair that was shaved on the sides and long on top, slicked back but clearly as thick and black as Noah's. His ears stuck out from his head like jug handles. A tight black T-shirt and jeans plus matching black boots were the only things he seemed to own aside from the tattoos covering his tanned arms.

As he slid into the seat across from me, he gave me a huge grin.

"Hello," he said, in a thick accent that made the H sound like a cat's hiss.

"Hi," I said. Next to me, Cass crossed her arms. I knew that look: she was sizing up the competition. The young man gestured vaguely to himself.

"Karakatsa," he said, or that's what it sounded like.

"What language is that?" asked Noah. His new seatmate looked over at him and shook his head, then indicated himself again. "Karakatsa."

"Russian, maybe?" said Cass.

"Nice to meet you, Karakatsa," I said to him. I was no-where close on the accent, but he seemed thrilled nonetheless as he barked out a laugh and slapped me on the knee. "Linnaea," I said, pointing to myself. It felt weird to be using our gamertags, but this guy obviously was, and he seemed to be a fellow adventurer. "Sepharad. Jessamine."

"Time to go," said our driver from the front seat. He pressed a button on the dashboard, and the engine came to life with a purr. The limo pulled away smoothly, leaving the little plane behind, and turned onto a two-lane road that wound around one of the nearby lakes and headed into the hills.

"Is this gonna be a problem in the Summerlands?" asked Cass.

"Is what?" I asked.

"Languages," she said. "People come from all over the world. How does everybody talk to each other?"

"You wanna take this or should I?" I asked Noah with a smile.

"Go ahead," he said. He had edged over in his seat to put space between himself and Karakatsa. The young man slumped in his seat staring out at the scenery, tapping the window idly with one knuckle.

61

"Very long story short, no, it's not gonna be a problem," I said. "Apparently, once you're in the Summerlands, everybody can understand each other. Nobody's really sure how it works, and obviously, it doesn't apply to the feeds—you ever try to watch Valkyrie's stream? It's all in Icelandic. But if you're there, you just understand."

Cass glanced at Karakatsa, then back at me. "Wasn't there a whole thing about translating the Elvish writings they found, though?"

"Maybe it doesn't work on Elvish," I suggested.

"Weird," said Cass.

"Magic," said Noah.

★★★

Our nervous silence lasted unbroken for nearly half an hour. I mostly stared at the window at the yellow landscape rolling by, but every now and again I would look over to find Karakatsa staring at me. I was just debating saying something to him when the limo stopped and the driver said, "Checkpoint."

We piled out of the limo to find that we'd pulled up at a steel gate in a high concrete wall that stretched for at least half a mile in either direction. From the top of the wall, guards stared down at us at intervals of fifty feet or so. They reminded me of how Porter had come dressed the night he killed Jason, with riot gear strapped over T-shirts and big black rifles.

"Good luck," said the driver as the gate rolled open in a slow, stately motion. Beyond, a row of armed guards waited to receive us. The driver rolled up his window, backed the limo up to the edge of the road, and drove back the way we'd come. Soon he was gone amongst the hills, leaving us alone with the guards.

"Step forward," one of them said. Noah went first, and Cass and I followed. Karakatsa trailed behind us. We passed through the gate. Beyond it was an asphalt yard, maybe a hundred feet square, surrounded on all sides by what looked to be the guards' quarters. Directly across from us, a small archway opened on a path that led further into the hills.

"Place your belongings here." The guard pointed to a yellow square painted on the asphalt. Cass set her duffel bag down and Karakatsa spread his hands to show he had nothing on him.

"Fine," said the guard. "Put your feet together and your arms out." We complied, holding the pose as guards patted us down while others searched Cass's duffel.

"At least buy me dinner first, huh?" said Cass. I rolled my eyes. The guard who was currently running one hand around the inside of her waistband said nothing.

"Okay," said the guard who seemed to be in charge. He pointed to the archway across the yard. "Pass through that door and take the path there. Do not leave the path. Do not stop walking until you reach the complex. You can expect to be there in twenty minutes."

"What about our stuff?" said Cass.

"What about it?" asked the guard.

"Can we have it back, please?" The tone of Cass's voice was sharply at odds with her polite phrasing.

"No," said the guard. "Everything you brought with you is forfeit at this point. Your clothes will be taken from you at your medical examination. After that you'll be given your starting equipment."

"I'm cold," said Cass. "I need a sweater from my bag."

"Fine," said the guard. "It will be taken at the complex, though."

"Fine," said Cass. She unzipped the duffel and began to rummage through it. There wasn't much to pick through; we'd known our stuff would be taken eventually, so we'd only packed what we needed for the trip itself. Cass pulled out a threadbare heather-gray athletic sweatshirt and tugged it on over her head. It had "HECZ SD #12" printed on the front and was much too big for her.

It was Jason's.

63

★★★

The walk from the checkpoint took us along a gravel path that wound between the low hills that characterized this part of Lewis. The uplands of the island were fairly unwelcoming, at least at this time of year. Patches of wavy gray stone stuck up from the yellowed grass, the only things to break the monotony besides a few scraggly shrubs. In some places the hills were scarred with rectangular lines that Noah said were the remnants of peat-cutting operations. Under the flat gray sky, it was cool enough that I found myself wishing for a sweatshirt of my own.

As we walked, Noah gave us a brief history of the island, which seemed to have been mostly the domain of sheep-farmers before Expedition bought it. Karakatsa made himself a part of the conversation despite the obvious handicap of not understanding a word we said; he listened attentively to Noah's lecture, nodding and smiling as Noah pointed out the landscape around us. I didn't pay much attention, though, too wrapped up in pondering the decision to make new players walk a mile between the checkpoint and whatever waited for us at the complex.

Twenty minutes of walking brought us to a final bend where the hills fell away to reveal a low, rambling structure nestled in a dell below us. It was two stories in most places but only one in the center, which seemed to hold an open courtyard. The whole thing looked like the buildings Expedition had put up in Wellpoint, a sort of faux Elizabethan design with lots of exposed beams and white plaster.

I paused where the path began its descent into the dell, and Cass stopped at my side.

"You okay?" she said.

"Yeah," I said. "Just nervous, you know?"

"Don't worry, we'll be famous streamers before you know it."

"I think I'm gonna keep my camera off," I said. "I just want to make enough money for your dad."

"More fans for me." Cass slapped me on the back and set off down the hill. Noah, Karakatsa, and I hurried to catch up, and we came down the last stretch of path as a group, huddled close against the wind that followed us from the hills.

The gravel petered out at a heavy door set into the near wall of the complex. It looked like wood with iron bands across it, but as we neared, it swept up into the ceiling. The building itself was a charade too; the wood and plaster were actually painted concrete.

The room that awaited us was bright and white, almost blindingly so after the dim sun outside. Sitting in plush chairs along one wall were two men in colorful patterned shirts, shorts, and sandals. One of them leapt up as we entered and nudged the other, who looked no better than half awake.

"Alan! They're here! Alan, get up!" The peppier of the two men crossed the room to us, his hand stuck out. He was tall, with a large belly beneath his shirt, which was printed with multi-colored birds. His face was red and only a few black hairs stuck out from the top of his head.

"Pleased to meet you all! I'm Neal Markan, Dr Neal Markan, but you can call me Dr Neal, ha!" He shook our hands one by one, and stopped in front of Karakatsa. "Now, you, sir, Greek, isn't that right? We don't have an interpreter, I'm afraid, but I'm sure we'll muddle through."

Karakatsa just grinned back at him.

"Now," said Dr Neal, "this is Alan Brodie, our resident man of the law. Ha! Say hello, Alan."

"Miss Keats." The lawyer waved sleepily from his chair. His accent was like the limo driver's.

"Now then," Dr Neal said with a clap of his hands. "We're going to double-team you to get this over as quick as possible. I draw the blood and Alan sucks it, huh? Ha! Just a joke, Alan, you know I love you. Seriously, though, what's going to happen is a combination medical exam and final body search. I'm sure you've heard the stories. Apologies ahead of time. We've got nurses for the ladies, by the way. Ha! While we're doing that, Alan will give you the paperwork. Plenty of that.

Here's the deal. Here's the deal. We're just looking for your basic congenital defects, cancers, flat feet, pregnancies, that sort of thing. Just kidding about the feet, by the way! Really just looking for anything that would kill you before the hell rats do. Okay! Any questions?"

"Uh, what's with the shirts?" asked Cass.

"Oh!" Dr Neal laughed. "Hawaiian day in the office, don't you know."

★★★

The next few hours passed much as Dr Neal had promised. Noah and Karakatsa were promptly taken to a separate room by the jovial doctor, but I was relieved to learn that Cass and I would be allowed to go through everything together. Two laconic nurses drew our blood, checked our eyes and ears and throats, tested our reflexes, and searched every cavity in as invasive a manner as possible.

As the nurses did their thing, Cass and I forged our way through reams of paperwork provided by Alan Brodie and his aides. With a yawn, Brodie detailed a young lawyer to stick around and patiently explain page after page of disclosures and releases. I signed away my right to sue and swore that I understood what I was getting into. I learned for the first time that all feeds were on a ten-second delay and Expedition Games reserved the right to censor any content they deemed inappropriate. I acknowledged the extremely limited rules of the game: no player-versus-player violence or other crime, no teaching magic to anyone who wasn't a paying player, no approaching the wall that bounded Expedition's territory in the Summerlands. I gave the lawyer my gamertag and had to spell it for him twice. He told me my feed would be set up and added to Expedition's tracking immediately, so I could start streaming as soon as my drone was synced up.

Finally the paperwork was done. Cass had worn Jason's sweatshirt through it all, taking it off only as directed and putting it back on as soon as she could. The last round of body searches required us to switch into hospital gowns, though, and she sat twisting the sweatshirt in her lap as Dr Neal came back in.

"One more procedure," he said. "Then you'll be set loose to seek your fortunes! Ha, always so exciting to induct our latest band of adventurers. Best part of my job, this."

From a cabinet on the wall, Dr Neal drew out what looked like the older brother of the gun that had pierced my ears at the mall when I was a kid.

"RFID chip implantation," he said. "They'll give you your drones on the other side. I'd say it won't hurt a bit, but you and I both know it's gonna sting. Still, it beats a bite from a trash snake, eh?" He waggled his free hand at us and I saw a large white scar in the shape of a set of teeth.

"You've been in the Summerlands?" asked Cass.

"Sure have," said Dr Neal as he walked behind us. "Started as a player, actually. Thought I'd make a fortune as a doctor, but it turns out the old needle and thread can't compare to healing magic. Wasn't much cut out for magic, wasn't a big fan of getting bitten in the sewers, so I talked to the woman upstairs about a change of jobs. Turns out they were just looking for a new head doc and here I am. Okay, you might want to bite down."

There was a snap and a searing pain in the back of my neck. "Ow!" I yelped. I slapped my hand over the burning spot and felt a small square lump that hadn't been there a moment before.

"Your turn," said Dr Neal to Cass. I watched as he pushed his implement against the back of her neck and pressed a trigger. With a sharp click, the gun implanted Cass's RFID chip under her skin. She gritted her teeth and stayed quiet, though her hands were wringing Jason's sweatshirt almost into a knot.

"All done!" said Dr Neal. "Now, don't pick at them for a day or so. It'll itch for a bit and then you won't even know it's there. Okay, that's everything from me. Got all your paperwork done? Good! Let's go find the boys. It's time for you to meet the woman upstairs."

Apollonia Blomhaugen, CEO of the largest company in the world, met us in the central courtyard of the Expedition Games complex. The woman who'd taken the reins from Dr Agony had long white-blonde hair, high ruddy cheekbones, and wrinkles around her eyes; a pin-striped jacket and pencil skirt hugged her willowy frame. She was trailed by a gaggle of aides who seemed to write down everything she said and every now and then she'd murmur something to one or another that sent the aide scampering away.

The courtyard stood in stark contrast to the clean, white rooms we'd gone through during our checkup. The entire complex was built to house the well that held the portal to the Summerlands and a few hundred square feet of land around it had been left undisturbed. We waited barefoot on soft, smoky-scented peat as a gentle rain pattered down from the square of gray sky above us. Noah and Karakatsa had appeared a few minutes after us in hospital gowns, rubbing their necks, and I'm sure we looked the same. Cass still held Jason's sweatshirt, but other than that we'd given over everything we had.

The well itself was unremarkable, not much more than a half-collapsed pile of stones. I didn't have the nerve to get any closer to it, let alone peer in. I was surprised to see what looked like a dozen tree roots, as thick as my leg, emerging from it. There were no trees in the courtyard; instead, the roots ran to points along the walls of the complex.

"Data uplinks," said Blomhaugen, as though she'd read my mind. She had a sort of lilting accent that made me think of stone and snow. "They run through the portal to the drone station on the other side. Nothing you need to worry about."

I nodded.

"Now then," Blomhaugen continued. Cass, Noah, Kara-katsa and I stood in a line before her, and she surveyed us like an army officer inspecting her troops. "You are about to be issued your starting equipment. A basic set of clothing has been made to your measurements. You will also receive fifty copper coins. This is enough to pay for food and lodging for about a week. If you wish to live in any sort of comfort afterwards, you will be fending for yourself. Do you understand?"

The members of Hearthammer nodded, but Karakatsa didn't seem to realize a question had been asked. According to Noah, Karakatsa had been taken away during their checkup to go through all the legal forms with a telephone interpreter. I hoped he understood what he had agreed to.

"Here they are now," said Blomhaugen. One of her aides returned with a pile of clothing, atop which sat four leather pouches. The aide passed them to us smoothly then retreated back behind Blomhaugen.

"Please get changed," Blomhaugen continued. "I will speak as you do." Cass and I shared a look, but Noah and Karakatsa were already stripping. Despite being a spellcaster, Noah had put on a lot of muscle in the last few years, and I was reminded of the evening not so long ago when I'd watched Jason get changed for work.

Karakatsa was much smaller, but lean and tough-looking, with about zero body fat. His entire torso was covered in tattoos. There were a few bigger pieces depicting chains, swords, and dragon's heads, but most of the ink seemed to be words and numbers. I suddenly noticed Cass was half-naked, so I hurried to untie my paper gown as Blomhaugen talked.

"You have paid for the privilege of entering the Summerlands," the CEO said. "How you use that privilege is your decision. Expedition Games does not interfere in the game. Do not expect us to save you if you get in over your heads."

I tugged on tight-fitting leather breeches that covered me from ankles to belly button. The shirt was a lighter material and slipped on easily over my head. I tied it closed over my chest and sat to pull on a pair of soft leather boots.

"Still, we do have one request of you," Blomhaugen went on. "Give us good streams. What that means is up to you, but if you give us good television, you will be well taken care of. Now then." She stopped in front of Cass, who was fully dressed and looked born to wear the faux-medieval garb she'd been given. "Miss Keats, I am afraid you must relinquish your brother's sweater."

I stood up as Cass stared at the CEO with tears in her eyes.

"Entering the Summerlands, you are born again. You are given a new life. You must let go of all artifacts of the world you are leaving behind." Blomhaugen's voice was soft, almost a whisper. She spoke to Cass alone. "Now is not the time to fear change."

Cass handed Blomhaugen the sweatshirt, which the CEO passed to an aide behind her. Immediately, Noah and I wrapped Cass up in a bear hug that only broke up when Blomhaugen said, "Ready."

Cass took my right hand and Noah my left as we walked to the well. Their hands were slick with sweat, and I'm sure mine were, too. Soon we stood peering over the lip of the well. A few yards down, a ring of moss glowed among the muck.

"We'll never forget him," I whispered to Cass. "No matter what happens."

She nodded and bit her lip. Her eyes were locked on the glowing portal, as though if she just stared hard enough she could see into the Summerlands on the other side.

"I'll go first if you want," said Noah. His voice was steady, but his hand was shaking in mine.

"No, I'll go," said Cass. "If that's all right. I'm party leader, after all." I let go of her hand and watched her climb onto the rim of the well.

"Wait," I said. Cass looked over her shoulder at me, and Noah turned as well. "I just… promise me that you'll watch my back."

"And you'll watch mine, right?" said Cass.

"Of course," I said. "Of course I will. Just promise me, okay?"

"I promise," Cass said.

"Jump," said Blomhaugen behind us. Cass turned back to the well, gave us one last glance over her shoulder, closed her eyes, and jumped. The moment her head cleared the stone lip I leaned forward to watch, but she was already gone.

Noah squeezed my hand, then clambered up onto the well. He gave me a smile, turned, and leapt down after Cass.

I looked at Karakatsa, who had come up next to me to watch the others go through. He gestured politely towards the well, but I shook my head. He nodded and climbed up. Still facing me, he crossed his arms over his chest and hopped backwards into the darkness.

I was alone. I looked at Blomhaugen for encouragement, but she had her back to me, conferring with her aides. After a moment she looked up as though she could feel me staring, and our eyes locked, but she returned to her huddle without acknowledging the moment.

"Goodbye," I said, looking up at the sky. A few orange clouds twined through the dismal gray pall. It was ugly, but it was the only sky I'd ever known. I took a shaking step up onto the well, and then another. The moss ring glowed beneath my feet. It looked tiny from up here. The well seemed to go down for miles and miles into the earth. It hadn't seemed so far when I was standing on solid ground.

"For Jason," I said. "For Keats."

I stepped off into open air.

PORTAL SQUARE

I fell through stars and woke with the sun in my eyes. Somebody was screaming. Everybody was screaming. The sun was dazzling white in a sharp blue sky and I blinked away tears.

A shadow fell over me and I felt hot breath on my face. It smelled horrible, like a sewage leak. I tried to roll away from the smell, but I couldn't move. I opened my eyes to see a long green tongue rasping over white needle teeth, shedding little sparks. The fangs gleamed along their razor edges.

"Linnaea, move!" A compact black shape tumbled over me, taking the green tongue and glinting teeth with it. I lurched to my feet. It felt like I'd just spent an hour tumbling around in a clothes dryer, but I was able to keep my legs under me as I tried to get my bearings.

I stood beneath an arched stone gazebo on a colorful bed of flowers. My feet were in the exact center of a greenish ring of moss. All around me, people were shouting, fighting, and running across the cobblestone plaza that surrounded the flowerbed. In among them were maybe a dozen creatures about the size of boars, with flat faces, spiny backs, and green tongues lolling around gleaming rows of fangs. Most of the boar-things were chasing fleeing people, but a few faced off against adventurers who held swords and spears in their hands.

I was in Portal Square, the heart of Wellpoint. I was in the Summerlands. I was also in a whole lot of danger.

To my left, Karakatsa was struggling with a boar. It was up on two legs with its front hooves on his shoulders. It snapped at his throat as he tried to shove it off. He must have been the one who'd gotten the thing off me: I hadn't recognized his voice

72

because he'd been speaking English. Spinning around, I discovered that Cass and Noah were nowhere in sight.

Images of the fight in the Keatses' apartment flashed through my mind, holding me frozen in the moss ring as I watched them play out again. Jason kicking in the locked window. Porter with his Armalite in one hand and Cass's twisted wrist in the other. Jason's body lying motionless on the floor, his blood creeping toward me as I stood as helpless as I was now...

I was supposed to be past this!

"Linnaea!" Karakatsa shouted as he fell under the weight of the boar. He put up his arms to cover his throat and face and the boar-thing roared in anticipation of a bloody meal.

A massive, armor-clad form strode past me, a bloody sword in his hand. He was dressed like a medieval crusader, in battered plate armor and a white tabard bearing a huge red cross, and spattered all over with green gunk.

Without thinking, I grabbed his free arm.

"Hey, you have to help me!" I shouted over the noise of the fight. He turned his helmeted head slowly, then flipped up his visor to peer down at me. His face was deeply lined and weatherworn, with a gray mustache, and I recognized it immediately: St George, legendary monster-slayer and notorious religious wackjob.

"My friend needs help!" I yelled, pointing to where Karakatsa was barely keeping the boar-thing away from his throat.

Without a word, St George slammed his visor shut, strode over to the struggle, and drove his sword through the back of the boar's head. The gory tip erupted from its mouth, spraying blood over Karakatsa's face.

"With the holy cross I slay thee, demon!" roared St George. "In Christ's name I consign thee back to Hell!" He tore his sword out, sending brains and blood flying in a wet arc, then stalked off.

"Thanks," said Karakatsa heavily. I ran to him and helped him up. He stood wiping blood from his eyes for a moment, then looked me up and down and flashed the wide grin I'd already gotten so familiar with. "And thank you, too."

"You're welcome, Karakatsa," I said. I watched St George wade back into the fray, his sword swinging, shouting in what sounded like Latin. "It's nice to be able to talk to you."

"Kara—" He looked confused for a moment, then barked out a laugh. "Magpie! It's Magpie."

"Emma!"

I whirled to see Noah waving frantically from behind a wide column of the gazebo that surrounded the flowerbed. I grabbed Karakatsa's—Magpie's—hand and dragged him towards the scanty cover.

We found Noah and Cass with their backs pressed to the stone pillar, making themselves as small as possible. Noah looked relieved to see me, but Cass's eyes were wide and white. Her throat fluttered as she panted with short, shallow breaths.

"Is she okay?" I asked Noah.

"I think she's having a panic attack," he said.

"I don't blame her," I said. I took a deep breath to make sure I didn't do the same. "What the hell is happening?"

"It started right as we got here," Noah said. "There was a grating in the ground—I think for sewer access—and it blew open and those things came out. I asked Jessamine what to do and she started breathing like that so I pulled her over here. Was that St George?"

"What?" I said. "Oh, yeah. He saved us. This is Magpie, by the way."

"Nice to meet you," said Noah, and stuck out his hand. Magpie shook it vigorously as Noah went on, "Is *Karakatsa* Greek for Magpie?"

"Yeah," said Magpie.

"I'm Sepharad," Noah said. He pointed to me, then to Cass. "This is Linnaea. She's Jessamine. Do you think—"

"Later," I said, putting a hand on Noah's arm. "How do we survive this?"

"I don't think that'll be a problem," said Magpie. He was peering around the shelter of the column. "Those guys are cleaning up."

"Who?" asked Noah. We poked our heads out to see that the vibe in the square had changed considerably. Where there had been chaos and panic, a group of four adventurers had taken charge. A musclebound, dark-skinned man was crushing boars with a maul nearly as big as Magpie. A slender, pale woman with raven hair stalked behind him, slitting the throats of any monster that so much as twitched. A small man perched on an overturned cart, apparently talking to himself. In the middle of the fray, shouting orders and pointing with a bell in his hand, was a tall man with a salt-and-pepper beard and red robes. Around them, four camera drones swirled and dove like warrior angels as they hurried to keep their owners in frame.

"Golden Apple," I whispered.

"Wolfheart looks older in person," said Noah.

★★★

Golden Apple blew in like a whirlwind and disappeared as quickly. In the space of moments they took command of the battle in the square. Rad and Valkyrie killed off the boar monsters while Dr Agony directed the panicked mob to safety. As far as I could tell, neither he nor Wolfheart had cast a spell.

With the last of the boars slain, Golden Apple was gone again, leaving a bloody, stinking mess behind. No one seemed to have been seriously hurt, but the gore was unbelievable. The dead monsters lay with their skulls shattered, limbs broken, and guts spilling out. Insects descended in buzzing mobs on the remains. I thought they were flies until I realized they were flashing faintly red, their glow washed out by the bright sun.

I stood in shock for a while, wondering if Portal Square would ever be clean again, until I noticed people creeping back into the plaza. They came out of hiding from behind the doors of shops and around alley corners. Most were dressed in bland, fantasy-medieval clothing, but some wore brighter colors and carried weapons.

Slowly, Portal Square came back to life. A group of workers in simple clothes began hauling the boar corpses to one side of the square and heaving them into something resembling a pile. Two young men, holding hands and laughing, strolled through the carnage to a shop across from me. A hushed argument broke out amongst a group of mussed, bloodied adventurers, apparently over who had killed a particular monster.

"Come on," I said. "Let's go help."

Soon Cass and I were lifting a dead boar by its legs. Its mouth fell open and its long green tongue lolled out. We hauled it to the growing corpse pile as it leaked sludgy brown blood on the cobblestones. The panic had left Cass's face and she was moving normally, but she hadn't spoken.

"It's okay," I said. She looked up at me with burning eyes.

"I choked," she said. Her voice cracked with bitterness.

Before I could respond, a chipper voice broke our reverie. "Hey there! Haven't seen you two around town. New NPCs?"

I turned to see a heavyset woman about Keats's age watching us haul the boar corpse. She wore a clean leather apron over a loose blouse and a kilt in a red, green, and black pattern.

"Adventurers," said Cass without looking up. "Not that you'd know it."

"Ah," said the woman, "apologies. It's just that adventurers don't usually help with the cleanup."

Cass and I shared a look as we swung the corpse onto the stack of its comrades.

"Who are you?" asked Cass.

"Oh!" The kilted woman perked up visibly. "You could call me the welcoming committee. Donna Markan, Expedition Games. I expect you've met my brother Neal. I run the Expedition Hall here. If you're all done hauling meat, why don't you come back with me?"

"Noah!" Cass yelled. Noah looked up from where he and Magpie were scrubbing blood off the cobblestones. Cass waved him over and Magpie followed. "Apparently we don't have to clean up. Come on, we're going to the Expedition Hall."

As we crossed the cobbles, I tried to take a moment to properly appreciate the scene around me. I'd seen it in streams a thousand times, but actually being in Wellpoint was another thing entirely. The buildings looked bigger, the colors brighter. Picking my way around the impromptu cleanup crews, I realized I was also seeing the social strata of the Summerlands for the first time. There were adventurers present, paying gamers, with weapons and armor and camera drones humming around them. Their clothes were nicer, their hair neater, their skin cleaner. They showed no interest in helping with the aftermath of the fight in the square. For the most part they seemed not even to notice the people Donna had jokingly referred to as "NPCs."

The term, a holdover from tabletop and video games, was short for "non-player characters", any character in a game not controlled by a real person. These NPCs were as real as me, though; they'd earned the nickname by filling all the support roles that were needed to keep us paying adventurers happy and fed. These were the people who had signed over their lives to Expedition Games for the chance to serve in the Summerlands. They cooked, cleaned, cut hair, made shoes, sewed shirts. Everything except adventuring: they weren't allowed to fight unless in danger and under no circumstances could they learn magic. Any gold they found out in the wilds would be immediately confiscated.

I blinked away a few tears. My eyes had adjusted, but I was still astonished at how bright the sun was. It wasn't too hot, though, much milder than our long summers in the HECZ. In fact the air was so clean that it felt cold in my throat as I took glorious deep breaths. Was this how our ancestors had lived, before gray and orange clouds choked the sky nearly every day of the year?

Portal Square was surrounded on all sides by buildings. They were the first built by Expedition Games, back when they were setting up the town, and had always been the most desirable real estate in Wellpoint. They were designed in an

77

Elizabethan style, but under the clear sun I could see rich reds and purples in the beams of local wood, and even subtle tints of blue and yellow pastel in the plaster walls. Those colors had never shown in the feeds.

Expedition Hall was plain in comparison, built of rough-hewn timbers and slapdash plaster, but as I passed through the heavy wooden door that Donna held open for us, I had to admit that it had a certain frontier charm. It was dim and low inside, like a tavern from the dark ages, and my eyes appreciated the break from the Summerlands' sun. A group of adventurers, a man and four women with weapons draped over battered white leather, clustered around what looked like a TV off to one side, but I didn't get a good look before Donna's chipper voice turned my head.

"Now then," she said with a clap of her hands that reminded me sharply of her brother, "let's get you set up! Wait right here, please." She ducked through a doorway and returned a moment later with four camera drones. "I'll just get these keyed in to your signals."

As Donna worked, I peered over the shoulders of the adventurers across the room. They were indeed watching a flatscreen that showed a long, scrolling list of names and numbers. I focused in on their murmured conversation and picked up bits and pieces as they argued in hushed tones. The TV showed feed rankings: viewing numbers for each individual adventurer's stream. From their dusty clothes and weaponry, I guessed that this bunch had just come back from a sortie into the wild. If their muted attitude was anything to go by, their feed numbers weren't what they were hoping for.

I was lucky. I didn't care about ratings.

Donna seemed to be having some issues getting Cass's drone to sync with her RFID implant, so as we waited, I moved over next to Magpie.

"Hey," I said quietly, "I just wanted to thank you for getting that thing off me. I was really disoriented, and… yeah."

"No problem," he said, waving his hand as if brushing away my gratitude. His eyes lit up as he went on. "Pretty amazing, isn't it? The sun is so bright. Did you notice how the air feels in your nose? So clean! It's a wonderland."

"It's pretty incredible," I agreed.

"Are you in a hurry to go out adventuring? I'm not. I'd rather see how long these fifty coppers can last me."

I shook my head. "You'd be out on the street in a week!"

He shrugged. "Eh, there's worse streets to be out on, wouldn't you say?"

Something in his tone caught my attention. "Where are you from, anyway?" I asked.

"Hell," he said with a laugh. "Also known as the Hellenic Austerity Zone. And here we are in heaven. Might as well enjoy it, no?"

I thought of Keats, sitting in pain in his wheelchair back in the real world. In the chaos of our arrival and the wonder that followed it, I'd forgotten all about him. A pang of guilt stabbed my heart.

"I guess."

"There we go!" said Donna. I looked over to see a camera drone following Cass like a hovering dog as she moved slowly around the room. It rotated as she paced back and forth, keeping her in frame, and it held a fairly steady distance when she tried to move too close or too far away.

Satisfied, Cass rejoined us as Donna set to work on my drone. She put a hand on my shoulder and the other on Noah's.

"Okay, Hearthammer." She was starting to look like herself again. "We're here. Now, where the hell are we gonna spend the night? Noah, what do you think?"

"Well," Noah said, "there are two parts of town we could afford right now. Bad Luck Alley and Home Street."

"One of those sounds a lot more appealing than the other," said Cass, and I had to agree. "What's the catch?"

"Price," said Noah. "Bad Luck Alley is called that because it's where adventurers end up when things go badly for them. So it's cheap. But the rooms you can get there aren't too nice, I think. I've never seen inside it."

"And Home Street is nicer…"

"But more expensive." Noah nodded. "It's pretty normal for new players to go there, though. They call it Noob Street."

"Okay, let's be noobs," Cass said. "We've got a little spending money, so let's spend it. We're gonna be swimming in coin soon enough anyway."

"Wait," I said.

"What?" said Cass.

"Shouldn't we be saving our money? I mean, we need to save up for… you know." I glanced around, but other than Magpie standing behind me, nobody seemed to care about our conversation. "For your dad."

"Emma—" Cass began.

"Linnaea," said Noah.

"Fine, Linnaea. We've been through so much to get here. Why can't you just relax for a few nights while we get the lay of the land?"

"I'm sorry," I said, "I just don't feel great about spending money on luxuries."

"Sepharad, what do you think?" said Cass. "Tie-breaker vote." Noah looked at the floor. He licked his lips as he pondered. Nobody was better than Noah at self-discipline, but if he had to make a decision he tended to shut down.

"I think Linnaea is right," said Magpie.

"Nobody asked you!" Cass snapped. She straightened to her full height, which put her a few inches over Magpie's head. "In case you forgot, you're not part of Hearthhammer. We shared a limo ride. That doesn't make us pals."

"Cass, wait," I said. "Jessamine, I mean. Sorry. Okay, listen. I know Magpie's not one of us. But he saved my life when we came through the portal."

"I thought St George saved you," said Noah.

"Before that," I said. "Magpie wouldn't have been in trouble if he hadn't gotten that thing off me first." Cass crossed her arms and looked down her nose at me. I knew that look. She knew I was right; she just didn't want to admit it. I soldiered

80

on. "He's been nothing but chill since we met him. I'm not saying we make him a part of the Hammer, I'm just saying... we don't have any other friends here. I'm not about to kick out the one we've got."

"Fine," said Cass. "We'll take in the stray. You have any useful skills, Magpie?"

Magpie smiled. Being talked about openly didn't seem to bother him at all. "Yes," he said, "as a matter of fact I do." He held up his coin pouch. Then he held up another one, and a third.

Cass's eyes went wide as she slapped at her belt. Noah looked down at his. My pouch was still in place, looped to my belt by its leather thong, but Magpie had taken the others'.

"Give that back!" said Cass, and Magpie tossed it to her. The smile hadn't left his face. He handed Noah his pouch and folded his tattooed arms across his chest.

"I'm also good with locks," he said.

"Magpie," I said, "what exactly did you do for a living in the Hellenic Austerity Zone?"

"If you're staying with us, I expect you to contribute," said Cass before he could respond. "Since we're letting in a fourth, we can afford Home Street. And you're gonna work, too. When we go out of town, you come with us. Deal?"

"Deal," said Magpie.

"Good." Cass nodded, looking as satisfied as if it had been her idea all along for Magpie to join us. "Linnaea, what time is it?"

"By the sun, it was about three in the afternoon when we arrived," I said. Timekeeping in the Summerlands was a fascinating subject, one that I hoped to explore more now that we were here. "So maybe four thirty?"

"Perfect," said Cass. "Sepharad, where can we get food?"

"Meat Street," said Noah. "Most of the restaurants are there."

"Great name," I said, but Cass ignored me.

81

"Here's the plan. Split up for the rest of the afternoon. At seven we meet on Meat Street to get some food."

"Split up?" Magpie asked. "Can't we eat now? I'm starving."

"Nope," said Cass. "One more thing we need to do before we settle in. The four of us need to join our guilds."

THE RED WIZARD

I crossed Portal Square, my camera drone buzzing happily behind me, its solar panels drinking in the light that still made me squint and rub my eyes. The Red Wizards' Guild Hall occupied one corner of the square, in a multi-storied building of deep red hardwood and black iron decoration. It sat like a rich shadow against the whites and pastels of its neighbors.

Active drones weren't allowed in any of the guild halls, so the interior was a mystery to me, but I knew the face of the building well. The door itself was of blood oak, a tree known for its anti-magical properties. It had been harvested from a nearby forest by Dr Agony himself. The exposed beams were red heartwood, beautiful but mundane. The iron was said to ward off supernatural forces, though none of the sources I'd read could agree on whether that was true in the Summerlands or just a superstition carried over from our world.

I caught myself holding my breath as I grasped the wrought-iron door handle. Assuming I was inducted into the guild, this place would be like a second home to me. The wizards here had unlocked mysteries of Summerlands magic that those of us educated only from books and blogs could scarcely imagine. If I paid my dues, literally and figuratively, that knowledge would be mine.

The door was heavy but silent as I pulled it open. My first impression was one of wealth. The thick carpet that quieted my footfalls was woven with arcane symbols intertwined with old-fashioned arabesques. Deep leather reading chairs sat here and there, each in its own pool of light from an individual red-shaded reading lamp atop a small wooden side table. A fire crackled in a large stone hearth, but it was no warmer in here than outside. The rich smell of woodsmoke and leather filled my nose.

A bar ran along the right side of the room, seemingly made from a single massive slab of crystal that glowed with a warm red light deep within. A few stools with leather seats and brass legs made a neat row beneath it.

The room was empty. I took a few more steps in and the door shut behind me, turning the room's many shadows to black. My mouth was dry and I licked my lips uselessly.

"You must be Linnaea." I jumped at the voice behind me, and turned to see a man standing between me and the door. He stood about my height in a simple red tunic and breeches. His hair was lank and brown, his beard scraggly, and he smelled a bit of sweat. Only his eyes stood out: one was blue, the other green. That detail jogged something in my memory; I'd seen him on the feeds, but as I racked my brain I couldn't come up with his name.

"I am Belphegor," he said, "lead tutor of the Red Wizards' Guild. It is also my duty to administer tests for admission and ranking. I imagine that is what has brought you here today?"

"Yes." I cleared my throat. "Yes, exactly. We just crossed over. I'm Linnaea. I've been practicing in the real world and I'd like to join the guild."

"My dear," said Belphegor with a flourish that took in the room around us, "this *is* the real world."

I blinked. The empty leather chairs were now full of men and women who sat reading, practicing magical passes, or talking quietly. A middle-aged woman with long blonde hair in two Viking braids stood behind the bar, cleaning a glass and chatting with a pair of patrons on the stools. As I gaped, I realized that I recognized some of them, well-known red wizards whose feeds I'd studied, hoping to pick up a trick or two.

"How—how did you—" I stammered to a stop. I'd seen monsters and swords already this afternoon, but this was my first taste of true magic.

"A simple charm, really," said Belphegor. "Not the true invisibility that the white magicians can create, but close enough." He held up a small, clouded diamond between two fingers of the hand that had made the flourish a moment ago. He rubbed the fingers together and the diamond disappeared. "We have many such secret arts. Perhaps you'll learn them someday."

"That would be a dream come true," I said, hoping that the sincerity in my chest would overflow my heart and spill into my voice. This was what I had come to the Summerlands for. There were mysteries here, buried only inches beneath the fertile earth, just waiting for me to dig them up.

"Come," said Belphegor.

★★★

The Room of Trials was a large, windowless chamber at the heart of the Red Wizards' Guild Hall. The floorboards were wide, straight boards of blood oak. The walls were white plaster, hung with wooden plaques, on which the names and ranks of every guild member were painted in gold leaf. In the center of the floor sat a copper coin, a sword, and a small iron bell. Belphegor knelt on one side of these magical implements and I sat on the other, facing him.

"Do some magic for me," he said.

I looked at the items in front of me, trying to remember the spells I knew. Or thought I knew: there was no telling if the years of practice I'd put in would actually mean anything here in the Summerlands. I'd been memorizing nonsense words and performing random acts of sleight of hand for so long without ever seeing a result.

The bell reminded me of the day not so long ago when I'd first earned my ticket fee, sitting inside the merch machine at the Expedition store. That life was quite literally a world away now. I wondered how Keats was feeling, what he was doing. Had he found our drone feeds? Was he watching Cass walk across a courtyard or duck down an alleyway even now? Was he happy for us? I picked up the bell.

"Do you have a candle?" I asked. Belphegor watched me, unblinking, but said nothing. Okay, he was obviously going to be no help. He must be putting pressure on me, testing how I could perform under stress. It made sense when you remembered that you'd eventually be expected to cast spells while monsters were trying to eat you and your friends.

I thought for a moment, then pulled the lacing from the front of my shirt. The neckline fell open into a shallow vee that exposed a little more of my chest than I would have liked, but there wasn't much I could do about that. Plus, I could retie the lacing pretty quickly once we were done.

I formed the lacing into a coil on the ground in front of me, then took a few deep breaths to steady myself. I never believed in anything supernatural or religious in the real world—I considered myself a scientist, devoted only to the empirical method—but it was hard to deny the sense of destiny that settled on me as I prepared to cast my first spell. So many years of hard work had led me here. So much pain and suffering.

Promising myself that I would come back to these feelings—promising never to forget everything I'd lost along the way—I put them out of my mind. I lifted the bell in my right hand, testing its weight. It was heavier than the bell I'd always practiced with, which was just thin sheet metal pressed into shape. This was real iron, probably forged by a local blacksmith. I gave it an experimental ring, and its sound was full and deep compared to the flat clinking I was used to.

My eyes locked with Belphegor's. For a moment it seemed as though his blue eye watched my face while his green eye watched my hand. I refused to look away, though.

I began to sweep the bell gently in a figure-eight pattern as I intoned a few quiet words in the language we called Elvish. At the apex of each turn, I flicked my wrist a bit to let the clapper of the bell strike its inner wall and as I drew the bell back in I silenced it with a quick finger. Soon, I had a feel for the motion, and I began to exaggerate my movements. Swirl and snap, swirl and snap, with an even rhythm that produced a steady cadence of sound and silence.

I spoke the Elvish words louder and more confidently, interweaving them with the ringing of the bell. The anxiety in my stomach had been replaced with something else, something warmer. It began as an unsteady feeling in my gut, but soon it burned up and out along my arms. I realized I was sweating when a few salty drops touched my tongue, which I had clenched between my teeth in concentration. The burning sensation reached my hands and flew along my fingers.

"Ow! Shit!" I dropped the bell, which landed with a dull clank. I stood and stumbled backwards from the bell, shaking my hands as though I could wave away the imaginary fires that had scorched them. Carelessly, I hooked one foot behind the other ankle and tripped myself. I landed painfully on my ass on the hardwood.

Belphegor began to laugh. His face grew red and his body shook as he cackled, his head thrown back. The wizard went on for a solid minute before regaining control of himself. Finally he stood, clapping.

"Burnt your fingers, did you?" He reached out a hand to me and I pulled myself up.

"I had no idea it would feel like that," I said. I made a show of brushing myself off, but the Room of Trials was immaculately clean. Really, my pride was hurt more than my butt.

"You still have no idea," said Belphegor. "But. I must admit that you've obviously practiced, much more than most who come here hoping to learn magic. Pay your dues, listen to your superiors, and you'll get along fine, I think. Welcome to the Red Wizards. First week is free, one silver per week after that."

"That's it?" My heart leapt in my chest. "I'm in?"

In reply, he stepped to the side and gestured at the floor behind him, where a spiral of ash sat smoking.

★★★

"I like what you've done to your shirt," said Cass. "Should bring in the twelve-to-twenty-nine crowd."

I tugged the neck of my shirt closed as we rounded a corner onto Meat Street. We'd smelled food for the last five minutes as we made our way down narrow alleys between boarding houses and small apartment complexes. The scent was hard to describe. It had depths. On top was a mouth-watering mixture of every meat I'd ever eaten, though lacking the usual tang of chemicals and salt, and much more I couldn't identify. Underneath was something solid and real.

The complexity in my nose was nothing compared what met my eyes as Meat Street opened before us. It was packed as densely as our old apartment block, but instead of exhausted workers and snoring squatters, the street teemed with adventurers. Signs, flags, and awnings competed to draw the eye with the brightest possible colors. Many of the shops had tables and chairs set outside, most of them full with patrons enjoying the ever-present sunshine.

I felt a wave of anxiety crash over me as I contemplated finding our friends in this mess, but then Cass yelled "Hey!" and I saw Noah waving to us from a stall near our end of the street. Magpie was handing over a few coins in return for a row of meat cubes on a skewer. He took a bite and rolled his eyes in mock ecstasy as we approached.

"Try this." Magpie waved the meat skewer in my face. The meat looked like chicken, but with flaky layers that showed it was real rather than from an extruder. Brown marinade dotted with seeds dripped enticingly from the cubes and ran down Magpie's hand. I leaned in and bit one of the cubes off the skewer.

It was chicken, but more so. It delivered on every promise made by the smells of Meat Street. I closed my eyes as I chewed. The sun was lowering in the sky and in the long shadow of a nearby awning the temperature was perfect. For a moment, I wondered if Magpie had been more accurate than he intended when he called the Summerlands heaven. Others had made the suggestion sincerely and I understood why.

"I'm hungry," said Noah. We set off down Meat Street, reading out loud from menus as we passed.

"Steak! Real steak!"

"Dosa, what's that?"

"Look, tacos—wait, we had tacos at home."

"Spanakopita, gyros... Magpie, isn't that Greek?"

"Sweet and sour pork pizza? Do you think it's good?"

"Somebody pick something—"

"Another steak place—"

"Okay, here!" Cass stopped in front of a narrow storefront. A wooden sign above the door clattered in the evening breeze, showing a sort of witch's cauldron with painted steam rising from it. The words *Open Seasoning* were painted below the cauldron. "I'm hungry, we'll have plenty of time to try everything else, and this smells good."

Nobody could argue with that. A scent liked salted steam led us through the door. A single row of tables and chairs lined one wall of the cozy restaurant. A knot of adventurers crowded around the counter at the far end and I took a few steps in that direction before stopping dead. Noah bumped into my back.

"That's Golden Apple," I said.

"Holy shit," Noah agreed.

They seemed to be having an argument with the owner of the restaurant. She was a square young woman in a dirty apron. She had dusky skin, thick black eyebrows, and bright pink hair. Cass shoved me and I stumbled farther into the room.

"I don't care if you're an elf come back from the dead, you still have to pay!" the owner said.

"Being seen eating here is payment enough," boomed Rad, the huge warrior of the party. "You'll be trending tomorrow." None of their drones seemed to be visible.

"I gotta pay for that meat, you know," said the owner. "That shit ain't free."

"It is if you go kill it yourself," said Wolfheart.

"Then get out there, bring me some back, and I'll cook it up for you. On the house." Standing with fists on her hips, the owner didn't seem at all intimidated by the power arrayed in front of her. "Until then, pay up or stay out. You're all certainly rich enough."

"How about this?" said Dr Agony. His voice was more nasal than it sounded on the feeds. "You can give us the meal for free, or I can let Blomhaugen in on your little secret."

The owner's face went pale. She opened her mouth and shut it, then turned away, her shoulders slumped. She waved a hand in defeat.

"Fine. Fine, go ahead. See you next time you're in town." She disappeared into the kitchen as the members of Golden Apple turned to leave. We were between them and the door, and as they brushed past us, Valkyrie's pale blue eyes locked with mine and lingered there. Her war paint was smeared and runny, and her short black hair stuck out wildly.

Dr Agony was the last to leave; he held the door open and turned back to the four of us gaping at him and his party.

"Word of advice, noobs," he said. "Don't let these NPCs push you around. They'll take you for all you're worth if you let them. Adventurers are the big fish here. Don't forget it."

The door slammed behind him.

"Asshole," said Cass in a voice that was louder than conversational. Noah picked up a little bell from the counter and rang it, which reminded me that I had something to show off to my friends.

"Check it out," I said, digging into my pockets. I came up with two metal bells of my own, as well as a tiny red gem that glittered enticingly despite being smaller than my pinky fingernail.

"Magic stuff?" asked Magpie. I nodded.

"I didn't even have to pay for it," I said. "Not yet, at least. The Guild said I can pay them back over time."

"They're charging you?" Noah asked.

A door slammed as the owner of the restaurant appeared from the kitchen, two menus in each hand, and waved us towards a table.

"Does Golden Apple harass you often?" asked Cass as we were seated.

"Ooh, sorry you had to see that." The young woman wrinkled her nose. "They're usually out in one of the border towns, but every now and then they like to come back to Wellpoint to slum it with the new kids. Bit sad, you ask me, like going back to your old high school." She shrugged. "It's only a little coin."

"Did you hear about the monsters in Portal Square?" asked Noah. "Seems lucky that they were here."

The owner laughed. "You must be new. That kinda shit happens all the time. Sometimes somebody gets hurt, but usually there are enough adventurers around to put 'em down quickly."

"Where do they come from?" asked Magpie.

"Today, it was the sewers, I think," said the owner. "I heard they were digging a new line, somebody knocked in a wall and there was a nest there. You know how it is. Well, I guess you don't. I'm Naila, by the way."

We all introduced ourselves, giving our gamertags, which didn't seem to faze Naila. I was starting to get used to the idea of everybody here going by a fantastical name.

When she wasn't being extorted, Naila was a sweetheart. The meal, a sort of spiced stew, was fantastic, so good that we forgot to ask what exactly it was made from. Eventually we all settled back in our chairs, letting the exhaustion of the day wash over us.

"Can we go to bed?" asked Noah. We were all thinking it, or at least I was.

"Yeah, we'll decamp to Bad Luck Alley in a minute," said Cass. "One more thing, though. Things went pretty quick at the Guild Hall, so I spent some time exploring the town. I bought something. It wasn't cheap, but I think even Linnaea will approve."

"What is it?" I asked. Cass dove a hand into her shirt and pulled out a rolled-up sheet of parchment. It was crumpled and had a large brownish stain.

"Apparently, some adventurer recently went out on a solo in the wilderness. He made it back to town, but only just barely. He died on the outskirts of town. I met the man who was there when he died. He heard his last words. And he was given this."

She unrolled the parchment and smoothed it on the table. It was a sketch in faded black ink, showing a little collection of houses, a few ragged triangles for mountains, and a dotted line. For a moment, I was a kid again, huddled over a gameboard spread across Keats's kitchen table.

"Cass, what are we looking at?" I asked.

She looked up at me, grinning. "It's a treasure map."

SCRAPS

"The man you bought it from—what did he look like?" Naila stood over us, her arms crossed and a rag in her hand.

Cass looked up at her. "Oh, older guy, short white beard, pretty tan. Why?"

Naila shook her head. "Silver chains around his neck?"

"Yeah, *why?*"

"You got scammed, I'm afraid." Naila pulled up a nearby chair and dropped into it wearily. "That's Andronus. He's well known for taking advantage of new players."

"He seemed pretty sincere," said Cass, her eyes narrowing. "He actually dropped his price when I told him I only had my starting copper."

"No, he made you think he dropped his price." Naila rolled her eyes quickly upwards, as though seeking strength from above. "What did you end up paying?"

Cass looked at the table and kept her eyes down as she murmured, "Forty coppers."

"Oh, shit!" Magpie stood up, covering his face with his hands. Noah stared out the window, expressionless. I was caught somewhere between the two reactions and ended by standing up halfway, sitting down again, and finally just putting an awkward arm around Cass's shoulders.

"It's okay," I said. "We'll get by."

Naila stood and flung her rag over her shoulder, then began to clear our dishes. "Looks like I'm comping two meals to-night."

★★★

Bad Luck Alley was as crowded as Meat Street, but smelled much worse. It reminded me of the halls of our apartment block that my parents had ordered me to avoid, the ones more or less abandoned to squatters and addicts, and the others agreed.

"This sucks," said Cass. "I'm oh for two in the Summerlands and now we have to live in this shithole. The Summerlands was supposed to be better than home, not worse."

Thanks to our free meal, only Cass and I had used any money. Magpie had actually turned up an extra silver piece somewhere, though he wouldn't say where. Between the four of us, we had the equivalent of a hundred and forty-five coppers.

We found a decent enough place to stay, a boardinghouse run by a man with a pink, drooping burn scar covering half his face. It was dusty inside, but the smell was tolerable, and we didn't get a bad vibe from anyone as we watched adventurers with dirty faces and threadbare clothing come and go. They rented beds in a long common hall for a copper a night, but we all agreed to pay five a night for a small private room we could share. We handed over a week's worth, paid equally by everyone but Cass.

Our stomachs full and our rent paid, we agreed wordlessly to retreat to the corners of the room, spread out the bedrolls we'd been given, and let the longest day of our lives end at last.

★★★

"I don't think I'll ever get tired of this." I blew out the melted candle stub in front of me and settled back. My bell clinked in my fingers and a moment later a wan flame flickered to life from the candle's black wick.

"Give me ten fireballs in a row, then I'll be impressed," said Cass.

"I healed a scratch on my arm last night," Noah said. "I'd show you, but it's healed."

The breakfast our landlord provided was dismal compared to the meal we'd had on Meat Street, gristly and gray and

94

lukewarm, but it still outclassed the processed extruder fare we were all used to. Two solid meals in a row filled our spirits as much as our stomachs; even Cass was content and seemed ready to put her mistakes of the previous day behind her.

"First things first," she said, putting down a wooden bowl to which a few grains of rice clung. "We need gear. Noah, what's that gonna cost us?"

"New?" Noah paused with a spoonful of rice halfway to his mouth. "More than we have. The best weaponsmith is Dahluhn—he has a storefront on Portal Square—but his minimum is a hundred gold per item. The other big name is Blackrazor, but he—"

"TMI, Noah!" Cass laughed, her hands up in mock surrender.

"Whoops," Noah said.

"It's okay, it's okay," Cass said. "What do new adventurers usually do?"

"Most people buy used gear," Noah said. "Either from other adventurers or their guilds."

"Well, I couldn't afford the Warriors' Guild prices and I don't see any yard sales around," said Cass. "What else?"

"The scrap dealer?" Magpie said.

"The what?" Cass said. Noah cocked his head.

"I saw it last night." Magpie pointed to an alleyway a few blocks from where we sat in the morning sun. "Down there, just around the corner. They have weapons and armor."

"When last night?" I asked.

"Late," Magpie said, a twinkle in his dark eyes.

★★★

The scrap dealer didn't have a sign, just a cracked glass shop window that showed battered armor pieces and dull swords. A bell jangled as Cass pushed through the door. Inside, the shop was dim and dusty. Tottering stacks of all kinds of adventuring gear were piled into little islands, between which wound narrow aisles. We spread out, picking our way cautiously among the junk, looking for price tags.

"How do you like Bad Luck Alley?"

I jumped as a man came around the corner of one of the scrap piles, sticking out his hand for a shake. He was about my height, heavyset, with a round, clean-shaven baby face and a snub nose. His black hair was thin on top of his head but thick on his arms and chest. Unsure what else to do, I shook his hand.

"I'm Linnaea," I said. "We're Hearthhammer. We're looking for gear."

"What do you think of Bad Luck Alley?" the man repeated, as though I hadn't spoken.

"It stinks," said Cass. "I'm Jessamine, party leader. This is Sepharad and Magpie."

"Do you know why it's called Bad Luck Alley?" the man asked.

"Adventurers who are down on their luck live here," said Noah. "Because it's the cheapest area in Wellpoint."

"Wrong!" The man pointed at Noah. "Propaganda. The rats out there"—he pointed at the door—"that's what they *want* you to think. Not one of 'em will tell you the truth: *I was a coward. I didn't watch my six. I didn't practice enough.* Go ahead, ask 'em. To a man, it's, *Oh, I'll be back on my feet soon. I just had some bad luck.*"

"That's not us," Cass said. "We just—I just—made a mistake, that's all."

"Sure you did," said the man. "I'm Wayland. Pleased to meet you all. I'm sure you'll be a regular bunch of Golden Apples soon. How can I help?"

"We need weapons and armor," said Cass. "A bow for me and some good tough leather. Sepharad, what do you want, a sword? Mace?"

"Sword, please," said Noah.

"A sword and steel armor," Cass said. "Linnaea, what do you need? You should have a dagger or something. And leather for her, too."

"Terrific," said Wayland, looking us over. "And for the quiet gentleman?"

"Oh, right," said Cass. She glanced at Magpie, who was examining a flat leather case. "He's paying for himself."

"He has more money than any of us," I whispered.

"Then he'll be fine," Cass replied.

Magpie held up the case. "I'll take this and two knives."

"Slow down," said Wayland. "Let me see what I've got. No computers, you know. Managing my stock is always a bit of a balancing act. You need leather too, thief?"

"No thanks." Magpie gave a crooked smile. "Never learned to fight in armor."

Wayland set off down the narrow aisles, talking to himself quietly, occasionally stopping to pick through a pile or count under his breath.

"This is exciting," said Cass.

"Do I really need a weapon?" I said. "I'll be in the back, right? We could save some money."

"Yes, you need a weapon," said Cass. "Be real."

"Here we are," said Wayland, balancing a tottering stack of weapons and armor in his arms. He dropped it at our feet in a clatter of metal. "Sword, shortbow, a dagger, two leathers, and I found a steel breastplate from someone about your size. Oh, and I'll get you some arrows, I assume you want arrows. That'll be six gold and a silver, all told."

"What?" said Cass. "That's insane!"

"You should see what the big guys charge," said Wayland with a shrug.

"Yeah, but that's all new and custom-made," Cass said. "This is... not." I knew she wanted to say something like *junk*, but had stopped herself. She wouldn't have been wrong, though. The armor was scratched and stained, with some loose seams and missing ties. The sword was missing a scabbard, its blade pitted and missing a triangle chip along one edge.

"And another thing," said Cass. "I didn't say *shortbow*. What am I, a kid? I may be a girl but I can draw sixty pounds when I want. I use a longbow."

"Terrific," said Wayland through gritted teeth. "Seven gold even."

"We can't afford that," Noah said.

"No shit," said Wayland. "And before you ask me to cut my prices down, the answer's no. This gear may be used but it ain't free for me either. Add in my payments to Expedition every month, I'm this close to losing money on the whole thing. So, wanna talk about what you can buy with fifty coppers each?"

Cass and I shared a glance.

"Look," I said, "maybe we could make a deal."

"What kind?" Wayland's eyebrows went up.

"Well, uh, we're adventurers." I spread my hands. "We just need to get started. Let us use the gear now and we'll pay you back. With interest."

"Ah, *that* deal," Wayland sighed. "Last time I made *that* deal, I lost a lot of good gear."

"What happened?" Noah asked.

"What do you think?" Wayland snorted. "They never came back."

"So they're still out there somewhere?" I asked.

"Their bodies are, sure," said Wayland.

"Okay then," I said. "We'll go get your stuff back."

★★★

We left town with weapons in hand and empty pockets. I'm not sure what I was expecting as we set out on our first quest as a fledgling adventuring party. An ominous stone gate leading out of town? Cheering townsfolk come to see us off? Whatever it was, we didn't get it. The ruin where Wayland's old customers had died was roughly to the north of Wellpoint, so we wound our way out of town via a neighborhood nicknamed "the

Burbs," where the very richest players owned proper houses. Each member of Golden Apple had their own place in the Burbs, as did Pixie and Meteora, though mostly the houses were shared by adventuring parties.

Past the Burbs, the cobblestone street that ran between the houses turned to gravel, then dirt, and finally petered out at the edge of a lush, rolling grassland spotted with flowered shrubs. Just like that, without fanfare, we'd left Wellpoint and were officially on an adventure.

My armor pinched my armpit, and I twisted it into a new position. The leather had been worked a little, forced into a somewhat fantasy-looking shape and imprinted with a scrolled-leaf design, but it was basically just big stiff slabs over half an inch thick, tied together with leather thongs. My dagger—Wayland's dagger—bumped on my hip as I walked.

So far, adventuring was a bit uncomfortable.

I was sharply aware of my armor, my weapon, my pouch full of magical implements, even the weather. The Summerlands were cool compared to the endless heat of the HECZ, but I felt sweat prickling my back all the same as the shade of the Burbs became a memory.

It was possible, too, that that was anxiety making itself known. I'd seen a shocking amount of bloodshed in the last few weeks, but walking towards it with my eyes open was a first. I'd frozen when Porter shot Jason and nearly done it again in Portal Square. Cass had collapsed completely. Why did we think the next time would be any different?

And yet… the flutter in my stomach and the quickening of my pulse didn't feel like fear. We'd spent five years training. I'd cast a real spell. I was walking towards danger, but also towards my chance to save Keats. Who cared about a little discomfort? I was in the Summerlands.

"I wish Wayland hadn't taken all our money," I said.

"It's just collateral," said Cass. "We'll get it back."

"I know, I just really wanted to get a sketchbook." I waved at the grasslands around us. "Look at all this! I should be taking notes."

"You could record it," Noah pointed out. "Everything that goes out on a feed gets saved on a server somewhere, so you could use your drone to take notes."

"Oh yeah." My camera drone still followed me everywhere, buzzing away, but I'd never turned on my feed, and I'd quickly tuned out the noise.

"Do it!" said Cass. "Maybe you'll actually get some viewers. Apparently nobody wanted to watch me walk around town."

"Okay," I said. "Okay, let's try it." I snagged my drone, which was hovering about a foot above my head, hit the big red Stream button, and let it go. Immediately, the drone spun into position, its camera eye focusing on my face. The sound and image it captured were sent wirelessly back to the Expedition Hall in Wellpoint thanks to a series of repeaters installed by the ranger teams. From there, the data passed down thick fiber-optic cables, through the portal to the real world. Somewhere in the Expedition Games complex on the Isle of Lewis, a content-distribution server woke up and began sharing my feed out to the world, spreading across Expedition's massive network like fire running out the branches of a tree.

"Hello," I said. "This is Em—this is Linnaea, making my first stream." I looked at Cass, uncertain, and she made a *go on* wave with her hand.

"Okay, so we're Hearthammer," I said. "This is Jessamine, that's Sepharad, and Magpie in the back there." Magpie looked away from the camera as soon as he realized he was in the frame. "We're Hearthammer and we're about to go on our first quest. Uh, actually, we're already on it. We're here in the Near Plains right now and we're going to recover the bodies of some adventurers who died recently in the White Chasm. Uh, you've probably seen it before. But that's where we're going. Anyway, I just wanted to make a record of some of the stuff we're seeing here. It's pretty amazing, actually. Here, look at this." I actually waved to the camera, which kept pace with me as I crouched by a bush speckled with blue flowers.

"They look like roses, don't they? Look at how the petals curl around. Here, let's look inside." I gently pried open one of the flowers, revealing neat red markings on the inside of each petal, totally hidden from outside. "Oh my God. It looks like a bell, doesn't it? And look, this one is like a dagger. I mean, can you imagine? These are red magic symbols, *in red*, just right here on the petals! Has anyone ever seen this before? Are there white magic ones, too? What do we even call this? Magic rose? No, that's cheesy. Uh, bell rose? Bell-and-dagger? Oh, no, this one looks like a coin. I mean, this can't be natural, right? The elves must have cultivated these…"

"Emma," Cass murmured. I looked up in surprise. She stood over me, eyebrows raised, arms crossed. "Time to move."

"Oh, right, sorry," I said. "I guess I got a little distracted."

"You think?" said Cass.

"Sorry, sorry!" I stood, brushing grass and dirt off my pants, then looked into the camera. "Okay, we're moving on."

We headed deeper into the Near Plains, judging direction roughly by the sun overhead. The White Chasm was due north of Wellpoint, at the point where the grasslands fell away suddenly to be replaced by a chalky gray land called the Battle Plains. At the bottom of the Chasm was a collapsed structure, probably an old fortress, that was among the first to be raided as soon as the Summerlands were opened to players. Still, it was a massive complex riddled with secret doors and winding passageways and clever players were always finding new secrets hidden within its crumbling halls. It was there that the dead party we were chasing had gone, following some rumor of forgotten treasure.

The thought that whatever had killed them might kill us, too, had definitely crossed my mind.

To distract myself, I kept talking. There wasn't much in the Near Plains other than grass and flowers, at least not that I'd ever seen on the streams, so most of my endless monologue was theories about plant life. I spent half an hour on the role of chlorophyll in a world where sunlight was pretty much guaranteed sixteen hours a day.

Nobody responded, of course, and even if there were comments coming in I'd have no way of knowing. Running a stream, it turned out, was something of an act of faith. You just had to assume that somebody was listening on the other end. Luckily, I was making these recordings for myself, not for some theoretical audience. In a way, I hoped nobody was watching. I was rambling, going off on tangents, making dumb jokes, getting distracted and losing my train of thought: all conduct unbecoming of a professional streamer. I was glad I wasn't one.

As the sun reached its zenith, we passed by a large patch of discolored grass. It was a rectangle, with straight rows of brown circles running parallel its long edges. A few flat stones were visible within the rectangle, buried in the overgrown grass.

"What's that?" I asked Noah.

"I don't know." He frowned. "Nobody's ever named it. I don't think there's anything there to explore."

"Are those paving stones?" I said. Noah shrugged.

"Come on, it's just some old elf ruin," Cass said. "If there was anything there, it's gone now."

"Is it?" I paused, letting my camera drone take in the long, yellowing spot. "The elves mostly built with stone. This looks like something made of wood used to be here, but rotted away."

"So it's older," Cass said. "Maybe it was prehistoric elves. Cave elves."

"I think these were posts," I said, gesturing to the circles. "If the rectangle was the body of the building, the posts would have held up the roof. It almost..." I trailed off, shaking my head.

"Almost what?" asked Noah.

"It almost looks like a Viking longhouse," I said.

"But that's impossible," said Cass.

"Yeah, obviously," I agreed with a sigh. "Okay, let's go."

★★★

"Wow, that is *deep*," said Cass. We stood at the edge of the White Chasm, gazing down to where the ruined fortress lay a hundred yards below. A steep set of switchback stairs, carved into the wall by an early ranger team, descended to the canyon floor. The chalky white stone of the steps had been worn smooth by five years of adventurers' boots and faint depressions were starting in the center of each stair.

Cass went first, her bow strung and an arrow nocked. She moved like she'd been born to wear armor—maybe all the time she'd spent making cardboard mockups from Jason's old factory boxes had actually helped—and any fear she'd shown in Portal Square was hidden away now.

Noah went second. His armor clanked as he walked, but it wasn't as noisy as I'd feared. His sword hung from his belt; he wore mismatched gloves, one white and one black, and carried a long, straight wand of wood. His arms were bare between the short sleeves of his starter tunic and the gloves, but instead of looking goofy, it just showed off his muscles.

I was third, safely in the middle. I had a bell in my left hand and my dagger in my right. It was silly, but I felt better holding it. Doing real magic in the safety and quiet of the Room of Trials was one thing, but out here in the field would be something else entirely. I knew how to use a dagger, though.

Magpie was last, a knife in each hand. Other than that, all he had was his money, his starter clothing, and the leather case he'd bought, which had turned out to be a set of lockpicks. He had a look on his face that I hadn't seen before: his mouth was a thin line and his eyes never stopped moving. He kept a tight grip on his knives.

We reached the floor of the canyon and set out for the ruined fort. Noah had asked if we needed a history, but every Summerlands fan knew the White Chasm. The best anyone could tell, there had been a massive battle on the chalky badlands just north of the fort. They were called the Battle Plains because they were still littered with broken weapons, shields, and bits of armor. Scrap dealers like Wayland and desperate adventurers like us had picked the place over for anything usable, but every now and then somebody turned up a gleaming sword or lost gem.

The popular theory was that the fort itself had been hit with some powerful magic, then dropped three hundred feet into the chasm that opened beneath it. As we approached, I saw no reason to doubt it. The fortress had been massive and a surprising portion of it was still more or less standing, a testament to the long-gone elves' building prowess. Still, it obviously hadn't been built down here: its towers slumped, its walls crumbled, and the whole thing was sunk a few feet into the white earth.

"Okay, cameras on and look sharp," said Cass. "Wayland said they were planning to head for Athan's Rest, so that's what we'll do. It's still a harpy haunt, so look sharp."

"You already said that," said Noah.

"Well, you all better look really damn sharp, then." Cass had reached the most popular entrance to the fort, a heavy wooden door that hung half-open in the wall of a circular stone tower. She pushed through it into the dimness beyond and we followed.

A spiral staircase led in both directions from a landing just past the door. We headed up, passing another landing and door as we ascended to the top floor of the tower. Our drones buzzed in single file behind us, the only sound aside from our footsteps. The staircase ended at a third door and Cass opened it without hesitation.

A long hall pierced with arrow slits stretched about fifty feet down the length of the fortress wall, and ended at another tower. I knew it well from years of feeds: Athan's Rest, named for an early player who'd been killed there. The roof was collapsed, leaving it open to the sky, and a brood of giant raptors used it as sort of rest stop to eat and shit on their way to and from their nests in the canyon cliffs.

Athan, a swordsman from South America, had been the one to discover the birds and nickname them "harpies", right before they tore out his guts and ate them.

We paced down the hall in silence, the history of the place weighing on all of us. Cass tried the door at the far end and it opened. We moved out onto the wide platform of the open tower, blinking in the sunlight, our feet crunching on years of harpy crap.

"There," said Magpie, gesturing with his chin. Three bodies huddled against the right-hand curve of the wall, about where it met the next fortress wall, which ran away at an angle from the one we'd come through. They sat half in the shadow of a large section of unbroken wall, but even from the doorway it was clear they'd been torn nearly to shreds by the harpies' claws.

"Whoof," said Cass, putting the back of her hand to her nose. "Smell that. Actually, don't."

"Look at this." Magpie moved into the shadow where the bodies lay. He nudged one gently with his boot and it toppled over into the light. It was a young man, maybe mid-twenties. One of his eyes was missing, torn out and leaving a gaping hole behind. I leaned over for a few deep breaths as Magpie clarified that he hadn't just wanted us to see the mangled body.

"There's a door here." He was right. It had been built flush with the wall from matching stones, so it would have been invisible if you hadn't known what you were looking for. Magpie pulled it open a few inches until it stuck on the corpses. "This must have been what they were looking for."

"They found it too late," said Noah. He looked unusually pale.

"Okay, Hearthammer," Cass said decisively. "This isn't pretty, but we've got a job to do. Let's get Wayland's gear and get out of here."

"It's a secret room," Magpie said. His voice dropped to a whisper. "Oh, okay."

"What?" I asked.

"Treasure," he said. "Somebody's stash." He shoved the door the rest of the way open, dislodging the bodies, which collapsed with a clatter of armor. Reaching into the dark space beyond, he pulled out an open-topped wooden box about the size of a shoebox. It was nearly full of copper coins.

"Wow," said Cass.

"Look out!" Noah shouted. He was pointing into the sky with his wand, where three birds nearly as big as me were diving out of the sun. He flicked the wand and shouted something in Elvish, but nothing happened.

Cass stepped forward, pulling an arrow from the quiver on her back. In one quick motion she settled the arrow on her bowstring, drew it back to her ear, and let fly. The lead bird screeched as the shaft tore through its wing, and its dive turned into an off-kilter spin. I jumped back as it crashed into the stone floor of the tower just a few feet from me.

"Cass, what's the plan?" I called, but she didn't answer. She hadn't choked; instead, it was like the rest of us didn't exist. "Cass!"

Magpie and Noah glanced at me as the two farther harpies drew closer.

"Stay back," I said. "I'll cast a spell."

Noah went one way and Magpie the other as I fumbled my bell from my left hand to my right. My dagger clattered to the floor. Finally, I had a decent grip on the bell, and I began to swing it as I tried to remember the right words.

Cass put another arrow into the fallen bird as the other two swooped in, their claws leading. They were coming too fast. One crashed into Cass and they went down in a jumble of feathers and muscle. The other beat its wings once, slowing its dive so it hovered just over the broken edge of the tower. Its eyes roved over us all and settled on me.

I leapt for cover behind Noah as the harpy rose a few feet then dove like a falling missile.

I hit the ground just behind Noah's feet and dropped my bell, imagining that I could already feel the harpy's claws tearing into me. They tore into Noah instead. He got his hands in front of his face just as the bird hit him talons first. He screamed as the harpy grabbed hold of his arm and beat him around the head with its wings. His wand clattered to the floor and he kicked me in the arm as he took a steadying step backwards, but he didn't fall.

106

Somebody was shouting, one of the boys. Magpie stepped over me to help Noah. He had both knives in one hand and was trying to grab the huge bird with the other. Noah got free suddenly and his sword came up and caught the harpy beneath one wing. He pressed forward, driving the blade deeper into the bird with his right hand, as somewhere in the back of my mind a voice said that was wrong. Magpie came after him, making darting stabs with his knives wherever he saw an opening.

By the time I managed to sit up, it was all over. One bird lay with two arrows in it, another with a broken neck, and the third chopped half to bits. Cass had a long, shallow gash down one arm and marks all over her leather armor. Magpie seemed untouched. I was about to thank Noah when he turned, holding his left hand up in front of wide eyes. It was a mangled mess, pulsing with blood, the fingers all sticking out at different angles.

He fainted.

★★★

"*Lest Darkess Fall*," whispered Noah.

"Are you *still* arguing about books?" Cass said.

"It's definitely"—Magpie grunted as he shifted his weight to get his shoulder back under Noah, who was starting to fall again—"it's definitely *Incomplete Enchanter*."

"De Camp didn't even..." Noah paused for a long, wheezing breath. For a moment Magpie was doing all the work for both of them as he dragged Noah across the grass, leaving a trail of bright blood spatters behind. Noah's eyes fluttered, then shut, and his head began to roll forward.

"Didn't what?" Magpie said. "Didn't write it alone? So what? It's still his best book."

"Just let him have this!" Cass snapped.

Noah's eyes opened, showing unfocused and wandering pupils. His skin was ashen beneath his tan. He'd lost a lot of blood on the hike back. "...maybe in Greek."

"There's Wellpoint!" I exclaimed, pointing. I set out across the grass at a sprint as Cass helped Magpie drag Noah after me.

"Medic! We need a medic!" My throat was raw from screaming by the time I reached the first cobblestones of the Burbs.

"Keep it down, huh?" said a voice from somewhere above me. I looked up to see Wolfheart, the white wizard of Golden Apple, peering down from the second-floor balcony of an airy white house. He was in clean white robes, but he was unshaven, with ratty stubble down his neck.

"Help us!" I called back. "Please! You're a healer."

Wolfheart sighed. "I'll be down in a minute and we can talk."

My friends caught up soon enough, but the rest of Golden Apple appeared before Wolfheart did. First Rad, then Valkyrie, and finally Dr Agony emerged from side streets, converging near Wolfheart's house and paying us no attention at all. They all wore backpacks bulging with gear and looked dressed to travel. Finally, Wolfheart's door opened and the white wizard appeared, clean-shaven and changed from his robes into simple traveling clothes and carrying a pack of his own.

"These noobs asked for my help," he sighed as he noticed the rest of his party waiting for him. "Let me see if they can pay, and then we'll get going."

He crossed his front yard to us, shaking his head.

"Harpies?" He pointed to the scratches across Cass's armor. She nodded, stony-faced. Wolfheart made a show of peering at each of us from his spot on the grass. "Four faces, eight eyes… eh, you were lucky. They love the taste of them, you know. So who needs the heal?"

"Sepharad," said Cass. She helped Noah show Wolfheart his shattered hand.

"Ouch," said Wolfheart. He crossed his arms. "Well, whatever I charge you, it'll be worth it."

"We don't have much," said Cass.

"What's that?" Wolfheart gestured with his chin to the box of coppers, which we'd taken turns hauling up the steps from the fortress and across the Near Plains along with the gear stripped from the dead adventurers. I cleared my throat, and he looked at me with a raised eyebrow.

"We can pay you a quarter of it," I said. "Sepharad was hurt protecting me and that's my cut, so..."

"Very fair-minded," he said. "Fine. Come here, kid."

Wolfheart pulled a white cotton glove from his belt and pulled it on, snapping it like a surgeon. He touched the gloved hand to Noah's shattered one and began to murmur.

"Hurry up!" shouted Rad. The rest of Golden Apple was standing a few yards out onto the dirt track and they looked impatient.

"Where are you guys headed?" Cass called back.

"Rangers just uncovered a big dungeon out by Wyatt Falls," said Rad. He was even taller than he looked on the feeds. "It's wild country up there. Not safe for noobs."

"Can we come with you?" Cass asked.

"Absolutely not," Dr Agony interjected. "Rad, shut the hell up. Wolf, make it quick. We need to be at Dann's Teeth by nightfall."

"Come on," Cass said. "We can help."

"No tagalongs!" Dr Agony snapped. "No noobs, no poseurs, and especially no fangirls. Wolf, time's up. We're leaving."

"Coming, bossman," said Wolfheart. He glanced up at the drones hovering around our heads. "Enjoy the new hand, kid."

The white wizard sauntered back to his party, pausing only to scoop up a big double handful of our coppers and dump them into his backpack. Golden Apple set off into the wilderness, leaving us to watch in awe as Noah held up his hand, which was clean, straight, and whole.

COMPANY TOWN

"Damn, money tastes good," Cass sighed, tossing a spoon onto our table at Open Seasoning. It bore the wreckage of a huge celebratory meal, paid for from the box of coppers we'd found. In fact, we'd insisted on paying double, to cover the meal that Naila had comped us the night before.

"Shouldn't we count it?" Magpie asked.

"In a minute, haircut," replied Cass.

"I'll count it." Magpie dove a hand into the box and began to make neat stacks with the coins he pulled out.

"Noah, how does your hand feel?" I asked. He was staring at it, closing and opening it in front of his face.

"Tight," he said.

"Tight?" I cocked my head.

"Like new shoes." Noah put his hand in his lap.

"We'll do some passes tonight to break it in," I offered, and he nodded.

"Anybody need seconds? Thirds?" Naila called from the back counter. Noah and I shook our heads, and Cass just put a hand on her stomach and groaned. Naila smiled. "Just leave the dishes. I'll get 'em after."

"Two hundred fourteen coppers and three silvers," Magpie announced. "They were hiding at the bottom."

"Not bad for our first day, Hearthhammer," said Cass. "You too, Magpie."

"What's that worth on Earth?" I asked. "I never got a clear sense of the exchange rate. Noah?"

"I don't know," Noah said. "There doesn't seem to be a clean exchange. I think Expedition takes a cut if you don't spend the money in the Summerlands."

"It's like company scrip," I said. "That's devious."

"Golden Apple are obviously doing just fine, the assholes," Cass said. "We could've used that extra coin. Anybody get that on stream?"

"You're the only one who kept your camera on," Magpie said.

"Seriously?" Cass rolled her eyes to the ceiling.

"He really healed me," said Noah. "It would have cost a lot more at the White Magic Guild."

"I think they knew, though," I said. "You can tell if a drone is filming by how it moves, right?"

"Wolfheart did seem to stay back from Jessamine," Magpie agreed.

"I've certainly never seen them act like that on the feeds," I continued. "It was the same thing when we first bumped into them here at Open Seasoning. All our feeds were off then."

"Public image," said Cass with a sneer. "I bet you're right. In fact, I *know* you are. Okay, Hammers, new rule. Whenever we run into GA, everyone's camera stays on."

We nodded. Life in the Summerlands was turning out to be a lot more complicated than we'd expected. Out of everything we'd had to navigate so far, the sortie to the White Chasm had been the simplest of our challenges, even if it was the most terrifying and painful. There was clearly a whole thicket of unwritten rules here to be navigated and despite Cass's righteous anger, I was a bit relieved that we hadn't made enemies of Golden Apple.

"Okay," said Cass, leaning forward. "We don't know how much this treasure would be worth to my dad, but we're set for food and lodging for now. I say we enjoy the cash. We're gonna need a hell of a lot more, so let's use this to get set up while we look for a bigger score."

"Do you mean—" I said.

"That's right." Cass grinned. "Shopping montage."

★★★

I stepped out into the scented evening, absorbing the sights, sounds, and smells of Meat Street at night. During the day, it was like a market, crowded and bustling with shoving, shouting vendors. After nightfall—9:07 pm sharp, just like every day in the Summerlands—it became more like a public square. The lanterns and windows of the restaurants cast a golden glow on the sidewalks, where adventurers sat long into the night, sipping coffee and swapping stories. This was the time when the walls between rival adventuring parties broke down and the humans in the Summerlands, the daring and the wild, the rich and the famous, joined together in awe of what they'd accomplished by coming here and surviving.

I already loved it.

But there was a sour note in the melody the beautiful Summerlands were weaving around me. Jason was missing. I'd been able to put the pain away temporarily in the whirlwind of our arrival, but his absence had been painfully obvious at Athan's Rest. He'd been our heavy fighter, our tank; he should have been up front with a sword and armor, not Noah. Maybe then Noah wouldn't have gotten hurt. And as far as whose fault that really was, I had no illusions.

"Hey." Cass put a hand on my arm. She'd come up behind me while I was lost in my reverie, moving more softly than usual.

"Hey," I replied.

"We need to talk," she said. She glanced down the street, to where Noah and Magpie were chatting with a couple of female adventurers. One of them pointed to an empty wooden cup on their table; Noah passed his hand over it and when I could see it again it was full of water. "Just us."

"I know what this is about," I said, "and I'm really sorry." Cass's brow furrowed, so I plunged on. "I really sucked today. I was useless—worse than useless. I understand if you're pissed. Do you think Noah is mad at me?"

"Noah—*Sepharad*, shit—couldn't hold a grudge if you put it in a bucket for him," Cass said. "Actually, I think he's too excited about getting healing from Wolfheart." She gave me a tired half-smile. "But you're right. You sucked today. I love you, but that was awful. I wasn't sure we'd be able to find your bell after you dropped it."

"I know, I just—"

"Don't." Cass sighed. "Em, you're my best friend. You're my sister. But I'm also your party leader and I need you to step it up, okay? This isn't us practicing out in the dust field. Noah was really hurt today." She looked back at the boys, who were laughing. Magpie had pulled up a chair, though Noah still stood stiff-backed like a soldier under review. "I'll admit Magpie came through, though. Who knew he was as obsessed with old books as Noah?"

I looked at my boots, which were spattered with brown dots of dried blood. There was a strange feeling fluttering in my chest and I discarded a few hypotheses before pinning it down: I was annoyed at the attitude Cass was putting on.

I wasn't the only one who'd messed up against the harpies: Cass was supposed to be party leader, but when I'd asked for orders, she wasn't there. The boys and I had stumbled all over each other as a result. She was acting the part *now*, which is what had triggered my irritation, but in the White Chasm she'd been like a solo player.

I took a breath, trying to figure out how to tell her without breaking her heart. When I looked up, she was gone.

★★★

Bad Luck Alley was empty and silent under a blue-tinged midnight moon. I stifled a yawn as I surveyed the implements set out on the sidewalk in front of me. Two simple bells of dull iron, a tiny red gem, Wayland's dagger, and three copper coins: all the tools of a real red wizard.

It was time to see what I could do.

I was determined not to screw up like I had at the White Chasm, but more than that, it was high time I figured out what spells I actually knew. I'd spent five years reading and practicing, but that didn't mean I could just toss out magic at will. For one thing, I'd already discovered that casting spells in the Summerlands went deeper than just making the motions and saying the words. There was also the matter of fake spells.

It was an unavoidable side effect of the market. Any Summerlands spellbook that wanted to sell had to either offer something new or collect from sources that had. Sometimes this meant a licensing deal with a player who'd actually discovered or mastered an unknown spell, but less scrupulous publishers were happy to pad out their books with spells born in the imaginations of writers who'd never set foot in the Summerlands.

Most fake spells were easy to spot. For one thing, they tended to make lurid promises, like a series of bell passes from *The Real Red Book* that would supposedly fill any listener with unsuppressable lust. Others fooled even the hardcore fans for at least a little while; one notorious video claimed to show a red wizard summon an invisible servant to open a locked door for him and that player's stream rocketed up the charts until somebody noticed the tip of a wand making the telltale motions of the white magic spell for levitation in the corner of the frame.

I picked up the dagger and got to work.

The first spell I tried went off with gratifying ease: with the right grip, a few taps with my fingers, and a murmured word in Elvish, the weapon began to glow with a pulsing white light. I gave it a few waves and it left an afterglow that hung in the air for a few seconds, illuminating the implements by my feet.

The other light spell I knew involved rolling the little red gem quickly over my fingers, muttering to it until it gave off sparks. It took me a few tries to get the movements right, but when I did, the jewel spat lights like a firework. The glowing white motes danced before my eyes and when I blew on them, they flitted out over the narrow street, where they reflected in a puddle until they faded into the blue night.

I wasted the next half hour on two spells that simply wouldn't go. One, which claimed to shoot a beam of fire from the face of a coin, was probably fake: no matter how exactly I performed the motions and spoke the words, I couldn't feel even a flicker of heat in my stomach. The other had to be real, because I'd seen it in action: a spell to create an illusion from a jewel similarly to how I'd drawn out the light. That spell, or some more advanced version of it, probably explained the trick Belphegor had pulled on me at the Guild Hall. But try as I might, I couldn't make it happen on even a small scale, and eventually I resigned myself to the thought that I simply had the words or motions wrong.

I was burning with curiosity about the freezing spell I'd watched Dr Agony perform over and over in the clip from his feed, but I had no monster to test it on. Instead I turned to the last spell on my mental list, the signature of every red wizard and probably the most beloved piece of magic ever seen in the Summerlands.

Fireball.

All it took was a copper coin. I plucked one from the ground and began to roll it over my fingers like I'd practiced so many times in the dust field behind our apartment block. The coinage of the Summerlands was thicker and heavier than the quarters I'd used, but it was still easier to manage than the little jewel. Soon I had the copper piece moving smoothly back and forth across my knuckles.

With the motion down, it was time to add a little Elvish. The words had been etched into my memory for years, and they came easily when paired with the familiar motions of the coin.

I gasped and almost dropped the copper piece: it was drawing lines of warmth on my fingers as it passed over them, and its growing red glow stood out sharply against the night. My nostrils flared as I willed myself to ignore the stinging heat. Soon the coin was nearly burning my skin and I had to squint against its light.

It was time.

The last motion of the spell was to flick the coin away, hopefully at some target that you wanted to blow up. Casting around in rising panic as the copper piece scorched my fingers, I saw a wooden barrel tucked between two narrow stone buildings at my back. I sent the glowing coin spinning toward it without a second thought and I almost hit it, but the coin pulled to the right at the last second and smacked into the stone corner next to the barrel.

There was a flash of fire and a much louder *whump* than I expected as the coin burst into a blossoming ball of blue-and-white flame that lit up the night for a single glorious moment.

Three stories above the scorched and smoking corner of the building, a window slammed open to reveal a scowling, bearded face.

"Shut the hell up! People are trying to sleep!"

★★★

We were all up early the next morning. It was like Christmas. We had money and we meant to spend it.

Well, the others had money. I knew I'd done the right thing by paying for Noah's healing; insisting on using my cut of the treasure had been a balm to my conscience, but it was hard not to feel a pang of jealousy as Cass and Noah compared notes on what to buy. Magpie was as quiet as I was, though, which somehow made me feel better.

Our first visit was to Wayland, the scrap dealer. My immediate impression as we walked through the door, the dead adventurers' gear split between us, was that he was surprised to see us, but he quickly covered that with a brisk, professional demeanor that was miles more accommodating than his edge the day before. As agreed, he let us keep the gear he'd lent us, which in the light of morning was clearly not as nice as the stuff we'd retrieved for him.

From there we split up to do our own shopping, agreeing to meet back at the Expedition Hall on Portal Square at lunchtime. With only a few coppers to my name, I headed back in the direction of Coin Street, thinking it might be fun to torture myself by watching the high-end blacksmiths hammer away at weapons I could never afford. I had my camera on again and I was talking about the quality of the sunlight as I walked backwards through the winding alleys off Meat Street. So I wasn't paying attention at all when I collided with someone in a crash that sent us both tumbling to the cobblestones.

"Oh my God, I'm sorry!" I said, getting to my knees and dusting off my armor. My drone buzzed around my head to keep my face in focus and I could feel a blush rising in my cheeks. "Good thing nobody is watching this."

"You never know," said Naila, who was picking up vegetables from the street, brushing them off, and returning them to a big wicker basket.

"Naila!" I said stupidly. "Hey! Uh, sorry about that. Here." I began grabbing vegetables and trying to clean them on my pants.

"That's okay," she laughed. "By the way, I heard about what happened at Athan's Rest yesterday. You should have said something at dinner."

"Oh, we're fine," I said. "Sepharad got healed by Wolf-heart, did you hear that?"

"Unfortunately, yes," Naila said. "I think your boy told everybody on the street last night. Classic newbie motormouth. Come on, help me up."

I did, and once we were both standing she slapped me on the shoulder in thanks.

"Hey, if anything like that ever happens again, let me know, okay?"

"What do you mean?" I felt my brow furrow.

"If anybody gets hurt," she said. Her eyes flickered up over my shoulder and I realized she was looking at my drone. I made a snap decision, snagged it out of the air, and hit the Stream button to shut it off. Naila sighed dramatically.

"Much better," she said. "I hate those things, no offense. I always feel like they're watching me even when they're not."

"What's going on?" I asked. Naila's mouth quirked in a little smile.

"You're sharp, you know that?" She shook her head, a little gesture of resignation. "Come on, I want to introduce you to someone."

★★★

"Wayland's all right, as far as it goes, but he's an ex," Naila said as she led me down a long alley between Meat Street and Coin Street, where most of the shops were. We'd dropped off the basket of vegetables at Open Seasoning before setting out for whatever introductions she wanted to make, and with her hands free, she gestured expansively as she talked.

"Ex?" I asked. "Did you guys…?"

"Ha!" Naila laughed. "Not an *ex* ex. An ex-adventurer. Shopkeeps in Wellpoint are split between NPCs like me and retired players like Wayland. And by retired here, I definitely mean failed. Folks who couldn't hack it, got injured, whatever, but for whatever reason didn't want to go back to the real world. Not that I can blame them. Who would want to leave all this?"

The sun was just cresting the roofs above us, warming the morning shadows of the alleyway for what promised to be another perfect day.

"Better to serve in Heaven than rule in Hell," I ventured and Naila laughed again.

"Exactly! Anyway, the exes, they don't really get it, you know? They tend to be bitter and they take it out on noobs like you. They can't give up the Summerlands, but they still feel like failures."

"Unlike the NPCs?"

"Unlike the NPCs," Naila agreed. "We actually appreciate being here, you know? Even the ones who came here hoping to earn tickets are happier than the exes who went the other way. But hey, enough about your poor choices in shopping. What brought you to the Summerlands?"

"Oh." I wasn't sure I was ready to talk about Jason and Keats yet, but at the same time, I liked Naila and didn't want to lie to her. "We have a friend back home who needs money."

"Trying to save up, huh? Well shit, good luck. Enjoy the exchange rates."

We walked on in silence for a while, pushing our way past workers hauling crates of food and hungover adventurers stumbling home.

"Earn tickets?" I asked. This was all totally new to me. Expedition Games didn't exactly advertise the mechanics of their player support systems.

"Sure," said Naila. "That was the promise Expedition made to the first round of NPCs. We came here for free and they helped us set up shop. Then, if we saved up enough for a ticket, we could buy in and become players."

"I don't get it," I said. "How does Expedition make money off that? Aren't they paying you, too?"

"Hell no!" Naila stopped in the middle of the narrow alley, forcing the other early-morning shoppers and workers to split around us. "Being here is payment enough, that's what they said, and honestly I don't disagree with that part. But did I say they 'helped us' get set up? What I mean is they leased us land and sold us equipment on credit. Extended by them. At interest rates that they set. Of course as a restaurant owner, I need to get my supplies somewhere, and guess who's ready to sell me fresh meat and veg from their factory farms back on Earth?"

"I had no idea!" I said. "Wait, what about fetch quests? NPCs pay adventurers to go get them herbs for potions and sunstone for smithing and stuff."

"Oh yeah, we're not allowed to go get it ourselves. Gives the players something to do, and gets our coin back in circulation. There are a ton of rules like that." Naila made a sound somewhere between a sigh and a snort. I was starting to get the distinct impression that she'd kept all this bottled up for years.

119

"Really they just want to keep the money moving around. The whole thing is a little bottle economy other than the money that flows up to Expedition."

"But you'd rather be here, wouldn't you?" I said.

Naila smiled. "Better to serve in Heaven. Come on, we're holding up traffic."

As we reached the intersection with Coin Street, another thought occurred to me. "There must be a black market," I said.

"Sharp!" Naila wagged a finger at me. "Didn't I say I wanted to introduce you to someone?"

★★★

Dan Seidenberg ran his little potion shop from a sort of medieval wheelchair. He looked a bit older than Keats, with a deep tan, a bald head and an overgrown goatee. His left leg was cut off at the knee, the pants leg tucked and stitched. The wheelchair was based on what looked like two wagon wheels and a leather cushion, but far from seeming makeshift or jury-rigged, it had clearly been built with love and care. The cushion fitted the seat perfectly, the arms were padded, and as Seidenberg rolled down the wide aisles of his shop straightening bottles and blowing dust off labels, his ride was smooth and silent.

He didn't acknowledge us until he'd tidied up to his satisfaction and then he only looked at Naila.

"Need something?" he said. His voice had the rasp of a lifetime smoker, though tobacco was forbidden in the Summerlands.

"I wanted to introduce you to somebody," Naila said. Seidenberg turned away with a flick of one wheel, shaking his head, and rolled towards the low counter at the back of his shop. Naila went after him. "Seriously. Come on, you know I don't like it when you turn your back on me."

That stopped him. He looked back with narrowed eyes. "Sorry, kid. But you know how much I enjoyed the last person you introduced me to."

"Touché," Naila said, her hands in the air. "But still. This is Linnaea. She and her party are new."

"They always are," said Seidenberg.

"I comped them for a meal and they actually paid me back," Naila said.

"Really?" Apparently that got Seidenberg's attention, because he turned his wheelchair to face us head on.

"Her archer called Agony an asshole," Naila added. "Loud enough for him to hear."

"Okay," said Seidenberg. "All right. Maybe I do want to meet her." He looked at me for the first time. "What do you think of the Summerlands, kid?"

"Well, it's interesting," I hedged. He didn't want the prepackaged noob answer, that much was obvious. What was he looking for? "It's a lot more complex than I expected."

"Complex?" Seidenberg gave Naila an *are you kidding me?* look.

"The feeds don't show much other than the players," I said. "You only see a little fraction of what life is really about here. It's weird, actually, when you think that NPCs outnumber players like three to one."

"NPCs?" he raised an eyebrow.

"Oh, I'm sorry—" I started, but he laughed.

"Just messing with you," he said. "It's dehumanizing, but that's the lingo."

"Tell him what you think about the economy," Naila prompted me.

"Oh, I just said there had to be a black market," I said.

"Why?" asked Seidenberg.

"Well, it's a company town. Expedition basically owns everything, right? Plus they control what people can and can't do, how they can spend their money... there's gotta be a black market running to serve everybody who isn't a paying player."

"She's sharp," Seidenberg said to Naila.

"That's what I said!" she laughed. "She's pretty much figured it out for herself, so where's the harm?"

"Fine." Seidenberg looked at me, frowning, as though he could bore two holes in my skull with his eyes. Finally, he reached out his hand, which I shook. It was large, dry, and covered in old scratches and scars. "I'm Dan Seidenberg, potions guy."

"Oh, I know," I said. "You've been here since the start. Golden Apple used to come here."

"Weren't those the days?" Seidenberg rolled his eyes. "Naila, shut the door. Her cam is off, right?"

"Of course," Naila said as she gently closed the front door. The shop sank into sudden dimness; Seidenberg was like an old statue of a president in his chair. "Linnaea's white wizard was hurt yesterday," she went on. "His hand was busted up by a harpy. They ended up paying Wolfheart to heal him, if you can believe it."

"That's charitable," said Seidenberg.

"If you say so." Naila wrinkled her nose. "Look, Linnaea's party is just starting out. In forty-eight hours they've managed to get tangled up with Andronus, Wayland, and Wolfheart. Matter of fact, I think the only honest person they've given money to is me. If they have to pay Guild prices every time they screw up a fight, they'll be slumming it in Bad Luck Alley before the week is out."

I kept my mouth shut about that.

"Christ, the Guild," said Seidenberg. "You ever been in their guild hall?"

"The White Wizards?" I shook my head. "Uh-uh."

"Big waste of space. Anyhow, if you need healing, come see me, okay?"

"I can't afford any potions," I said. "I'm sorry. I wish!"

Seidenberg's eyes drilled into mine. "I'm not talking about potions."

"What?" I blinked as my brain caught up. "Oh! Isn't that illegal? Or, wait, are you an ex?"

"Hell no!" Seidenberg laughed. He gestured at his missing leg. "I got this in Afghanistan a long time before you were born. I've never seen so much as a gold dog in the Summerlands. And yes." His face got serious. "It's very illegal for me to do magic. But I do it anyway. So if anybody asks, shut the hell up, huh?"

★★★

"There she is!" Cass shouted as I strolled across Portal Square. "Linnaea, come here!"

I stopped halfway through a description to the camera of what going through the portal felt like, which I'd gotten on after seeing a smiling, chatty Donna Markan leading three men in starter clothing towards a weapons shop near the White Wizards' Guild Hall. I spotted Cass in front of the Expedition Hall, waving with both hands as though despite the volume of her voice and the fact that we'd been best friends since middle school I wouldn't be able to pick her out.

"Linnaea!" That was Donna, catching up with me as she returned from her errand. "I was just talking to your friends. How do you like the Summerlands?"

"Come on, come on," Cass urged as we got close. "Hey again, Donna."

"Hey again!" Donna patted me on the shoulder. "Don't be a stranger."

Cass spared a wave for Donna as she headed back into the Expedition Hall, but Noah didn't seem to have noticed her. He was poking in fascination at something in his hand, and I craned my neck to see what it was, but Cass put herself between me and him, practically bouncing with excitement. "Okay, do you want the good news or the good news?"

"Huh?" I said.

Before Cass could respond, Magpie appeared from the mouth of an alley at a near-sprint. At first I thought someone must be chasing him, but then I realized that he was as giddy with excitement as Cass. Apparently spending a little coin had recharged everyone's batteries until they overflowed.

"I have an idea!" he exclaimed, stumbling to a halt in front of us. "What if we went after Golden Apple?"

"Went after?" Cass said, frowning.

"Not like that." Magpie shook his head frantically. "I mean, what if we go where they're going? Wyatt Falls! They obviously know something that everybody else doesn't and if they're rushing out of town it must be a fat score."

"He's got a point," I said. His excitement was contagious and he did seem to know what he was talking about when it came to money.

"Huh." Cass tapped her chin. "Okay, let's say we do go to Wyatt Falls. We don't know where the ruin is, right? And you heard what Rad said, it's dangerous up there. It hasn't been tamed like the area around Wellpoint."

"How's your arm?" I said, and Cass looked down at the long scratch that was starting to scab over.

"Point taken." She nodded. "Okay, let's do it. If Magpie is right, maybe we can get all the money for Dad in one big haul. That would be…" She glanced away, blinking, and cleared her throat. "That would be good."

"Didn't you say you had some news?" I said, taking a page from Keats's playbook on how to change the subject.

"Right!" Cass brightened immediately. "Check this out." She stepped aside to reveal Noah, who was still fiddling with a little black object that looked like a phone.

"It's Noah," I said. He looked up, gave me a flash of a smile, then went back to fiddling.

"It's a handheld!" said Cass.

"A what?" I said.

"For our drones!" Cass looked at me expectantly. "To turn them on and off! And we can track our viewership!"

124

"Why would we want to do that?" I asked. I knew I was being a bummer, but I was already worrying about how we'd get to Wyatt Falls ahead of Golden Apple and their massive head start, and anyway it didn't slow Cass down for a second.

"Because of this," she said. "Noah, show her."

Noah tapped the touchscreen of the handheld a few times, then flipped it around and handed it to me. I looked down to see my own name, LINNAEA, in big letters across the top of the screen. Below that was a line that glowed green: an email icon and the text 103 NEW MESSAGES.

Next came a line graph, with the last twenty-four hours across the bottom and VIEWERSHIP written vertically along the left side. A bright red line showed a steady climb from the time I'd turned on my camera in the Near Fields, peaking when we fought the harpies at Athan's Rest, and dropping off to nearly zero when I turned it off on our trip back. The line jumped back up each time I had streamed that morning, and was currently holding steady…

At 12,442 viewers.

I looked up at my camera, down at the handheld, back up at the camera, and finally back down. There was one more thing on the screen: a big red button labeled END STREAM. I hit it as fast as I could.

HARD PASS

"I'm here in the Near Plains with the Einstein of the airwaves herself, the first, best, and only scientist of the Summerlands, the legendary Linnaea!" Cass ducked towards me and her camera followed. "Say hi, Linnaea!"

"Hi," I said, forcing a smile. "How long did it take you to come up with that, Jessamine?"

"Only all night," said Cass. She took a long step over to Noah. "Now let's check in with our wonderful white wizard..."

"Are you okay?" Magpie sidled up to me as Cass rambled on. She'd turned her camera on the moment I turned mine off and it had been on ever since, chronicling our so-far uneventful venture back into the wilderness on our way to Wyatt Falls.

"Yeah," I said. "Thanks." I held up a little notebook, rough white paper bound in leather. "I've been feeling better since I got this. No more streaming for me."

Magpie laughed. "Cass is doing enough for the rest of us."

"It's good!" I smiled at him. "This is how she always wanted to play the game. She's welcome to it."

The only rock in Cass's shoe as we made our way towards the White Chasm was her numbers, which were nowhere near what I'd hit. She'd topped out around two thousand, though that was a big jump from her previous high of a hundred or so. Her hope had been to pick up my viewership and it had worked, but only up to a point. She was working those two thousand viewers as hard as she could, though, somehow coming up with a never ending stream of jokes, observations, and confessions. It was actually pretty entertaining to watch as long as she kept the camera pointed away from me.

I was happy with my notebook, though it had cost me more than I'd expected. There were no ballpoint pens in the Summerlands, but pencils were allowed, and I now had a stash of those along with a little pocket knife to keep them sharp. I'd started our sortie making sketches while we walked—I'd gotten the whole layout of the Viking-looking ruin while the others took a pee break—but I found soon enough that I couldn't keep up with Cass's pace if I was drawing, so I stowed my pencil. I didn't want to put the notebook down, though.

"There's the White Chasm," Noah said. We were tracking roughly northeast, planning to skirt around the edge of the canyon on our way into the Battle Plains. The White Chasm was ahead and to the left, meaning I'd steered us more or less perfectly. Despite the fact that we'd been walking for hours, I found a new spring in my step.

★★★

"Look at this!" Noah held up a battleaxe that had been split straight down the middle, the shaft and double-headed blade broken into two perfect halves.

"Worth keeping, you think?" asked Cass.

"Probably not." I looked up from a pile of broken arrows, their red fletching bright against the gray dust of the Battle Plains. "It would be a pain to reforge and it would probably break along that same line when you tried to use it. Maybe we could have it made into two single axes?"

"Nah," said Cass. She waved to Noah. "Toss it!"

"We should keep moving," Magpie said. He was maybe ten yards ahead of us, pacing in the dust as we picked through the shattered weapons and armor all around us. "Golden Apple has a full day on us."

"About that," Cass said, gesturing for us to huddle up. "What about Hard Pass?"

"Hard Pass?" Magpie looked lost.

"The normal way to Wyatt Falls is to skirt east around the foothills of the Wyvern Range, through a rock formation called Dann's Teeth," said Noah. "But there's a pass between two of the lower mountains that lets out at the top of the Falls. It would probably save about a day."

"Great, let's do that!" Magpie said. "Come on!"

"Wait," I said. "It's called Hard Pass for a reason. A couple players died there in the early years, including Wyatt Sheridan, who the falls are named for."

"Not much of a gamertag," Magpie said.

"Hell of a fencer, though," said Cass.

"He was an Expedition employee, actually—" Noah began, but Cass held up a hand.

"I think it's worth a shot," she said. "Otherwise Golden Apple is going to loot the new ruin before we can even find it. If we can get to Wyatt Falls when they do, we'll have a chance at the treasure."

"Wait," I said. "I wanted to suggest something." I glanced up at Cass's drone, which was quietly humming a few feet above her head. "Maybe we should turn the cameras off."

"What? Why?" said Cass.

"Well, I'm just worried about spies," I said. I dropped my voice to a whisper despite knowing perfectly well how sensitive the mics were on the drones. "We don't want some GA fanboy sharing our plans with them."

"You're paranoid," said Cass.

"It happens," said Noah.

"She's right," said Magpie. "Information is power. We don't know how many players know about the new ruin. We should be trying to keep that number down."

"Fine." Cass nodded. "Noah, kill my feed, would you?"

Noah pulled out the handheld and tapped it a few times. Cass's drone backed off into a neutral position, no longer concerned with good angles.

"Thanks," I said. "I think we should go for Hard Pass."

"Sure," said Noah.

"Perfect!" said Cass. She set off at a trot, headed for the distant mountains that made a faint blue line on the horizon. Noah followed her and I was just setting out when I heard Magpie mutter from behind me.

"I agree too."

★★★

"You know," Cass said between wheezing breaths, "I used to do my homework during these parts."

Hard Pass was a long, shallow uphill slog featuring lots of rocky scree and a path obstructed by boulders. Sometimes the boulders blocked the way and we'd have to climb over them while hoping they wouldn't shake loose under our weight and start one of the short but terrifying rockslides we'd learned to expect.

It was exhausting, it was unwelcoming, and most of all, it was boring. On the shadeless side of the Wyvern Range, sweating our way uphill, the welcoming sun of the Summerlands became a glaring white fireball. Our usual banter died away and was replaced by nothing but muttered curses as we toiled up the pass. Cass's quip was the first thing anyone had said in over an hour.

And it was true, I reflected as I clambered up the side of a boulder taller than I was. Back on Earth, watching the feeds, it was so easy to skip these parts. If you were watching live you could hit mute and do something else. After the fact, there was the fast-forward button. Highlight reels cut this stuff out entirely.

I reached the top of the boulder and paused to wipe the sweat from my eyes. Then I blinked, because something was coming down the pass towards us. Under the bright sun the shape soon resolved itself into three people. One of them was limping badly, supported between his comrades.

"Hey!" I called, waving. "You guys okay?"

They looked up as they came near and exhaustion was written plainly under the streaks of blood and filth on their faces. Two women about our age supported a man who hopped on one leg; he was at least twenty years older than they were. Their gear was battered and dirty, but mostly whole.

"What's going on?" Cass shouted up to me. She was behind me, peering up around the curve of the boulder. I slid down her side.

"Other players," I said.

"Don't—hey!" Cass put on a big smile as the strangers rounded the boulder. Even up close I didn't recognize them. They weren't major streamers. Cass put out a hand, which the man shook. "We're Hearthhammer. I'm Jessamine, party leader."

"Merric." His hair was long and lank, a flat brown. His face was pale beneath his tan and his cheeks were sunken. "And what's left of Merric's Angels. I don't suppose you have a healer?"

"Sepharad, any chance you could help out?" Cass said.

"I'll try," said Noah. He knelt down by Merric's feet and pulled a left-handed leather glove from his pack.

"You're going up the pass?" said Merric.

"That's the plan," said Cass.

"Don't," Merric said. "The wyverns have been breeding. We got hit last night, more than ever. I lost two girls and barely made it out myself."

"Okay, try your leg," said Noah. Merric set his foot down gingerly, testing it. His eyebrows went up, and his face cleared as he settled his weight.

"Not bad, kid!" he said. "Shame you aren't a girl, or I'd take you in a second. Anyway, you guys wanna head through the Teeth. Forget the Pass."

"Thanks," said Cass. "We'll think about it."

"Which means no," Merric laughed. "Shame, I could've used an archer... tell you what. You survive, look me up in Wellpoint. Just promise me you'll find shelter for the night, okay?"

★★★

We may have ignored Merric's warning about the pass, but we took the news of wyverns seriously. We'd had enough trouble fighting off the harpies that we didn't want to tangle with another flying monster just yet. As night drew down and we neared the crest of the pass, we began looking seriously for shelter.

It was Noah who found it, a pentagonal hole cut into the ground halfway beneath a small boulder. Shoving the rock aside took all four of us and caused a minor landslide of its own, but it revealed a drop of about six feet onto the landing of a staircase that led down into blackness.

"Did you know this was here?" Cass asked as she unslung her backpack.

"No," said Noah. "I don't think anyone's found it before."

"God, I wish we were streaming right now!" Cass rolled her eyes to the sky. "Okay, Magpie, get a torch going. I'll go first, then you, then Linnaea and Magpie last. Oh, wait. Tie up a rope so we can get out easily in the morning. Good? Good."

We set to work and soon the four of us stood on the stone landing, staring down the stairs into murky dark. As promised, Cass went first, torch in one hand and my dagger in the other. The staircase led straight down for a while, then hooked to the right at something wider than a ninety-degree angle. This happened three more times before we finally reached the bottom.

"Oh, wow." I dug for my notebook as I took in the chamber at the end of the stairs. It was a single rectangular room, but absolutely massive, on a scale I associated with sports stadiums. Ten columns of stone statues stretched away into the darkness. I could see at least a dozen rows in the flickering torchlight, but there was no telling how far back the chamber went.

"What is it?" asked Magpie.

"Look at this," said Noah. He was peering at one of the statues, whose head was cracked. He picked at the stone, flaking away a few shards. "I think there's hair in here."

131

"Hair?" said Cass.

"Definitely," said Noah. "And a skull. I think it's a corpse."

"Okay!" Cass said, a little too loud. "I think that's enough exploring for today. Let's make camp and get some dinner going. Emma, make a fire, please."

The corpse statues loomed over our shoulders as we worked, but the familiar routine of camping took over, and soon enough we had a little fire going, sending smoke up to the high ceiling of the tomb. We'd spent plenty of nights camping under the orange glow of the night sky, so even in this alien place, the evening had a nostalgic air. Soon we unfurled our bedrolls and let the exhaustion of the day carry us away as the fire burnt down to embers.

★★★

I woke with a start to the sound of scuffling feet. The fire was low but still alive, and there were shadows moving around it. My mind was too fuzzy to panic until a whisper of sound told me that one of the shadows had drawn a sword.

"Wake up!" I screamed. Magpie sat bolt upright and his knives flashed red in the firelight when they appeared from somewhere nearby. Cass was next; she leapt to her feet while I was still on my knees. Noah sighed and rolled over.

I turned my backpack over and shook it. The contents spilled over the cold stone of the tomb: food, flint and tinder, two torches, a few coins. I threw one of the torches onto the remains of our fire, where its oil-soaked wrapping promptly burst into flame.

Cass faced off against the intruders, crouched low and ready to spring in any direction, my dagger in her hand. There were three of them, in black leather armor, their faces wrapped with bandanas. They all carried swords and they were spreading out to flank Cass.

I snatched a copper coin up from the ground and began to roll it across my fingers, warming it up. It fell, but I snagged it before it could hit the floor and started again. I was muttering under my breath, Elvish words, their meanings obscure but their power obvious now as the coin began to glow a faint crimson that made wobbling shadows on the floor as it tumbled over my fingers.

The attacker on Cass's right lunged for her and suddenly Magpie was there, his long knives slicing through the air. One caught the man's sword as the other darted for his face, but Magpie's opponent ducked back at the last second and Magpie stumbled forward, overreaching.

Camera! I thought as Cass bullrushed the swordsman before he could take a swing at Magpie. The two went down in a crash and tumble as Magpie leapt clear. I glanced around frantically. My drone was hovering outside my reach, dangerously near to another of the attackers. I dropped my coin, scrambled around the fire and turned over Noah's backpack, shoving away his rations and magic gear.

"Looking for this?" said the man nearest me. He held up Noah's handheld just long enough for me to register what it was, then threw it in a high arc far out among the statues. I didn't hear it land.

"Shit!" I yelled. The man drew his sword and started for me. Casting around for anything I could use, I saw the dull red light of my half-magicked coin on the black floor. I snatched it up and began to roll it again, but it had lost most of its heat. The attacker advanced, his eyes locked on me and glittering in the firelight.

Noah sat straight up with a snort, his head crashing into my assailant's hip.

The coin in my fingers burned hot and bright and I flicked it at the third man, who was squaring off with Magpie. It hit him in the chest. A sphere of flame about the size of a basketball flowered where the coin struck, sounding a dull thump that echoed in the tomb. He stumbled backwards and hit the ground, his armor scorched and smoking.

I jumped to my feet. Noah was up, too, his sword whipping up to catch an arcing slash from the attacker he'd bumped into. He brought his blade back down in a neat counterattack that caught his opponent on the sword arm.

"Run!" the wounded fighter yelled, slapping his free hand over the fresh cut. His two companions responded instantly; Cass's attacker disengaged from her and bolted for the stairs, while the one I'd scorched stumbled after him.

"Yeah, run!" Magpie shouted as the apparent leader followed his men. Soon they'd disappeared up the stairs, leaving us panting and bewildered.

"Everybody okay?" said Cass, brushing dirt from her pants. "Nice fight, Hammers. MVP goes to Linnaea, though. Clutch fireball!"

"Thanks," I said. "But what the heck was that about? PvP is illegal. Were they trying to steal something?"

"Probably. Anything missing?" asked Cass. We spent the next few minutes sorting and repacking the gear that had scattered all over the floor. Everything was there. Noah took a torch and found the drone controller out among the statues where it had been thrown, its screen cracked but otherwise fine.

"I'm not going to be able to sleep," I said.

"Me neither," Cass agreed. "But—what the hell is *that?*" Her eyes were fixed on the archway where the staircase let out. Water was sluicing down the steps and spilling across the floor of the tomb.

Magpie laughed. "It's raining!"

★★★

We packed quickly, leaving the fire behind, and took the rain-slick steps as fast as we dared. The water came thicker as we climbed and soon we emerged panting into a torrential downpour.

"This is new!" shouted Cass over the lashing roar of the storm.

"It's the Summerlands, not the Sunshinelands!" I yelled back. Thunder boomed as a sheet of lightning illuminated the boulders and mountain slopes around us. "Come on, let's move!"

Any hopes I had of the descent down the far side of Hard Pass being easier than the climb up were soon washed away in the storm. The pass swiftly became an impromptu streambed as the rain rushed downhill, lapping at our ankles and making the rubble floor of the pass shift erratically beneath our boots. We stumbled our way through the darkness, crashing into boulders that loomed up out of the darkness to scratch and rasp against our questing hands.

"Sound off!" Cass shouted for the third time in maybe ten minutes.

"Here!" I called back.

"Here!" That was Noah.

A few empty seconds passed. I stopped, bracing myself against a rock, and let another long moment go by before I began to panic.

"Magpie!" Cass's voice cut through the hiss of the rain. "Magpie, where are you?!"

They tumbled out of the darkness, two figures locked in desperate combat, just as another blaze of lightning showed them like a photograph. One was Magpie—I saw his knives flash—and the other had one hand on his sword and the other on Magpie's collar. Then they were gone among the boulders further down the slope.

"That way!" I shouted, but nobody could see where I was pointing. I plunged after them, bouncing off rocks and slipping in the rain-slick scree.

"Emma, don't—" That was Cass, her words lost under another boom of thunder. But it was too late. I'd lost him in the darkness and the rain muted any sound of the fight. Magpie was gone.

★★★

Hard Pass ended at the top of Wyatt Falls, where a rain-swollen river tumbled down from the left-hand peak and spilled over the sheer cliff edge in a glittering rush. There was a rainbow in the mist, pale colors against the faraway blue sky, and framed under its arc we saw the little frontier town also called Wyatt Falls alongside the little lake at the base of the cliff.

A wooden scaffold ran two hundred feet from the top of the cliff to its foot, supporting a rickety staircase whose planks squished and bent under our feet as we picked our way down. We were all as soaked through as the staircase, still dripping and shivering in our soggy clothes despite the morning sun. There were only three of us and we made our way to Wyatt Falls in miserable silence.

The town itself was like something from a Wild West movie. It lacked the cobbled streets and stone buildings of Wellpoint; instead, two dirt tracks made a cross between a few wooden structures that looked about as sturdy as the stairs we'd come down. There was a little inn for players, an Expedition Hall that held the wireless signal repeaters and a single small TV, and a general store, and that was it.

We headed for the inn, praying they'd have space. We needn't have worried. The innkeep, a yawning NPC, seemed surprised to see us. Apparently rumor of the rangers' discovery had gotten out and the adventurers based in Wyatt Falls had all spread out into the wilderness to hunt for the new dungeon. Despite the bad news, we were much too exhausted to turn around and head back into the wilds, so we handed over our money and tromped upstairs to strip and dry off.

We had no extra clothes, of course, but just being out of my waterlogged leather pants gave me the best feeling I'd had in days. We took turns with a small, scratchy towel provided by the innkeep, and soon lounged around our small single room wrapped in the sheets from the beds. We barely said a word to each other. Cass was especially subdued, her eyes locked on the floor and her voice little more than a mumble. I knew what she was thinking: she'd lost another one.

There was a knock at the door.

"Noah, can you…" Cass said, but he was already on his feet, his sheet around his waist. He shuffled to the door and turned the handle.

The door burst open and Magpie tumbled into the room. He took in our near-nudity in a glance, paused for half a second to wonder at it, then dove for the backpack at Cass's feet.

"Magpie, what the hell—" she started.

"Map! Map!" He was tearing through her bag, tossing stuff to either side as he dug for the bottom.

"What?" said Cass. "What map?"

"This map!" Magpie held it up, his grin nearly blinding. It was the fake treasure map Cass had bought from Andronus back in Wellpoint. Magpie shook it open one-handed, then flipped it over and held it out at arm's length. He sprang to his feet.

"Yes! Yes! Yes!" He was practically jumping around the room. I put a hand on his shoulder.

"What is it?"

"The map is real! It's real! And I know where the treasure is!"

AN AWFUL LOT

"Are you sure this is right?" Cass asked, her gaze flitting between the map in her hands and the woods around us.

"Absolutely," Magpie said. "I just came this way."

"You gonna tell us what happened?" I said, pulling a branch out of the way for Noah. Wyatt Falls was built on a lake, but it backed on a dark, tangled forest through which Magpie was now leading us with the help of the treasure map.

"What's to tell?" Magpie flashed me a grin. "We got separated and then that asshole from the dungeon attacked me. It was still dark when I found the staircase, so—"

"What happened to the guy you were fighting?" Noah asked.

"Well, he found the staircase for me," Magpie said, "by falling down it. It was still dark when I found his body at the bottom, so I figured the best thing to do would be to stay near the cliff. I walked for a while, but I was pretty worn out, so I grabbed a catnap. Woke up, got a good look around, and realized I'd seen the place before."

"Okay, so what exactly are we looking for?" Cass asked.

The trees fell away suddenly, revealing the cliffside. On our left, maybe a mile away, was the waterfall itself and the rickety stairs just beyond it. Just in front of us, a grove of what looked like crystal trees erupted from the white earth at the base of the cliff. They rose in sharp, stiff angles to glitter blue and silver under the noon sun. The glinting facets of each branch made lines of light on the ground, like the inverse of shadows. It was nearly blinding to look at.

"Not bad, right?" said Magpie. He pointed to a clump of angles on Cass's map. "See? There's the cliff and that's the grove."

Cass squinted at the tangle of ink. "Mmm... I guess so. Okay, let's take a look around."

We headed into the crystal grove. It was easier to see under the glassy eaves, where the reflections were muted and the light was a soft blue glow. The map suggested that the treasure, whatever it was, was hidden right at the angle where the cliff met the valley floor, so we started our search there. We picked between the smooth blue roots for maybe ten minutes before Magpie gave an excited shout.

"Look at this!" He waved us over with a flash of something red.

"What is it?" I asked. Magpie held a scrap of rich crimson cloth with a few stitches of silver thread trailing from one edge. It looked familiar, but I couldn't place it.

"It's from Dr Agony's robes," he said and he was right. It was part of the robe Agony wore on the billboard near my old apartment block, the one I'd seen every day for years. "It was hooked on this root here. I think it tore off."

We stood beneath the largest of the crystal trees, which was so wide that it would have taken all four of us to get our arms around it. Its roots stuck up and plunged into the earth at sharp angles, leaving gaps big enough for a person to climb under. As we passed the red scrap around, a leaf separated from its branch high above our heads and fell to shatter on the ground with a faint tinkle.

"So they were here," Cass said.

"They certainly weren't in town," I agreed. "This must be it. But where's the entrance?"

"Wait, before we do that." Cass held up a hand. "Cameras on, guys. Linnaea, I know it's not your favorite, but we've been caught with our pants down twice now. Shit, we almost got PKed last night and we've got no proof! We're doing it right this time and that means making sure we have a record of whatever goes down in the dungeon."

I peered up at my drone, which was hovering uncertainly among the branches. "Can I borrow the handheld?"

"Sure," said Noah. He dug into his pack and pulled out the little controller. He tapped the screen a few times, then his eyebrows went up.

"What?" I said. "You're making me nervous."

In response, he flipped the handheld over and put it in my waiting hand. I saw my tag at the top, then the green NEW MESSAGES line and the red viewership graph. It took me a second to register what I was seeing: my inbox, which had contained maybe a hundred messages the last time I looked, now had over a thousand.

"You're popular," Noah said.

"Oh no," I said.

"Read them!" said Cass. "Or at least check 'em out. Come on, superstar."

I took a deep breath and hit the email icon. The screen switched to a long, scrollable list of unread messages. I swiped through them at high speed, but it was easy to see what they were about from the subject lines that swept past: "You OK?" "Don't die!!!" "WHERE IS LINNAEA??"

"Well?" asked Cass.

"I think people were worried about me," I said.

"Of course they were!" Cass said. "They love you and you disappeared without a trace. You left them on a cliffhanger. It's kind of genius, actually."

"It's terrifying," I said.

"Well, you better give them what they want." Cass waggled her eyebrows at me. "Superstar." Before I could stop her, she leaned in and tapped the big START STREAM button at the bottom of the screen.

My drone swooped down obediently and oriented its camera at my face. I glanced down at the handheld and tapped back to my viewership graph. The red line was already climbing.

"Uh, hi," I said, and gave the drone a little wave. "Linnaea here. Sorry for the radio silence. We, uh… we didn't want to

140

give away our secret plan. But I think it worked, so here we are. Thanks for hanging in there, guys. Okay, check this out." I gestured to the glittering grove. "We're just outside Wyatt Falls, here in these amazing trees. Or are they actually trees? I'm not sure. Anyway, it's beautiful. But that's not why we're here. We heard the rangers found a new dungeon outside Wyatt Falls and we're pretty sure this is it. So, let's check it out." I glanced at the roots of the big tree where Magpie had found the scrap of Agony's robe. "This is either gonna be really cool or super embarrassing. And, uh, if we don't come out, send somebody to get our bodies, okay?"

I got to my knees by the mass of jutting roots. I could definitely fit in there if I just stayed low... I shuffled forward on all fours. My drone swept down and closed in and I could imagine perfectly the exact shot my viewers were now getting of my butt.

It was dark under the roots, the same deep blue as the evening sky in the Summerlands. I could still see a little, but my hands found it first: a pentagonal hole in the earth. Reaching in, I could just barely touch a stone step maybe a foot beneath ground level.

"This is it!" I shouted. I wasn't about to crawl in on my belly, though, so I backed out from under the root system.

"You found it?" Cass was twisting her hands over and over each other.

"I found it," I said. "Another staircase like the one in the pass. It's gonna be a pain to get in, though."

"What's life without a little pain?" said Cass.

★★★

"At least there aren't any corpse statues," I said. At the foot of the stairs, a long, empty stone hallway stretched in both directions. We were blind until Noah lit a torch and even with its flickering, smoky light we could only see a few yards in each direction.

"Yet," said Cass, and she waggled her eyebrows at me again.

"What do you think this place was, though?" I asked.

"What do you mean?" said Noah.

"Well, it's not like the elves just built dungeons for us to have adventures in, right?" I caught my drone tracking me out of the corner of my eye. "The last one was clearly a tomb of some kind, so what about this place?"

"Hopefully a treasury," said Cass. "Come on, let's go this way."

We set off at random down the hall, four camera drones buzzing happily behind us. I was reminded of the last video I'd watched, the day Jason was killed. Four adventurers, a low, enclosed space, the promise of danger and reward everywhere. Golden Apple had looked so cool in that video, so professional, but so far Hearthammer had just muddled through, broke and chasing rumors without any real idea what we were doing. And yet I suspected that on the other side of the camera, we looked better than I thought.

The walls were etched with line drawings of elves, a perfect example of why we all used that name for the lost inhabitants of the Summerlands. The pictures reminded me of ancient Egyptian art, with flat, slender figures, only these had long, pointed ears sweeping back from their heads. Strangely, their skin seemed to be covered in polka dots, a detail that had never shown up in the other art I'd seen.

I pointed out details to my camera as I went: the high boots on one elf, the crown on another. The drone's black eye relayed every word to my invisible fans. I paused at one curious carving, where a figure stood with its right hand raised, facing another elf with a very different look. His build was stockier, and he had what looked like a beard under a heavy helmet. Rather than the narrow, curving sword that most of the elves had, this one carried around shield and a long-handled axe. I stepped back to give my camera a better view.

"Stop," said Magpie. I glanced down the hall to see him standing with a hand raised. Cass and Noah paused a few feet behind him. Magpie stood at the end of the corridor, with a door in front of him and one on either side. All three were identical: smooth, neatly-fitted stone with metal hinges that gleamed yellow in the torchlight. I lifted my hand to turn off my camera, then remembered that this was exactly what people wanted to see. So instead I moved down the hallway to give my fans a better view.

"Just pick one," said Cass, coming up behind me.

"Look at this," Magpie said. He pointed to the floor. Faint scratches marred the otherwise smooth stone, straight lines that extended from the left- and right-hand doors.

"Are they from the doors opening?" Noah asked.

"I don't think so," said Magpie. "The doors are too well fitted for that. Plus that would make an arc, not a straight line."

"Then what?" said Cass.

"Not sure." Magpie knelt down and pulled his lockpick set from a pocket. He chose an implement that looked sort of like a long, flat dentist's pick, and tried to slip it between the door at the end of the hall and the wall it closed into. There was no room. "See? It fits perfectly." He took a long breath. "Okay, everybody move back."

We moved back. The elves set traps, everybody knew that. Like the ancient Egyptians, Mayans, and others in our own world, whoever these lost builders were, they'd been concerned with people stealing their stuff after they buried it. Over the years, greedy adventurers had fallen prey to pits covered by false floors, tumbling rocks, automatic crossbows, even poison gas. Apparently the elves had been as paranoid as they were rich. So if Magpie thought the doors were trapped, I intended to take him seriously.

The center door sighed as he eased it open a fraction of an inch and slipped his lockpick into the open space.

"Ah—" he breathed, and after a moment, "ha." He pushed the door shut.

"What?" said Cass.

"I almost died," said Magpie. He looked back at us, grinning. "But only almost." He tapped the center door with his lockpick. "See this door? Not a real door. It's just a trigger that pops the other two open. I would guess that whatever comes out of them isn't very nice."

"So if you open one of them—"

"Same result." Magpie stood up. "This is a dead end."

"Seriously?" said Cass. "It's been one long hallway other than this."

"Maybe the other way?" I suggested. "That must be where Golden Apple went."

"Well," said Magpie, "unless you wanted me to do this."

He leapt towards us, away from the dead end, and in the same motion yanked the left-hand door open. Its match across the hall crashed open, too, and as Magpie stumbled forward, a glittering blade swept down from each archway. The doors themselves stopped moving after ninety degrees, making a neat wall that blocked off the hallway behind him just as the arcing blades bit into the floor, fitting perfectly into the long scratches on the floor.

"Holy shit!" shouted Cass.

"Did you know that would happen?" said Noah.

"Are you okay?" I asked.

Magpie flashed his smile. "Just fine, thanks. I thought it would be something like that. But now..." He gently pushed the right-hand door, which swung silently in. Its blade retracted back into the open shadows of the doorway, timed so that it would be fully reset when the door closed. Magpie slipped through the little gap between the open doors. "You were right, boss!" he called. "There's more back here."

★★★

There was another short hall, then a series of doors and corridors that seemed to turn back on themselves in an endless fractal loop. We marked the corners, scratching little arrows into the stone with our daggers, but any anxiety was soon reduced to tedium as we had to stop for Magpie to check and double-

check every new door. As we waited at yet another intersection, I pondered whether this whole part of the complex was a
devious invention of the elves to send us in circles until we
starved to death.

"Linnaea?" said Noah. Lost in my thoughts, I didn't realize
he was talking to me until he said my name again. "Linnaea.
You should see this."

"What's up?" Noah had his handheld out, and by the com-
bined green-red glow on his face I knew he was checking our
rankings. He passed it over to me without a word. I gave it a
quick scan: more messages, a graph with an upward curve…

There was something new on the screen, near the bottom.
A little image of a trophy, glowing gold, and the word
CONGRATULATIONS! But for what? I tapped it and the
handheld played a tinny little tune as digital fireworks exploded
beneath a new message that took up the entire screen.

CONGRATULATIONS, LINNAEA! YOUR STREAM
HAS REACHED THE TOP TEN FOR THE FIRST TIME!
YOU ARE CURRENTLY NUMBER 9 IN THE WORLD!

I dropped the handheld, which clattered to the floor as its
celebratory music played out. The firework animation sent
multi-colored shadows shifting across the walls and floor of the
hallway.

"What?" said Cass and Noah together. I opened my mouth
to respond, but Magpie caught my eye with his sudden movement as he stumbled away from the door he'd been working
on, staggered to his feet, and began to run.

"Gold dogs!" he shouted. "Move!"

They came snapping and scratching out of the door he'd
just opened, a wave of rust-colored scales and claws. Gold dogs
were the great pests of the Summerlands. They were strange
creatures, not like dogs at all aside from being quadrupedal and
having teeth; in fact I always thought they looked more like
giant armadillos with insect heads and long, searching antennae.
They were famously *good news/bad news* creatures: they hung
around piles of gold, hence the name, but for whatever reason
they defended treasure with their lives.

"Sepharad, move up!" I yelled. "Make a wall!"

Noah shoved past me, sword in hand, to form up with Cass and block the hallway. She had her bow out and an arrow nocked.

"Linnaea, bomb 'em!" Cass ordered.

"They're fireproof!" I called back. Magpie skidded to a stop between Cass and Noah and the gold dogs, which were spilling down the hallway in a tumbling rush. There were at least a half-dozen of them.

"Fine, genius, you think of something!" Cass's bow hummed as she sent an arrow into the mass of monsters. It was impossible to miss, but the gold dogs didn't slow down as arrow after arrow stung them. I caught a glimpse of Magpie's face as he ducked between Cass and Noah. He didn't seem to be panicking, and frankly, he was right to run. He had no armor and only knives for weapons, which wouldn't put much distance between him and the gold dogs' snapping jaws. He stopped by me and turned to face the monsters roiling towards us.

My mind riffled through my list of spells like the pages of a catalog, checking and discarding each in turn. There was only one that might help, and it was the one I hadn't tested. I ducked both hands into my bag of magic implements and fumbled around until I had a bell in each. It was time to see what I'd learned from Dr Agony.

"Hold them back," I shouted. "Buy me some time!"

The spell was as tricky as any I'd ever learned. I stuck my arms straight out, almost punching Magpie in the face. I began to roll the bells in little circles, one forward, the other backward. They clanked faintly under the sound of the skittering gold dogs. I tried to let half my mind focus on keeping them in motion—roll, snap, reverse—as the other half dredged around for the right incantation.

I found the words, painstakingly memorized by rote from Dr Agony's feed. I had never noticed how well they fit the movement of the bells, locking into spaces between rings to make a hypnotic polyrhythm. I focused on the gold dogs, now only a few feet from my friends, will them to slow, slow, slow… stop. Freeze. Hold.

My arms were burning. Holding them rigidly out was bad enough, but the motion of the bells was wreaking hell on the tendons along my wrists. My left arm started shaking, then my right. Everything was blurry except the trembling mass of gold dogs, which strained in sharp focus as they battled my will. Cass's arrows soared in leisurely slow motion, their fletching riffling in the stale dungeon air, and Noah's sword arm rose and fell like a long, heavy pendulum. I could feel the monsters' massed rage pressing against my mind. They hated me for holding them, caging them, forcing them to stay still when they wanted so desperately to run rampage and paint the hallway with our blood.

My left arm gave out as the bell in that hand came around in a loop and my hand spasmed open. The bell arced over Cass's head and disappeared among the gold dogs. The world snapped back into place. The monsters screeched as they charged.

"Run!" Cass screamed, and I ran. I sprinted down the hall, hared around the first corner, and ducked through an open doorway. A swift *thunk* made me turn: the door had closed, or some other panel had cut off the hallway. It seemed important, but panic had taken over, and I kept running. All these little twisting halls intersected; I could find my friends again if I just kept my head. Maybe I could even get behind the gold dogs, take them from the rear with some better magic, if only I could think of a spell.

I took another corner at a run, bouncing off the far wall as again a sliding panel thudded into place behind me. Two open doors loomed up, one on either side. I nearly fell over as I skidded through the opening on the right. It was dark in here and suddenly it was deep black as the doorway closed itself off.

"Shit," I hissed. I pulled my dagger from my belt and held it pommel-up in a finger-twisting grip. I tapped the weapon with each finger in succession as I whispered a few Elvish words, then flung it down the hall. It trailed a fat white line of light that stayed hovering in the air even as the dagger clattered to the floor somewhere far away.

In the new glow, I saw the glinting black eyes of a single gold dog, staring me down from a T-junction at the end of the hall. A glance behind me showed that I was trapped. The gold dog twitched its antennae, snapped its mandibles twice, and charged.

I had lost one bell and just thrown away my only weapon. I didn't have time to heat up a coin, and gold dogs were notoriously resistant to fire magic anyway. I eyed the gold dog's approach, took half a breath, and jumped.

I hit the ground just beyond it, stumbled, and landed on my shoulder. I scrambled to my feet and set out at a run as the gold dog behind me skittered around to chase me. A few long strides took me to the end of the corridor. I hared left. My heart was beating in my ears, nearly drowning out the sound of the monster's claws on the stone floor.

I dared a look over my shoulder. The thing was closer than I'd thought, much closer. Its antennae were reaching out for me. Were they venomous? Suddenly I couldn't remember, but—

Thunk.

A panel slammed down from the ceiling, neatly severing the gold dog's snapping head from its body. The head rolled a few feet and came to a stop, its quivering antennae inches from my face.

I sat down on the stone floor, trying desperately to catch my breath. My brain rifled through a pile of pressing questions: where was I? Where was everyone else? Why could I still see?

My dagger lay cocked in the corner of the hall, near where the panel had come down. It was still glowing with a faint white light, nothing compared to the hovering fluorescent beam it had made when I threw it, but still enough to see by. I picked it up. There was no way to know where my friends had gotten to when I didn't even know where I was. We'd broken the first rule of adventuring: never split the party.

I gave myself two minutes to settle down, then I set out, holding the dagger at arm's length ahead of me to light my way. I quickly found myself at another dead end, with a single door in the wall before me. I was tempted to sit down and wait; thoughts of the traps Magpie had uncovered taunted me as I imagined opening the door that barred my way. Eventually, though, I decided that I couldn't count on the others to come find me. There was every chance that they were in just as much trouble, hoping I might show up with light and fire to save them. I had to take my chances with the door.

It opened easily, swinging silently on ancient hinges. I stepped through into a space that was clearly too big to be another hall. My little light was lost in a vast, echoing darkness, or I thought so until my eyes adjusted and I began to pick out faint gleams of ruddy yellow bouncing back at me from the shadowed beyond.

I took a cautious step forward and my feet rustled something. A coin, no, a handful of them. The edge of a pile, a slumping mound of gold and silver that sat in the heart of what must be a treasury or tomb or storehouse. Gems glinted red and green and blue in the metallic mass. My mind reeled, trying to count it all, calculate its volume, its value, how many meals and shirts and shoes and bells and nights at the inn it would turn into.

Another light appeared, white and warm. It bobbed as it came into the room from some other entrance out in the blackness. It floated at chest height, and illuminated a swathe of red robes and the face of its bearer, white, bearded, and lined: Dr Agony. He turned green eyes to me.

"That's an awful lot of treasure, isn't it?"

NUMBER ONE

"It's mine," I said. "I got here first, and—"

"I know," Dr Agony said. "I made that rule." He was right, of course; he'd set it down at the very beginning to discourage player-versus-player fights over treasure. Whoever saw it first had claim to it and that was that. The treasure, all of it, was mine by rights.

"Okay then," I said.

"But," said Dr Agony, "can we talk?" His little light flared, making me squint as it filled the room. It was a pentagonal chamber with a door on each wall, about twenty feet high and thirty across. In the center of the room was a sort of dais raised about a foot off the floor, also pentagonal but with its angles offset from those of the room. This platform was absolutely heaped with treasure, some of which had spilled off as far as the doorway where I stood.

"About what?" I asked.

"Money, of course," said Agony. "Moving it, storing it, spending it, exchanging it."

"Well—"

"I'm just worried," he cut me off, "that you don't have a good support system in place yet. You want to send money home, isn't that right?"

I glanced at my camera drone. "That's right."

"Here, look." He pulled a handheld drone controller like ours from a pouch on his belt and held it up to me as though I was a scared animal. "You seem nervous. I'm sorry about that. Let me turn my camera off." He hit a few buttons with the handheld screen still facing me, and his drone moved into a neutral position. "There, that's better. Do you mind turning yours off? Then we can talk."

"I'd rather not," I said. "My party leader wants me to keep it on."

"Jessamine, right?" He nodded. "Hell, I'll admit it, I'm impressed. She's a smart cookie. You guys didn't waste any time finding this place and you obviously know new dungeons are like crack to the fans. Cameras on was the right call. But here's the thing—I guarantee you we're being censored right now."

"Censored?" I'd never heard of a feed being censored.

"Sure," said Dr Agony. "You agreed to it in your legal packet before you went down the well, remember?"

"I thought that was for, like, curse words." I hadn't thought about it for longer than it took me to initial that page of the contract.

"Really? There are players streaming hardcore porn, you think Expedition cares if we drop a couple F-bombs?" Agony laughed. "No, it's legal cover so they can blank out conversations like ours. Right now your viewers are seeing 'no signal' or 'technical difficulties' or something, guaranteed."

"Why?" The whole conversation was making me nervous, despite how friendly Agony was being.

"Oh, preserving the mystery, of course." Dr Agony gestured vaguely at the treasure chamber. "Real danger, real treasure, but in the end, it's all a game, remember? Nobody wants to know how the sausage is made."

"The what?"

"Expedition doesn't want details about the in-game economy leaking and they *really* don't want viewers being reminded that there are parts of the fantasy that aren't too fantastic. So they censor conversations like this. Which is all a long-winded way of saying that you may as well turn your camera off so we can just go ahead and talk."

With one eye on Dr Agony, I reached out for my drone and hit the Stream button. My camera spun around to hover a foot above my head. Agony's shoulders slumped, his body relaxing visibly.

"Thank you," he said. "Now, can I give you some advice? One red wizard to another. Belphegor had some nice things to say about your trial at the guild, by the way."

"Thanks," I said. "And sure."

"Let me ask you a question." Dr Agony moved into the room and kicked idly at a few loose coins at the foot of the dais. "How much do you think this is all worth?"

"Well, I—" I paused, trying to make a hasty calculation, then gave up. "I have no idea. A lot."

"Let's say there's five thousand gold here," said Agony. "Give or take, converting the silver and gems I see to their gold-piece value. Obviously, you're set for life here in the Summerlands, but that's not your goal. You've got someone at home who needs this money. So you figure you'll send it back to Earth. Well, how do you do that?" He looked back at me, an eyebrow raised.

"Through Expedition, right?" I ventured.

"Righto. Now, they'll be happy to exchange this all for you, once you get it back to Wellpoint, of course. Just talk to Donna at the Expedition Hall. But they're not running a charity, are they? So they'll take a bit out as a handling fee. That's only fair. Oh, and they'll set the exchange rate. Let's say... seven or eight points below the spot price on the Euro market. That's not great, but what can you do? But okay, now you've got cash out of it. Expedition will hold that in your name, no problem, but you'll need to put some aside for the recapture fee."

"The what?" My head was spinning. I sat down on the dais, starting a little cascade of coins behind me.

"Oh, you haven't heard about this? If you die out here, there's a recapture fee to get your stuff to your next of kin. Your money, your gear, your corpse, that sort of thing. Flat fee plus a percent of savings. So that gets escrowed out of your holdings with Expedition. Okay, do you have a bank account?"

"Yeah."

"Good for you!" He actually looked impressed. "So they transfer the rest of the cash to your account. Well, there'll be a little transfer fee. And you just made a lot of money, so of course you'll get taxed on the income. What's the flat tax at now? Still twenty percent? There goes that. Okay, no problem. Now we just transfer it to your friend—there's another transfer fee—and we're done. Oh, except he has to pay taxes on it too, since it's income for him as well. Did I miss anything?"

"No clue." I had a headache.

"Look, I know it's a lot," Agony said. He sat down next to me. "I hate to be the bearer of bad news. But since Apollonia took over, this is how Expedition makes their money, you know?"

"Sure," I said, "but how are we supposed to make ours?"

Dr Agony laughed. "Great question, kid. It seems impossible, doesn't it?"

"A little."

"Well, here's where the advice comes in. I've got two tricks for you. One: make as much as you can outside the Summerlands. Sponsor money and royalties don't go through Expedition, they go straight into your bank account. That's the real secret to getting rich off this game."

"What's the other one?"

Agony looked away. "The other what?"

"The other trick," I said. "You said there were two."

"Oh, right," he said. "I really shouldn't."

"Shouldn't what?"

"Well, it's illegal, for one. I could get in a lot of trouble just mentioning it." He stood up and held out a hand. "Come on. We should go find your friends."

I took his hand and pulled myself up. "What's the other trick?"

"You really need this money, huh?" He looked me straight in the eye. His were grey-flecked green, with pencil-thin crow's feet and... a little flaking eyeliner? "It's that bad at home?"

"Worse," I said.

"Okay." He let go of my hand. "I tell you what. Over the years, Golden Apple has been able to negotiate a bit with

Expedition. We're their biggest earners, after all, and I'll admit that it helps that I'm still friends with everybody over there. They like to keep us happy. So we've got our own prize agent on the outside that handles everything and Expedition takes a much smaller cut from us than they would from you and your friends."

"So, what, I give you the treasure and you exchange it for us?" I squinted. "Why would you do that?"

"Well, look." Agony shrugged. "I'm not offering to do it for free. There's too much risk for me. But let's say we take twenty percent. We'll process the whole thing then transfer you your share. Or we send it right to your friend on Earth, whatever you want. Up to you."

"How do I know I can trust you?" I said.

"Hm." Dr Agony smiled. "You're a smart cookie, too. Tell you what. We'll get our guys in here to box up the treasure and haul it back to Wellpoint. You'll come with us the whole way. Once we get it to the Expedition Hall, we'll have Donna Markan handle the exchange. We'll just tell her Golden Apple is investing in a promising new adventuring party. It'll be good PR. You know Donna, right?"

"Right." The thought of the cheery, welcoming kilted woman being in on the plan settled my nerves considerably.

"Okay, perfect! It's a deal." He stuck out his hand and I shook it. He put a hand on my shoulder and guided me towards the door I'd come through, which he opened with a flick of his hand. "Let's go find your friends. And on the way, I've got some tactical tips for dealing with gold dogs."

★★★

It took a whole day to get all the gold up from the dungeon. Golden Apple took point, leading teams of NPCs with bags and boxes down to the treasure room I'd stumbled into. Each trip was accompanied by at least one member of Hearthhammer, camera on of course, and usually two since Cass didn't trust

154

them and Noah kept volunteering. If the seasoned adventurers were annoyed by his constant questions, they didn't show it.

Dr Agony and I had found Hearthammer and Golden Apple together, in the midst of a heated argument about which door to take. Noah actually jumped when I tapped him on the shoulder. I was relieved beyond words to discover that my friends had all made it out unharmed, but it had been close. The shifting walls of the dungeon had separated them almost immediately, with gold dogs hard on their heels. Cass's face was like stone as she described how she'd run out of arrows and just about resigned herself to being eaten when Valkyrie of Golden Apple appeared around a corner and plunged both her knives into the gold dog's brain.

Rad, Valkyrie, and Wolfheart had indeed gone the other direction in that first hallway at the bottom of the stairs. If they hadn't, they would have reached the treasure first; instead they spent an hour exploring dead ends. They'd turned around to look for Dr Agony and discovered Hearthammer fighting for their lives. It seemed that if Golden Apple hadn't shown up when they did, I'd be heading back to Wellpoint a solo act.

It was a slow hike around the Wyvern Peaks, through Dann's Teeth, and back to Wellpoint. The NPCs hauling our treasure couldn't move as fast as we all wanted, but Dr Agony flatly refused to let us share the load and give our hirelings a break.

Cass kept her stream up the whole way home, which was a relief, because after the head-spinning events of the last few days all I wanted was privacy. Golden Apple didn't chat much along the way and mostly kept their cameras off as well, other than nightly check-ins that coincided with prime time back home. Around the after-dinner campfire, they answered messages, checked stats, and posted to social media, their faces blue-white masks in the electronic glow of their handhelds.

We arrived in Wellpoint at the end of our third day on the road, sweaty, dusty, and sore. At least I was. Cass insisted that we go straight to the Expedition Hall and Dr Agony only put up token resistance as we passed his house in the Burbs. His three partymates disappeared promptly into their own homes.

Donna Markan lived on the third floor of the Expedition Hall in an apartment about the size of Keats's back home, as I discovered when Dr Agony let himself in and began shouting for her to wake up. She appeared from a back bedroom in a knitted wool robe, looking disheveled and pissed off.

"How many goddamn times, James—oh, hello, darling!" She had noticed me, standing halfway hidden behind Dr Agony, my eyes roving over her homey apartment. "And the gang's all here!" Along with the NPCs hauling the treasure, all of Hearthammer had come up, unwilling to leave Dr Agony alone, afraid to be separated from our money and each other.

Donna put her fists on her hips. "Well?"

"We're sending some gold out," said Agony. "GA's usual channels, you know the deal. The kids here are getting eighty."

"Eighty!" Donna's eyebrows went up. "Awful generous."

"They found it," said Agony. "We're just helping out."

Donna yawned. "Can't send their gold through your channels, James."

"Linnaea is signing it over to me first," Agony said.

"For this you had to wake me?" Donna rolled her eyes. "Unbelievable. All right, I'll get the papers together. Where's their bit going?"

Dr Agony gestured for me to step up. "Linnaea has a bank account back on Earth. She'll give you the details."

Donna disappeared downstairs and returned a few minutes later with a stack of paper and a few decidedly un-medieval ballpoint pens. She dealt the forms out between me and Agony, who dashed off his signatures without bothering to read anything. I tried to focus enough to untangle the legalese in front of me, but exhaustion was crossing my eyes and it seemed straightforward enough.

My stomach somersaulted as I finished reading the first packet, which gave control of my treasure to Agony, and uncapped my pen. If there were a perfect moment for a betrayal, this was it. Donna must have seen the anxiety on my face, because she caught my eye and gave me a smile that untangled the knot in my guts somewhat.

"I don't like this," Cass said.

"What?" said Dr Agony.

"What's to stop you from screwing us over as soon as Emma signs that?" Cass's eyes were narrow as she stared at the red wizard.

"Donna is here," Agony said.

"The contract would still be binding, though," Cass insisted.

Agony sighed. "Fine, okay. How about some collateral?"

"Collateral? Like what?"

"Um…" Agony glanced around the room, then apparently realized he couldn't give away any of Donna's stuff. He sighed and stuck a hand into an interior pocket of his robe. "Like this."

Glittering in his hand was a necklace, a string of rich sea-green emeralds. I knew that necklace: he wore it on the billboard near my block.

"That?" Cass was nonplussed.

"I'll need it back," Agony said. "For wizard reasons. Linnaea understands." He walked over to me and opened his hand; the necklace slithered like a jeweled snake onto the stack of papers in front of me. "Now, you satisfied? I'd like to take a bath."

"Yes," I said, uneasy about trying Agony's patience any further. I quickly signed the packet that handed over our loot, then filled in the next few pages with information on how to send the money directly to Keats.

Donna collected the mass of paper and tapped it into a neat pile on her kitchen table. "All set. The usual channels, James?"

"Yep," said Agony. He turned to us where we stood by the pile of boxes and leather sacks that held our new fortune. "We good?"

"Yes, thank you," said Cass. "I hope we can do business again sometime." She stuck out her hand. Dr Agony looked at it, glanced at Donna, and shook it.

★★★

157

"We're going to try another restaurant eventually," said Magpie.

"I'd rather you didn't," said Naila, setting down four bowls of steaming soup. "Now that you can pay, that is." Open Seasoning was empty except for us, which was just how I liked it. Naila pulled a chair over from an empty table, flipped it around, and sat backwards with her arms draped over the back. "So, dish. Tell the thrilling tale. Sepharad, how's the hand?"

"Fine, thanks." Noah smiled, and suddenly I was smiling, too. I'd learned to read his expressions over the years and I could tell when he was pretending to smile and when it was spontaneous, genuine. With Naila, he meant it.

Cass told the story, though she let me cut in for a minute to tell how I'd been separated from the party after the gold dogs broke through my spell. Naila was a perfect audience, laughing and shaking her head and gasping in surprise at all the right moments. Her emotions played across her face like a projector screen as I described the gold dog chasing me down the twisting halls and losing its head at the last second, my trepidation at the final door, and the massive pile of gold gleaming under my dagger's dying glow.

So there was no way to miss the fall of her face when I reached the arrival of Dr Agony, our conversation, and our ultimate deal. I'd thought she'd be pleased, or proud, or something, of my clever evasion of the Expedition rules that she clearly chafed under as an NPC. Instead, by the time Cass wound up with an account of Donna Markan in her bathrobe, Naila looked as though we'd just stepped on her cat.

"You didn't," she whispered.

"Oh no," said Cass. Her face was pale. Magpie and I locked eyes across the table, and I knew that we'd reached the same conclusion. It was as though the floor had dropped away, opening a great dark pit under my chair, and I was falling, falling, tumbling through shadows, waiting to hit a bottom that never came.

"What?" said Noah. Nobody spoke, so he repeated himself a little louder. "What?"

"I'm so sorry," Naila said, "but you'll never see a penny of that money."

"Wait," I said. "It's okay, Donna is setting it up."

"Her?" said Naila, shaking her head. "There's hooves under that kilt. She's as crooked as a busted antenna. Agony gives her a few percent to do his dirty work."

"We had—" I had to clear my throat to get the words out. "We had a deal. Agony and I. We shook on it."

"I'd rather shake hands with a hell rat," said Naila. "At least it'll attack you from the front. God, I wish you had asked me first. Or Seidenberg. Or anybody! They'll tell you. Everybody knows not to do deals with Golden Apple."

"*We* didn't know," said Cass, her eyes narrowed.

"I know," said Naila. "I'm sorry. I should have warned you ages ago. I just thought... oh, hell, I don't know."

"We got collateral," Noah said.

"The necklace!" I straightened up, stuck my hand into my pouch, and drew out the string of emeralds. "Right! Naila, look, Agony gave me..."

In my hand was a line of gray stones tied together with twine.

I blinked. "Wait." I could feel tears stinging my eyes. "No. He gave me... you guys saw it!"

"Glamored," Naila said. "I knew it."

"Well, if you know everything, how do we get our money back?" Cass stood up. She looked like she wanted to deck the chef. I expected I'd be next in line.

"You can't," said Naila, unintimidated.

"What do you mean, we can't?" said Magpie.

"Well, how would you?" Naila spread her hands. "Sue? There's no court. You can't go crying to Expedition, Agony is their golden goose."

"We'll kick their asses, then," said Cass.

"And get kicked out for PvP? Or stomped into paste?" Naila spread her hands wide. "Shit, even if you won it wouldn't get your money back. It would be hilarious, but it wouldn't help anything."

"God dammit!" Cass yelled. "God *dammit*, Emma!" She turned her burning eyes on me. "Why would you agree? *Why would you do that?*!"

"Easy, killer!" My chair clattered over as I stood up. "You were all for it until five seconds ago! Don't act like you wouldn't have done the same!"

"Girls—" said Magpie.

"Shut up!" Cass and I barked in unison.

"Look, you should have heard him," I said. "Turning gold into real money is nearly impossible. They have a whole system set up—the exchange rate—there's taxes, and—and—the real money is in streaming! That's what he said!"

"And you went ahead and trusted him." Cass's lips were pulled back in a snarl, and she spoke between gritted teeth. "Just like that? I guess you're party leader now, is that it? Did I miss the vote or did you just declare yourself queen for life? You obviously don't have a problem bossing everyone around when a fight breaks out."

"I wouldn't have to," I snarled, "if you could do your damn job."

Cass took a step back as though I'd hit her. Her face was red, her hands shaking, and her mouth moved noiselessly as she searched for a comeback.

"Okay, let's just take a breath," said Naila.

"Emma," said Noah.

"Why don't we just eat our soup?" said Magpie.

"*Emma*," Noah said again.

"I don't want soup!" Cass shouted.

"*Why does nobody ever listen to me?*" Noah roared. His voice reverberated into a sudden silence in the restaurant as we all looked down at him, sitting with his hands on either side of his handheld, flat on the table. His face was red. He took a long, deep breath, and then he nodded to the handheld. "Linnaea," he said. "When was the last time you turned your camera off?"

160

"In the treasure room," I said. "When Agony wanted to talk. He turned his off and asked me to do mine, so I did."

"So about four and a half days ago," Noah said.

"Yeah, why?" I picked up my chair and sat down.

"For about twenty minutes before you turned it off, you were the number one feed in the world."

"Oh," I said. "Shit."

"You topped out at three million, fourteen thousand, six hundred and eleven viewers," Noah went on.

"Emma," said Cass, "I am *very* sorry I got mad at you."

"Now you're sorry!" I coughed. "Now you—of course you…" I couldn't do it. I couldn't pretend to hold a grudge, not now. I was laughing too hard, and I was sobbing, too. Everyone was laughing, even Naila, and it went on and on and on. I hugged Noah, and Magpie hugged me and kissed me on the cheek, and Cass hugged Naila, and everybody hugged everybody else. Our soup cooled, forgotten, on the table.

"Congratulations," said Naila, wiping away a tear. "That's a really big damn deal."

"Yeah," I said.

"Every nerd in the world must be watching you," Cass said. "That must be it. People really wanted a boring stream about plants and art. You're the hero they've been waiting for."

"I don't think that's it," I said. "I mean, you're right, you're definitely right. That's how it started, that's what set us apart. But the numbers didn't go crazy until we were in that dungeon, right?"

Noah checked his handheld again, then nodded. "Right."

"So what?" Cass asked.

"So, I had some viewers, not a lot, but some. Then we hit the dungeon and they were able to spread the word." I shook my head. "You know how it works—somebody's watching a stream, something exciting happens, word gets around, everybody hops on because nobody wants to miss it."

"And suddenly you're number one," said Cass.

"Until Dr Agony convinces you to turn off your camera," Naila put in.

"He said we were being censored." I blinked. "You think he knew?"

Naila shrugged.

"So what do we do?" said Magpie.

"What else can we do?" I said. "Let's give them what they want."

UNCHARTED TERRITORY

Give them what they want... easier said than done. We spent a day posted up on the sidewalk outside Open Seasoning, just talking through our plans. We tossed out any hope of getting the money we needed in treasure, big or small. We weren't going to luck into another hoard like the one by Wyatt Falls, and even if we had, there was truth in Dr Agony's patter about all the ways Expedition Games would cut out chunks from our winnings. If a massive pile of gold wouldn't pay Keats's medical bills, there was no way the handfuls of coppers and little art objects scattered throughout the wilds around Wellpoint would do it.

Streaming, that's where the money was. I needed a sponsorship that would put cash directly into my bank account, quickly. To do that, I needed to keep my numbers up. We talked it over all day, going in circles as we argued about the best way to leverage my sudden popularity.

Cass thought we had to keep putting ourselves in danger, pointing out that our trips to Athan's Rest and the dungeon by Wyatt Falls had been my best streams as well as our most nearly lethal adventures. Her favorite idea was to go get revenge on the harpies of the White Chasm by drawing them all into a huge fight.

Magpie suggested that what fans really wanted was to see us succeed. In his view, people watched streams to imagine themselves in our boots, to live vicariously through our victories. He suggested we make up a schedule of sorties to well-trod adventure sites and rack up a string of easy wins.

In the end, it was Noah who hit on the answer. He sat sipping a tall glass of clean, cold water as Magpie reiterated for the dozenth time that return trips never got ratings as good as the first time a party hit a new spot.

"Doesn't that mean you're both wrong?" he said, wiping condensation from his lip.

"What?" said Cass and Magpie in unison.

"Magpie is right that viewership drops when parties go back to the same place," Noah said. "Even if they have a new mission or have to rescue somebody or something. That's just what the data says."

"So we go with my plan," said Magpie with a nod.

"Well, no," said Noah. "Viewership also goes down if you go somewhere other parties have been."

"We got good numbers at the White Chasm," Cass said.

"At Athan's Rest," Noah persisted, "where nobody's been in five years. Plus they were nowhere close to the numbers for the Wyatt Falls dungeon. Like not even on the same order of magnitude."

"So what, then?" said Magpie.

"Novelty," I said. Noah gave me a little smile that said *thanks for translating.*

"Explain," said Cass.

"Fans want something new," I said. "Our numbers at Athan's Rest grew slowly while I was streaming my notes. You said it yourself, Cass, all the nerds on Earth were waiting for a feed like that. It was new. And then at Wyatt Falls, it was a brand-new dungeon *and* we were racing against Golden Apple. Head-to-head stuff like that is rare."

"So we need to do things nobody's ever done before," Magpie said.

"Exactly." I nodded. "Forget the White Chasm and the Battle Plains and all these places that have been picked over a thousand times. What around here *hasn't* been explored? Noah?"

"All the dangerous places," he said.

"Ha!" Cass slapped the table.

"I mean, anywhere with a bad risk/reward," Noah went on. "Places with lots of monsters and no treasure, like caves."

"We have to go to caves?" said Magpie.

"Noah, make a list, please," I said. "Anywhere around here that hasn't been explored already. The flashier the better. Anywhere with a good story attached to it, like Athan's Rest. Cass, we'll go wherever you want from the list, okay?" I smiled at Magpie. "We can even make a schedule."

"What are you gonna do?" said Cass.

"I have a lot of email to catch up on."

★★★

The first decision I made was that there was no way I could ever reply to everyone. I'd started at the very bottom of my inbox, the first few messages that had trickled in from fans picking up my earliest streams from the Near Plains. Even if I got back to each of them with just a few words of thanks, it would have been the work of days to clear out every one. How did the big streamers handle it? Maybe they didn't. Maybe they had interns or something. I took a deep breath and told myself it was impossible.

Scrolling up the list, I could see the meteoric growth of my popularity mirrored in my messages. They seemed to come in three basic categories: fan mail, trolls and weirdos, and sponsorship offers. The fan mail grew steadily. The crazies jumped up considerably around Wyatt Falls then fell off again; I guessed these were people who would harrass whoever was popular in the moment. The sponsor messages started at the same time, but they hadn't stopped.

I opened one at random, just to get a taste. For twenty bucks a day I could rent them my face for a line of acne cream. Annoyed and wondering whether I should be insulted, I deleted the message. Flicking through the others, they were all like that: small offers from small companies. If I'd had the time and inclination to handle them all, I could have built a decent little passive income, but that wouldn't help Keats. We needed money fast, and a lot of it; twenty bucks a day wouldn't cover his rent, let alone the surgeries that might let him walk again. The second decision I made was to ignore the little offers for now.

I sighed. Just deleting them all would take an hour or more. My head was already hurting from staring at the little handheld for so long. I'd just made up my mind to put it all aside for later when the handheld dinged and a new message alert popped up, glowing a cheerful green.

I recognized the sender immediately: Uncharted Territory, the biggest producer of Summerlands memorabilia after Expedition Games themselves. Their bestselling *Spells You Don't Know* series had filled in many of the gaps from Dr Agony's original *Book of Elvish Magic*. I tapped the alert.

```
Linnaea -

Big fan of your work so far. Looks like
you've found an untapped market of
fans. Want to work together? I'm think-
ing books, video lectures, a speaking
tour back on Earth.
A little bird tells me you have some
money problems at home. I can make
those go away.

Let me know ASAP.

Dave Davies
Uncharted Territory
```

A book of my own. I'd forgotten all about it. I set the handheld down, leaned back, and looked up at the sky, as wide and blue as ever. A few thin white clouds rolled across the sun. A few minutes passed as I watched them go by. When the sun was fully back in view, I picked up the handheld and hit REPLY.

```
Mr Davies,
```

Thanks for reaching out. I'd love to
work with Uncharted Territory. How did
you know about our money problems?

Best,
Linnaea

I sighed, stood up and stuck the handheld in my belt pouch,
where it promptly dinged again. To my surprise, Davies had
already gotten back to me.

Linnaea-

Don't take it personally. We keep tabs
on everyone in the Summerlands. Listen,
my bosses give me a lot of leeway to
make deals, but they want proof that
you can deliver. So here's the offer:
we'll do the books and everything and
as an advance on future earnings, we'll
pay all Mr Keats's medical bills. But
first you need to get your feed to #1
again. Just say yes and I'll get you a
contract.

Dave

I blinked away tears as I tapped REPLY.

Yes.

Linnaea

★★★

My next stop was the Red Wizards' Guild Hall. I was proud of
myself for pulling off Dr Agony's paralysis spell, but I'd come up
short when it counted and I didn't want that happening again. It
was high time that I got my money's worth as far as my Guild
dues.

167

The interior of the Guild Hall was as dim and clubby as ever and as crowded. The patrons who sat reading, practicing, or quietly chatting weren't invisible this time. A few of them, including a pale young man I recognized as Kronos from a group called Question Cross, nodded or lifted a greeting hand to me.

Belphegor met me by the glowing crystal bar. His face wore deep lines and his mismatched eyes darted around the room as though he expected something to be watching him from the shadows beyond the reach of the hearth. He raised a hand to cut me off before I could speak. His lank brown hair fell over his eyes as he dug into a pouch at his belt. He pulled out a silver coin, which he tossed on the bar.

"Here, that's your dues for the last week. Take it and go."

"What?" I pushed the coin back towards him. "No, I need to learn."

"You can't do it here," Belphegor insisted. "I'm sorry, but we cannot allow you as a member."

I looked around the common room. The other wizards all had their eyes locked doggedly on their reading, the fire, or the floor. Finally, I turned back to Belphegor, who stood eyeing the silver piece. "This is about Dr Agony, isn't it?"

"He is—" Belphegor cleared his throat. "He is the head of the Guild, after all."

"Fine," I said. The coin clicked as I snatched it off the bar. "Tell Agony thanks for the free lesson."

★★★

My next stop was Dan Seidenberg's potion shop on Coin Street. He hurried his few customers out as I wandered the aisles, pretending to read the labels on various oils and salves. Soon we were alone and he shut and locked the door while I double-checked that my camera was off.

"I was expecting you," he said.

"Can you teach red magic?" I said. "Or do you know someone who can? Agony kicked me out of the Guild."

"It's not that simple," Seidenberg replied. He peered up at me from his wheelchair, eyes narrow. "White magic is easy to keep quiet. If you can hide an injury until you get it healed, it's like it was never there. Red magic tends to be a lot noisier."

"Is that a no?" I asked.

"It's a maybe. What do you need to learn?"

"Well," I hedged, "I'm not sure."

"Then why are you so hellbent on bothering me?" Seidenberg turned away with the spin of a wheel.

"Because I know your secret," I said. He stopped, but didn't turned back, didn't speak. "You're a white wizard, a healer. You could regrow your leg any time you want, couldn't you?" In the shadows of the shop, Seidenberg's back became hunched and tight. "But you don't. The question is why. So I thought about it, and I realized that if you did, it would be obvious pretty quickly that you'd used illegal magic. There's no hiding a new leg. And then you'd be kicked out... which means that however much you'd love to walk again, you love the Summerlands even more."

"You're too damn sharp by half," muttered Seidenberg. "But what's that got to do with you?"

"I'm the same way," I said. "Look, I don't know why you came here originally. Maybe you thought you'd get your leg back and leave. But this place... it's special. People like Dr Agony want to hoard it all for themselves. He's holding onto magic like it's money, which I guess it is. But he obviously thinks that he weakens himself by sharing it. I don't agree. If we ever want someone else to take Agony's spot as king of the hill, people need to be empowered."

"So what's your plan, then, kid?" Seidenberg turned back to me, with a look on his face that I'd never seen before.

"Me?" I put my hands on my hips. "I'm going to start a lecture series."

***

And that's exactly what I did. While Magpie, Cass, and Noah worked out an adventure schedule, I set up the Summerlands' first lecture series under the shockingly creative title *Linnaea's Lectures*. It was easy to do; the persistent good weather meant I didn't need to rent space, and A/V was taken care of by my drone, so all I really needed were topics. I sat in Portal Square with my notebook and pencils and soon I had a list that covered both sides of a dozen pages.

I started with broad topics and big questions. The blazing neon question mark was magic: what was it, actually? Where did it come from? Why did it work? It was so regimented, split into two schools with such a clear distinction between them that once you learned to work with one, you could never use the other. Was this a natural law, like gravity or relativity on Earth, that the elves had merely described with the spells they'd uncovered? Or had someone built magic, designed it like a game or a legal system? Whatever the answers, I could at least share the spells and secrets that Dr Agony and the Red Wizards' Guild had been hiding behind the blood oak door of their hall. After all, I wasn't a member any more.

I drifted onto the topic of the elves themselves. There was so much we could learn from their art and architecture alone. There had never been any sign of why they'd disappeared or where they'd went, but maybe I could at least uncover some clues to how they must have lived and what they had believed before they left the Summerlands. Maybe some of them actually had spots.

I took a swing through biology. Did evolution occur in the Summerlands the same as back home? If so, what could we learn from the animals we'd discovered so far? What did their adaptations tell us about the environment? Could we construct an evolutionary tree based on their shared characteristics? How did they combine with the plants that bloomed all around us to form a complete ecosystem and how did those plants evolve?

170

I went on and on, letting my mind run free. There were ten thousand lifetimes' worth of topics to be covered and not for the first time I wondered what would have happened if the Summerlands had been found not by a game designer but by a scientist. It was the greatest case of wasted opportunity in all of human history, but I intended to do my part to fix things.

My list grew so massive that I had no idea where to begin. I needed something great to kick off my lectures, a big question that I could tackle head-on and, if not answer, at least say something meaningful about. As I watched adventurers going in and out of the Expedition Hall, my mind drifted back to Hearthammer's conversation about language in the limo on the Isle of Lewis. It was the perfect question: everybody asked it, nobody answered it. And as I sat listening to the people around me chatter away about their adventures, their rankings, and their lives, I realized I might have at least part of the answer.

★★★

I started Hearthammer on a strict schedule of risking our lives the very next day. Noah had made an exhaustive list of all the least popular adventuring locales near Wellpoint, and we hit them one by one. Our feeds followed a programming schedule that fit neatly with prime time in the major world markets on Earth: seven a.m. in the Summerlands was also seven a.m. in the New England Regional Command District, perfect for morning commuters, as well as 9 pm in Tokyo, right when the automated curfew was locking doors citywide. That meant we had to be up with the sun at 5:14 every day and on our way out of Wellpoint by 6, since even the nearby adventure sites were a few miles distant.

It turned out that if you ignored the ranger-approved paths and well-worn treasure spots like the White Chasm and the Battle Plains, the Summerlands were completely lousy with danger. The better part of the wilderness around Wellpoint was forest and field, but a half-hour's walk to the southeast was the edge of a swamp that absolutely stank with the stomach-turning

171

stench of rotten meat. The elves had obviously had the common sense to stay away from this place, which was overrun with monsters and totally devoid of treasure. It was perfect.

We spent a few days testing the strength of a gang of creatures we quickly nicknamed swamp porcupines. They were reminiscent of the boar-like things we'd fought on our first day through the portal, but they were covered in needle-sharp spines that they could shoot a shockingly long way when threatened. Cass was happy to retaliate with arrows and a few choice curse words, but soon enough we discovered that they were highly susceptible to fire. My skill with exploding copper pieces grew accordingly.

One benefit of working ourselves to exhaustion was that we had no energy for arguments about the party pecking order. I found the boys looking to me for orders both in and out of combat and it was growing rarer and rarer to see a smile on Cass's face. When she did speak, it was often to disagree with me during our planning sessions, but when a fight broke out she shut her mouth and sent arrows where I pointed.

The swamp porcupines learned to avoid us, which made sorties into the marsh dull, and our rankings slumped. I aimed Hearthammer at the next item on Noah's list: the Thing Cave. The notorious monster called the Thing had only been sighted once, by the single surviving member of an early adventuring party called the Duke's Own. Players had avoided its domain ever since.

We knew better than to actually fight the Thing, but we wanted to get it on camera for the first time since it had eaten the Duke's Own's drones along with their weapons, armor, and corpses. We succeeded after three days spent making suicidal amounts of noise at the mouth of the Thing Cave. It finally woke up and came out to see whether its harassers could be made into breakfast, roaring from three lizard-like heads as its tentacles tried to grab us and get us in reach of its mouths. The monster proved as impervious as a gold dog to my fire magic and Cass's arrows were equally useless. She and Magpie were well out of reach by the time Noah and I dashed up the long slope that led from the cave mouth and we scattered among the trees of the surrounding forest, leaving the Thing roaring in impotent hunger.

That one got us back in the top ten.

★★★

The next day, I gave my first lecture. We'd discovered the remains of an amphitheatre not far from Wellpoint, little more than grassed-over stone benches rising in shallow tiers from a small central yard, but perfect for my purposes. I advertised on my feed every chance I got, making sure to remind my viewers that if they couldn't catch the lecture live, there would always be video-on-demand after the fact.

I showed up to the amphitheatre an hour early, unsure of what to expect. I'd tried to spread the word locally as well, but none of the other players I'd talked to had seemed particularly interested. I reminded myself firmly that the lectures weren't for them, but it was hard not to be disappointed. Speaking to an invisible audience was lonely work.

Five minutes before my scheduled start time, as I paced my thousandth circle around my makeshift stage, a far-off movement caught my eye. My heart leapt in excitement; then I realized it was just Cass, Noah, and Magpie come to support me. Still, having them there made me feel brave. I flipped through my notes one last time and turned on my camera.

"Hey fans!" I forced my voice to sound chipper. "Just five minutes until the first of Linnaea's Lectures! Don't miss it!"

"Thank God, there are still a few seats!" I turned to see Naila smiling at me, Seidenberg scowling at her side. A long double line made by his wheelchair cut through the grass, leading roughly east back towards Wellpoint.

"You came!" I said.

"Wouldn't miss it," said Naila.

"This place really needs an access ramp," said Seidenberg.

"I'll tell the manager," I laughed. I glanced up at the sun. "Oh, shit, time to start!"

Five friends made a paltry audience, but it sure beat being alone. I stepped out onto the grass stage, cleared my throat, double-checked my notes, made sure my camera had a good view, and dove in.

"Listen to my words," I began. "What do you hear? If you're at home, you're hearing me speaking in English. And that makes sense—I'm American, after all. But would you believe me if I told you that that's not what my audience here in the Summerlands is hearing?"

My tiny little audience, said a little voice in my brain, but I told it to shut up.

"As streamers, we talk so much that I think we forgot how to listen. Well, I've been listening, and get this: I'm not speaking English right now."

On the first tier of seating, Cass raised her eyebrows and Naila cocked her head. Noah wore a look of fierce concentration. Magpie lounged back on the row behind him, but his eyes were on me.

"One of the big questions of the Summerlands has always been how we talk to each other. Adventurers from America, the EU, and Japan come here and the language barrier just disappears. But *how*?"

I waved to Magpie, who looked a bit surprised. I hadn't run this part by him.

"Magpie, can I get a hand?" He stood and joined me on-stage, within view of my camera. "Thanks! Okay, say something, anything."

"What should I say?" he said.

"Perfect, thanks," I told him. "Everybody on Earth just heard a sentence in Greek. But I understood him perfectly—he just asked me what I wanted him to say, by the way. But here's the thing. *That wasn't English*."

"No, it was Greek," said Magpie.

"No it wasn't," I said. He squinted at me like I'd just told him the sky was pink. "Listen to what I'm saying. Not the meaning, that doesn't matter. Listen to the words—you need to

174

hear them as they hit your ears, before your brain gets a chance to process them. We're speaking Elvish."

★★★

The lecture was a hit. The feed itself was a bit of a dud, but the VOD numbers were crazy. I had no way of checking, but I could imagine the recording spreading on the same forums and chatrooms I'd once frequented as a fan. When I gave my second lecture a few days later, I immediately jumped back into the top hundred feeds. My third made the top forty.

I was feeling pretty good as Hearthammer strolled into Portal Square after my latest talk, where I'd demonstrated the paralysis spell I'd used on the gold dogs. Heading for my accustomed seat on a bench near the Expedition Hall, I caught a glimpse of Donna Markan watching me from her apartment window. Our eyes met for a moment before she dropped the curtain, but my curiosity was interrupted as a handful of players from my most recent audience shouted my name and waved from across the square. I smiled and waved back, Donna already forgotten.

"Little Miss Popular," Cass said. "Check the ratings."

As I pulled it out, the handheld pinged, and a cheerful green alert popped up on the screen: I had a new message from Dave Davies. I tapped it.

```
Linnaea-

Not bad. Save some for the book! I like
these numbers but my bosses are still
focused on that #1 spot. The forums
want to see more flashy magic. Help me
out here! Let's get this thing to the
top. What have you got for me?

Dave
```

"Is that from UC? What's it say?" Magpie peered shamelessly over my shoulder.

"Dave wants me to do flashy magic," I said. "I think people are starting to get bored."

"Or they just love the way you roll those coins," said Magpie. "Well, what've you got?"

"For flash?" I glanced at Hearthammer's drones one by one, double-checking that they were off. "Not much. Fireballs are kind of old news."

"You said Seidenberg could hook you up, though, right?"

"Right," I agreed. "I'll ask him again. But I think we have to step it up. We've only broken the top ten once since Wyatt Falls and it wasn't with lectures."

"I'm not fighting the Thing, if that's what you mean," said Cass.

I laughed. "Don't worry, I like living as much as you do. They want to see magic? I think we should try for Hero's Bane."

"That's suicide," Noah said.

"Not if we survive."

HERO'S BANE

The arching stone bridge between us and the sword was littered with corpses. Noah knew every one of their names: Shekto, Tarquin, Talon, Daerloth, Gamblewise. Adventurers, every one of them, lured by the promise of the glittering silver blade that stood plunged halfway into a black stone, killed by the traps that guarded the bridge.

"Are we sure about this?" asked Cass.

"Noah, numbers?" I said. He checked the handheld.

"We're in seventh place," he said.

"Just waiting for the action to start," I said. "Come on, Cass. For your dad."

She blew out a breath and set her eyes on the bridge.

"It's magic time." I stuck my arm straight out. Pinched between my fingers was my little red gem. I began to murmur in Elvish, wondering what the words meant. It was strange to think that I was hearing Elvish all the time, yet when it was actually spoken I couldn't understand it. Pushing that little mystery out of my head, I focused on the spell. Unlike so many others, it required no fancy sleight of hand, just the right words and the confidence that it would work.

The bridge spanned a chasm whose murky deeps were untouched by the faint light from my dagger. In that black, something stirred. Soon, a wind picked up, ruffling our hair and moving the dust on the bridge.

"We're on," I said. "Magpie, you're up."

Magpie nodded and stepped forward. At the foot of the bridge he adjusted his belt and cracked his neck. Noah put a hand on his shoulder.

"Remember," I said, "ignore the arrows. Don't step on copper. And keep count."

"Okay," Magpie said.

"Go!"

Magpie set out at a sprint, running up the long arc of the bridge. The arrows, heralded by a series of swift clicks, started just as he dodged around the first of the corpses. I threw my gem straight out toward the bridge as a dozen arrows soared towards Magpie from either side. The breeze from the chasm became a roar, and my hair flew around my face as the air in the cavern swept after the gem in an invisible vortex. Magpie stumbled, buffeted by the sudden rush, but righted himself. The arrows flew in all directions, scattered by the wind. Magpie kept running.

I had Seidenberg to thank for that spell; it was one I'd seen performed on feeds, but I'd never been able to make out all the terms to vocalise. I'd hoped to learn it from Belphegor at the Red Wizards' Guild, but instead an eyepatched Japanese man had taught it to me in the back room of his ramen joint.

A second flight of arrows met the same fate as the first, spinning away into the chasm as they faltered against my spell. Magpie passed the third and fourth bodies, moving on tiptoe like a dancer as he picked his way among swirling arabesques of copper embedded in the stone of the bridge. It had taken freeze-frame analysis of the video of two deaths to figure that trap out: stepping on any of the copper decorations triggered booming fireballs, an apparent variation of the spell I was so familiar with.

Magpie reached the apex of the bridge and started down the other side. Even from here I could see his lips moving as he counted the seconds since he'd reached the top. Beside me, Noah was doing the same thing under his breath.

"Jump!" Noah yelled, a split second after Magpie kicked off from the bridge, leaping forward into open air. The next moment the far half of the bridge simply disappeared. The last of the corpses—Tarquin, I thought—hung half off the lip where the top of the arch had been, then suddenly slumped over and slid off into the waiting darkness.

The missing half of the bridge reappeared just as Magpie came down. He hit it at a run, stumbled a few steps still at full speed, then jumped again as the stone blinked back out of existence.

This time he landed on the solid earth on the far side of the chasm. He skidded to a stop only a few feet from the black stone where Hero's Bane, the silver sword that had cost so many players their lives, stood glittering in the gloom.

Magpie looked back at us, raised his eyebrows, and waved.

There was a moment of absolute stillness. I let out the breath I'd been holding since Magpie put his first foot on the bridge. On the other side, he took the last step toward the stone, put his hand on the hilt of Hero's Bane, and pulled.

The sword slid out in total silence. Magpie turned back to us, holding the sword up, a massive grin splitting his face.

"Got it!" he called.

"No shit!" I yelled back. "Now get back here in one piece!"

The black stone unfolded like a toy robot until it stood in the rough shape of a human, but seven feet tall and totally featureless. It raised a boxy arm and brought it down at Magpie, who must have spotted the horror on our faces and threw himself blindly to one side as the golem's black fist crashed into the earth inches away, shaking a shower of dust from the bridge and sending a spiderweb of cracks down the wall of the chasm.

As the golem recovered, Magpie ducked around it and onto the bridge. The sword waved wildly in his hand as he began to run up the far slope.

"Jump!" Noah yelled, the only one who'd thought to keep count. Magpie looked up, his eyes white circles, and made a stumbling jump towards us just as the bridge flickered out under him. It came back a moment later and he hit it chest-first, slipped halfway over the side, and let his feet fall as he wrestled both arms onto the flat of the bridge. The sword skidded a foot back down toward the golem, which was now advancing.

Magpie's drone swooped in for a dramatic closeup of his face as the stone automaton took a step onto the bridge.

"*Jump!*" Noah screamed. Magpie made a helpless sort of lurch with his arms, then the bridge disappeared. Hero's Bane flashed once in the light as it tumbled spinning into the chasm. The golem followed it, falling in silent stupidity to shatter somewhere in the darkness below. Magpie fell, too...

And grabbed his drone, which lurched a few feet into the depths before it righted itself under its new burden. It began to spin slowly, trying to track Magpie's implant without understanding that he was hanging off it.

"Sepharad!" he called as he came around to face us. "Handheld!"

Noah stared at Magpie blankly for a second, then understanding dawned on his face. He began tapping at the handheld with a look of fierce concentration.

"Drop it!"

We all spun at the voice behind us. Three men in black leather armor, their faces hidden by bandanas, stalked towards us from the gloom: the same men who'd attacked us in the tomb at the top of Hard Pass. If we'd hurt them in our last fight, it wasn't apparent; the one I'd blasted with a fireball even had shiny new armor.

"You again?" I shouted back. "Didn't get enough last time? Sepharad, do your thing. We'll handle these guys."

They came toward us slowly and I thought with satisfaction that maybe they'd learned a hard lesson in our first fight. Something was bugging me, though.

"How'd you find us?" I called, expecting they'd ignore me, but to my surprise the lead fighter caught my gaze. His eyes crinkled as he smiled under his bandana.

"You should be more careful where you open your big mouth."

With that, the men in black charged, but I had just the thing. I pulled both bells from my pouch and began to swing them in opposite directions as I spoke the words of the spell. After using it on the gold dogs, it was easy to find the spell's rhythm again, and I quickly had the bells' ringing interlocked with my chanting.

Our attackers kept coming. They didn't seem to notice that I was using powerful magic on them. Cass sent an arrow at the lead fighter, but he slapped it out of the air with his sword. I kept chanting and swinging the bells, but the spell just wasn't working; the sensation of slowed time that I'd felt when I froze the gold dogs wasn't there.

"Any time now, Linnaea!" said Cass. She shot another arrow that scored a white line across the leader's armor as it deflected away into the shadows.

"It's not working!" I gasped. My arms were burning again. I let the bells clatter uselessly to the cavern floor and pulled out a copper piece. The attackers were a few feet away now; Cass was backing up as she pulled another arrow from her quiver, but there was only so much space between her and the lip of the chasm.

I backpedaled as well as I started rolling the coin over my fingers, willing it to heat up. The fighter on my right noticed and sprinted forward, his sword up. It was hard to tell, but I thought he was the one I'd scorched last time. My coin was barely warm, but I threw it anyway, and my attacker flinched away as the copper piece bounced harmlessly off his armor without even a puff of smoke.

I pulled my dagger from my belt, trying to steel myself for a real fight. The man coming after me was a few inches taller than me and had a sword, but maybe I could trick him into falling into the chasm or running into the traps on the bridge.

He realized he hadn't been hurt and came at me even faster, one hand out to grab me and the other bringing his sword back for a lethal overhand chop. A glance to my left showed the other two fighters advancing on Cass, who had an arrow nocked but couldn't choose where to send it. I couldn't see Noah or Magpie.

The fighter farthest from me grunted in pain as Cass's arrow stuck into his leg. The other man on her lunged, but I didn't

181

have time to watch as my own attacker closed with me and brought his sword down at my head.

"*Cleave!*" Noah screamed. The sword slicing toward me spun off into the chasm along with the arm holding it, which had separated neatly from its owner. I stumbled to the side as the man who'd been about to cut me down toppled forward, his remaining hand over the bloody stump at his shoulder, his face pale under his bandana. He hit the ground and didn't move.

I turned to help Cass, but she didn't need it. One of her opponents was still trying to pull the arrow from his leg as the other turned and ran. Noah pointed at him with a long wand of bleach-white wood, blinked, then put his arm down. Behind him, Magpie let go of his hovering drone and dropped to the cavern floor. The drone rose a few sudden feet before catching itself, then stayed still.

"What the hell spell was that?" Cass gasped. She spared one glance for the gaping maw of the chasm only inches behind her, then joined us at the foot of the bridge.

"I think it's supposed to be for surgery," said Noah.

"Yikes," said Magpie.

"And what—" I shook my head. "Are you okay?"

"Fine," Magpie said. "Thanks to Sepharad. You can control drones manually from the handheld, you know."

"Jesus Christ," sighed Cass. "Linnaea, super job with the magic. What happened?"

"I don't know," I said tightly. "I cast the spell properly, I know I did. It just didn't work."

"No harm, no foul," said Cass, turning away. "So much for Hero's Bane."

Magpie laughed and scratched his head. "Yeah, sorry about that. Maybe we can come back with a ladder."

"You can go first," said Cass, then her head shot up and she grabbed an arrow from her quiver. "Freeze, PK!"

The would-be player-killer with an arrow in his leg stopped dead in the gloom of the cavern, where he'd been trying to limp away while we talked. He slowly turned, favoring his hurt leg, and put his hands in the air.

"Time to find out what these assholes want," said Cass. "Sepharad, Magpie, strip him."

"Strip him?" Magpie's eyebrows went up.

"Not completely!" said Cass. "Just his armor and weapons. Jeez."

Magpie kicked the man's sword away and unwrapped his bandana as Noah set about unbuckling his armor. The wounded fighter kept his hands up and let it happen, clearly resigned to his fate. My first impression of the face beneath the bandana was that he sort of looked like Magpie: olive skin, though pale with the pain of his wound, and thick black hair. But I wasn't ready for what was revealed when his armor came off. His scarred, muscular body was covered in tattoos just like Magpie's, little strings of words and numbers.

"Shit," Magpie said.

"Tie him up," said Cass. "And then I think it's time for an explanation."

★★★

"They're here for me," said Magpie. The tattooed fighter was safely tied up near the edge of the chasm; we sat in a little circle farther away, lit only by the glow of my dagger, our cameras turned off. Cass had her bow and an arrow near to hand.

"Why?" I said. "What are those tattoos?"

"Hell—sorry, the Hellenic Austerity Zone—isn't a good place," Magpie said. In the faint upward light his face looked gaunt and pale, his bones obvious beneath the skin. "There's no government there anymore. No laws. Athens is a warzone."

"Who's fighting?" asked Cass.

"Criminal families," said Magpie. "There's endless skirmishing and raiding and every once in a while, a proper battle. But mostly there's the normal sort of crime: drug deals, shakedowns, hits, that kind of thing."

"What do your tattoos mean?" asked Noah.

"I'm getting to that." Magpie smiled, but his eyes were in shadow and his grin had lost its flash. "I grew up on the streets. An orphan. I think my mom was a junkie, but that's just an educated guess. Anyway, pretty much the only way off the street is to make yourself useful to one of the families, so that's what I did. I went to the family that controlled my neighborhood, Vyronas, and I signed up as a contract boy."

"Contract boy?" I said.

"When two thieves do a deal it's hard for them to trust each other. Paper contracts are easy to forge, lose, change..." He flashed another smile, this time with the faintest hint of his usual easy attitude. "Plus it's hard to get paper when there's no infrastructure. So they use kids like me. They tattoo the contracts on us: names, numbers, that sort of thing. We follow the bosses around like a posse. The older contract boys act as bodyguards if they have to, but mostly it's so the bosses always have their contracts at hand."

"That's crazy," said Cass.

"I guess." Magpie shrugged. "It was a good job for a while. You're protected by the family and you don't really have to do much as long as you don't mind going under the needle all the time."

"Did they teach you to read?" Noah asked.

"That's a weird question," Cass said.

Magpie laughed. "No, it's a good one. The answer is no. They don't like contract boys knowing what's on them. I taught myself to read." His eyes were vague and far away. "I spent so many hours in the library, or what was left of it. As it happened, the science fiction shelves all survived."

Noah smiled, his real smile.

"You make it sound almost okay," I said. "What changed?"

"Well..." Magpie ducked his head, and for a long moment his entire face was lost in shadow. "I decided to get out. They don't like their contract boys leaving, but I thought if I could get to the Summerlands, they wouldn't be able to follow me."

"How did you afford a ticket?" asked Noah.

"How do you think?" said Magpie.

"You stole the money," I whispered. "From a mob boss. Oh, Magpie…"

"It's easy when you're at every meeting," he said. He blew out a heavy breath and looked up at the cavern ceiling. "Guys, I'm so sorry. I'm putting you all in so much danger. They're not going to stop coming until they get me. I'm not going to hand myself over. I'm not. But I'll leave you alone." He put his hands on the floor, getting ready to push himself up.

All three of us, Cass, Noah, and me, reached out at the same time to stop him.

"Like hell you will," said Cass.

"You're our friend," Noah said.

I patted his knee. "Welcome to Hearthhammer."

★★★

Uncertain what else to do with him, we left the hitman tied up at the base of the bridge. A cloud of questions still hung around the whole thing: when had they come through? How did they always know where to find us? How were they resistant to my magic? Why weren't they being punished for attempted player-killing? And as good old sharp-eyed Noah had pointed out: where were their drones?

More than anything, though, we wanted to know if we'd hit number one. As we headed for home under a low-slanting sunset, Cass had her head bent over the handheld, tapping through the screens.

"We better have," she murmured. "That one had it all, drama, magic, traps, extreme PvP violence. We better have, that's all I'm saying."

"Well?" said Magpie. He walked with a spring, almost a bounce, in his step, far peppier than I would have expected from someone who'd stared death in the face less than an hour ago.

"Oh my God," Cass said.

"Did we do it?" Magpie said. "We did it, didn't we? Did we?"

"I have a message from my dad," Cass said.

That stopped us all dead in our tracks, and we clustered around Cass, trying to see the handheld screen.

"How did he afford it?" asked Noah.

"Didn't he have to turn in his phone when he was fired?" I asked.

"Everybody shush!" said Cass. "I'm sure he'll explain. Back off, I just need—give me some space, okay?"

We gave her her space, but Noah and Magpie paced nervously and I fiddled with a coin as Cass read the message. It took a few minutes, and when she finally finished, she looked up with tears in her eyes.

"Is he okay?" I said. I hadn't meant it to, but my voice came out as a whisper.

"He didn't say anything about the pain," said Cass, just as quietly. "Which means it must hurt more than ever. But he's okay. Mr Vogler helped him get to the library to use a computer there."

"The library?" I said. "He can't afford a library card, right?"

"Yeah, funny thing about that," said Cass. "He said it cost him the last of his money."

"The last of his money?" I repeated dumbly.

"Well, how much have we sent home?" asked Cass. "Assuming Agony cheated us, which I think is a pretty safe bet at this point."

"None," I said, "but—"

"And how long have we been here?"

"Twenty-nine days," said Noah.

"Which means…" Cass wiped the fledgling tears from her eyes, which had the same iron look that I'd seen at Jason's funeral.

"Oh no," I said.

Cass nodded. "Time's up," she said. "He's gonna be evicted in three days. His medical bills are piling up. And guess what?"

She held up the handheld, showing me the glowing screen. "We're number two."

★★★

We split up when we reached Wellpoint. I said I needed to touch base with Naila and Seidenberg, and I did, but first I had a message to send. I borrowed the handheld and sat on the stoop of our flophouse on Bad Luck Alley, where we'd never bothered to move out. A few ragged adventurers watched me through disinterested eyes as they shambled down the alley, but nobody stopped.

```
Dave,


I saw we hit #2 today. Can't that be
good enough? We're regularly in the top
ten now. Most parties take years to get
the kind of following we have. We did
it in a month. I've done everything you
wanted. I even found a way to learn new
spells. I'm trying to play the game and
make the fans happy but we could really
use your help. Please. Keats is count-
ing on us.


Emma Burke (aka Linnaea)
```

I hit SEND and put the handheld down. Leaning back on the stoop, I could just see the last sliver of the Summerlands' red sunset over the shingle roofs of Wellpoint. As I watched, it disappeared, leaving the alley in blue shadow. A few lights went on in windows around me. Somewhere far away, on some other street, a woman laughed.

Bad Luck Alley, they called it, where adventurers went when their luck ran out. Bad Luck Alley, because it was never their own fault. I had been so sure that we could reach number one again so easily. I was giving my viewers what asked for, wasn't I? Lectures for the nerds like me, dangerous exploits for everyone else. What more did they want from me? What more could they take?

The handheld pinged softly, and the screen glowed in the failing light: 1 NEW MESSAGE.

```
Linnaea,

I hear you, I do. I really want to help
but I've got to keep my bosses happy.
You know how it is. I know you've got
something really great for me. Give
yourself some credit, Linnaea, you're a
superstar. Let's prove it and then
they'll let me make all your problems
go away.

Think big!
Dave
```

I sighed and set the handheld on the stoop. There was already so much I should have done differently. I'd managed to make the wrong decision at almost every opportunity, and now I was out of ideas.

Well, almost all out. I shook my head, trying to drive away a thought that had been scratching at the back of my mind since we'd first decided to fight for rankings instead of treasure. I'd been able to put it aside before, but this time it wouldn't leave me alone.

It was a crazy idea that would involve breaking at least a few of Expedition's rules of the game. We'd have to leave all the comfort and safety of Wellpoint behind, striking out into the wilds of the Summerlands where only the ranger groups had penetrated. Those same rangers would be looking for us as we went, trying to stop us by absolute decree of Expedition Games. There would certainly be no treasure at the other end. But if we did it, our numbers would explode. I was sure of that. More than that, we'd be legends, written into the history of the Summerlands forever.

It was a crazy idea and the rest of Hearthammer would almost certainly shoot it down, but it was all I had left. Even if they didn't want to, I could always go alone... Before I realized it, I'd made up my mind: I was going to the Wall.

INTERNATIONAL RELATIONS

"What's the Wall?" asked Magpie.

"Seriously?" I said, setting down my empty bowl. Naila had really outdone herself this time, with pan-fried noodles and spiced meat that melted in our mouths. "It was in the legal stuff we signed."

"I didn't understand most of that," Magpie said. It was just us at Open Seasoning, at least until Cass and Noah came back from the Expedition Hall. "It didn't really seem important."

"Me neither," I admitted. "But the Wall is a pretty big one. Basically, it's the boundary of Expedition's territory in the Summerlands, at least to the north."

"Why'd they build it?" Magpie said around a mouthful of noodles.

"Dunno," I said. "But it must have been bad, because they don't mess around about it. We're not allowed to get within five miles."

"So your plan is to…"

"Go there and touch it, yeah." I shrugged. "If that doesn't get us to number one, I give up."

"Well, I'll follow you anywhere."

"Thanks." I could feel heat creeping up into my cheeks. Magpie's grin had gone into hiding and his dark eyes were locked on mine.

"Actually," he said, "I wanted to—"

"That absolute *bitch*!" Cass stormed into the restaurant, Noah close behind. The door slammed shut behind them, nearly knocking the little welcome bell from its hook. "That stupid, kilt-wearing... oh, hey, guys." She flipped a chair around and dropped heavily into it, her elbows over the back. Magpie suddenly got very interested in his food and Noah was at the back of the shop with Naila, leaving me alone with Cass's mood.

"Not good?" I ventured.

"Remind me," Cass growled, "are we allowed to kill NPCs?"

"No, but we're not allowed to kill each other, either," I said. "Are you telling me she isn't going to do anything about it?"

"Nope," said Cass. "She said there was no proof we'd been attacked by people."

"No proof?" I felt my eyebrows go up. "There's four feeds of it!"

"She said she doesn't have access to those." Cass made a noise somewhere between a laugh and a cough. "As though Expedition doesn't save everything."

"Jesus," I said. "You'd think she'd care that her company had been infiltrated by organized crime."

"We really are on our own." Cass shook her head. "Next time those bastards come for Magpie, I swear to God..."

"Emma has a plan," said Magpie.

"A plan?" Cass blinked, her conversational train derailed.

"To get to number one," Magpie said.

"Oh, lord," Cass sighed. "Here we go again."

"Just hear me out," I said. "I really think this one will work."

"That's what you said about Hero's Bane," Cass said. "And the Thing Cave. And your lectures, though at least those didn't almost get us all killed."

"This one's not even dangerous," I said. "You know, comparatively."

"Then it won't get us ratings!" Cass slumped forward, her chin on her hands. "It's hopeless, Em. You need to give up on the get-rich-quick stuff. Get some of those little endorsement deals set up. We'll start going for treasure again and just send home what we can... it won't get Dad out of debt or anything, but maybe we can cover his rent."

"You haven't even heard her idea yet," said Magpie.

"I don't need to," Cass said. "Dad is getting evicted in three days. It's over."

"What if I told you it would really piss off Donna Markan?" I said.

Cass spread her hands and looked up at the ceiling as if seeking divine intervention. "Fine." She snorted. "I'm listening."

★★★

Cass didn't really seem to care how confident I was that going to the Wall would be a ratings blockbuster; she put aside her concern that we'd end up like the Lost Expedition and got on board as soon as she realized what a black eye it would be for Expedition Games. Noah was as willing as always to go along and Magpie reiterated that he would follow me, though that odd gleam in his eye had gone.

The first decision I made was to keep our cameras off for the journey. There was something to be said for streaming the whole thing, since we'd be passing through a lot of unexplored wilderness, but ultimately there was just no telling how closely Expedition could track us by watching our streams. If we were going to elude the ranger patrols and make it to the Wall, we needed every advantage we could get.

Provisioning came next and we split up to cover the preparatory ground more quickly. Cass bought the food. There was none of the decadent restaurant food we'd gotten used to, which was too big and would spoil quickly; instead, she stuffed her backpack full of nutrient-dense protein bars that opened the floodgates on a tide of suppressed memories of all the dismal extruder meals of my childhood. Noah upgraded our camping gear with proper bedrolls, tarps for rain, even miniature pillows. Magpie insisted on doing the clothes shopping.

That left me to go find Seidenberg. I thought he'd want to know what we were up to and I had one more request of him and his network of NPC spellcasters. Watching Hero's Bane spinning away into the darkness had been a heartbreaking moment—we'd come so close to owning the Summerlands' first magic sword—but it had lit a fire under me to master a spell I'd seen a few times on the feeds. It was an enchantment that brought out the best in any sword or dagger, giving it supernatural sharpness for a day or so. Naila knew that a few NPCs could cast it because they occasionally did so on her kitchen knives in return for a free meal.

We met at sundown on Meat Street for one last meal at Open Seasoning. We ate quietly, even Magpie, though he kept glancing at a stack of packages wrapped in brown butcher paper that he'd brought in with him and refused to explain.

Maybe because she caught the heavy feeling of fate that hung over our meal, Naila outdid herself on our dinner, grilling up four fat, pink steaks that came out gridded with fat black lines in steaming juices. The smell reminded me of the juicy, fat-dripping patties on Regional Manager Roger Sorolla's grill, a lifetime ago and a world away.

"Is this cow?" I asked Naila as she cleared our empty dishes.

"Cow?" She laughed. "No."

"Oh," I said, feeling my cheeks flush. "What is it?"

She paused halfway back to the kitchen, two big, greasy plates in each hand. "It's food."

"What does *that* mean?" asked Cass.

"It means don't worry about it," Naila said. She turned away as Hearthhammer shared a look. Cass stood up.

"Naila, what have you been feeding us?"

The chef looked back with the tiniest hint of a smile on her face. "Well, hell rat is great in fried rice. Harpy is a nice low-fat option. But for steak, it's gold dog or nothing."

"We're eating *monsters*?" Cass looked green.

"You're eating animals," Naila huffed, and her eyes narrowed. "If you prefer extruder meat, you're welcome to go home."

Cass's mouth opened, shut, and opened again. Her face was the red of a coin ready to make a fireball.

"Or," said Naila, "you can sit down and let me bring you dessert."

Cass sat down.

"What's in the packages, Magpie?" Noah asked.

"Oh, yes!" Magpie put his hands flat on the table. "I think it's time. You guys are going to love this. Noah, would you, please?"

Noah fetched the packages, which were labeled with our gamertags. The three of us unwrapped them as Magpie watched, his excitement written plainly on his face. The butcher paper slid open easily, revealing a folded black bundle. I shook it open to discover a slim black shirt with red stitching. Embroidered over the left breast was a little symbol in silver and gold thread: a long-handled warhammer over a heart.

"Magpie, did you—" I started.

"What on Earth?" said Cass.

"It's a Hearthammer!" Noah said. His shirt was black as well, with white accents where mine had red. His smile of wonder was matched only by Magpie's open glee.

"Not bad, eh?" he said. "An adventuring party should have proper outfits, that's what I think." His eyes flickered over to me. "Do you like them?"

"Are these bracers?" said Cass, holding up a matched pair of leather greaves.

"To protect your arm from the bowstring," Magpie said.

"You absolute madman," Cass said, smiling for the first time in days. "You crazy, wonderful little thief."

Magpie grinned, but his eyes were on me.

"I love them," I said, and I meant it.

★★★

We set out that night, moving under cover of darkness in the hopes of attracting as little attention as possible. Given that, my last act before we left Wellpoint behind took on a special irony.

"This is Linnaea, coming to you live from the road out of Wellpoint," I said to the black eye of my camera drone. "I have to sign off for a while. But don't think of this as goodbye. It's more of a *see you soon.* Keep an eye on my feed, you guys. Because the next time it comes on, I'm going to show you something that I absolutely, positively guarantee you have *never* seen before. I'll be back in a few days—I don't know exactly when—but in the meantime I want you all to spread the word. Tell your friends. Tell your mom. Tell your mom's friends. Tell the world. The next time this feed comes online, you'll want to be there."

I held up the handheld, my thumb over the Stream button. "This is Linnaea, signing off... for now."

I tapped the button and tossed the handheld back to Noah, who stowed it in his backpack. I took a long look back at Wellpoint, through the big white houses of the Burbs back to the town proper, then turned and followed Noah to the spot where the cobblestone street became gravel and Cass and Magpie stooding waiting with their hands on the straps of their packs. The Summerlands' moon hung huge and low in the sky, making blue shadows that pooled around our feet.

I patted Cass on the shoulder. "Here we go."

We walked for hours in silence. The night was warm, of course, and there was enough light from the moon that we hardly had to watch our steps as we crossed the low, rolling hillocks of the Near Plains. We reached the White Chasm around midnight and camped near its eastern edge.

The next day was as bright and clear as ever, and we made good time on our way toward the Wyvern Peaks. We'd decided not to dare Hard Pass again; we'd been lucky to make it through the first time and had no intention of exposing ourselves to attacks from hitmen, wyverns, or anyone else by trying the crossing a second time. Instead, we spent the next two days reversing the path we'd hiked with Golden Apple, through

Dann's Teeth to Wyatt Falls. We moved faster this time without all the treasure weighing us down and it was hard not to feel that our world had gotten smaller since the day we'd arrived in Portal Square.

We reached Wyatt Falls just as the last red sliver of the sun sank away in the west. Lights were coming on in the town, far more than I'd expected. Wyatt Falls had been nearly a ghost town the last time we'd been there, but now it was showing signs of life. The dirt road into town was lined with tents and studded with campfires where adventuring parties sat sharing dinner.

The center of town—little more than a crossroads where the inn, Expedition Hall, and general store sat at the intersection of two short packed-earth streets—was even more crowded. The inn looked full and its patrons overflowed onto its front porch and from there onto the street. They drank, laughed, and shouted in the light of a few dozen torches stuck into the dirt in a lopsided circle.

A shape came swaggering up to us out of the flickering shadows and resolved itself into Merric, the adventurer we'd met at the base of Hard Pass, with his arms around two new Angels, both in white leather armor.

"You survived!" he slurred. Even if he hadn't had a bottle in each hand, it would have been obvious how drunk he was. "And you look great!"

"What's going on?" I asked. "This place was dead last time we were here. Did something happen?"

"You happened, girlie," Merric said. He gestured at me with a sloshing bottle. "Can't climb the charts that fast without people noticing. And what do I always say about success?"

"What?" asked Noah.

"Uh…" Merric looked at the young women in his arms, but they both shook their heads. "Uh, I forget. But the point is, we're doing what you're doing. Everybody is. Meteora's here, Lord Blackmore… I even saw St George lurking around. He's not much of a partier, though. All on the Linnaea plan now. New"—he belched—"new discoveries. Very popular. Good job." He drummed his fingers against his bottle in a sort of half-clap.

"Did you discover a new type of liquor?" Cass said.

"What, this little shindig?" Merric glanced back over his shoulder. "You get all the big names in one place, there's gonna be a party. Casualties have gone up forty-four percent since you got here, did you know that? Folks are taking risks again. Well, excuse me if I want to get drunk and get lucky before I go risking my life to find a weird new bug in a cave." With that piece of philosophy, Merric staggered off back towards the torchlight, his Angels propping him up as surely as when he'd been injured on Hard Pass.

"It's like the Olympic Village," said Cass.

"The what?" said Magpie.

"Something my mom told me about when I was a kid," Cass explained. "They used to have this big sports event called the Olympics every couple years. All the best athletes from around the world would get together and compete. I guess they'd all stay in this makeshift town called the Olympic Village, and there was lots of partying and... you know. International relations."

"Your mom told you that?" There was a deep furrow between Magpie's brows.

"I did some independent research," Cass said.

"It makes sense," I said. "From a sociological standpoint. I mean, think about it. You take a bunch of young, healthy people predisposed to risk-taking behavior, put them all in one place with no supervision, and stir it up with a healthy threat of death and dismemberment. It only stands to reason."

"Okay then, professor." Cass slapped me on the shoulder. "Who are you hooking up with tonight?"

★★★

The answer, as it turned out, was nobody. As we unpacked in one of the little inn's few remaining rooms, it occurred to me that I had no particular desire to spend the night with anybody other than Hearthammer. We'd been through so much in the Summerlands, been knocked down so many times, but all those indignities had bound us together more tightly than any of our victories could.

Our impotence in the face of Dr Agony's theft was infuriating, and despite the improvement in Cass's mood I knew that sooner or later she and I had deal with the fracture it had caused in our friendship. She would come around, I thought, once she admitted to herself that I made a better leader than she did.

The thought that Magpie's past was still chasing him scared me, too, Expedition's refusal to acknowledge the problem even more so. But the fact was, the string of disasters had given us an enemy, put a face to the forces that had held us down since childhood. Hearthammer had our problems, but as long as we could point our anguish at Dr Agony and Donna Markan and Apollonia Blomhaugen, it was us against the world.

The story of Magpie's life made my tension with Cass seem so small in comparison. As I settled into my little feather bed, I decided that he'd earned a spot in Hearthammer before he'd ever set foot in the Summerlands. He wasn't like the other players, who had almost all been rich or famous or both before they joined the game. He was one of us. He could never replace Jason, either as a fighter or a friend, but it was good to have a full party again.

The thought of Jason pushed a sudden stabbing pang of loss into my chest. He would have loved it in Wyatt Falls. It was beautiful everywhere in the Summerlands, but it was different here than in Wellpoint, which sat among flowering meadows. Wyatt Falls was a little frontier town cut out of the dark woods and that would have warmed the soul of a boy who'd named himself Yukon. As I stared at the shadowed beams of the ceiling, I could see him swaggering out of the inn, down the porch steps, and out into the torchlight to make friends with everyone he could reach. He would have had no trouble finding someone to spend the night with, I thought, as a prickle of heat crept up my neck.

It felt good to sleep in a real bed, though, even if I was the only one in it.

★★★

The wood was silent except for our footfalls in the heavy leaf cover. The trees here were huge, wide enough that Noah and Magpie could barely touch hands around one, with layer upon layer of thick leaves that turned what little of the sun penetrated them to a deep golden green. They were also ruler-straight, in perfectly spaced rows that made a neat grid aligned to the cardinal directions.

It made navigation easy, but it was unnerving. It was clearly unnatural, and I found myself wishing I could turn my camera on and chatter about how it must have been the handiwork of the elves. Instead I kept my thoughts to myself and walked straight into a trap.

I stumbled over something hidden in the underbrush and fell to my knees with a curse, but had only half a moment to catch my breath before the ground gave way beneath me.

"Help!" I shouted as the leaves and dirt under me began to slide down into an opening pit. Magpie was already running, one hand outstretched, but there was no way he'd make it in time. I felt myself slipping as the slide became a cascade in which I was being pulled along.

I flopped over onto my belly and reached out with both hands, trying to grab a stone, a tree root, anything that would give me purchase against the rush of dirt trying to drag me down. My left hand closed around something thick and mossy: a vine?

Whatever I had grabbed gave way with a snap as the ground collapsed completely in a sudden rush, dumping into a dark pit that went deeper than I could see. I swung forward and slammed into the near wall of the pit, slid a few feet down as the slick, moss surface in my hand sloughed away and finally came to a shuddering stop hanging by one hand over a wide, dark mouth that had swallowed all the dirt it was given and wanted to swallow me, too.

Magpie's head appeared over the lip of the hole, shadowed against the thin light from above.

"Emma!" he called.

"I'm here!" I shouted back. A thin trickle of dirt started up, sliding past my cheek and falling away into the dark.

"Just hang on!" Magpie called as Cass and Noah peered down on either side of him.

"I've only got one hand on—what is this, anyway?" I said.

"It's a rope," said Noah. "It looks really old. It's covered in moss."

"Okay, I need to get my other hand on it—"

"*Don't!*" Magpie and Cass yelled simultaneously.

"What?" I called up. "Why?"

"Uh, don't worry about it," said Magpie.

"*What?*" I shouted.

"It's kind of coming apart," Cass said.

"We're going to find something else," Magpie called, and his head disappeared.

"Well, hurry!" I shouted back. Cass and Noah retreated as well, leaving me dangling alone, or so I thought. When a new voice called up to me from the depths of the pit, I almost let go of the rope in surprise.

"You there!" It was a man's voice, deep and commanding. "Girl!"

"What?" I shouted down into the void.

"Are you an adventurer?" the man called. The voice was familiar, but I couldn't place it.

"Yeah, you?" I replied. The whole thing had a faintly ridiculous air, like I was chatting in Portal Square and not about to fall to my death.

"I am a weapon of God," the man said primly and I instantly knew who I was talking to: St George, the Crusader of the Summerlands. He was my mom's favorite player, but more importantly, he'd saved Magpie's life in Portal Square when we'd first come through.

"Are you stuck?" I asked.

"Indeed," St George called. "I was trapped here by some devilry! The earth gave way, tumbling me into this mouth of Hell, and before long the open sky above had sewn itself shut again. Look, even now it grows closed!"

I glanced up, and was horrified to see that St George was right. The ground around the pit was moving, reaching out dirty roots to make a lattice over the opening. As I watched, a few leaves fell from a high-up branch to land exactly over the hole, hiding a sliver of the sunlit canopy.

"Guys?" I called.

"Have your companions free us!" shouted St George.

"No shit!" I yelled back. "Guys!" There was no response.

The ground closing above me was like a shroud of panic being laid over my mind. I shook my head to try to clear it away and make myself think properly. I was a wizard, after all.

My grip on the rope slipped a few more inches, sending another miniature avalanche of dirt and rotten leaves into the pit.

"Okay, I'm gonna try something!" I called down into the dark. With my free hand, I flipped open my belt pouch, pulled out a copper coin, and began rolling it over my fingers. It was just starting to grow warm when it rolled off my pinky into the open air and tumbled down into darkness. I didn't hear it land.

"It's no hope!" St George's voice was firm. "Drop down here and seek an exit with me."

I ignored him and took a long, slow breath, forcing my jackhammering heart to slow. I reached back into my pouch and felt around: bells; pencil; a few coins that felt too big… was I out of coppers? No, there was one more, hidden halfway inside the mouth of a bell. I slid it free.

I braced myself against the dirt wall as best I could, trying to keep my free hand level, and began to roll the coin. Soon it was warm and not long after that it began to glow a dull red. I gave it a few more seconds, letting it get bright and almost white, then held my breath and flicked it straight up to the grid of wan light that marked the closing mouth of the pit.

The coin ticked off a tangled root and burst into a ball of flame. I shut my eyes against the sudden glare as a rush of heat buffeted me. When I opened them, green sunlight greeted me from the reopened hole. My heart leapt in sudden hope, then the rope in my hand gave way.

A second rope, weighted with a fist-sized rock, swung down from the opening and nearly hit me on the head. I grabbed it with both hands just as the pit wall collapsed and fell away, leaving me swinging in the gloom. There was a moment of lurching terror as I fell a few feet; then the rope went taut and I jerked to a stop.

"Pull!" someone called up above. I rose a few sudden feet, clutching the rope in a terrified grip. "We've got her! Pull!"

Slowly, I rose towards the opening, which was already beginning to weave itself shut with new reaching tendrils. As soon as my head crossed the lip, I reached out a hand to Magpie, who stood sweat-streaked and filthy with his feet braced against the ground and the rope in both hands. His face split in a huge grin as he grabbed my arm and heaved me up onto solid ground.

"Oh, thank God—" he started.

"Someone else!" I gasped, rolling onto my back. "St George! Rope!"

Magpie blinked, then kicked the rock at the end of the rope and let it tumble into the darkness as the rope slid loosely through his hands. His palms were a bright, angry red, rubbed raw as he'd clung so tightly to my lifeline.

"George!" I called down into the pit. "Grab on!"

A silent moment passed, then something in the darkness gave the rope two sharp tugs, and Magpie began to pull. I climbed to my feet to help and saw that behind Magpie, also hauling with fierce concentration on every face, were Noah, Cass, Merric, and his two new Angels from the night before, as well as the two we'd met on Hard Pass.

I ran for the end of the line, but before I could even get my hands on the rope, St George appeared at the mouth of the pit, red-faced and spitting dirt. Magpie hooked him under the armpits and hauled him the rest of the way out, until they collapsed in a clatter of weapons and armor a few feet from the hole.

"Ah," Magpie said between gulps of air.

St George stood, straightening his sword belt and brushing filth from his heavy armor, which I noticed he hadn't bothered to take off. His tabard was stained and torn, the wide red cross dulled and the white changed to a blotchy brown. He flipped down the visor of his helmet, then flipped it open again.

"My thanks," he said to Magpie. "What brings you to this wood?"

"Uh," Magpie said. He sat up and blew on his hands. "Ow."

"What brings *you* here?" asked Cass, stepping forward. She'd never liked St George on the streams; she thought he was too violent and way too crazy.

"I seek to slay Hell's demons, as ever," the knight replied. "I assume that is not so for you, archer, as you travel with a witch."

"Oh, here we go," Cass said. "Spare me the sermon, buddy. If the next thing out of your mouth isn't *thank you*, we're leaving."

"Magic is the Devil's—" St George began, and Cass spun on her heel, gave us a *round-'em-up* wave with her hand, and set off into the forest, watching where she put her feet.

★★★

"You really should carry rope," said Merric, spearing a sausage on a long stick and holding it out over our campfire. "Fifty feet at least. Silk if you can afford it, hemp if not."

"Thanks again for the assist," said Cass and Merric shrugged.

We'd made camp at the first place the unchanging forest showed us anything other than a perfect grid of identical trees. A single trunk had been carved with an image that reminded me of the pictures we'd seen in the treasury near Wyatt Falls. It was a simple relief of an elf, with long hair past his shoulders, one thin hand held up palm forward, covered with what looked like spots or sores.

I was studying it and wishing I could turn my camera on for just a second when Dahlia, one of Merric's new Angels, came up behind me with a tin plate of food.

"He looks sad," she said.

I cocked my head. There wasn't much detail in the carving, but there was something about the lines around the elf's eyes, the set of his mouth, that made me think Dahlia was right.

"Here," she said, offering me the plate.

"Thanks." I took it and gingerly touched a sausage, which was sizzling hot. Dahlia looked back at the carving. Her hair was long and blonde and plaited into a single thick braid that she pulled over her shoulder and rested on her chest. She began to stroke it idly.

"When's your next lecture?" she asked.

"Oh," I said, "I don't know. We're kind of on hiatus."

"Until when?" Dahlia's eyes were a deep brown and her eyebrows were thick and dark. She wore white leather armor like the other Angels, and there was an ornately carved shortbow and a quiver of arrows with her pack.

"Whenever we get back to Wellpoint, I guess," I said.

"Where are you headed?" she asked.

I opened my mouth to answer, but caught myself. Instead, I gave her what I hoped was a sympathetic smile. "Sorry, I can't tell you."

"I understand," Dahlia said. "I'll leave you alone—oh, wait, one more question."

"Shoot."

"Have you and Magpie talked about his feelings?"

"His what?" I blinked.

"His *feelings*," she said. A moment passed. "For you."

"We're friends," I said. "So what?"

"So, you should have seen him when you were stuck in that pit. He was this close to melting down. That's more than just friends."

"Well—" I cleared my throat. "Well, what's the deal with Merric? Are you guys, like…"

"His harem?" Dahlia laughed. "Hell no. That's all marketing. He has a wife back on Earth."

"Seriously?" I felt my eyebrows go up.

"Her name is Karen," said Dahlia. "He talks about her all the time. Sends her all his money. Hey, if whatever you guys are up to doesn't work out, you should find me. Being an Angel is one of the most stable gigs in the Summerlands."

"Linnaea!" Magpie called from the fire. "Did you get food?"

"Think about it," Dahlia said.

★★★

The campfire had long since died to embers and the straight trees all around us trembled with Merric's noisy snoring. A surreptitious glance at the handheld showed me the time, about five minutes after what would have been midnight on Earth.

Time in the Summerlands was strange. Every day was exactly the same: the sun rose at 5:14 AM and set at 9:07 at night. It was like the same day looped over and over again, but with an added wrinkle: thirteen o'clock. Days in the Summerlands were twenty-five hours long, with an extra hour of darkness between 11 PM and midnight. The time from 12 to 13 AM, also known as Summerlands midnight, simply didn't exist on Earth. During that hour, feeds and other data sent home were simply lost. On Earth, when the clock ticked over to midnight, anyone watching a feed would see it jump ahead an hour instantly.

So even if I'd had my camera on, nobody back home would have seen Magpie sit down beside me at the glowing remains of the fire, scoot in until our legs touched, and twine his warm fingers with mine.

"Hi," he said.

"What's your real name?" I asked, my eyes on the campfire.

"Magpie," he said.

"No, really," I said. Despite the warm night air and the embers a few feet from us, his leg felt hot against mine. "What was your name before the Summerlands?"

"Magpie," he repeated.

"Really?" I said. I still couldn't look at him.

"That's what the boss called me," he said. "I never thought to ask why. I was so happy just to finally have a name."

We sat like that for a few minutes, our fingers interlaced, our legs pressed together with unnecessary closeness.

"Dahlia said the funniest thing before dinner," I said.

"You too?" He snorted a little laugh and shifted his weight against me. "What do you think?"

"About what she said?" I was hedging, stalling, and we both knew it. Magpie squeezed my hand.

"About what she said," he agreed.

"I think…" I started, and then I looked at him at last, and his face in the firelight was a mask of flushed red and shadowed black, with a wide-eyed stare of fear and hope that made him look so young that all I could do was put my free hand on his cheek and my lips on his.

After that we were a tangle of limbs and clutching hands, locked together as we stumbled off into the dark forest. Eventually he picked me up—he was stronger than I'd guessed from his slight frame—and I wrapped my arms around his neck as he carried me to a private spot far from our sleeping companions.

I was still wearing my dirt-stained, sweat-infused armor and as Magpie fumbled with the laces I pushed him away and dragged his ragged linen shirt over his head. In the green dimness I ran my fingers down his chest and over his lean, flat stomach, letting snatches of his tattoos catch my eye in single words and chunks of numbers that I forgot as soon as I read them.

Until I saw something that stopped my heart. The blood it put out to my body with its terminal beat was ice water, freezing my limbs and making me shake. My gentle fingers became rigid claws that jabbed Magpie's flesh.

"What?" he whispered. Just above his hip in sharp black ink were three lines that wavered before me like the remnants of a nightmare that cling on in the darkness long after the dream has ended.

Brayden Porter - HECZ
USD 40.000
Jason Keats - HECZ - Assassination

THE WALL

"Explain this," I said, standing. "Now."

Magpie didn't need to look to know which tattoo I meant. "Emma, I'm sorry—"

"Oh my God, there's another."

There was. A second tattoo, not far from Jason's, had caught my eye. It was another name I knew.

Pablo X - EU
EUR 31.000
Terra Almeida Santos - EU - Assassination

Terra, Jason's friend, the one who'd sent him that mysterious file the day before he died. She was dead too. In my growing panic a lurid scene played out across the screen of my mind: the assassin standing over Terra as she bled to death, her phone cradled in red-smeared hands, pressing send on the email that would immediately condemn Jason to the same fate. A thousand questions buzzed like wasps through my head, making me stumble dizzily. I needed answers before I passed out or puked. I jabbed a shaking finger at Magpie.

"*Explain this!*"

Magpie slumped. "Okay. But please believe me, I was going to tell you. I just… After we lost Hero's Bane, you asked me what changed. Why I decided to go on the run. Well, it was because of your friend."

"Because of Jason?" I whispered.

Magpie nodded. "When you're a contract boy, you're invisible. The bosses, they'll talk about anything in front of you like you're not there. So I heard everything… someone came from Expedition Games, a lawyer. They were looking for someone to kill a kid in America. I guess he found out something he shouldn't have and they wanted him silenced. It happens all the time with the big corporations. Or maybe they just always came to us, I don't know. The family I worked for has people all over the world and a good reputation for keeping our silence, so we did a lot of contract work for companies."

"So the police officer who killed Jason…" I was shaking.

"Was a hitman." Magpie nodded, his eyes on the ground. "Hired by Expedition Games. And I'm the contract."

"That must be why they want you back so bad," I said. Then another realization came like an aftershock. "And Expedition must be helping them. But I still don't understand why you ran away."

From his seat on the ground, Magpie shrugged. He still wouldn't meet my eyes. "They were going to kill a kid. I couldn't do it anymore."

"But you knew, this whole time." I could hear my voice getting louder and I couldn't stop it. "You knew it was Cass's brother, our friend. And you didn't say anything! You weaseled your way into our friendship. We made you a part of Hearthhammer—you took Jason's place—and you knew the whole time!"

"Emma—"

"*Don't call me that!*" I screamed, and that's when the rangers appeared from the trees all around us, silent in black leather, swords painted black, their faces grim in the wan moonlight.

"I've got them!" one called over his shoulder. "Right where he said they'd be."

"Who said?" I said, squaring my shoulders as a half-dozen rangers made a circle around us. Half the lacings of my armor dangled loose and Magpie was holding his stained shirt over his bare chest with one hand; the other was moving slowly through the rotting leaves on the forest floor, looking for anything to use as a weapon.

"The Jesus freak," said the ranger. He gestured to Magpie with his sword. "You there, get up."

"St George sold us out?" I shook my head. "So much for chivalry."

Magpie stood and started to pull his shirt on, but three rangers stepped forward at this motion and he stopped with his head through the neck and the shirt dangling over his shoulders. The rangers herded us back towards the camp, where another half dozen had Noah, Cass, and Merric and the Angels on their feet with their hands on their heads. The rangers began lighting torches that sent shadows shifting across the camp.

"Where the hell were you?" Cass asked as we came in sight, then she caught a glimpse of Magpie with his shirt half-off. She shut her mouth, but her eyes stayed wide.

"What's going on?" Merric said. "We didn't do anything."

"Hearthammer is wanted for player-versus-player violence and player-killing," said the ranger nearest him. He looked like a model dropped down incongruously into the wilderness, with thick black hair, black stubble on a square jaw, and deep-set eyes of a piercing light blue.

"That's bullshit!" shouted Cass. "We were attacked; we defended ourselves. Check the feeds if you don't believe me!"

"Shut it," said the ranger. "We have our orders. Merric, you and the girls are free to go. Hearthammer, you will come quietly."

"Like hell we will," Cass muttered.

"Angels, get your gear," said Merric. "We're outta here." They packed slowly, taking their time tidying up their campsite to the obvious annoyance of the rangers, but eventually the Angels set off between the trees, heading south. Dahlia was the last to leave and as she passed between two wide trunks she turned back and gave Magpie a leer.

"Nice tattoos," she said, and was gone.

"Finally," said the blue-eyed ranger. "Hearthammer, you will pick up your gear and follow us back to Wyatt Falls. You will not attempt to escape or resist." As we gathered our things, he turned to address the other rangers. "Third ranger Group, keep them in line. Fourth, you're running interference. I don't want to see any other players on the way."

As if on cue, an arrow thunked into a tree trunk a foot from the ranger's head. His men immediately dropped into fighting positions, scanning the dark forest for the source of the attack. With a *whack*, another arrow appeared in a tree across the camp.

"Whoever's out there, stop and show yourselves!" shouted the lead ranger. "We're authorized to use lethal force in self-defense!"

His only answer was two more arrows in succession, from opposite sides of the camp. I thought I saw a flash of white among the trees, but it was hard to be sure in the gloom. The ranger barked a command and his men began to spread out into the forest, heading toward the sources of the arrows.

"I think they forgot about us," Noah said. I looked around and realized he was right; the rangers were so focused on the new threat that they'd let their cordon around us come loose.

"Time to go," I said. I set off at a run and the others followed. The only plan I could think of was to get as deep into the wood as possible, opting for speed over stealth and hoping to lose the rangers in the darkness beneath the canopy, but we made such a clatter as we dashed between the trees that the rangers immediately realized what they'd done. Somebody shouted orders and a few men bolted after us.

"Scatter," Cass hissed.

My hand was grabbed and I found myself running with Magpie at full tilt. We flew together between the trees, packs banging on our backs. I glanced back; the red torchlight at the camp was already diminishing into nothing.

We pounded through the underbrush until Magpie skidded to a sudden stop and I crashed into his back, nearly toppling him.

"What is it?" I whispered. Then I saw her, standing in a beam of moonlight that broke through the heavy canopy, dressed in white leather armor with a short sword in each hand, her long blonde braid hanging over her shoulder and down her chest: Dahlia.

"Thank God—" Magpie began.

211

"On your knees, traitor," said Dahlia.

"What?" Magpie's voice was hoarse.

"You think you can just walk away from the family?" She took a step forward, and Magpie moved to keep himself between her and me.

"Who are you?" he said.

"I'm the one they call when the regular goons can't get the job done." Dahlia smiled. "You know, I never wanted to go to the Summerlands. The whole thing is so stupid, playing pretend like this." She shrugged. "The weapons aren't bad."

"Leave him alone." I stepped out from behind Magpie and slipped my pack to the ground.

"So faithful." Dahlia shook her head and tightened her grip on the sword in her right hand. "I thought for sure my little plan would work." Her voice got high-pitched and sickly sweet. "*Ooh, Linnaea, don't you know how much he loves you? You should take his shirt off...* I'm just sorry you didn't get a chance to have a proper fight before those idiots from Expedition showed up and ruined everything." She sighed dramatically. "Oh well. Out of the way, girlie. I don't get paid extra for you."

I got the dagger from my pack just as Dahlia darted forward, leading with one sword and bringing the other back for a stab at Magpie. She must have discounted me completely, because she looked genuinely surprised when I sank my dagger into her ribs. She stumbled to the side and I fell with her, crashing down on top of her as Magpie jumped clear of our tangle.

Dahlia said nothing, just looked up at me with a clenched grin that was equal parts pain and glee. Thin, watery blood showed on her white teeth. Her bloodshot eyes flickered to her left, and I followed their glance to see her fighting to free the sword arm I had pinned under me. I shifted my weight in that direction and immediately realized my mistake as she tugged her right arm free. Her sword flashed up in the moonlight and came down.

It clashed against a black blade that appeared as if from no-where and deflected down to plunge into the earth inches from my neck. I rolled off Dahlia and scuttled backwards through the leaf cover as she leapt to her feet, my dagger sticking from her side, and faced off with the handsome black-haired ranger from our camp.

"Drop the swords," he ordered, but Dahlia ignored him. Her eyes were locked on his and her bloody teeth still showed in her vicious grin.

She moved first, feinting with her right-hand sword; the ranger glanced in that direction as Dahlia brought up the sword in her other hand. Then she dropped it again, real pain flashing across her face. The ranger darted in and brought his sword up into her belly. It tore through her armor to stick out of her back, dripping red. He let go, and Dahlia slumped to her knees, coughed once, and fell onto her side.

He turned to me and Magpie. "She attacked me first."

"Us too," I agreed. "Did you hear the part where came to kill Magpie?"

"I heard enough." The ranger looked troubled. "If I go back to the feeds, will I see something similar from your last PK incident?"

"It's all there," said Magpie. "And you might want to ask your bosses who paid for her ticket."

The ranger nodded. In the moonlight I could see the lines on his face, the gray in his hair. "I'll call my men back. Your friends aren't far away. Get out of here."

★★★

It didn't take long for Magpie and me to find Cass and Noah, which was good, because neither of us knew how to start the conversation we so badly needed to have. The feeling of betrayal still burned inside me, like a wasp stinger that had gotten lodged between the folds of my heart, every effort to dig it out just shoving it deeper. Magpie was the one who had to perform the operation, but I would have gladly told him how if I'd only known.

Our friends hadn't gotten much farther than we had before being caught, and we found them by walking against the stream of rangers who now filtered back through the trees toward our camp. Noah heard us first, looking up from where he was fiddling with a tinderbox, trying to light a torch that he held between his knees.

"Are you okay?" He straightened up and the torch fell on the ground.

"We're fine," I said. "You?"

"Fine," said Cass. "I thought the rangers had us for sure, then they just stopped and turned around."

"We finally got their captain to listen to us," I said. "All it took was Dahlia nearly killing me."

"Dahlia?" Cass blinked. "The Angel?"

I nodded. "Yup. She worked for Magpie's crime family."

"She seemed really nice," said Noah.

"She was a sociopath."

"Was?" Cass's eyebrows went up.

"I don't want to talk about it," I said.

"Fine," she replied, kneeling to fix a strap on her backpack. She paused and glanced up at me. "I'm glad you're okay."

I looked away. "Okay, Hearthhammer, let's get to the wall."

"Anybody know which way is north?" Magpie asked.

"That way," Noah and I said together.

★★★

We walked all night, too flooded with adrenaline to sleep. As dawn came green and gold among the leaves, we curled up in exhaustion on the soft forest floor. The sun was high overhead when we woke and, wordless, set out again. The forest seemed to go on forever, as the rest of the day and another night passed with no apparent change to the endless rows of trees.

I made the trip in near silence. I'd been severed from two of my three friends, and I didn't have the heart for one of Noah's monologues. I was sure the rift between me and Magpie had to be glaringly obvious, but then, I was relying on the two most oblivious members of our party to pick up on it. Really, it was my duty to tell them, but every time I tried to work up the courage I discovered a new excuse not to. Cass would blame me, my dark thoughts said, or it would renew Cass's trauma, or it would distract us during our most important quest yet, or it would tear the party apart just when we stood on the brink of victory.

Help Keats first, I told myself. *Then you can collapse.*

I woke before dawn on the third day, feeling restless, and as I shuffled around our campsite I saw my friends opening gummy eyes and stirring in their bedrolls. We got underway in silence, and as we set out again between the trees I found myself wondering if the wood would ever end, or if we'd been trapped in some sort of magical loop.

The forest fell away just as the sun appeared in the eastern sky and we found ourselves at the top of a long incline of gray rock that ran down and away for miles. Just at the horizon was a thin line of darker gray that divided the earth and sky.

"Is that the Wall?" Cass asked, shielding her eyes.

"That's the Wall," I said. "We did it."

"You said we were going to touch it," Noah put in.

"Okay, picky," I said, "let's go."

It took over an hour to descend the slope and my thighs and ankles ached from the persistent tilt by the time we reached the Wall. It was about thirty feet high, solidly built of the same gray stone we'd just crossed, cut into neat blocks that seemed fitted together without the aid of mortar. As we drew near, we were able to get a view over it, where the gray stone continued for maybe another mile before trending back to forests. The Wall itself was about a yard thick, with no indication of any guard posts or other habitation. Just a big, blank stone face, stretching endlessly in both directions.

I stretched out my hand and laid it flat on the smooth stone. It was a bit cool to the touch.

"Now we did it," said Noah.

"Cameras on?" Cass said.

"Cameras on," I agreed. Noah slipped off his pack and began rifling through it for the handheld, but I had already snagged my drone from where it hovered loyally nearby and hit the big red button. It tugged itself out of my hand and rose, turning, to an angle that captured both me and a stretch of the Wall at my back.

"I'm back," I said. I gave the camera my best tired smile, wondering just what I looked like after days of endless travel and nights on the dirty ground. "I know you've missed me. And I missed you, too! Now, you might be wondering just what I've been up to all this time. And I'm sure you're wondering why I started streaming again in such a boring place. Well, guess what? It's not boring at all."

I glanced back at Noah, whose eyes were locked on the handheld. He must have felt me looking, because he caught my eye and gave me a thumbs-up. Our numbers must be coming back, but I still wanted to stall a bit longer before the big reveal.

"I grew up on the forums, so I know what kind of crazy speculation you guys get up to. I used to love doing it. Is DragonLass29 still taking bets on ElfBoard? I don't think I ever won one of those pools..." It had only been a month since I was one of those Summerlands fanatics arguing over famous streamers' next moves on the most popular forums, but it felt like the world had moved on into an entirely different era in human history. I smiled at the memories. "But somebody's about to win the 'What Is Linnaea Up To?' betting. You ready? I'm ready."

I took a deep breath as the weight of what we'd just done came crashing over me like a wave. Going to the Wall was expressly forbidden by Expedition Games, everybody knew that. Just coming within five miles was grounds for expulsion from the game. Now we were flouting that rule in the most public possible way, turning it from a sacred law to a ratings gimmick.

It was too late to turn back. I put my hand on the Wall, enjoying its coolness in the growing heat of the day.

"We're at the Wall," I told my camera. "It took about two and half days from Wyatt Falls. There's a huge forest, and the trees—well, I'll do a lecture on that soon. But for now, yeah, here we are. This is the Wall. We're not supposed to be here, but so far we haven't seen anything worth hiding."

I faced the camera head-on. "Now, I need to shut off for a minute, but don't go anywhere. I'll be right back, I promise."

As I turned around to ask Noah to shut off my stream, Cass threw her arms around me in a hug that squeezed all the breath from my lungs. She was somehow simultaneously hugging me and jumping up and down, squealing. Over her bouncing shoulder I could see Magpie and Noah sharing a serious handshake, which quickly became a hug of its own when Magpie pulled Noah in and thumped him on the back. There were tears in both boys' eyes. Finally, I pushed Cass away, my hands on her shoulders.

"Did we—" was all I managed before the other three members of Hearthhammer began shouting all at once.

"We're number one—" Magpie was shaking his head in wonder, his eyes wide.

"You did it! You did it!" Cass looked like she was about to hug me again, but instead she just slapped my shoulder. "You're a genius, Em. I never would have thought—you're a genius!"

"Look, look, look—" That was Noah, shoving the handheld into my hands. My screen was up, showing a bright red line swooping up in a steep climb and leveling out at the very top of the graph. Digital fireworks were just dying away, trickling down under fake gravity to the bottom of the screen, where the words CONGRATULATIONS! YOU ARE THE #1 STREAMER IN THE WORLD! burned in red.

The green NEW MESSAGES line was lit up as well and the counter next to it was ticking higher and higher with every passing second. I had thousands of messages and more were

217

flooding in as I watched. Suddenly the handheld displayed an alert I'd never seen before, which took over the entire screen: PRIORITY MESSAGE. PLEASE OPEN.

Alarmed, I tapped the alert. A message from Uncharted Territory opened on the screen.

```
Go over the Wall.

Dave
```

My breath caught in my throat, and I felt pinprick tears start in the corners of my eyes. I hit REPLY.

```
That wasn't the deal. We hit #1.

L
```

The response came in almost instantly.

```
New deal. You want the money, go over
the Wall. Not joking.
```

In a daze, I passed the handheld to Cass.

"What is it?" she said, glancing down at the screen, where my chain of messages with Dave Davies still showed. "Oh, shit. Is he for real?"

"I think so," I said.

"What is it?" Noah asked.

"Dave from Uncharted," I said. "He says we have to go over the Wall if we want the endorsement deal."

"If we do it, will he pay Keats's bills?" Noah asked.

"Yeah," I said. "I think."

"Then we should do it," Noah said.

"What's out there?" Magpie asked.

"I don't know," I said. "Nobody knows except Expedition, and apparently it was worth building a Wall to keep us from finding out."

"He's playing us," Cass said. "You guys seriously can't see that? We did everything he wanted and now he's stringing us along for more." She shook her head. "Look, we're all desperate to find some way to help my dad. You have no idea how bad... but this guy is using it against us. He's never going to give us what we want, can't you see that? I'm not dancing for some marketing jackass anymore. I say no way." She folded her arms. "Magpie?"

"I'll do whatever Emma wants," Magpie said, giving me an apologetic half-smile.

"Yuck," said Cass. "Okay, Linnaea, that's one for and one against. You're the superstar, you decide."

I already knew the answer.

★★★

Anticlimax followed, as we all turned our cameras on and set out along the Wall, looking for anywhere that we might cross it. The smooth, fitted stone was unclimbable, and the blank gray rock at the foot of the Wall offered no trees that might help us up. As we walked, I tried to keep my audience entertained with my thoughts on the terrain of the last few days. I even mentioned our run-in with the rangers, though I left out the details of our escape, saying only that we'd slipped away in the night and fled north.

In the end, in was pure luck that made our plan possible. As we slogged along the Wall we saw a break in its clean, gray line about a mile ahead. We spent the next fifteen minutes debating what it could be, until we finally came close enough to realize that, against all odds and all logic, the Wall simply ended.

Cass thought it must have been knocked down by a storm, and I was inclined to agree, until we reached the spot where the Wall petered out. It wasn't a clean line, as though the builders had decided they'd come far enough and finished the project, but it also wasn't a jagged hole smashed by a stormborne tree or rolling boulder.

The Wall was still under construction.

Huge blocks of neatly-cut stone stood all around, and on the far side of the Wall, a wooden scaffold was raised where the builders must have just finished placing the highest blocks of the most recent stack. A single gray cube stood flush with the end of the Wall, clearly the first to be placed in a new column.

"Okay, uh…" I stared at the black eye of my camera, which stared back. "Well, we found a way past the Wall. It looks like Expedition is still working on it. So, we're just going to go around, I guess. Here we go."

I went first, with Cass and Magpie close behind me and Noah watching our backs, his sword drawn. I clutched a copper coin in my right hand, ready to start a fireball rolling at the first sign of danger.

Instead, we found a camp. It was set only a hundred yards back from the Wall, and was far larger than the little campsites we'd made on our journey. It reminded me of the nomad camps of the ancient Mongols: five large tents, all brightly painted in different colors, stood around a large central fire pit. The tents were made from thick canvas on long wooden poles, substantial but clearly moveable.

"It's deserted," Cass said, lowering her bow, and then the flap of the nearest tent opened and an elf stepped out.

There was nothing else he could be. He was tall, maybe six and a half feet, with thin, pale features and long pointed ears that swept back from his head. His hair was long and bone-white, almost a match for his skin. In high boots, tight pants, and a loose sort of half-toga of rich purple cloth, he looked just like the art we'd seen scattered around the Summerlands, though I noted that he didn't have any spots.

"Holy shit," Noah said.

"Put your weapons down," I said, and they did. The elf watched us from the mouth of his tent, his face a blank. The copper piece was hidden in my right hand as I stepped forward and raised my left in greeting.

"Hello," I said.

The elf ducked back into his tent, and I made out a few faint words in the musical language we called Elvish. He reappeared a moment later, accompanied by a second elf dressed similarly, but with a long golden vest over his outfit.

I pointed to the Wall behind me. "Are you building that? Did you build the Wall?"

The first elf's eyebrows went up in a surprisingly human gesture. He raised his left hand with the palm towards us, reminding me of the carving we'd seen in the forest, and spoke. His voice was like a song, flowing through what had to be words and sentences with no indication where one ended and the next began. The cadence was familiar—it was the same language that we used for magic, I was sure of that—but the words were alien and inscrutable.

I shook my head and tried to look apologetic.

Now the second elf leaned in and murmured something in the ear of the first. As he spoke, he held his right hand up with the back facing the first elf in a posture that looked somehow commanding and subordinate simultaneously. He indicated us a few times with nods of his head and at one point they both paused their conversation to give us a long, appraising look. The second elf finished his speech with a sort of half-bow and a sweep of his hand back down to his side. A look flickered over the face of the first that, if he had been human, I would have pegged as guarded annoyance.

The first elf shouted something, a single word, I thought, and the camp came to life. From the tents came more elves, with long, curved swords and bows of red and purple heartwood, another dozen in all. At the edges of my vision I could see the other members of Hearthhammer readying their own weapons. Cass lay an arrow on her bow as Noah raised his sword warily. Magpie had his hands on the knives in his belt.

"Wait," I said. "We don't want to fight. We just want to talk to you."

The first elf cocked his head at an elegant angle and spoke again, but all I could do was stare back blankly. He took a languorous breath, the nostrils of his long nose flaring, then glanced at the elf in the gold vest who still stood attentively at his side. That elf said something solemn, and the face of the first

221

hardened. He looked back at me, catching my gaze and holding it with mismatched eyes of blue and green.

Then he barked out a command, and all around us, the elves attacked.

I fell back as the archers loosed a flight of arrows that fell just short of us—a warning shot, maybe?—peppering the ground with long, red-fletched shafts.

"Form up!" I shouted. Noah darted forward, sword in hand, and Magpie joined him, putting himself between me and the camp. Cass nocked her arrow as I began to roll my copper piece over my fingers, murmuring the Elvish magic words as quickly as I dared.

Another rain of arrows fell, all of them landing neatly behind us this time. The message was clear. But if the elves expected us to surrender, they were disappointed, because Cass responded to the arrows with one of her own. It flickered out in a laser-straight line to slice the cheek of the elf in the golden vest, who slapped a hand to his face that came away smeared with blue-green blood.

"Dammit!" Cass grunted as she pulled another arrow from her quiver. The two elven leaders backed away as four swordsmen advanced, spreading out to try and surround us more surely than the archers could. Magpie turned warily, both his daggers gleaming in white-knuckled hands; Noah stood stoically with his sword in a ready position.

The swordsmen dashed in, moving faster than I'd ever seen a human move. They split into pairs; one duo came straight at Magpie and Noah while the other cut around to come straight at Cass. As much as I hated the idea of fighting the elves only minutes after we'd met them, the threat was obvious. All we had to do was survive long enough to escape; then we could try to lose them on our side of the Wall. And if a fight with elves didn't satisfy Dave Davies, it would be time to give up.

The first pair of elves hit the boys in a whirlwind of blades. The grace of the elves was incredible; they moved together like dancers, if those dancers were identical twins who had practiced together every day of their lives. One cut low as the other slashed high, then they spun back-to-back and came apart to dart their swords around Noah's guard, pricking him in the arms. Magpie tried to counterattack with his daggers, but each stab at one elf was blocked by the other, as though every motion had been choreographed beforehand. As the boys fell back in the face of the coordinated onslaught, it was all they could do to keep from being cut to ribbons.

I had to look away as the other pair of elves came at Cass and me. Cass loosed an arrow at them. With a flick of his sword, one of the elves cut it out of the air. Cass's mouth hung open as we watched the two halves of the arrow spin away to either side of the advancing swordsmen. She stood as still as if she'd been enchanted, a new arrow dangling from one hand and her bow held limply in the other.

The copper piece was still rolling over my fingers, almost under its own power, and I suddenly realized that it was blazing hot. The elves raised their blades for a dual slash at Cass, and I flicked the coin at them, hoping to force them back with the explosion even if I didn't hurt them outright. It whistled past Cass's shoulder, making a red smear across my vision.

Then it stopped, hanging in midair.

The swordsmen split around the frozen coin and came back together as Cass raised her bow in a desperate attempt to stop the coming swords, which chopped the bow into three pieces and swept down to bite through her leather armor, cutting deep into both shoulders. Cass dropped to her knees, her eyes wide, her mouth moving in silent shock.

I put my hands up, trying to show that they were empty, but one elf wrenched his sword from Cass's shoulder and swept towards me, raising his weapon. I dropped to my knees and ducked my head behind my raised arms as the sword came down. It bit into my right arm with a *thwack* and hit bone. There was a flash of cold, and then a searing burn like a line of lightning as blood ran down to drip off my elbows. Tears blurred my vision as the elf raised his sword again, spraying blood in the sunlight.

The commander barked a single, sharp word and the swordsman lowered his weapon. I crumpled over, holding my shattered arm. From my bed on the stone I could see Magpie on his knees; one elf stood with a sword at his throat as the other disarmed Noah with a flickering twist, sending his sword spinning to skitter across the ground a few yards away.

Beyond the boys, the two commanding elves stood watching the fight with impassive faces. The elf in the golden vest had his left hand up with two fingers raised, then made a flicking motion as though shooing a fly or brushing dust from his shoulder. My paralyzed coin flew off to one side and burst harmlessly in the distance.

After that, it was just a matter of mop-up. Cass was conscious, but her face was pale and she couldn't stand under her own power. Two elves hauled her to the center of camp and dumped her on the stone, where she sat slumped to one side, breathing shallowly. They tied the rest of us up with slender rope that bit into my wrists as they pulled it tight and looped it around my upper arms until I could hardly breathe, let alone act. My ruined right arm hung dripping at my side.

They sat us near Cass, then ignored us as they set about catching our hovering drones with nets of the same tough material as the rope. As they dragged the buzzing machines to the ground, I thought they would smash them, but instead they tied them all up into a sack and tossed them into the commanders' tent.

I felt a hollow blossom of loss in my chest as I watched my drone disappear. It was my lifeline to the outside world, but more than that, I'd grown sort of attached to the little thing. It had been a faithful companion through all the madness of the last month, and if not for its camera, Hearthhammer would still have been scraping for coins with the other adventurers in Wellpoint, hoping to make enough for food and shelter and wondering how we could afford to send any home to Keats. In my pain-wracked state, the loss of the drone felt as momentous as Jason's death, and I sobbed openly.

After a few self-pitying minutes, I tried to rally my smeared senses. If only we could survive this, I told myself, we'd be okay. I didn't need Noah to tell me that the ratings on our little scrap with the elves, however terrible it had been, would be through the roof. Our discovery would change everything; we just had to make it home to reap the rewards. That the elves hadn't killed us outright was surely a good sign; the only reason my head was still attached to my body was that the one in charge had reined in his warrior. And hadn't the commander almost seemed like he would have preferred a conversation to a fight...?

The soldiers came back for us eventually, yanking us roughly to our feet and indicating that we should start walking away from the Wall, deeper into the unknown. I felt a wave of exhaustion crash over me, but came out from under it suddenly as Cass lost her balance and stumbled into me, sending a sharp lance of pain up my arm. It was all I could do to keep my feet as she slumped against my shoulder. Her eyes were bloodshot, her face as white as a skull, and her voice barely a whisper.

"Good job, superstar."

The elves detailed to help her along grabbed her and pulled her away. I glanced around and realized Noah and Magpie were gone, and as I watched, Cass was dragged off in one direction as prodding swords forced me to go another. Stripped of our weapons and gear, relieved of our drones, battered and bloodied and defeated, we were now being separated.

THE BLACK CANDLE

"At least they gave you a candle," Jason said.

"Two would have been nice," I whispered. There was just one candle in my cell, and otherwise it was darkness. I'd stared at the tiny, flickering flame for so long that it was burned into my vision. I saw it when I closed my eyes, a white smear against black, and when I slept I dreamed of it.

"How much has it burned down?" Jason asked. He stood over me, visible despite my blindness.

"Stop asking me that." I rolled onto my side to face the wall. "I don't know how long candles are supposed to burn, I don't know how tall it is, and I don't know how long I've been here."

"Don't get mad." Jason knelt and put a hand on my cheek, but I couldn't feel it. "You're burning up."

"They made us walk…" I paused as a violent shiver racked my body. My shirt and breeches, the only things the elves had left me with, were damp with sweat. "They made us walk for a day. To their war camp. My arm hurts."

"What did it look like?" Jason whispered.

"My arm?"

"No, Emma. The war camp. Describe it to me."

I took a long breath, finding the strength to speak. "Big. So big. It filled the whole valley. Lines of… of tents, all different colors. And so many campfires in the dusk."

"That's bad," Jason said.

"What's happening?" I rolled back to look at Jason, who crouched over me. He looked just as he had on the day he'd died, but his eyes were hollow. "It's off the rails. Why?"

"You tell me."

"I made them go over the Wall," I whispered. "I could have told Dave Davies no. I should have…" I laughed wheezily, but it turned into a cough. "…said I'd sue. Breach of contract."

"Good luck finding a lawyer in the Summerlands." Jason smiled.

"Okay. Okay. But it was my idea to go to the Wall. Getting viewers instead of treasure."

"The party agreed."

"My idea. Starting with my mistake. I gave Dr Agony everything."

"Cass was mad," Jason agreed. "She's party leader, after all."

"Not me," I said.

"Not you."

I lay shivering in silence for a while, watching Jason pace the confines of the cell. He paused at the candle, which burned with a still, straight flame.

"Starting with my mistake." My voice sounded far away even in my own ears.

"You said that." Jason turned away from the candle, but it wasn't Jason, it was Jamie Bullard, the hunting knife in one white-knuckled hand, the other reaching out to take my paycard. "You got me in a lot of trouble. You should have kept your mouth shut."

He kneeled in front of my face, Jason again. "You should have kept your mouth shut. Porter found me because you made me come to the police station. He was hired to kill me and you helped him do it. Why?"

"I'm sorry," I said.

"Why did he kill me?"

"The file Terra sent you."

"*Why?*"

227

The door opened with a click, and I flinched away from the light. A blurred shadow with long ears placed something on the floor of the cell, then paused as it straightened up. I blinked away tears and the scene swam into focus long enough for me to understand that he had stopped to look at the candle. It was tall, the length of my forearm, and jet black. The elf glanced from the candle to me, then shut the door.

In the returned darkness I felt my way over to the bowl of food the elf had put down. There were no utensils, so I touched it gingerly and found my fingers in a lukewarm sort of porridge. I shoveled a handful into my mouth, then realized I had no appetite at all and let it slop back into the bowl. I set the bowl down and returned to watching the candle, alone.

★★★

Jason never came back.

The same elf brought me food every so often. I thought he was coming twice a day, but that was little better than a guess. Each time, he would check the candle and glance at me before shutting the door. I was no threat, that was obvious, and no escape risk. I forced myself to eat, but my arm was still ruined, and my fever hadn't broken. The candle, though, it was burning down, slowly but surely. It was a bit lower every time my captor checked it, a bit more misshapen with dripping wax. There was a sense of impending doom about the black candle, as though it were counting down to something terrible that would occur when it finally gave up and died.

On one visit, I tried to start a conversation. My voice was raw and whispery as I asked where I was, how long it had been, why I was being held like this. The elf only shook his head and said something in his own musical tongue.

I thought back to my first public lecture, when I'd said we were all speaking Elvish to each other. Obviously it was some magical effect of the Summerlands, but there was a real biting irony to the fact that while I could communicate flawlessly with somebody who'd grown up speaking Icelandic or Greek or anything else from Earth, Elvish itself remained as alien and incomprehensible as ever.

★★★

I kept my eyes shut as the door opened. I'd learned to recognize the scrape of the lock, the scuffle of feet in the hallway beyond, and knew better than to let the light dazzle me and start tears in my eyes again.

So I jolted painfully in surprise when something touched my shoulder. It was a gentle touch by a warm hand, accompanied by something murmured in Elvish. That wasn't the voice of the elf who'd been bringing me food, though; it was new yet familiar.

I opened my eyes. Looming over me was the outline of an elf crouched before me, silhouetted against the flame of a torch stuck in the dirt floor of my cell. Behind him sat a leather case about the size of a shoebox. As my vision cleared and my eyes adjusted, I realized he was the elf who'd commanded the camp we'd stumbled on just beyond the Wall.

He said something and touched my arm, the shattered one. He obviously wanted to examine it. I inched my way up into a sitting position with my back against the wall across from the door, then straightened my arm in a moment of teeth-gritting pain.

The elf nodded, his eyes on mine, then bowed his head and began to examine my wound. His concern was obvious, a human expression on alien features. In the torchlight, I could see that the gash was badly infected. There was a white flash as he prodded the cut gently and I bit my lip to keep from swooning when I realized I was looking at my own exposed bone.

The elf caught my eye and pointed to the black-and-purple flesh of the infection. He made a short chopping motion with his hand, which I interpreted to mean that he wanted to cut away the infected flesh. I forced myself to nod, hoping that my face didn't show the sick fear welling up in my stomach.

He drew a slender wand of purple heartwood from his belt and pointed it at my arm, which he still had clamped in his other hand. His eyes flickered up to catch mine for one last affirmation that I understood what was about to happen.

"Cleave," he said.

A line of magic cut into my arm like an invisible scalpel, slicing away the throbbing necrotic flesh. I hissed in pain and shut my eyes, searching my mind for anything to think of but the meat falling away in black chunks from my wound.

My thoughts clamped onto a single word, which I had just heard spoken. *Cleave.* It was the same spell Noah had cast when we were fighting the hitmen at the bridge, and then as now, I'd understood the word. It wasn't like speaking English on Earth, and it wasn't like hearing Magpie speak Greek here in the Summerlands. It was Elvish, in its original, unaltered, unmagicked form.

Understanding went off in my head like a camera flash. It made no sense at all, and yet, at the same time, under the illogical laws of magic it made absolutely perfect sense. I had gotten so close to the truth in my lecture.

In the Summerlands, every spoken language became Elvish and from there, became understood. Whatever deep magic worked this miracle was clearly for benefit of the denizens of the Summerlands, who spoke Elvish already... any language put into the black box of the spell would come out handily translated, except Elvish itself!

And yet all this time, all these weeks, I'd been hearing Elvish spoken day in and day out by everyone I met. Sure, it had been translated before it hit my brain, but the words underlying the ideas were all in the language of the Summerlands. I'd never had to pay attention, never had to care, but the words had been there all along. Which meant they were somewhere in the hazy blue ocean of my memory, if only I could fish them out. I had to start small, with something simple, something I'd heard plenty of times. If I could hook onto that, I might be able to pull up the whole lexicon.

"*Eme Linnaea as,*" I said. *I am Linnaea.*

The elf looked up, his eyes wide, his arched brows high. The hand with the wand froze, and his grip on my arm tightened.

"*Emeas Scytri*," he said. The verb form was different, but it was obviously just a variant. *I am...* a doctor? No, it had to be a proper noun, his name. *I am Scytri.*

I glanced down at my arm. Not only was the infection gone, but the gash as well. The skin was tight and shiny, as though he'd closed a tear in a lump of clay by smoothing it with his thumb.

"*Atka... atka as ven.*" That was *thank you*, or something like it. Scytri laughed, a genuine sound accompanied by a genuine smile. Something I'd said was funny to him, but he wasn't laughing at me. He tucked away his wand and held up his right hand, palm facing me.

"It is my duty to help," he said, using a phrasing I'd thought was just *you're welcome* but was clearly something more complicated. "The work"—work? duty? healing?—"is done."

"I am glad you understand me," I said, though it took me the better part of a minute to put the sentence together.

"We always understood you." Scytri smiled. "You did not understand us."

"Magic makes you understand?" I asked.

"Yes," he said. "But magic does not work the same for your people."

"No," I agreed. "Why did you attack us?"

Scytri looked away. "We had to. I regret it."

"I do, too," I said. "We don't want to fight you."

There was a long silence as Scytri sat back on his haunches regarding me.

"What is the candle?" I finally asked. Scytri glanced back at the black candle, which was still burning and looked to have lost about two thirds of its height.

"An implement of judgment and *asteri*," he said.

231

"*Asteri*?" I echoed, shaking my head. I didn't recognize the word. Scytri's brow furrowed.

"A time for thought," he said at last. "To consider what you have done wrong and, if you want to, to repent."

"When the candle burns down, the time is up?"

"Yes." Scytri nodded. "And then you are taken to the Eldest for judgment."

We lapsed into silence again. It felt stingingly unfair that I should be judged for doing nothing wrong. Things had gone so horribly askew that I found my mind sliding away from any contemplation of what that judgment might mean for me and my friends, if they were even still alive. I found myself in sudden desperate need of small-talk.

"What do your people call yourselves?" I asked.

"We call ourselves people," Scytri said, using the same word I had. "Why? What do you call yourselves?"

"People," I admitted. Scytri laughed. "Or humans, maybe that's better. We call you elves."

"What does it mean?" Scytri asked.

I blinked. I'd never really thought about it before. "It's an old word in our language. Elves are... creatures like people, but magical."

"Do they look like us?"

"Well, they're not real," I said. "They're..." I had no idea what the word for mythical was, or legendary, or imaginary. "They weren't real until we found the Summerlands. We thought we were alone."

"So did we, until your people came." Scytri shook his head. "My children would be amazed to learn that I'm speaking with a human."

"Children?" I repeated.

"Yes." Scytri raised his chin, a proud motion. "Two sons. I haven't seen them in a year, since I was sent to the Wall."

"You must miss them," I said. Scytri's eyes were shadowed in the torchlight, and I thought suddenly of Keats and the tired smile he wore whenever the topic of his single fatherhood came up.

Behind Scytri, the door swung open, almost clipping the torch he'd stuck into the ground. In the light from the hall stood the elf in the long golden vest who'd been there when Scytri's men attacked us. He raised his right hand, with the back facing Scytri.

"I would like to know if your work is finished," he said.

Scytri raised his left hand, palm forward, in a gesture of thinly-veiled annoyance. "She is healed. She will be ready for judgment by the Eldest."

"I am glad to hear it," said the other elf. "I must say, I do not see the purpose in using your talents on her. Her judgment will surely be death."

"Until then, she is our guest," Scytri replied.

The gold-clad elf gave me a long looked from narrowed eyes. I stared back, trying my best to look ignorant and innocent. He pursed his lips, then turned back to the door. The black candle caught his eye, and he examined it with exaggerated interest.

"Not long now, I would say."

"Do you need anything else?" said Scytri.

The elf moved out into the hallway, then turned, his right hand raised again. "Thank you for your time." He shut the door with a decisive click.

"Who is he?" I asked.

"He is Eneri," said Scytri. "He serves the Eldest. Come, can you stand?"

He knelt and put a hand on my shoulder just as he'd stirred me earlier. I wondered if he woke his sons the same way when they overslept.

"I think so," I said. My head still felt hollow and airy, like an overfilled balloon, and I was punch drunk, almost giddy, with relief at the lack of pain.

I stood uncertainly and followed Scytri into the hall, squinting against the light of torches that guttered along the wall. The whole structure seemed to be made of wood, roughly cut and hastily assembled. I would have sworn that my cell had walls of cold, damp stone, but now I wasn't so sure.

Scytri closed the door of my cell gently behind us and we set out down the short corridor, passing half a dozen identical doors on both sides.

"Are my friends in there?" I asked.

"I do not know," Scytri replied.

"Where are we going?" We reached a heavy, iron-banded door at the end of the hall, which Scytri opened to reveal a long dirt tunnel leading sharply upwards, with a rough, crumbling staircase cut into its floor. I vaguely remembered being hauled down similar stairs in a feverish haze when I was first taken captive. We ascended and passed through an archway into bright sunlight. The exit had been cut directly into the side of a low, grassy hill, and elven guards stood stony-faced on either side.

We were in the military camp I'd seen on our approach, near the back of a valley made by two high stone ridges. Colored canvas tents filled the intervening flatland from ridge to ridge, and stretched farther than I could see in front of us. Unlike the little camp we'd seen near the Wall, which had been dead and still until Scytri appeared, this one bustled with activity all around us. Tall elven soldiers in long shirts of painted chain mail sat by cookfires, conferred at the flaps of tents, and sat buffing the rust from their long, curved swords and gleaming spears with long shafts of magic-resistant blood oak. The chatter of Elvish sounded everywhere like a forest full of birdsong.

We set off down the central aisle of the camp, a dirt path that had been pounded as hard as stone by thousands of passing feet. Most of the soldiers ignored us, but some stared openly at me as we passed. I hadn't felt so watched since the day I'd gone to the police station with Keats. I much preferred the anonymous viewership of my stream.

"Where are we going?" I asked Scytri as we turned off the main path into a cul-de-sac made from a dozen tents painted with bright images of harpies pierced with arrows.

"To speak with my progenitor," he replied. A few soldiers hailed him with their right hands, and he replied with his left, like a general returning a salute.

"Is that the Eldest?"

Scytri stopped and turned on me; his gray eyes caught me and held me pinned like a bug under a magnifying glass.

"No," he said. "You will see the Eldest when the candle burns down."

"Then who's the progenitor?"

"*My* progenitor." Scytri started off down the muddy path again, talking as he went. "The Eldest leads us all. My progenitor leads my *imru*."

"*Imru?*" That was a new one.

"The *imru* is the progenitor and all his children, and their children, and so on."

"So the Eldest is like a… high chieftain?" I had to use the English words, but Scytri seemed to understand. "Is he a progenitor, too?"

"He can be. The Eldest is a title, given to the oldest person who leads an *imru*, but he need not be the progenitor of that *imru*. Whichever *imru* has the oldest progenitor is the most esteemed, but not every *imru* has a living progenitor. Certainly not anymore. You see?"

I didn't really, but we seemed to have reached our destination, which was a tent at the back of the cul-de-sac. It was remarkably plain compared to the others, with no decoration, though it was easily the largest of the group. Scytri greeted the guards who stood holding spears on either side of the open flap, then ducked into the tent.

I followed him and found myself in a dim, cool space where a single elf stood over a table covered in maps and papers. He turned as we came in and I nearly gasped. His face was pitted with scars like little divots taken from his flesh and his right eye was swollen and droopy. Otherwise he showed no signs of being any older or more infirm than the other elves I'd seen. He wore the same mail armor as his soldiers, with a long red vest over it.

Scytri approached him and raised both hands, palms forward; the other elf touched the backs of his hands to Scytri's palms in greeting. They exchanged a few murmured words, then the progenitor's eyes drifted over Scytri's shoulder to me.

"Welcome, Linnaea," he said. His voice was husky and soft. "It has been nearly a decade since I've seen one of your people. I am sorry we had to meet under such circumstances."

"I'm honored," I replied. "I think we got off on the wrong foot with your people."

"The wrong foot?" The progenitor cocked his head.

"A human expression," I said, and the progenitor smiled. "It means, um… we had a bad first meeting. Which I would like to fix."

"As would I." The progenitor turned back to his papers, and waved for me to join him. "As you can see, we are planning a war."

I took in the pile of maps and orders written in neat Elvish script. Translating any of the writing would have taken serious effort, but the maps clearly showed the land between the Wall and Wellpoint, with geographical features like the Wyvern Peaks draw in neat black ink and a small star for the town of Wyatt Falls.

"Why are you telling me this?" I asked.

The progenitor took a long breath in through his nose and blew it out. "Do you remember when your people first came here, eight years ago?"

"Eight?" I blinked. "It's been five years."

"Five years since your second group came through," the progenitor said. "The first came three years before that."

I shook my head blankly.

"They were different from you. It was a small group of men, rough and dirty. Their weapons and armor were similar, though their language was different. They claimed the land where they came through and built a great hall in the meadows there."

Something clicked over in my memory: the Viking-looking ruin I'd seen outside Wellpoint. It all made sense, the pieces coming together in a rush. Time worked differently in the Summerlands; they'd discovered that when the First Ranger Group disappeared through the portal for three days and came back insisting they'd only been in the Summerlands for ten minutes. Expedition Games had found a way to keep the portal permanently open, forcing time to run the same in both worlds with the exception of the missing hour, but it hadn't always been that way. So if three years had passed here before humans returned—I did some quick mental math—it would have been something like a thousand years on Earth.

"You met Vikings," I said.

"Vikings?" Scytri raised an eyebrow.

"An ancient warrior culture from our world," I explained. "From a thousand years ago. Time doesn't work the same way here. What happened to them?"

"We came to greet them," the progenitor said. "All of the progenitors went—nobody wished to be left out. The meeting turned hostile, then to bloodshed. We killed them all, and returned to our *imrua*, thinking the matter had been settled. But then the plague began."

"The plague... your scars?"

The progenitor nodded. "I am the lucky one, the one who survived. I am the only living progenitor. But our society is in upheaval and the plague stills ravages our people."

"You can't cure it? Scytri fixed my arm. He saved my life."

"I can't cut away an infection I can't see." Scytri shook his head sadly. "And our callers cannot reach the spirits of the disease. It is the same with you humans, as though you have no spirits at all."

I was reminded of the times my magic had failed against other humans. Did we lack something that the creatures of the Summerlands had, something that red magic needed to latch onto? White magic seemed to work well enough, which was a mercy considering how heavily adventurers in the Summerlands relied on magical healing.

"This is all incredible," I said, "but it still doesn't explain why you're planning a war. Or why you're telling your enemy about it."

The progenitor tapped the maps in front of him. "This war is the work of the Eldest. We are sworn to obey him, but... the Eldest was given his title after the plague took all the other progenitors. He was not at the parley with the Vikings. He does not know how that moment balanced on the edge of a cliff, how a single wrong word tipped us over into killing. He sees the pain and death caused by the plague and he blames the humans. Eight years ago he set us to build a great wall in case any more of your people should come through, but the wall was not completed, so now he commands us to kill you all."

"But you don't agree," I said.

"I do not," the progenitor agreed. "I wish only for peace and an end to the plague. This is why I volunteered Scytri to guard the wall, in the hopes that when humans came, we might be the first to meet them. Of course the Eldest, suspecting my motives, sent Eneri to enforce his will. Scytri has told me how Eneri ordered him to attack you. Though we are the highest *imru*, when the Eldest speaks, even we must obey."

★★★

Scytri returned me to my cell, where the black candle had burned down to a tiny stub. Every now and then it flitted out of existence, then sprang back to life as some bit of wick or wax caught fire again.

My judgment at the hands of the Eldest was coming, soon, and from what I'd been told, I had no reason to expect mercy or reason from him. Scytri and his progenitor clearly felt powerless to resist him. I needed a plan to keep myself alive.

In the waning light of the candle I noticed a dark shape on the floor: Scytri's leather case. He'd forgotten it in his hurry to bring me to the progenitor after Eneri's visit. Squinting in surprise, I flipped it open and felt around its shadowy interior. It took me a moment to realize what I was touching, but when I did, I gasped aloud: surgical equipment, scalpels and little saws, Scytri's backup plan in case his magic hadn't worked on his human patient.

I grabbed a straight, slender knife and slipped it into my pocket just as the black candle went out.

The door opened, but it wasn't Scytri. Instead, two soldiers I didn't recognize grabbed me roughly by the arms and pulled me to my feet. As they dragged me into the hallway and shut the door, I tried to keep my body between them and Scytri's case, and if they noticed it they didn't react. I got my feet under me in the hallway and by the time we made it up the stepped tunnel to outside, the guards had let me go and were merely flanking me with swords at the ready.

It took half an hour to walk the length of the valley, during which time the sun disappeared over the western ridge and blue night came. A faint chill had crept in by the time we arrived at a tent that was more like a pavilion, huge and round with guards encircling it and torches burning in a line to the entrance like lights on a runway. My guards led me down this path and through the dark opening into the tent of the Eldest.

He stood on a low platform of blood oak, wearing a heavy robe made from patches of various muted colors. He was the only elf I'd seen who bore any signs of age, just a few lines on his face and faint crow's-feet at the corners of his eyes. His hair was glossy and black, and as long as Scytri's.

Cass, Noah, and Magpie stood at the foot of the platform, and my thoughts reeled drunkenly as I was shoved past a few spear-wielding guards to stand with Hearthammer. My friends looked up at my arrival; Magpie gave me a wan smile and Noah's face was carefully blank, but Cass stared at me with rage burning in two eyes swollen nearly shut with bruises. She had purple and green marks up and down her arms, and her shirt was torn and filthy.

The knife in my pocket felt like a stone. It seemed incredible that it hadn't dragged me to the ground with its dangerous weight, and yet there I stood, only a few feet from the Eldest, with a weapon at hand. I slipped a few fingers into my pocket and touched the knife's handle. The words of the spell I'd learned from Naila's NPC friends rose in my mind: an enchantment to give a weapon supernatural sharpness and an almost-intelligent capability for finding a target's vital spots. With it, I could turn the little surgeon's knife into a deadly weapon. All I had to do was jump onto the platform, close with the Eldest, and cut him down.

I felt the idea calling to me, drawing me like gravity, as though I'd fallen into a well headfirst with nothing left to do but watch the ground rush up to break my neck. If I survived, I would be a hero, the girl who killed the enemy general. I would carry a credibility that someone like Dr Agony, with all his little adventures under his belt, could only dream of approaching. He would be nothing next to me, a poseur.

My ratings would go through the roof.

"You are here for judgment," said the Eldest in round, deep tones. His words filled the room without him so much as raising his voice. "Your crimes are the crimes of all your people."

Another thought reared up in my mind, standing like a black stone as the foaming waves of my dreams of glory crashed and broke around it. If I killed the Eldest, it would validate every terrible thing he must be saying about humanity. The war would start with his death and it wouldn't stop until every human in the Summerlands had been cut down. I could see the curved swords of the elves rising and falling like sickles, see the flames leaping from house to house in Wellpoint, see the bodies stacked like firewood in Portal Square.

Or maybe the humans would beat back the elven army and carry the war back over the Wall. There was no telling what Expedition Games would do to protect their investment. For all their magic, the elves would be doomed the moment Apollonia Blomhaugen decided to start importing machine guns and missiles. The green grass of the Summerlands would run red as the place turned from heaven to hell.

I took my hand off the knife. If there were any chance to protect the innocence of the world we'd found, I had to take it, even if it meant my own death.

"Sepharad, Jessamine, Magpie." The Eldest spoke in tones of finality. "I sentence you to death for your crimes of violence against us. Scytri, you will carry out the sentence." I glanced over my shoulder in surprise to see that Scytri had come in behind us, Eneri at his side. Scytri hung his head obediently.

"Linnaea." The Eldest turned his gaze on me. His eyes were deep black pools. "I sentence you to act as sole survivor. You will ride to war with us and see your people slain, then carry the news back to your world."

I tried to face him, to stare back without fear, but I couldn't. I lowered my eyes.

"Scytri, Eneri, Teneru, Imhan." The elves he named straightened to attention. "If these humans have found us, others cannot be far behind. We must go to war immediately. Make ready to ride in the morning. And Scytri... do not shirk your duties."

★★★

Scytri and his soldiers brought us back to his *imru*'s corner of the camp. Hearthhammer walked in silence, afraid to meet each other's eyes. I wanted desperately to apologize, to try to explain. But every time I found myself about to speak, I remembered that telling my story would mean admitting that I could understand the elves, and that would mean telling Noah, Cass, and Magpie that they were sentenced to die while I survived.

The decision was taken out of my hands as soon as we entered the tent of Scytri's progenitor. The plague-scarred elf beckoned us to his table and took my hands.

"I have been told of your sentence," he said. "I am sorry."

"I'm worried about my friends," I said.

"We will see what we can do for them," the progenitor replied. "Though I do not know that it will matter in the end."

241

"Um, Linnaea?" That was Cass, leaning around Magpie, who stood open-mouthed, and waving for my attention. "Em? Emma?"

"Yes," I said. "Sorry."

"Can you speak Elvish?" Noah asked.

"A bit," I admitted.

"Her speech is very good," said Scytri in Elvish.

"What did he say?" said Noah.

"He said I'm pretty good at Elvish."

"Uh, are you guys friends?" Cass asked. "What exactly is happening right now? Who was that old guy? Are we in trouble?"

"Yeah," I said. "We are. And I'm so sorry, because—"

"*You speak Elvish?*" Magpie burst out. He began to laugh. "How? How? You're a genius! We've only been here a month!"

"I just listened," I said, feeling my face flush.

"You just listened." Magpie shook his head. "Unbelievable."

"I believe you were in the middle of apologizing," said Cass tightly.

I put a hand on Magpie's chest and pushed him gently out of the way so I could face Cass head on.

"I should have listened to you," I said. "A bunch of times. I got... I was really enjoying success."

"You think?" One eyebrow stood in a dire arch on Cass's face.

"Too much," I said. "It's addictive, I guess, I don't know. That's no excuse. We decided years ago that you were party leader, but then we got here and I just thought I could do a better job than you, and... now we're in so much trouble."

Cass's superior expression collapsed as she took my hands. "You *did* do a better job than me."

I laughed in disbelief. "Are you *kidding?*"

"I tried, believe me," she said. "But I choked. Every time. If I can't lead when it counts, I can't lead at all."

"You led us for five years," Noah said.

"He's right," I said. "We wouldn't be here if not for you. You made us learn how to fight, cast spells, survive in the wilderness... we all wanted to give up sometimes, but you never doubted yourself, not once."

"Until Jason died." Cass let go of my hands. "Don't you get it? He died trying to save me from my own stupid decisions. If I'd listened to him and run, he'd still be alive. Every time we're in danger I see him lying there on the kitchen floor... and I remember that I've got no goddamn right to tell anyone what to do."

I threw my arms around her and pulled her close as I tried to think of something, anything, I could say to take her pain away. How could I apologize for not seeing what she was going through all this time? How could I show her that out of everyone touched by Jason's death, not one of us blamed her? How could I possibly explain why on the day Cass and I met, just two six-year-olds on the block, I'd sworn in my heart to follow her to the end of the Earth?

"What kind of trouble?" asked Noah.

"What?" I blinked.

"You said we were in so much trouble," Noah said. "What kind?"

I let Cass go and though I didn't know whether the tears gleaming on her cheek were hers or mine, there was tiny fraction of a smile beneath them, and it was enough.

"The Eldest," I said to Noah. "That old elf who judged us. He sentenced the three of you to... to death." I shook my head. "He spared me, God knows why."

"Sole survivor," said Magpie. We all turned; I know I'd nearly forgotten he was there. "One person picked to warn everyone else. The families used to do it after a big purge..." His eyes widened in horrified understanding. "They're going to kill everybody."

"That's the plan." I couldn't look at him. "They're attacking tomorrow."

"If I might interrupt," said Scytri politely.

"What did he say?" asked Cass and Noah together.

"We have no desire to execute anyone," Scytri continued. "We can hide your friends for the time being, until we can find a way for them to escape."

"It is only delaying the inevitable," said the progenitor. There was a sort of scolding tone in his voice, like a teacher correcting a student who should know better. "When we reach the human city, the Eldest will demand we slaughter them all. The war will reach you all eventually."

"Yes, Progenitor," agreed Scytri. "But surely it is preferable to delay."

"Surely." The progenitor's mouth angled in a half-smile.

"What if we could stop the war before it started?" I said.

"I would if it were possible," said the progenitor. "In the name of peace, I am willing to defy the commands of the Eldest, as you see. But even if we were to raise our swords in open rebellion, it would not be enough. We are only one *imru*. It is true, we are the most revered. Perhaps others who do not want war would follow our example; in these times, it is impossible to know. But there would never be enough and we would be slaughtered along with your people."

"I'm not talking about a revolution," I said. "I just need a chance to talk to my people. I'm sure I can make them see."

"Then they will be cut down," Scytri said.

"Do the elves really want a fight?" I asked. Scytri looked away, but the progenitor kept his steady gaze on me.

"The Eldest does," he said. "You must remember as well that the first battle with humans is only eight years gone. The wounds are fresh. The plague is still found in some *imru*. The acts of your ancestors were not so long ago for us."

I squared my shoulders, steadying myself for my final pitch. "What if we could cure the plague?"

244

That one landed: Scytri looked up with wide eyes and the progenitor's hand made a claw that crumpled the papers on his table.

"What did you say?" asked Cass.

"Sorry, sorry," I said. "Here, I'll speak English. They can understand it, they just can't speak it."

"Oh my God." Cass buried her face in her hand. "Magic."

"Progenitor," I said in English, "ever since I saw your scars, I've been trying to place why they were so familiar. I finally realized it's not something we have on Earth anymore— I've seen those scars in a history book. The Vikings who came here carried something we call smallpox."

"And there is a cure?" Scytri's gray eyes glittered in the dimness of the tent.

"The disease was eradicated sixty years before I was born," I said.

"If you bring us this cure, war can be avoided," said the progenitor. "How swiftly can you get it?"

"Well, that's the problem," I said. "The company—there are people who control entrance to this world. They won't let me just bring the cure in. I'll have to convince them."

"How?" asked Scytri.

"I don't know," I admitted.

The progenitor sighed. As he leaned on his table, his eyes were on the many maps and orders there, the physical manifestation of the war he didn't want to fight. Finally, he looked at me.

"We have been extremely liberal in our treatment of you," he said. "Would you agree?"

"I'm very grateful," I said. "We're lucky you're the ones who caught us."

"I am grateful as well." The progenitor shook his head. "But hospitality and trust have their limits. You tell me everything I wish to hear and that makes me wary."

"It's all true," I said. "Please believe me."

"I want to, I admit it. But you must see that it is all a little too easy."

I snorted. "We'll see how easy it is when we get to Wellpoint."

The progenitor showed a hint of a smile at that. "Can you make some proof of your good faith?"

"I'll do anything," I said. "I just don't know... wait." I touched my pocket, where Scytri's knife still sat. I slipped it out and showed it to the elves, trying my best to look nonthreatening. "Scytri, you left your surgery tools in my cell. I pocketed this before we were taken to see the Eldest. And I'll admit... I thought about using it on him." Unexpected guilt welled up in my chest, and I looked away. "But it just seemed like the wrong thing to do."

"You thought to attack the Eldest with a surgeon's knife?" Scytri's brow was furrowed. "You would have thrown away your life for nothing."

"Well, I had a trick up my sleeve," I said. I shifted my grip on the knife and began to chant the words of the enchantment I'd been taught. As I spoke, a proud scientist's voice in the back of my mind pointed out that the musical magic words were just an antiquated form of Elvish, not so different from the language I'd mastered. Far from nonsense, the spell was actually a sort of polite request that the warrior spirit inside the knife give up some of itself in return for victory.

Apparently, the spirit was interested, because the edge of the blade began to gleam with a wicked blue sharpness. I could feel the eagerness of the knife to be used, to cut and spill blood. For a fleeting moment I felt the urge to drop it, lest I end up using it, but I got a grip on my thoughts and offered the glowing knife to the progenitor.

"This is what I would have used on the Eldest," I said. "But I didn't. I think we can win this war without bloodshed."

The progenitor took the knife gingerly and tested its edge with his thumb. He showed a flash of teeth as a line of blue blood stood out, then dripped a single drop onto the table. He stabbed the knife into the blood oak surface with a resonant *thunk*; it stood quivering next to the blue stain as its glow evaporated.

The progenitor put his right hand up, facing me. His palm was smeared with blue.

"May that be the last drop spilled."

SPIRIT CALLER

I tried to look defeated and dejected as my wheeled iron cage rattled along behind an elven wagon, itself pulled by four giant birds with iridescent black feathers. It wasn't too tough an acting challenge; there was barely room in the cage to sit down, so I'd been stuck in various stress positions for the last day and a half. So far, being a pretend prisoner was almost as bad as being a real one.

At least I had fresh air, though. The Eldest had ordered that, in my role as sole survivor, I be given a front-row view of the massive elven war effort. Thus my rolling cage was smack in the center of the elven column that tromped its winding way south from the Wall towards Wyatt Falls. Neat rectangles of infantry marched to either side, protecting a line of wagons that stretched apparently to infinity ahead of and behind me. As we passed between the pin-straight trees of the neatly gridded forest, I wondered what exactly the elves were afraid of. I certainly hadn't seen anything strong enough to take on their army.

My cage bumped over a rut in the dirt, making me bang my head against its bars, which alternated between black iron and blood oak. Rubbing the permanent sore spot I'd developed over the course of a few dozen such blows, I reminded myself that the rest of Hearthhammer had it worse. Noah, Cass, and Magpie were two wagons ahead, stuffed into straw-filled crates that purportedly held spears for Scytri's *imru*. Scytri had snuck them out the night before to stretch and relieve themselves, but otherwise they'd spent the better part of twenty-five hours in stinking claustrophobia.

A shout sounded from farther up the column and was passed back from soldier to soldier until it disappeared into the forest behind me: "Town ahead! Town ahead!" We had reached Wyatt Falls.

It was a few more hours before my cage rattled down the pitted dirt main street of the little frontier town. I stared around in fearful attention, looking for any sign of the players I knew had lived here less than a week ago. As bad as the coming war would be, I was terrified that it would open with the wholesale slaughter of everyone I'd run into on our way to the Wall: Merric and his Angels, the blue-eyed ranger who'd killed Dahlia, even St George. As I contemplated sitting caged and unable to intervene while I watched their deaths in sunlit detail, I wondered if the Eldest hadn't given me a worse sentence than the rest of Hearthhammer.

As it turned out, I had nothing to fear, at least not yet. The elven scouts returned quickly to report that Wyatt Falls was abandoned. The elves didn't seem concerned by that fact, and when word came down from the Eldest to make camp for the night, the caravan was swiftly consumed in a bustle of activity that left me alone to wonder where exactly the rest of humanity had gone. The best I could guess, and the best I dared hope, was that they'd been warned of the elves' coming and fled for Wellpoint. It wasn't like the noisy elven column had any hope of stealth, after all. Rangers could easily have seen the war-party coming and evacuated the town with time to spare, and if that thought left me feeling lonely and afraid, that was a problem for me and the long night to come.

Darkness fell, and the army settled into its familiar evening places, the soldiers in their popup tents and the officers bivouacked comfortably in the abandoned inn, dining on food and liquor looted from the general store.

Scytri came with food just as the last hint of sunset disappeared from the western sky.

"What do you call the west?" I asked between bites of porridge. Often when I ate, Scytri stayed with me under the public pretense of making sure I didn't hide away any silverware to be repurposed into a shiv or lockpick, though I got the distinct impression he enjoyed having someone he could talk to about his kids.

"The west?" He repeated the English word.

"The direction where the sun sets," I said.

"*Inan*," he said. "He was one of the first progenitors, a caller who spoke to the spirits in living things. Flowers bloomed where he walked and animals followed at his heel."

I ate in silence for a few minutes, scraping up the last little slivers of food from the corners of my bowl. As I handed the utensils back to Scytri, I whispered as loudly as I dared, "I need you to get my drone for me tonight."

"Drone?" He raised an eyebrow.

"The... flying machine that followed me. I can use it to get a message out, but I need it tonight."

"To warn your people?" Scytri asked.

"Not exactly," I said. "It's complicated."

The elf frowned. "Then explain."

So I did, as best I could. I told Scytri about the world I came from, the gray-orange sky and the terrible food and the poverty, how the Summerlands had seemed like Eden when we discovered it. I told him how Expedition Games had been the ones to find the portal and build a game in the Summerlands using technology far beyond what we or the ancient Vikings had revealed. And finally I described, stretching for the right Elvish words and finally resorting to English when I couldn't find them, how the drones were mounted with cameras that sent live video back to tens of millions of viewers on Earth.

If I'd expected him to marvel at our technology or think of it as some sort of magic, I would have been disappointed. Scytri merely nodded his understanding, his eyes narrowed in thought as he followed the threads of my reasoning.

"So," he said finally, "you think that if you turn public opinion against this war, you can leverage that to force the game-makers to give us the cure to the plague."

"Yes, exactly!" I would have hugged him if there weren't inch-thick bars of iron between us. "But if I wait until we get to Wellpoint, it'll be too late. I need to get a message to my viewers now so they know to tune in when the time comes. Hell, at this point they probably think I'm dead."

Scytri opened his mouth to reply, but at the same moment, an elven patrol came around the corner of the inn, their boots barely a whisper on the cobblestones. Scytri banged the empty bowl on my cage, making me start.

"You're lucky we give you this much, human!" he barked. "I don't want to hear any more complaining from you!" Without so much as a wink he turned his back and fell in with the patrol, chatting amiably with their captain as they marched off into the night.

★★★

Life in a cage was starting to seriously affect my ability to sit comfortably enough for sleep, but I got there eventually, and I was dreaming of Jason and Magpie in broken fragments when a soft *click* woke me in a thrashing panic.

"Hush!" Scytri hissed, grabbing my arm. He swung the door of my cage open silently. His hands were empty except for an iron key.

"Where's my drone?" I whispered. I was too fuzzy-headed to make myself simultaneously understand Scytri and find the Elvish words to reply, so I fell back on English.

Scytri shook his head. "I can't get to it," he said. "It's in the Eldest's armory wagon."

"Which I'm guessing is heavily guarded?"

"No more than the rest of the camp." Scytri made a few awkward hand signs I'd never seen before. "Besides, shapers have ways past guards. The problem is the spirit fence Eneri has put up."

"Spirit fence?" I echoed.

"A magical ward," he explained. "There is a radius around the armory that no elf can enter without alerting Eneri instantly."

"Shit," I said and Scytri's brow creased at whatever Elvish translation he'd heard.

"There is a chance," he continued. "If you go."

"Of course there is," I muttered. "Okay, how can I get past this spirit fence if you can't?"

"You are a human," Scytri said.

"What's that got to do with it?"

Scytri's pinned me with a searching gaze. "You are a caller. I saw you draw out the metal spirit from a coin at the wall. Tell me, can you hold the spirits of men?"

I blinked at him. Spirits...? Then I remembered the words I'd used to enchant the surgeon's knife before we left the war camp. I'd thought they were metaphorical.

"Are you saying there are literally spirits in everything around us?"

"Everything except you." Scytri's face was like stone in the deep blue of night. "Your people do not have spirits, nor do the things you bring from your world."

"And when you say 'hold the spirits of men—'"

"A spell known to callers, which freezes a man or an animal by distracting his spirit. It is effective on my people, but not on yours."

"I know that one!" I felt a rush of excitement like a flash fire in my chest, but it was instantly doused by the cold water of disappointment. "But I need my bells to do it. And even if I had them, it would be way too noisy."

Scytri held up a hand. "Let me finish. It works on my people because we have spirits. You do not. The spirit fence—"

"Won't recognize me!" I finished for him, the warmth rushing back into me. "So I should be able to just waltz through and grab my drone."

"I am sure you do not need to dance, but yes." Scytri nodded. "That is my hope."

"Well, it's worth a try," I said. "I mean, what have I got to lose beside my life?"

★★★

God, I wish Magpie were here, I thought as I crept barefoot across the cobbles. *Actually, I wish Magpie were doing this instead of me.*

Armed only with Scytri's directions, I headed for the Eldest's section of camp as quickly as I dared. I'd promised Scytri not to rat him out if I was caught, but anxiety on his behalf still scratched at the back of my brain; it wouldn't take a genius to figure out that he'd freed me.

I kept to the shadows, though they were few and far between. The Eldest had circled his wagons south of town, at the base of the cliff where Wyatt Falls, or whatever the elves called it, tumbled over the terminal edge of Hard Pass to crash down into a little lake that hid among the trees. That meant I had to leave the comforting cover of the inn and general store behind and duck from trunk to trunk in the spaces between the little camps of each elven platoon.

I found myself wishing for some sort of silence or invisibility magic, but that was the domain of white wizards. Scytri was one, though he'd called himself a *shaper.* And apparently I was a *caller;* I could only assume that elves followed the white magic/red magic split we did, under different names. Assuming I survived the night, I looked forward to picking Scytri's brain about it all.

Guard patrols were few and far between and I couldn't blame the elves for their apparently lax security. There was nothing out there in the night but the army and even if every human in the Summerlands had gathered at Wyatt Falls to fight back, they would have been outnumbered three to one. The elves had nothing to fear. This was their land.

I shoved the thought away and made myself refocus on the task at hand. Skirting the edges of the various campsites where elven soldiers lay snoring around burnt-down fires was easier than I'd expected, especially when I passed the pens where the elves' giant birds of burden squawked and squabbled. Soon I heard the rush of the waterfall. With that to guide me, I covered the last few hundred yards with newfound certainty.

How much of his life had Magpie spent sneaking around in the dark like this? He said the life of a contract boy was easy, but I had the distinct feeling that he wasn't giving us the full story. Well, of course he wasn't. He'd known who we were and what had happened to Jason the whole time, and hadn't breathed a word of it. A shiver spasmed up my back. The memory of what I'd been about to do when I discovered the truth—purely by chance—made me queasy. What else had Magpie lied about?

The trees fell away and the waterfall came in sight. The Eldest's wagons made a semicircle around it, protected by the sheer cliff of Hard Pass at their backs. A few dying fires glowed a muted orange within the ring, but the camp was otherwise still. According to Scytri, the armory wagon was up against the cliff on the right, just behind the one in which Eneri traveled and slept.

Wonderful.

The light from the camp was dim enough that I felt fairly invisible as I moved in a low crouch towards the cliff wall. Soon I was within a few feet of the armory wagon and I paused for a minute, breathing as shallowly as I could despite my pounding heart. I heard nothing other than the waterfall.

The spirit fence, a white circle of salt, stood out in the darkness. It circumscribed the armory wagon without much room to spare, but I had to admire how neat and even it was. Clearly Eneri had had some practice with red magic.

There was nothing left to do but cross the salt circle and hope for the best. If Scytri was right and humans really didn't have spirits, then nothing should happen. If he was wrong... I set one foot on the other side of the spirit fence and froze, listening. Nothing stirred in the camp and there was no new sound. I shifted my weight gently forward and brought my back foot across the line as well.

Something rattled in the darkness. I froze. Was that the click of a boot on stone? The sound of chain mail shifting? A spear bumping a pauldroned shoulder?

The sound didn't come again. I wished it would, just to know. But I had no choice: I forced my muscles to move and bring me to the back of the armory wagon. As far as I could see, there was no lock. Eneri had to be extremely confident in his spirit fence and I wondered whether it meant anything that he'd put up a powerful security system to keep out other elves and nothing against anyone else.

The wagon opened with a sound like a tired sigh. The interior was a deeper shadow against the night, black on blue. I could just make out the shapes of weapons hanging on the walls like prisoners chained up in a gloomy dungeon. Two layers of crates, identical to the ones where the rest of Hearthhammer hid, sat in the center of the wagon.

I reached out and gingerly touched the nearest sword. It didn't immediately bite me, so I tapped it with one finger at a time while murmuring a few words in Elvish. The spell wasn't so different from the enchantment I'd used on the surgeon's knife: it seemed to be asking the warrior spirit within the weapon to show some of its energy.

The sword began to glow, brighter than I'd expected. I scrambled up into the wagon and swung the door shut behind me, all as quickly as I dared. Another breathless minute passed as I sat waiting for any sound over the rushing waterfall, but none came.

I looked the crates over. Mostly they were long and narrow, clearly made for spears. One stood out to me, a bit boxier than the others. I took a breath and flipped the top open. Four drones sat stacked inside, their big red buttons only faintly luminescent in the glow of the sword.

Low battery, I thought. *Shit.*

I pulled the first drone off the stack and gave it a hasty look over. It was Magpie's, I thought, with a bent fin where he'd grabbed it by the disappearing bridge. Definitely not mine. The second and third also didn't have the pattern of nicks and scuffs

I'd gotten so familiar with over the last weeks. Of course mine was at the very bottom.

Sliding it from the crate was like seeing a long-lost friend. The big button glowed warmly at me. I pressed it.

The drone leapt promptly from my hands, seeking an angle.

"Shit!" I hissed. I grabbed it, pulled it down to eye level, and held it there against its struggles.

"Hey guys," I whispered. "Miss me?" I tried to look like things were under control, just another heroic adventure. "Did you see the elves? Pretty amazing, right? Okay, here's the thing. They're coming to Wellpoint. They have some serious bad blood with our ancestors—long story, I promise I'll tell it someday—and they're looking for a fight. I'm their prisoner for now. Look for my feed when we get to Wellpoint, and I'll—I'll—" The red light on my drone flickered and died and its buzzing engine whined away to nothing. It went limp in my hands.

"What is that thing?"

I looked up. The wagon door was open, and Eneri stood leaning halfway in, his face like a skull in the light of the glowing sword.

"Shit," I said.

"Put it down," Eneri said. "Slowly." I did what he said, laying the dead drone next to its companions. He watched me with eyes in black shadow. "Good. Now. How did you escape? Did Scytri help you?"

"Your little elven locks are no match for human magic," I said. It was a stupid lie, but it was the first thing that came into my head.

"Hm." It was more a laugh than anything. "You are no spirit caller, only a fake, a shadow. My children need less help than you. Now come. I expect the Eldest will want to behead you himself. Guards!"

There was something about the word he'd used to say *help*. It was more like... tool? Crutch? *Implement.* When Eneri had stopped my fireball, he'd done it with just a word and a gesture.

I put my hands up slowly, showing Eneri that they were empty, and as I did began to murmur a rhythmic incantation. My fingers twitched sympathetically, wanting to perform the motions I'd trained so painstakingly to lock in with the words, but if I was right, the motions weren't needed.

Time slowed.

The world blurred out; only Eneri's face was in focus, almost too sharp. The Elvish words that rolled from my mouth were old, ancient, but comprehensible. I spoke directly to Eneri's spirit, the soul that burned within him, commanding and beguiling it to be still. This was the hook that had been missing when I'd tried the same spell on Magpie's hitmen. I could feel it inside Eneri, fighting me, raging against me, falling back exhausted as I drowned it with my will, then roaring up again to rattle the bars of the magical cage I'd made around it.

A look of absolute hate was frozen on Eneri's face. It was more than hate; it was disgust. He was looking at me like a dog that had just shit on a brand-new carpet, as though I'd sullied something sacred by using the same magic he did. I could almost see the spirit locked behind his eyes straining to reach out and immolate me.

I took a slow step forward, keeping my eyes locked on Eneri's, keeping the words flowing from my lips. He did nothing as I crept closer. For all his hatred and all his power, as long as he couldn't move, I was safe. Soon I would move into his peripheral vision, then slip around him, and then I could back away into the midnight woods and run for my life.

Something moved in the blur around Eneri's face, then the wind crashed from my lungs as two armored elves tackled me, slamming me into the stacked crates at the back of the wagon and bouncing my head painfully from a sharp wooden corner. I slumped back, gasping like a beached fish, seeing stars as the world wavered around me.

The guards grabbed me by the legs and dragged me from the wagon, making absolutely no effort to be gentle. I hit the ground on my back; now the world wasn't spinning quite so badly and the stars I was seeing were real, but Eneri's face blocked them out as he leaned over me, and he was smiling as he spat the words of a spell I didn't know in precise, clipped syllables.

A shout carried from the forest, an alarm in Elvish. Another sounded, and a third, until the woods echoed with alarms. There was a scrape of metal on metal and a pained grunt, then the noisy clatter of swords meeting.

"Eneri!" The voice of the Eldest cracked like a whip in the clearing within the circled wagons. Eneri looked up sharply, his spell lost, giving me a moment to catch my breath. My head pounded, but a quick check of my body suggested it was otherwise whole, so I glanced toward the forest to see if I could make a run for it. Instead I discovered the glittering points of two spears an inch from my eyes.

"Take her back to her cage," Eneri told the guards. "Make sure it's locked with blood oak and check her for implements. Then stay there until I come for you—no one else." His eyes flickered to me. "And *watch* her."

"Eneri!" The Eldest called his name again and the wizard strode off across the yard, his long gold vest fluttering behind him.

"Up," grunted one of the soldiers, prodding me with his spear to show me he was serious. I pushed myself onto my knees and the other guard grabbed the collar of my shirt and hauled me to my feet. He patted me down roughly as his comrade watched the forest with narrowed eyes and a half-open mouth. The sounds of fighting had only increased; it sounded like the skirmishing had turned into an all-out running fight among the trees. The guard clearly wanted to join in, and if I was being honest, I couldn't blame him.

Who was out there?

The other guard finished his search and grabbed me by the wrists. Together they marched me back to Wyatt Falls, taking a direct route through the camp. We passed a dozen abandoned campfires and a few straggling soldiers still grabbing weapons and buckling on armor, but nobody stopped us or even seemed to care much who I was. They were all headed towards the fight.

The town square was similarly abandoned and I didn't resist as the elves shoved me into my cage and snapped the lock shut. It was made from iron inlaid with blood oak: Eneri had already accounted for my bit of magical skill. Even if I could pick the lock and disable my guards, with the camp on high alert I had nowhere to run, nor could I leave Hearthammer locked away in claustrophobic darkness, no doubt panicking at the sounds of violence around them.

I slumped back against the bars of my cage, then straightened immediately as a shape appeared from the treeline, running full tilt towards me. My first thought was that it was some member of Hearthammer, wearing the black uniform Magpie had bought, but as he moved into the light I realized it was the black-haired, blue-eyed ranger who'd killed Dahlia in the forest.

"Linnaea!" he shouted as the elven guards squared up, lowering their spears at his chest. He came at them at a fearless sprint, his black sword in one hand and a splintered wooden shield in the other. The elf on the left lunged, shoving his spear forward as his leading boot slapped the cobblestones with a sharp *smack*. The ranger rolled his shoulder under the glittering spearpoint and brought his sword up to cut the shaft neatly in two. The elf spat out some curse I couldn't translate and tossed away the broken spear, then drew his sword in the nick of time as the ranger closed with him, sword tip leading.

The right-hand elf stepped back, trying to get an angle of attack as man and elf crashed together in a scrape of steel. For a second their swords locked, sending a spray of black paint flaking away as the blades ground together, then the ranger shoved his opponent off and into my cage. I tried to grab his long hair through the bars, but the elf ducked away and aimed a warning cut at my fingers.

The fight split apart and again the single ranger faced off against two elves. They circled warily, like a trio of caged animals feeling out each other's strength, neither side daring to get within the weapon-reach of the other.

259

The spear-wielding elf shouted and lunged, stealing the ranger's attention as his companion darted in with his curved sword high.

"Look out!" I shouted, but it was too late. The gleaming sword bit into the ranger's shoulder, driving him to his knees even as he deflected the spearpoint that would otherwise have pierced his throat. I winced in sympathy. The elf's sword came down again and the ranger slapped it away with his own blade, but his reaction was slower with his injured sword-arm.

I had to help.

It was possible to do magic without implements. I had proven it by freezing Eneri at the armory wagon. But could I enchant a sword from yards away? Did I need to be touching it to imbue it with magic, or was I really talking to some sort of animistic spirit within the blade that merely needed a little convincing?

My voice was loud as I called the words of the spell, focusing on the ranger's black sword. I could feel it listening to me, pushing back against my request that it give up something of itself to win this fight. The combatants ignored me as I began to shout: maybe my voice was lost against the noise of clashing steel and shuffling boots, or maybe they had all just fallen into the total focus of a life-or-death battle.

A blue gleam flashed along the edge of the ranger's sword as he raised it to meet an overhand chop from the curved elven blade. The swords met and with a shower of sparks and a noise like a buzzsaw, the ranger's sword cut the elf's clean through. The elf barely had time to register shock on his pale face before the ranger flicked his wrist and brought his sword back around to sever the elf's arm between elbow and shoulder.

The ranger leapt to his feet, sword twirling in his hand. Two quick slashes cut the other elf's spear to pieces, leaving him nothing to defend himself with against the ranger's lunge that pierced his heart and sheared through his chest as he fell dead to the cobblestones.

The blue-eyed ranger captain approached my cage, keeping one wary eye on the elves as though he wasn't sure of the limits of their mortality.

"Leave me in here," I said as he raised his enchanted sword to chop the lock off my cage.

"Why?"

"The rest of my party is still captive. I need to stay to help them."

The ranger glanced back at the forest, where the sounds of fighting had died away. "We can free them and run for it."

"Trust me," I said. "We're safer where we are and we'd just slow your team down."

"My men are gone." The ranger dropped his hand and let the gleaming sword dangle from his grip.

"Then you can make it out," I said. "Just disappear. Head south and get to Wellpoint before this army does. Somebody needs to warn them."

THE LANGUAGE OF PEACE

From my iron cage I watched the miles roll by as the elven army approached Wellpoint. We skirted the Wyvern Peaks by way of Dann's Teeth, taking the same route so many human adventurers had trod in the last five years. As we crossed the gray landscape of the Battle Plains, the Eldest stopped the column for an hour to kneel and perform what looked like a ritual offering, burying new-forged weapons deep in the chalky dust and calling a long list of names to the sky.

We skirted the White Chasm without incident and entered the Near Plains. A few elven platoons, all of them with green-painted armor, paused by the blue roses I'd discovered on our first trip out of town. They seemed to be arguing about something, though I couldn't make out what as my wagon rolled past. Eventually they formed up again and fell in as the column marched over the gently rolling hills, trampling flat the grass beneath its many boots and leaving a muddy scar a hundred yards wide in its wake.

The army camped a mile outside Wellpoint and woke early the next morning. Scytri brought me food and water as the soldiers all around me polished their swords and spears, patched holes and replaced weak leather straps on their chain mail, and had their final meal before the battle that now felt as inevitable as sunrise.

I was desperate to ask Scytri about the rest of Hearthhammer, whether they were still safe and sane hidden in their crates, whether he'd been able to let them out for a break last night, but as platoons jogged past and Scytri's own men ran back and forth spreading his orders, I never got a chance.

As the chaos of the camp resolved itself into something approaching a battle-ready order, a shout rose up from the rear guard. My heart leapt and for a second I let myself hope that help had come in some unexpected form, but I quickly realized I was hearing the sound of joy rather than panic. Officers called for discipline as scattered soldiers broke off to go running north towards the back of the camp, then came straggling back in ones and twos. I was baffled until I realized that the elves hadn't returned alone: they were accompanied by gold dogs, which trotted at their heels and in some excitable cases, weaved between legs, yipping and snapping their pincers playfully.

The elves looked overjoyed to see the monsters. Even Scytri had one and as he passed me he drew a gold coin from under his red cloak and tossed it in the air; the creature at his heels snagged it midflight with its pincers and trotted it back to its master just like a dog with a stick. Apparently, our nickname hadn't been so far off the mark.

The officers shouted their men into a neat column at last and the army covered the last mile to Wellpoint, leaving its baggage train behind. My friends were in there somewhere and as my cage rattled along behind Scytri's men, all I could do for them was hope.

They marched through the Burbs, boots tromping in perfect time on the wide streets between the big white houses. There were no humans to be seen and at first I thought Wellpoint would end up being as deserted as Wyatt Falls. If someone had gotten a warning to Wellpoint, the blue-eyed ranger maybe, the hundreds of adventurers and NPCs and Expedition Games employees who lived in Wellpoint might have had just enough time to flee back through the portal to Earth.

Running didn't seem like Expedition's style, though, and my hunch was confirmed in dramatic fashion as my section of the column reached Portal Square. The town of Wellpoint had apparently chosen to make their stand there and they'd erected hasty barricades that split the square neatly in half, great piles of firewood, furniture, even a couple doors, behind which frightened human faces peeked out and disappeared as the elven army

263

filtered into the square and formed up into a line of interlocked shields bristling with long, gleaming spears.

True to his word, the Eldest made sure I had a perfect view of the slaughter to come. They rolled my cage up one of the narrow alleys that approached Portal Square, just on the elven side of the barricade, and left me in the alley-mouth, alone between the lines. When the fight came, I would be close enough to see everything in gory detail, but I expected that any spells I might try would be lost in the noise and chaos.

Eneri stepped forward from the elven line, flanked by two soldiers with tall tower shields that were obviously for the wizard's protection rather than their own. An expectant hush fell over the square and for the first time I heard the buzz of the drones that swarmed over the human lines like a cloud of attendant bees, so thick that they had to be giving the adventurers shade from the noon sun high overhead.

"When your ancestors came here, they brought violence and disease with them," Eneri called. His voice filled the square with perfect clarity and I suspected he'd used magic to amplify it. "We killed them all. Now we will do the same to you if you do not leave our lands. We have been gone too long from these places our progenitors made. They will be ours again!"

In the silence that followed, I wondered if any human other than me had understood a word of Eneri's speech. There was no reason to think so. Then a shout came from somewhere beyond the palisade: "Speak Japanese or shut up!" The adventurers gave a cheer and raised their weapons in defiance, swords, maces, spears, and more glittering in the sunlight.

"It would almost be exciting if we weren't all about to die." I half-turned, half-jumped in surprise to find Hearthammer filling the alley behind my cage. Three drones, rejuvenated by the bright sunshine, hovered around them. Magpie was working the lock, his tongue between his teeth, Noah was releasing my own struggling drone into the air, and Cass just stood looking up at me with her hands on her hips as though my whole imprisonment was just the latest inconvenience in her very annoying day.

The lock opened with a snap and Magpie threw it down the alley, then opened the cage door for me with a bow and an outswept arm. I hopped down to the cobbles, but found it too hard to look Magpie in the eye, so instead I grabbed Noah and Cass in a big double-armed hug.

"You're okay!"

"I'm pretty sore," said Noah.

"Beats being dead," Cass put in. "How's your master plan going, superstar?"

"I think I got a message out the night we stopped at Wyatt Falls." I rolled my shoulders and cracked my neck. "With any luck, when I start streaming, they'll be watching. You guys ready?"

Cass tapped the bow that she wore slung across her chest. "Turns out it's easy to steal your gear back when nobody's watching it."

"I hope I don't have to fight anyone famous," Noah added.

"If this works, we won't have to fight anyone at all," I said. "Let's go stop a war."

I turned back towards my cage and found Magpie standing between me and Portal Square. He was only inches away from me, his eyes hidden by the slanting shadows of the alley.

"Emma," he said.

"No," I said.

"No?"

"No." I shook my head. "Not this. Not here. Not now."

"But—"

"I haven't forgiven you," I said. "And considering that I'm about to walk into the jaws of death, I really don't have the time or the energy to start now." I sighed. "Magpie, I get it, I do. Trust me. We might be walking to our deaths, and you want to make it right first in case we don't walk out again. After everything we've been through, you don't want things to end like this... well, I don't either. But I can't do this now."

"Okay," he said.

I looked over his shoulder into the plaza, where two armies swayed like tall grass agitated by the motions of an invisible predator. "You want to make it up to me? *Survive.*"

★★★

The sunshine of Portal Square was eye-wateringly bright as we strode out of the cool shadows of the alley. In the moments of our all too short reunion, nothing had changed; the elves and humans still eyed each other warily across a few naked yards of cobblestone, one side waiting for the order to attack and the other dreading the storm about to descend on them.

My drone buzzed along behind me as I walked the empty swathe between the opposing lines. I heard a few gasps and murmurs from behind the adventurers' barricades. Someone said my name. I ignored it all, focused wholly on taking one step at a time until I reached the center of the square. I thought for sure that each step would be my last, that either an elven arrow would cut me down or I would simply break and run back to the safety of my cage in the alley. Only the feeling of Noah, Cass, and Magpie at my back kept me moving forward.

I reached the center of the square and stopped; the rest of Hearthammer formed up around me. Our drones swooped into position above us, all four cameras on and focused.

"Make it count," Cass whispered.

I put my right hand up, palm facing the elven line.

"Please listen to me," I said in Elvish. "I need to speak my language so everyone will understand. But please listen."

The faces of the elven soldiers were as stony and still as the corpse-statues we'd seen beneath Hard Pass.

"My name is Linnaea," I said in English. "My name is Linnaea, and I have one more lecture to give. I hope you'll listen, because I have a story to tell. It takes place a thousand years ago, on Earth, where we're from. A group of warriors called Vikings found themselves on an island called Lewis. Maybe they'd come there looking for plunder, or maybe they were shipwrecked, I don't know. But there they were.

"They set out to explore, and they found a glowing circle, a fairy ring. They stepped through it from our world into this one. It was a beautiful land, perfect for farming, so they made it their own, built a hall here. There was only one problem: it was already inhabited by the people we call elves.

"The leaders of the elves came to speak with the Vikings, but a fight broke out. The Vikings were all killed, but the elves got something even worse. The Vikings carried smallpox. The plague ravaged the elves, killing and mutilating. They're still suffering, even now."

I took a long breath, which sounded incredibly loud in the silence of the square.

"You might be wondering how I know all this. Well, I could point you to the ruins of a Viking longhouse just north of here. But there's better evidence: eyewitness accounts. Because on Earth, this all happened a thousand years before any of us was born, but time works differently in the Summerlands. We know that. Here, it was only *three years* before Expedition games came back."

I gestured at the line of soldiers, their spears making a ruler-straight fence, who still watched me coldly. "Every one of these warriors remembers that time. Some of them were probably there. This isn't the deep past to them, it's living memory. It's no wonder they hate us." I turned to face the elves head-on. "What happened was a tragedy, yes. It was a terrible misunderstanding. But to us it's ancient history. The men you fought eight years ago are as alien to us as they are to you. But most importantly, in that time we've been able to cure the plague."

That got a reaction. The elven stoicism collapsed into various expressions of surprise and doubt, some whispering to their comrades as others watched me with refreshed attention.

"Let us give you the cure," I said. "We can bring it here and teach you how to administer it. We can help you rebuild. There's no need for a war. There's no reason to fight."

"No reason?"

I knew that voice and my fear was confirmed when Dr Agony clambered over the top of the barricade and slid down to

267

the stones a few feet from me. He was dressed in his finest plush red robes, stitched with silver symbols of magic; a string of sea-green jewels—the real ones—made a perfect parabola on his chest. His salt-and-pepper hair was neat, his beard trimmed, and any wrinkles had been smoothed out by a little makeup.

"She says there's no reason to fight," Dr Agony called. "And I applaud her! I do. I was a newbie once, too. But then I gained some experience." He smiled at his little joke. The square was quiet. "I know all of you, and you all know me. You trust me. Well then trust me on this: there's so much more to the Summerlands than you know. There's a whole world beyond the Wall, waiting for us to take it." He pointed at the elven line. "But they're not just going to *give* it to us, are they?"

"No!" someone shouted from beyond the barricade.

"How do you know?" I said. "Have you tried asking? Have you tried talking to them? I have!" I switched to Elvish: "I can speak their language—can you?"

"As a matter of fact," Dr Agony replied quietly in Elvish, "I can." He raised his voice as he returned to English. "War!" He shook his head. "They say it like it's a bad word. But *war* is dangerous. *War* is thrilling. *War* is good for ratings!"

"What?" I said, my voice a strangled whisper.

"In a war, every man is a hero!" Agony called. "Think of the stories! Isn't that what we've all learned from Linnaea here? It's not about treasure, it's about telling a story. That's how this game is supposed to be played. Can you imagine what it's like back home right now? Millions of eyes glued to your feed as you stand in the front line of a great army facing off against the elven horde. The Summerlands has never seen a huge battle before! And guess what? This is our chance!"

A cheer rose from the adventurers beyond the barricade, and they began to climb, picking their way up the mound of junk until they had made their own ragged line atop it, facing the rigid elven army with ragtag bravado. I recognized so many of them: the rest of Golden Apple was up there, St George with his sword out and his eyes hungry, Meteora swinging her double-headed chain hammer, Belphegor and Kronos from the Red Wizards' Guild side by side, Pixie wearing armor for the first time I'd ever seen.

"Wait!" I yelled, patting the air with my hands in desperation. "Listen! Do you really think our fans just want to see blood and guts?"

"Yeah!" shouted someone I didn't recognize, a squat, bullet-headed man in chain mail with two short swords. A laugh rippled down the line of players. I was losing them; panic was opening up beneath me like a black pit. I took a breath and leapt.

"My name is Emma Burke," I said. "You all know me as Linnaea, but my real name is Emma Burke. I'm from the Hollywood Economic Cooperation Zone in America. Before I came to the Summerlands I had a shitty job fixing merchandise machines at the Expedition store." I gestured to Cass. "This is Cassidy Keats. Before we came here she worked with kids. Her brother Jason was killed by a crooked cop. This is Noah García Benatar. He was a high school student. Magpie was a contract boy for a Greek crime family.

"A month ago, we were just fans, watching the feeds back on Earth and cheering you on. The Summerlands was just a dream to us. Look around you! This place is paradise! We came here to escape the real world, and I'm betting every one of you did the exact same thing. Do you really want the Summerlands to end up like our world? Let me tell you, a war would be the fastest way to make that happen.

"How many elves do you think are here? How many more are waiting beyond the Wall for when these ones are killed? Do you think Expedition Games will just let them roll over us and run us out? Or will they start shipping in soldiers of their own— not adventurers, not players, *soldiers*—to fight back? How many people can they bring in? How fast? How long until they start sending in guns and Humvees and bunker busters? I've seen the way the elves use magic. We'd need guns just to even the odds.

"A war will destroy both sides and the Summerlands will get chewed up between them. There would be no dream left. If

269

we make the Summerlands like Earth, why would anybody watch the feeds?"

Silence fell over Portal Square as I ran out of words. The players on the barricade shifted their weight, swung their weapons, looked to each other, and did anything else they could think of not to meet my eyes. The elven line looked just as anxious, unsettled by my references to alien technology.

"Put down your weapons," I said. I didn't raise my voice, but I knew everyone was listening. "All of you. We can talk. I can translate. We can make peace."

"Well," said Dr Agony, giving me a slow clap. "That was quite a speech. Bravo. Thank you for sharing your story, Emma. May I share mine?"

I watched him warily, thinking he looked like nothing so much as a snake rearing its head back to strike.

"Sure," I said.

"Thank you." He gave me a shallow bow, then straightened up to address the adventurers. "This is the story of the Lost Expedition. You've heard the rumors, I'm sure. In the very early days of our exploration of the Summerlands, I led a group of rangers north. I came back, but my men didn't. I'd like to tell you what happened."

Agony spread his hands. "You all know that north of Wyatt Falls, there's a great wall. It's the one place in the Summerlands you're not allowed to go. I'm sure you all assumed that Expedition Games built it for one reason or another. I've heard all the whispers about what the Wall was supposed to keep out... well, they're not true. The elves built the Wall. I know, because I'm the one who found it.

"We set out from the falls and spent a few days in the forest before we reached a badland of gray stone. Cutting across the badland was a huge wall. We followed it for a few days until, much to our amazement, we reached a spot where it was still under construction." Dr Agony shook his head sadly. "The elves attacked us that night. Half my men were killed in their sleep. The other half tried to put up a fight, but we didn't stand a chance. I was the last one alive, and as I lay there on the ground with an elven sword at my throat, I thought I was a dead man. But they spared me. Why, I don't know. But until Emma and her friends broke the rules and went to the one place they shouldn't—and brought this whole mess down on our heads, I might add—I was the only living person to have met an elf. And believe me, they may look like us... but they're as much monsters as the gold dogs and the hell rats."

"It's true!" called a new voice, speaking Elvish. Eneri pushed his way through the elven line, gold vest fluttering over a shirt of golden chain mail. "Every word of it. I was there that day."

"You!" Fury distorted Dr Agony's face. He pointed a shaking finger at Eneri. "This creature was there at the Wall! He killed my men, then put his sword to my neck and told me to run! I swore I'd kill him if I ever got the chance. Well, this is my chance, and I sure as hell intend to take it! Come on!" He turned back to the players lining the barricade, their weapons at the ready. "*Who's with me?*"

With a roar, the adventurers rushed down the barricade, swept past Hearthhammer and Dr Agony, and crashed into the elven line in a shower of sparks and blood.

REVOLUTION

Cass grabbed my right hand and Noah my left and we held on to each other as the human line crashed and surged around us in their rush to fight. The sound when they met the elves was teeth-rattling, the roar of a thousand battle cries drowning out the shrieking of metal on metal as weapons and armor clashed.

The human wave passed us by and Hearthammer stood alone in the center of Portal Square, forgotten behind the scrum. We had suddenly gained a perfect view of the battle, where any pretense at tactics had quickly been abandoned by both sides as the fight devolved into a bloody shoving match between two disintegrating mobs. In the roil of color and chaos, miniature narratives rose up and sank again like a drowning man breaking the surface of a stormy sea as the fighters grouped up, made goals, achieved them or failed and broke apart again.

Kronos, the red wizard, was rolling coins double-handed and throwing fireballs that boomed on the tower shields of a squadron of elven heavy infantry. By his side, Belphegor seemed to be attempting something with a large iron bell that suddenly span off into the fray, along with three of his fingers, sheared away in the sweep of an elven sword.

In the center of the line, St George was singing a hymn as he laid about him with his longsword. It stuck in the shoulder of an elven spearman, whose weapon skittered off St George's armor as the knight planted a foot on the elf's chest and shoved him away.

Meteora was swinging her chain hammer in a wide circle, forcing elves and human alike to duck away and creating a radius of empty space with herself at the center. A flick of her wrist sent a hammerhead whipping out to slam into the back of a retreating elf, who crumpled to the ground. A gang of elven infantry with shields and spears formed a miniature shield wall and rushed her, forcing her to pull her weapon back, then darted in and pierced her from half a dozen angles at once.

A flight of arrows soared overhead, arcing over the cloud of drones that shaded the sky before they thunked into the barricade or broke on the ground beyond it; there was nobody left on the far side to get hit.

A squad of black-clad rangers, led by the blue-eyed captain who'd saved my life near Wyatt Falls, met a group of elven skirmishers in a whirlwind of swords. A few fighters on each side fell away and then the disciplined fight crumpled into a shoving match as the rangers forced the elves back towards their own line.

Dr Agony had disappeared in the first rush, but he appeared suddenly with the rest of Golden Apple at the heart of the melee, shouting orders and pointing. I saw Rad first; he rose up from a humped pile of bodies, throwing elves off him in all directions—I couldn't tell if they were alive or dead—and swung his maul in a sweeping arc that crumpled an elven helmet and the skull inside it. Valkyrie kept under the shelter of the huge warrior, darting out to slide her knives into necks, armpits, and groins where the armor of the elves was weakest, then retreating back into Rad's kill radius. Even Wolfheart was more engaged than usual; he'd apparently discovered the same violent use of the white magic surgery spell that Noah had, and his face was tight with focus as he lashed out in all directions with a wooden wand that left long red gashes like an invisible whip.

For a moment, it seemed like the humans stood a chance.

Something shifted up and down the battle; I caught a glimpse of Eneri in his golden armor running along behind the elven front line shouting orders, and whatever he told them proved effective as they slowly formed up into something resembling order. The entire elven line shouted as one, a remarkably sharp sound that cut through the ruckus, and shoved forward with their shields. With another shout and another step, they forced the disorganized adventurers back a foot or so and with that the momentum of the battle shifted and the players were forced into a chaotic fighting retreat that spilled back across the square toward me and my party.

"Stay together!" Cass screamed as the melee swallowed us. One of Merric's Angels, her white leathers sprayed with blood in blue and red slashes, bolted past me, and then the elven line reached us and we stumbled backwards with the other players.

Panic crashed down on me like a bucket of ice water. I spun in a helpless circle, looking for anywhere I could hide, or at least retreat to, to catch my breath and start working a spell. The elves in front of me were still pushing forward and the players behind were finally starting to push back, trapping me between hammer and anvil.

An elven spear lanced at my face and I ducked aside. Too slow: the tip made a burning line across my cheek. To my left, Noah deflected another spear with his sword, his teeth showing in a snarl of focus. Cass was struggling to get space of her own to nock an arrow; she managed to get one up but it was immediately dislodged by an errant sword and trampled. Magpie had his knives out, but could barely fend off the assault of elves with shields and a far greater reach.

I took another step backwards and my foot landed on something other than the flat ground. It was an elven sword, lost by someone somewhere, and I snatched it from the cobbles as the same spear that cut my cheek lashed out again and caught the empty space above my head.

I could feel the warrior spirit within the weapon, begging to be used, and mentally whipped it into order as surely as Eneri had done for the elven army; the curved edge of the sword flared red as the spirit leapt to my command. I came up swinging, cleaving an elven shield in half from bottom to top to reveal a startled soldier with a broad patch of his unprotected chest suddenly revealed. An arrow appeared there and he fell away, gasping.

"Come on! Come on!" someone was screaming and my throat was raw and I realized it was me. My sword left burning red trails in the air as I bulled forward, slashing through shields

274

and weapons all around me. I broke through the elven line; on either side of me Magpie and Noah turned my point into a wedge and Cass trailed in our wake putting arrows through elven armor at point-blank range.

I caught a flash of gold a few ranks back: Eneri. He disappeared into the melee, but I turned our vanguard in his direction and chopped into the next row of elves with renewed fury. Our drive bought us a few more bloody yards before I stumbled over something that checked my forward momentum. A body lay at my feet, black against the cobblestones: the handsome ranger from the forest. He'd saved me, but I hadn't returned the favor. I'd never even learned his name.

"Linnaea! Linnaea!" Someone was screaming for me. I ignored it. They could follow me or not; I had to get to Eneri and the Eldest.

"Linnaea!" The voice wasn't behind me; it was ahead of me, somewhere among the mass of elven infantry who blocked my way. A white face smeared with blue blood floated up and my sword flickered out of its own accord. I caught it at the last moment as I realized I was staring into the face of Scytri.

"Stop! Stop!" he shouted. A spearman bumped into him and Scytri shoved the other elf away. "Listen!"

"What?" I yelled back, struggling to be heard over the chaos. I jabbed my sword at a soldier who fell back with his shield up.

"You can't kill the Eldest!" Scytri had his face next to mine now. "This war will never, *ever* end if you do."

"It'll never end if we don't!" I replied. "He's forcing you to fight!"

"The caller in the red robes on your side—"

"Dr Agony," I snarled. "Now get out of my way!"

"He did the same for your people—drove them to fight—listen! Listen!" I was trying to push past Scytri, but he had his hands on my shoulders, keeping me in place by sheer physical strength. "If we can stop them both, we can stop this fight. Do you understand?"

The red sword in my hand was really a shield, I thought insanely. As long as I kept swinging and cutting, nothing would hurt me or my friends. So I would just cut my way to the Eldest and chop him apart too and then I'd be safe... but something in Scytri's eyes caught me and held me there more powerfully than his hands. He was as panicked as I was, but somehow he'd managed to keep his senses in a way that I really hadn't.

But Scytri was right. Killing the elven leader would only make things worse. I didn't want to win this fight, I wanted to end it, and I wanted to end the war of which this was only the first terrible moment.

"What's your plan?" I said.

"I'll kill the Eldest," said Scytri, and I saw in his eyes how serious he was. "When I do, my progenitor will become Eldest. You stop Dr Agony and tell your side to stand down."

"Kill Dr Agony?" I felt like the wind had been knocked out of me. Killing monsters was one thing, but killing another player...?

"Just stop him! It has to be one of you, don't you see?" Scytri's eyes were wide, and for the first time I could see that the gray in them was a raging, swirling stormcloud. "We stop our side, you stop yours. We both make that sacrifice to prove we're serious about peace."

"You're talking about revolution—"

"Just tell me you understand!"

Then the melee swept him up and carried him away from me as the elves surged forward, bristling with spears and thirsty for blood.

"What's the plan?" That was Noah at my left shoulder, falling back with me against the elven shields. His face gleamed with sweat and blood of both colors and his chest was heaving. He swiped his forehead with the back of one hand, then jerked suddenly to swat a spear away from me with his sword.

"Find Golden Apple," I said between gritted teeth, shoving back against the shield wall. A sword darted through a gap and I sheared it in half with my own enchanted blade. "Stop Agony. Scytri stops the Eldest. Battle ends."

"Over there!" Magpie pointed with a dagger to a break in the battle where Rad's hammer rose and fell as steadily as a pendulum. Cass grabbed my arm and pulled me away from the elven line, spinning around to take my place so she was now at the rear of our new wedge, aimed perfectly to drive towards Golden Apple.

I shoved Pixie out of my way as I bulled towards Dr Agony with my party at my heels. She sneered, opened her mouth, and shut it after a look at my face, and the roiling fray carried her off. The last of the elven line had disintegrated again, and the whole of Portal Square was engulfed by the melee, which seemed to be rotating slowly in a vortex of clashing steel.

"Halt, witch!" St George forced his way between two other adventurers to block my path. His tabard was purple with blood and torn nearly to shreds that fluttered around him. "I have seen you consorting with demons and speaking their tongue! Kneel and repent or taste my sacred blade!"

"Get out of my way," I growled. St George raised his sword. His eyes were wild with holy madness.

"And let you betray God's children? I think not!" He brought the sword down in a two-handed slash and I swept mine up into a high guard, hoping I could shear his blade in half and keep moving. The swords met, and a numbing shiver ran down my arms. His blade ground against mine, throwing red and blue sparks of magical force that sizzled where they hit us; obviously his hatred of witchcraft hadn't prevented him from having his blade enchanted.

Over his shoulder, I caught a flash of Dr Agony's robes disappearing farther into the melee. He was getting away while I wasted time toe-to-toe with my mom's favorite madman.

"This guy bothering you?" Merric stood by my side, his chest puffed out and his chin raised. He wore steel plate armor enameled white, though the enamel was chipping and flaking away, and he carried a battered steel shield and a mace with all its flanges badly bent. His long hair was plastered to his head by sweat, revealing how thin it was on top.

"He called me a witch," I said. "And he's in my way."

"Angels!" Merric barked. Three women with white leathers and dangerous expressions readied their weapons. "Clear a path! First one to knock him down gets a raise!"

They charged, attacking St George from all sides; he batted at them like a bear swatting away wasps. There was no time to watch, though, and I drove Hearthammer onwards towards the knot of fighting that surrounded Golden Apple.

They saw us coming and either somebody had warned them or they could read the look in my eyes, because Rad, Valkyrie, and Wolfheart formed a line between us and Dr Agony as the swirl of the battle dragged the fight away from us and cleared a little space in the square. The red wizard eyed me warily from behind his party. He'd taken a cut across the forehead and his face was smeared with blood.

"Move aside," I said. "Or surrender, that would be easier."

"Who do you think you're talking to?" Rad said with a laugh. His maul was black with gore. "Golden Apple never surrenders."

"Actually," said Noah, "you ran from some hell rats about three years ago, in that dungeon under the Crown Oak."

"That was a tactical retreat," said Wolfheart.

"I'm sure the rats could tell the difference," said Cass.

"Their souls weren't worth the harvest," said Valkyrie. "At least you will know the glory of Valhalla after you die."

"Is that a threat?" Magpie took a step forward.

"It's a promise," hissed Valkyrie.

"Show me," Magpie said. "Or are you afraid to fight a bunch of noobs?"

"We're not afraid of you," Wolfheart said.

"*Then show me!*" Magpie screamed, and Valkyrie attacked. It was incredible how fast she was, darting at Magpie with both knives leading, pricking at him from all directions in a flashing blur of steel. They came together and stumbled apart again. Their fighting styles couldn't be more different: Valkyrie moving with flashy precision like a fighter in a martial arts movie, Magpie like a back-alley brawler, ducking his face behind one elbow as he lashed out at Valkyrie's eyes with his free hand.

Cass had Wolfheart pinned down with arrows; he was trying to cast something, but kept being interrupted by near-misses that I suspected were going exactly where Cass wanted them to. That left Rad for me and Noah, and we stepped forward together to confront the huge warrior.

He went for Noah first, bringing his maul down in a double-handed blow that would crush its target into the ground if it landed. Noah dodged to the side and the maul crashed into the cobbles where he'd stood a moment earlier, cracking the paving stones with a bang like a gun. I stepped into the opening, swinging my elven sword, but Rad brought an arm up with surprising speed and, incredibly, caught the blow on one of his neon armbands.

"Yeah, they're magic," he said, waggling his eyebrows at me. He grabbed the blade of my sword, twisted it out of my hands, and snapped it over his knee. The last of the enchantment rose from the broken pieces with a puff of red and a sound like a gasp.

Rad grabbed his maul as Noah came back in and swatted Noah's sword away with a one-handed sweep of the huge weapon. Unable to check his charge, Noah fell to his knees and slid to a stop at Rad's feet. The huge warrior raised his maul for a killing blow.

"Don't be a PK!" Noah shouted.

"What?" Rad stopped, his brow furrowed.

"You already initiated PvP combat," Noah said in a rush. "Don't be a player killer, too."

"You attacked us, kid," said Rad.

"Not by the rules," I put in. "Valkyrie made the first actual attack. Then you tried to kill Noah."

"Fine!" Anger creased Rad's face. "So what? Expedition ain't gonna bring the hammer down on us. We're Golden Apple."

"It's not Expedition you need to convince," I said. I gestured upward, where something like a thousand drones swirled like a stormcloud. "It's them."

Rad looked up, dismay dawning on his face. He looked at Noah with disgust, then raised his maul and prodded Noah roughly in the shoulder with its tip. "You ain't worth the trouble, you little shit." He stomped off into the melee, looking for something he was allowed to kill, muttering, "Ain't no goddamn PK…"

"Well, that was—" A red line appeared on Noah's chest, parting his armor and the skin and muscle underneath. He opened his mouth like a fish and fell onto his back, gasping. I whirled around. Behind me, Cass stood with her bow in two pieces, looking stunned. Magpie and Valkyrie were locked together in a sort of death grip, frozen like a classical painting of two wrestlers with their free hands around the other's wrist, each straining to drive his or her knife into some soft part of the other.

Wolfheart stalked towards me, wand in hand.

"That's what I get for giving out discounts," he told Noah. "Now, you stay down while I deal with your red wizard."

My spells flickered through my mind, but they all seemed equally useless: I had no coin to throw, no weapon to enchant, no enemy spirit to hold. There wasn't even a breeze I could try to whip up.

A small smile blossomed on Wolfheart's face as he drew near.

"*Cleave!*"

The same spell that had lashed Noah now split Wolfheart from the shoulder to the belly button. He crumpled into a pile on the cobblestones, leaking blood.

"Holy shit, what—" I choked on my words as Scytri appeared from the throng, the wand he'd used to cut away my infection in his hand.

"I must admit," he said, "you humans are certainly creative in your use of spells."

"Did you do it?" I rushed to him. He was battered and bloodied, with a purple swell threatening to close off one eye, but he looked whole.

"No." Scytri shook his head. "The Eldest still lives."

"What are you doing here?" I wanted to shake him.

"I saw you in trouble." He caught the look on my face. "Don't worry. My progenitor leads the fight against the Eldest." He glanced at the drone-clouded sky. "There's revolution in the air."

"Thank you," I said. I gripped his shoulder for a moment, then a movement drew my eye, and I saw Dr Agony pull a bell from a pouch at his hip. "Look out!"

I pushed in front of Scytri, but it was too late: he was frozen, victim of Agony's spell. Valkyrie and Magpie tumbled past me, now fighting for control of a single knife that flashed back and forth between them. I leapt over them and ran for the red wizard. There was a sword on the ground and I grabbed in. In a flash of dizzy homesickness I realized it was the same one Dr Agony held in the billboard near my old apartment block.

Then I tried to kill him with it.

I reached into the blade with my mind, probing for its fighting spirit, ready to command it to give itself up for the cause, but the sword was empty. There was nothing there, just dumb metal.

"I know that look," Dr Agony said. His left hand was still swinging his bell, and he had a green gem in his left fist: he must have just plucked it from his necklace; there was a gap in the string right over his chest. Something warped the air around him, like the shimmer of a mirage.

I lunged. The sword caught on something and was yanked from my hand as though pulled on a string. It hit the ground at my feet and skittered a few feet to the side.

"Nice, right?" Agony opened his fist and jeweled green dust fell out, to get caught by the same force that had taken the sword from me. The gem dust swirled once in the air and flew off like a scarf taken on the breeze. "I call it *wind shield*. Doesn't last long, but it's a great surprise." He sighed dramatically. "I'll miss that sword, though. I saw you trying to enchant it. Bet you didn't know I bring all my gear over from the real world."

"Call off this fight," I said.

"Why?" Dr Agony shrugged. His bell kept on swinging, clattering tinnily as it looped back and forth. "So you can play diplomat with the natives? Nobody wants to see that shit. Blood and guts, that's what gets views."

"I'll kill you if you don't."

"Wow, you look serious!" Agony made a mock-impressed face. "But no you won't. I'm a superstar. I'm number one, kid, despite your pretensions. Do you have any idea how much money I make for Expedition? I'm untouchable. So piss off, hater." He waved a dismissive hand.

His little monologue had given me the time to find what I needed: a spirit I could latch onto. This one was in a coin, just a copper piece, that sat forgotten at the bottom of Dr Agony's belt pouch. It was a funny thing to try to talk to a piece of metal. The spirit wasn't very smart, but it was proud, and it resented being hammered into a flat, orderly shape. It wanted to burst out into the random fractal it had been when it was born deep in the earth, before the elven miners had come and cut it out, before the elven minter had melted it down and molded it into a little disc. All I had to do was suggest that maybe now would be a good time to break free.

The fireball exploded at Dr Agony's hip, incinerating his robe, scorching away half his armor and searing the flesh beneath, and sending everything else in his pouch spraying across the cobbles. The wizard shrieked in pain and stumbled to one side, then fell to his knees.

I stepped forward.

"Tell them to stop fighting. Tell them you changed your mind. Tell them whatever you want, but if you want to live, call this off."

He was trembling as he looked up at me. He had one hand clamped to his side, and the other he raised, shaking, like a beggar. His cracked lips opened, and his voice was less than a whisper.

"What?"

"I said," the wizard gasped, "I told you I bring all my own gear."

The hand beneath his robe flashed up and in it was a pistol, a heavy, black, blocky thing that froze me in sheer terror at the absolute *realness* of it. He pulled the trigger.

The world froze as the gun went off, a hundred times louder than any clash of swords. I shut my eyes, waiting for the pain, but it didn't come. When I dared to open them, I saw Scytri with his hands wrapped around Agony's wrist in a white-knuckled grip. Blue smoke wafted lazily from the muzzle of the pistol and blue blood spilled from Scytri's stomach.

"What—" said Scytri.

"No!" I dove past Scytri and came up with Dr Agony's sword, which I brought down in a glittering arc, severing the red wizard's hand from his arm at the wrist. He screamed and fell back, grabbing the spurting wound helplessly with his remaining hand. The pistol clattered to the ground, where Scytri picked it up.

"What is this?" His face was paper white and he was shaking.

"Scytri, please, you're hurt—"

"*What is this?*" he repeated.

"It's a human weapon," I said. "Please, just put it down. You need help."

Scytri put a hand to his own leaking wound, then raised his head to gaze out across the battlefield. The sound of the gun had drawn hundreds of amazed stares from elf and human alike, stopping half the skirmishes around the square with its roar.

At the far side of the battle, a knot of elves was still fighting. Eneri in his gold armor stood bloodied but unbowed with a sword in each hand. The Eldest huddled behind him, pale hands up in a gesture of self-defense. Some of Scytri's men—I recognized their red armor—were still battling their way towards the

Eldest, but they'd stalled out against an elven shield wall that looked unbreakable.

Scytri raised the pistol in a shaking hand, blew out a long breath, and squeezed the trigger.

The second bang of the gun stopped all fighting in the square. Every eye turned to us. As the elves and adventurers registered what had just been done, they looked as one in the direction the pistol pointed. I looked, too, and so we all watched together as the Eldest put a hand over the new hole in his chest, coughed up a gout of brackish blue, and toppled over, dead.

AMBASSADOR

Dr James Agostino glowered at me across the polished conference table. He'd cleaned up for the meeting, washed off the blood and filth of the battle and gotten clean, white bandages for his wrist, but in his reflection on the table I could see a spot under his chin that he'd missed while shaving.

The three of us—Agostino, Apollonia Blomhaugen, and I—sat in leather office chairs in a small room tucked away off the foyer of the Expedition Hall. A TV hung on one wall below an AC unit and a minifridge filled with bottled water hummed in the corner. It was easy to forget that we were in the Summerlands and not some corporate boardroom on Earth.

The existence of this room was a secret, Blomhaugen had told me as we waited for Agostino. A place for Expedition execs to hold their most sensitive discussions, the room was off-limits to all but Blomhaugen and her coterie, regularly swept for bugs, and had even been built as a Faraday cage to keep electromagnetic signals from entering or exiting.

We'd left our drones outside. They sat powered down in their own Faraday bags, under guard by two dozen black-clad rangers who filled the front room of the Hall to keep out curious adventurers. There were no cameras in this room, no phones, not even a pad of paper and a pencil. Cass had nearly rioted when she'd been told, but in the end, Blomhaugen had invited me and not her.

"Can we make this quick?" said Agostino. "I'd like to do a segment with the elves before I shut off for bed."

"Certainly we can." Blomhaugen's face was steady. "James, what are you hoping to get from this meeting?"

Agostino's mouth angled in a smirk. "I'm prepared to be merciful," he said. "All I want is a lifetime ban. Emma and her little friends leave the Summerlands and never come back, and I don't press criminal charges."

"I see." Blomhaugen folded her hands on the table. "And where would you take the game from here, if you were still in charge?"

Agostino crossed his arms and leaned back in his chair. His eyes were on me. "War. Let's not kid ourselves here: we've all checked the numbers from the battle, and we all know they aren't coming back unless we keep this thing going."

"The elves want peace," I said. I had to clench my jaw to keep from shouting.

"Oh, that's why they brought their army?"

"I already told you." My teeth hurt and I could hear the tightness in my voice. "The Eldest that Scytri shot was from an *imru* that supported the war. But now his progenitor is Eldest, and their *original* progenitor was a healer, so—"

"If you say so." Agostino rolled his eyes. "Well, it takes two to sign a truce. Let them limp back past the Wall while we get our strategy in place and then we'll show them how humans feel about being attacked."

"Emma," Blomhaugen interjected. "Do you agree about the ratings?"

"The ratings?" I blinked. "Well... no. I don't. Violence isn't all the viewers want; I've proved that. There's so much more we could be doing. Stream the rangers' exploratory expeditions, or just have players do it. More lectures. Language lessons. Cultural exchanges with the elves." I straightened up in my chair. "Ms Blomhaugen, I used to fix merch machines for Expedition. You're missing out on so much. Forget T-shirts, you should be selling textbooks to high schools and colleges. Let people visit short-term. You could export flowers—"

Blomhaugen held up a hand. "Thank you, Emma."

"You're not seriously listening to her?" Agostino's mouth hung half open as he gestured at me with one hand and one bandaged stump. "Attempted PK, going to the Wall, who knows where she learned some of that magic—I'd tick off all the rules she and her friends broke, but I can't because she cut my goddamn hand off!"

"And what are you hoping to achieve here, Emma?" Blomhaugen was as icy as ever, totally unfazed by Agostino's outburst, but there was something in her eyes I hadn't seen before. She almost looked... expectant?

"Well, stopping the war, for one," I said.

"Aside from that." Blomhaugen shook her head. "I mean personally. What do *you* want?"

"Oh." I glanced at Agostino, who had open disgust on his face, then back to Blomhaugen. "I want him in jail."

"You—you what?" At first I thought Agostino was choking, but then I realized he was laughing, a wheezy, uncontrolled sound.

Blomhaugen nodded. "I can do that."

"*What?*" Agostino leapt up from his chair. "You absolutely cannot!"

"I certainly can," said Blomhaugen, looking up at the red-faced wizard. "You can join Donna Markan after she testifies about all the fraud you two committed together."

"You never cared about that before," Agostino snarled.

"I'll admit it, I looked the other way on plenty of your little indiscretions." Blomhaugen shook her head. "And now I'm paying for that mistake. You brought a *gun* into my game, James."

"Your game? *Your* game?" His voice, always nasal, was rising to a shriek. "It's *my* game! *Mine!*"

Blomhaugen stood, and I found myself glancing back and forth between them like a kid watching her parents fight, unsure which one to be more afraid of. But instead of confronting Agostino, Blomhaugen turned and opened the door.

"Elting?"

A ranger stepped into the room, his hard eyes locked on Agostino. His head was shaved and plastered with a dirty white bandage and I guessed that the healers hadn't gotten to him yet.

"Take him through the portal, please. Security has been prepped on the other side."

The ranger nodded. His men followed him as he moved into the room, and together they manhandled Agostino around the table as the wizard struggled. They passed my seat, and his burning eyes on locked on me.

I raised my left hand, palm towards me and back towards Agostino. It was an elven gesture, one of many I'd started to unpack since the battle. It meant something like "I am above you in every respect and you'd better listen to what I'm saying," and of all the billions of human beings in this world and the other, Dr James Agostino was the only other one who could possibly understand just how insulting I was being.

"Have fun in jail," I said.

"You'll regret this!" he spat suddenly. He was looking at Blomhaugen; he didn't dare meet my eyes. "I swear to God you will! I built this place, I built your little company—they're all loyal to me, you'll see—you stole it from me!"

He kept shouting as the rangers dragged him across the foyer; I could hear his voice receding. I bit my lip. I'd promised myself—and Cass, and Noah—that I would play it cool in front of Blomhaugen no matter what happened. But this…

I leapt from my chair and turned to watch just as Elting opened the front door of the Expedition Hall. The bright sunlight of Portal Square picked out the dust swirling around Agostino, thrashing and yelling in the arms of three rangers, and even from across the foyer I had to squint. Beyond the door, out in the blinding white, I began to make out shapes: people, a whole mob of them, and above their heads, a hundred or a thousand drones swirling and jockeying for the best view of the action as Dr Agony was dragged mid-tantrum into the view of the entire world.

"It's always sad when a great man falls," Blomhaugen said softly. I turned in surprise. I'd forgotten all about her, but there she stood, looking as calm as if we'd just been discussing what to order for lunch.

She gestured to my chair, and I sat back down, feeling sheepish. So much for playing it cool... though compared to Agostino, I was doing just fine.

"What else do you want?"

"What?" I said, trying not to start stammering. "Really? Why?"

"As a policy, it's good business to keep my top players happy," Blomhaugen said. "Anyone who can unseat Dr Agony deserves to be taken seriously." She straightened her suit jacket and sat at the head of the table. "Besides, you saved us all from quite a slaughter. It was obvious which way the battle was headed."

"Don't start a war," I said. "Please."

Blomhaugen laughed, a sound like an ice cube hitting a martini glass. "Good God, what do you take me for?"

"You weren't...?"

"Not a chance." Blomhaugen snorted. "We sell fantasy. War is too real."

"Then why was Agony at this meeting at all?" My head was starting to feel fuzzy.

"If I hand him the rope, I'm not responsible for tying the noose." Blomhaugen folded her hands on the table, her face as still as the icy face of a frozen lake, and I suddenly remembered that she was most definitely not my friend. "What else do you want?"

"Why did you kill Jason?"

"I didn't kill anybody," Blomhaugen said.

"You know what I mean."

"Then let me apologize on behalf of Expedition Games. Further, let me assure you that the employee responsible for that tragedy has been dealt with."

"Who?" Inplexicably, my nerves had disappeared, replaced with a coolness that matched whatever Blomhaugen was projecting.

"A rogue lawyer," the CEO said. "Overzealous in his protection of our corporate secrets. Again, my sincerest apologies."

"*Who?*"

Blomhaugen cleared her throat. "Did you meet Alan Brodie on your way in?"

"Jesus Christ," I said. "All over what? Some files? It was about the elves, wasn't it? You wanted people to think they were all gone, but you had proof they were alive."

"I can neither confirm nor deny the contents of the files your friend received."

"Well, I hope it was worth it." I crossed my arms. "I'm still not sure why I shouldn't tell the world."

"I'll only ask one more time: what else do you want?" Blomhaugen's eyes bored into mine, but I refused to flinch. "I can try to chase down the money James stole from you, though I should warn you, it could take years. Finances in the real world aren't as simple as here, and even in prison, James will have lawyers."

"Sure." I waved my hand as though the offer were nothing. "Go ahead. But that's not enough."

"I'm listening." Blomhaugen leaned back in her chair, her hands still folded.

"There's a store manager I used to work for, back home. Mr Fessy. Get him his job back and fire his boss Roger Sorolla. Actually, give him Sorolla's job."

"Done."

"Okay, as far as here in the Summerlands. All of Hearthammer is forgiven for whatever rules we broke."

"Of course."

"Next…" I could feel a lump forming in my throat. We'd reached the things I *really* wanted. "I'm in charge of negotiations with the elves. I'll translate until other people can learn Elvish, and then I get to be, like…"

"Ambassador?"

"Exactly. Ambassador. Still a player, though, too, so I can fight, use magic, find treasure, everything. But I'm at all the peace talks, plus any delegations to the elves after that. Really, we should set up an embassy for them here, and our own in… wherever the elves actually live."

"You're rambling again." Blomhaugen straightened up. "Is that all?"

"Actually…" I licked my lips, which had gone suddenly dry. "There's one more thing."

★★★

A week later, I stood in the slanting red light of sunset, looking at the patch of ground where new players came through. It had been thoroughly trampled during the Battle of Portal Square, churned to mud and watered with the blood of human and elf. The stone gazebo had collapsed completely, reduced to a pile of rubble that sat nearby on the stained cobbles of Portal Square. Most of the buildings on the plaza were splashed with gore or scorched by fire.

A chipped metal pipe showed in the dirt at the edge of the glowing moss ring, which seemed to have survived the battle unscathed, and it occurred to me for the first time that there must be hundreds of miles of fiber optic cable buried beneath the soil of the Summerlands. On either side of the pipe, a few green shoots poked up a fraction of an inch from the earth. Someone had planted them just today: new bulbs to replace the bed of flowers I'd tumbled into when I arrived.

"They'll grow back," said Magpie.

I turned in surprise. I'd thought I was alone; almost every adventurer in the Summerlands—the ones who'd survived—was on Meat Street, drinking and eating in a party that had started the night after the battle and showed no signs of stopping a week later.

"How long have you been standing there?"

"Only a minute." He shrugged. "It was nice to see you looking happy."

"Look…" I caught myself staring at my boots and forced my gaze up to meet his. "I'm sorry I haven't been around much since…" I sighed. "I'm sorry I haven't been able to talk to you. I just don't know what I want you to say."

"There's nothing I *can* say." Magpie's Adam's apple bobbed as he swallowed. "But I can show you."

"Show me?" I blinked, but Magpie was already stripping. He had a clean black shirt on, and he pulled it over his head, mussing his thick hair as he revealed the lean muscles of his stomach and chest. My eyes caught immediately on the tattoo of Jason's name—then I began to laugh.

Magpie was doing the most ridiculous dance I'd ever seen.

"What the hell are you doing?" I choked. He was twisting like the love child of a stripper and a drunk snake, his hands over his head as he rotated slowly, giving me a good look at his battered body. A sudden thought made me glance up. "*Is your camera on?*"

"The world must see my dance of seduction," he said in a low voice that sounded ridiculous coming from his slight frame. He even had a sort of accent going on, like a lover from a hundred-year-old romance movie. "As must you. Drink it in. All of it. This is what you are giving up if you will not love me. If you will not have me…"

He stopped dancing with no warning, shifting back to himself as suddenly as if someone had flipped his crazy-person off switch. I opened my mouth, but he cut me off.

"And now that we're well past the time delay on live feeds, allow me to explain exactly what each one of these tattoos means to the Vyronas crime family."

"You—" My mouth was hanging open, and I let it stay there for fifteen solid minutes as Magpie went through his entire history as a contract boy. Line by line, victim by victim, he sold out his crime family with absolutely no shame, implicating every capo and thug he'd ever worked with, even inserting embarrassing personal information about them as it occurred to him. He reached Terra's tattoo, then Jason's, and when he'd finished the story of the Expedition lawyer with the accent who'd paid to have Officer Brayden Porter kill a seventeen-year-old boy, he finally looked at me with eyes so wide and empty that any anger I still felt was lost in them immediately.

"Turn off your camera," I said.

"It's a bit late for that, don't you think?" He smiled. "I'm not invisible anymore."

"Turn it off."

He did, and I kissed him.

We broke apart breathlessly a minute later and stood holding each other in the red sunset. It was another minute before I could find the courage to speak.

"They must have cut the feed as soon as they realized what you were doing. They had to."

"Doesn't matter." Magpie smiled. "I'm sure I got in at least one good turn before they tumbled to my plan. Every one of those tattoos is public knowledge now." He glanced up at the descending sun. "Good lighting, too."

"What happens next?"

"Chaos," he laughed. "For every damn one of them. And all the thugs and assassins, too. Can't be a contract killer if everyone knows your name."

"Porter will go on the run," I said. "He was a cop, you know. He worked with Cass and Jason's dad…" I shook my head. "But even Chief Bullard can't protect him if he's got the feds *and* a pissed-off crime family coming after him. But that's actually not what I meant." I smiled. "What happens next for *you*, now that you're not invisible?"

Magpie cocked his head. "I thought I might open a cafe."

"A cafe?" I blinked, uncertain if he was teasing me. "I don't know what I'll do next time I meet a locked door."

"There are other thieves." Magpie twisted his foot nervously. "I figured out I wasn't really meant for the adventuring life sometime after Valkyrie filled me with holes."

"It was very brave of you, taking her on like that."

Magpie shrugged, but wouldn't meet my eye.

"Let me ask you something," I said. "One last question before you retire. And I just want the truth, whatever it is. You knew about Jason the whole time. You knew who we were. Why didn't you just tell us?"

Magpie pulled away from me. "I never got a chance to tell you the whole story, even after you found the tattoo. When you got on the plane in Edinburgh, I recognized you immediately. The lawyer from Expedition showed pictures of all of you to my boss, said you were likely witnesses. Well, when I saw you on the plane, I immediately knew what must have happened. At first I just couldn't face you, but then I decided... I decided there was a reason I was on that plane with you." He turned to me, looking up with his eyes wide. "I was going to protect you. The three of you."

"You did," I said. "More times than I can count. But that still doesn't explain why you kept it all to yourself."

"I was ashamed," he said. Tears were pricking the corners of his eyes. "I was there for the whole plan. I could have done something, anything—gone to the media, stabbed my boss, I don't know. But instead I just ran away and convinced myself I was being brave. I was a coward. I could have saved Jason."

There's nothing I can say, I thought, *but I can show you.* I took his hand, and we stood in the quiet of the square for a while, just the two of us with our fingers intertwined as the daylight faded.

"About time," Naila called across the square, where she and Noah had entered by a side street.

"Don't tell me you shut down Open Seasoning!" I said. "You must be raking in the gold."

"Ran out of product." Naila shrugged. "All the adventurers are here, so nobody is supplying me. It's cool. We'll get back to normal after my vacation."

"How are the plans coming?" Magpie asked Noah.

"I'll show you!" Noah was beaming as he pulled a rolled-up poster map of the Summerlands, the whole radius of human control from Wellpoint to the Wall, from under his arm and unfurled it on the ground. He knelt down, and Magpie joined him as Noah began to explain the route he would take: starting in Wellpoint, he would visit every important site in the Summerlands. Old dungeons, famous fights, places discovered and named and fought over by the first generation of adventurers, he wanted to see them all.

"Vacation," I repeated. Naila was smiling. "So you're going with him after all?"

"I've always wanted to get out of Wellpoint," said the chef. "Besides, your boy can be very convincing when he wants to."

"You mean annoying," I said.

"I mean wonderful." She shook her head. "Hey, did you hear about Valkyrie?"

"Uh-uh."

"Finally gone. It took six rangers to get her through the portal."

"It took twice that many to pull her off Magpie when the fight was over," I said. "She was like a wild animal. It was horrible."

"Good riddance." Naila shook her head. "Where are they stashing her, anyway?"

"Blomhaugen told me they've got a prison contract somewhere."

"Think she she'll be with Dr Agony?"

"If she is, at least some of Golden Apple will still be together." I shook my head. "Wolfheart is retiring to become a commentator, did you hear?"

"I can't believe he's heading back to Earth." Naila looked at the sky. "It's such a shithole."

"I imagine when you have as much money as Wolf does, it's not so bad."

"Still, I'm surprised he didn't stay with Rad."

"Rad is going solo!" I laughed. "More camera time, I think."

"At least he's willing to fight!" Cass stormed across the square, waving her hands in annoyance. "You wouldn't believe the yellow bellies on these players!"

"Still recruiting?" I asked, pulling her into a hug.

295

"Trying." She snorted. "Everybody's spooked by the elves. I don't think there's been a proper sortie into the wilds since the battle. Whoever gets back out there first is going to be number one simply by default."

"And that'll be you, right?" Naila said.

"You bet your ass," Cass agreed. "From now until the rangers find the last dungeon."

I squeezed her shoulder. "I wish you'd come with me."

"Past the Wall?" Cass shook her head. "Your signature is on the treaty, Emma, you know it's a no-go for treasure hunting. There's plenty still in our territory, thanks."

"Gonna buy yourself a nice big house in the Burbs?" Naila asked.

"Shit no," said Cass. "I'm starting a scholarship."

"Seriously?" The chef's eyebrows went up.

"Yes, seriously." Cass crossed her arms. "For Hecker kids who want to be adventurers. Training and stuff. And then the best ones get to come here free."

"Huh." Naila looked Cass up and down as though taking her measure for the first time.

We waited in silence for a few minutes, enjoying the warmth of eternal summer. Across the square, the door of an expensive inn clicked open and another group entered Portal Square: Apollonia Blomhaugen and her entourage of aides.

"Still waiting?" she called as they crossed to us.

"Yep," I said.

"Travel is complicated," said the CEO. "We're heading back to Earth. On behalf of Expedition Games, let me just thank you again—"

"Save it." I put my hand up. To an elf it would have been a gesture of deference, but Blomhaugen knew how I meant it.

"I just wish you would appreciate what a coup this was for us," she went on.

"We get it," Cass said. "You haven't stopped talking about it since you got here."

"Nine hundred million unique viewers—"

"Won't bring my brother back."

Blomhaugen's facade of bonhomie melted away. She held Cass's gaze for a moment, then turned to her entourage. "Come along, everyone! Time to go home!"

One by one, her aides stepped into the mossy ring that had somehow, miraculously, survived the fight. One moment there they were, as solid and real as anything around us, and then they were gone, pitching through stars and darkness to arrive at the bottom of a well on Earth. Blomhaugen went last, and as she stepped into the fairy circle, she caught my eye one last time.

"It's going to be a very different game going forward," she said. "I'm looking forward to it."

And then she was gone.

"Have you talked to Scytri?" Noah asked. He was rolling his poster map back up; Magpie was brushing off his pants.

"Not outside the peace talks," I admitted. "He's been busy. But the wound healed over really well," I added. "You did a great job. I know he wants to thank you eventually; I think there's just a lot of work involved when your progenitor becomes the Eldest."

"Listen to you," Cass said with a smirk. "You nerd. You love this."

"I'm the human ambassador to an elven kingdom during a time of turmoil," I said. "How could I *not* love this?"

"Okay, ambassador," said a new voice. "Care to diplomatically explain why you made me roll all the way out here at nightfall?"

"Hi, Seidenberg," I said. Naila leaned down to hug him in his wheelchair, and the others waved their greetings.

"I'm still waiting for an answer," he said.

"Well, there's a couple reasons," I said. "But mainly I wanted to make you an offer."

"Which is?"

"Well, Noah and I had a chance to talk, and he's been practicing his healing magic. He's had plenty of opportunities, after all, and he's gotten really good."

297

Seidenberg stiffened in his wheelchair.

"Want to walk again?"

The shopkeep looked away, then spun a wheel to turn his back on me entirely.

"Seriously?" said Cass. "You should be grateful."

"I am," said Seidenberg. "Really, I am. But I have to turn you down."

"Why?" asked Noah, cocking his head like a curious dog. Seidenberg spun back to face us.

"Kid, I was eighteen when I lost my leg. The surgery took a bunch of my nervous system with it. Took me six months to learn to walk with crutches, then my other leg gave out and I had to start all over again with the chair." He snorted. "I put more time into learning to do this than I did learning to walk as a baby. You think I want to go through that shit again? No chance. This made me who I am. This *is* who I am. So thanks, Linnaea, all of you—but no thanks."

"Rude," said Naila and Seidenberg laughed.

"Now, is that all?" he asked. "It's almost dark and in case you hadn't noticed, I don't fit down alleys."

"There's one more thing," I said. "You heard I made a deal with Blomhaugen, right?"

"Well?" Seidenberg frowned.

"Just wait," I said, and he did. We all did, watching the last sliver of sun disappear over the rooftops of the square, pitching the town of Wellpoint into deep blue night. A gentle breeze picked up, and it brought, faintly, the sounds of the party on Meat Street along with a whiff of mingled food scents. My stomach growled. I'd hardly eaten anything during the last day of peace talks. I was looking forward to getting some food, but I wasn't quite ready yet...

A shape was there in the darkness, lying in the luminescent circle at the heart of Portal Square. It was a human shape, big, and for a moment it was still. Then its head rose up, and it took in the people gathered in the dusk, all waiting with held breath and an unbearable tension in our hearts.

"It's real," said David Keats.

"Daddy!" shouted Cass, and she fell to her knees and threw her arms around her father. She was sobbing openly, and Keats was, too, as his daughter helped him up into a sitting position.

He stared up at us from the ground in abject wonder, his eyes wide and his mouth hanging just a bit open. He'd lost even more weight, I realized, and the lines in his face were more pronounced, but the playful spark I'd known so well was still there, undimmed.

"Is this—" said Seidenberg.

"This is Keats," I said. "Jessamine's dad. Noah and mine, too, really, if we're being honest."

"This is the man you were fighting for," Seidenberg said.

"That's right."

"Well, help him up!" Seidenberg snorted.

"We can't," I said. "He's paralyzed from the waist down. His spinal cord was severed about six weeks ago."

"Oh," Seidenberg said. "You want me to help him…"

"Thank you, but I don't think you'll need to," I said, gesturing with my chin to where Keats sat in the dirt. Cass was stripping off his shirt as Noah kneeled behind him, probing his back with gentle fingers.

"Kids, kids," Keats was saying, but Cass and Noah were all business, and they ignored his wondering protests as they prepped him for magical surgery.

"Okay, Mr Keats, this is going to feel funny," said Noah. "You shouldn't feel any pain since the nerves are all dead down here, but there might be… pressure, maybe? I don't know, I've never had my spine reattached."

"How does this work?" Keats's voice was shaky.

"Well, I'm going to cut away a square of flesh and muscle where the damage is, and then—"

"Okay, okay, stop!" Keats shook his head. "I don't want to know how the sausage is made. If you say you can do it, that's good enough for me. Just… somebody distract me."

"We could tell you about the battle with the elves," Cass suggested.

"I saw it all," Keats said. "You need to learn to use a melee weapon, Cassidy."

His daughter barked an unbelieving laugh.

"I could introduce our new friends," I tried.

"That can wait until I can look them in the eye, thanks."

I ignored him. "This is Naila; she's the best chef in the Summerlands. Seidenberg makes potions. You're both old guys, so you should have a lot to talk about. And this"—I squeezed his hand—"is Magpie."

"How was your trip?" asked Magpie.

"Who are you, exactly?" Keats said, and then he saw how Magpie's fingers were laced with mine, and his face softened. "Never mind. Welcome to the family. The trip was fine, thanks. I definitely thought I was hallucinating when they found me at the homeless shelter, but after that it was first class all the way." He sighed. "How's it going back there, Noah?"

"Nicely," Noah said, almost cross-eyed as he focused on Keats's back. He was wearing white gloves now, stained and spattered pink with blood. "Mr Keats, do you remember that book you lent me, about the kids who find a portal to another world in a closet?"

"A wardrobe," Keats said. "Not a closet. What about it?"

"Someone stole it from me before I could finish it. I'm sorry."

Keats laughed. "Noah, that was years ago! Why would you bring it up now?"

"Well, I was just wondering how it ended." Sweat shone on Noah's face, and his tongue poked between his teeth as he worked. "Since I never finished it."

"How it ended? Well, let me think." Keats scratched his chin, which was hidden by a ragged beard. "There was a whole series, but I only ever lent you the first one. I guess I thought you didn't like it."

"No, I loved it," Noah said. "But they took it."

"Right," said Keats. His right foot twitched and then suddenly that leg bent at the knee and jerked up to make a triangle. With a look of fierce concentration, he dragged his left foot back towards his body and got it under him. He pitched forward, overbalanced, and almost toppled over, but he waved off help from Cass and Noah as he regained his balance. Then, his teeth gritted and his legs shaking, David Keats stood in the fresh, clean dirt that surrounded the portal between Earth and the Summerlands.

"As I recall," he said, "it ended with a miracle."

ACKNOWLEDGEMENTS

With all my heart, I'd like to thank my wife Molly, who always understands when "I'll put the kid to bed" really means "go play pinball, I need to write." Equal appreciation is due to my hilarious and weird son Jack for watching cartoons in my office as often as needed. Maybe someday he'll grow up and realize how many ideas I stole from his childhood ramblings... I also owe my parents a huge debt of gratitude (and probably money) for all their support over the years.

A tip of the hat to my brother Nick for teaching me to have good taste, a lesson which I have roundly ignored. A bump of the fist to my many best friends, including BBB, C-Slice, DA, Nutty, Talking to Walls, and Jesse, who doesn't have a nickname. Inspiration for any member of the Peninsular Expeditionary Group who reads this.

On the technical side, I couldn't have done it without my editor Conor Kostick, a great GameLit author in his own right, who constantly pushed me to do better and never accepted "good enough." Thanks also to my many long-suffering alpha readers from the Reddit LitRPG community, especially Rogue.

No thanks to any cat who insisted on being on my lap after I said no.

ABOUT THE AUTHOR

Nathaniel Webb, aka Nat20, is an author, musician, and game designer. As a lead guitarist, he has toured and recorded with numerous acts including Grammy-nominated singers Beth Hart and Jana Mashonee and Colombian pop star Marre. His published writing includes various short stories and novellas; adventures and supplements for the tabletop RPGs Shadow of the Demon Lord and Godless; and the Veil of Worlds modern fantasy novels. Expedition: Summerlands is his first GameLit novel.

A graduate of Phillips Exeter Academy and Wesleyan University, Nathaniel lives in Portland, Maine with his wife and son under a massive pile of cats. He can be found @nat20w on Twitter and Facebook, where he mostly talks about games, writing, and obscure 80s progressive rock.